INTO THE PIT OF BLACKNESS

As Wandor stepped up close behind her, Gwynna drew her sword, rested the point in the door's keyhole and thrust hard.

The door swung open, and it seemed to her that a blast of cold damp wind laden with grave-stenches poured out of it. All her awareness of Powers at work came awake, and she raised one hand to start a light shielding spell while she clawed at the buttons of her tunic with the other. A cry not in her own voice forced its way out of her throat. Then she felt a twisting and hammering of all the senses of her body—the floor tilting under her with a terrible squeal and grinding, Bertan's hand clutching her shoulder, his own cry telling her that he also felt void under him—at last air rushing past her as she plunged down into darkness . . .

ROLAND GREEN

WANDOR'S FLIGHT

▲ AVON
PUBLISHERS OF BARD, CAMELOT AND DISCUS BOOKS

WANDOR'S FLIGHT is an original publication of Avon Books.
This work has never before appeared in book form.

AVON BOOKS
A division of
The Hearst Corporation
959 Eighth Avenue
New York, New York 10019

First Avon Printing, June, 1981

AVON TRADEMARK REG. U. S. PAT. OFF. AND IN OTHER COUNTRIES.
MARCA REGISTRADA. HECHO EN U. S. A.

Printed in the U. S. A.

10 9 8 7 6 5 4 3 2 1

TO THE MEMORY OF MY FATHER

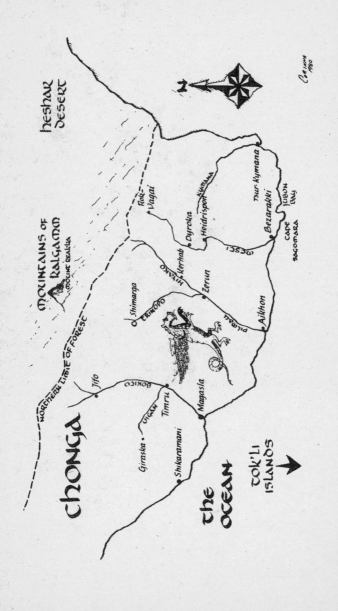

PROLOGUE

Year thirty-three of the reign of King Nond II in Benzos:

Bertan Wandor, Master in the Order of Duelists, came to stand before the Guardian of the Mountain beneath Mount Pendwyr. The Guardian of the Mountain, last of the Five-Crowned Kings of the Ancient Days, set him four tasks.

"Go and win Firehair the Maiden.

"Go and win the faith of Strong-Ax and Fear-No-Devil.

"Go and win aid from Cheloth of the Woods.

"Go and seek these—the Helm of Jagnar, the Ax of Yevoda, the Spear of Valkath, the Sword of Artos, the Dragon Steed of Morkol.

"Go among all peoples and through all lands and against all who torment and distress men, wherever you find them barring your passage.

"Go then to the house of him you call father and take up the talisman and watch, while Mount Pendwyr splits with fire, and the hills and woods rise into the sky and are scattered to the sea.

"Go then at last forth to battle and smite those who come against you with all your strength and cunning.

"All such will be your testing. The road is long. The testing is great. May your strength be great also."

The Guardian returned to the fires from which he came, and Wandor rode forth on his quest.

He took service under King Nond of Benzos and the king's good right hand Count Arlor, and was given for his own service Berek, a freedman of the Sea Folk. Wandor and Berek swore to each other the sacred Oath of the Drunk Blood.

Berek of the Sea Folk bore the warname Strong-Ax.

In this year Duke Cragor, called the Black Duke, raised plots and Powers against King Nond, seeking Nond's life and throne. The Viceroyalty of the East was already subject to Cragor, save in the South Marches, which Baron Oman Delvor held for the king. Wandor was sent to strengthen Baron Delvor against the Black Duke.

Cragor was watchful for such dangers. His sorcerer Kaldmor the Dark unleashed potent magic against Wandor, but the Guardian of the Mountain fought Kaldmor and defeated him.

So Wandor came safely to Delvor's stronghold and there met Gwynna Delvora, daughter of the baron and a woman of Power. In time he won her for his wife.

Gwynna Delvora was Firehair the Maiden.

Thereafter Wandor and Gwynna made a bitter journey across the River Zephas and the Silver Mountains, to win help from the fierce Yhangi who rode the Plains beyond the mountains. They were not received among the Yhangi as friends.

Cragor was an unsleeping foe, and in Wandor's absence his hirelings and vassals made war against the Marches. But the baron's friend Sir Gilas Lanor had sworn oaths with the Khindi who lived in the forests of the Viceroyalty, so they fought well against the Black Duke's men.

Year thirty-four of the reign of King Nond:

That spring Wandor faced a Testing before all the Yhangi, and fought in single combat against the proud Jos-Pran, War Chief of the Gray Mares. He defeated Jos-Pran in three combats, yet this was not enough. Wandor was bidden to ride the King Horse of all the Yhangi, which none had done before. He did so, however, and then the Yhangi swore to follow him.

He had great need of their aid, for that same spring Duke Cragor led a great army against the Marches. Seeing Wandor's danger, the Guardian of the Mountain opened the South Pass of the Silver Mountains for the Yhangi to enter the Marches. Cragor's army came to Delkum Pass, and Wandor met and defeated it by the strength of the Yhangi and by the sorceries of the Yhangi Red Seers and of his wife Gwynna. The greater part of Cragor's army perished, but Cragor and Kaldmor fled in good time, to work further evil.

Year thirty-five of the reign of King Nond:

In the spring, fresh allies of Duke Cragor came against the

South Marches, and now the Khindi would not leave their forests to join Nond's cause.

Meanwhile Cragor continued to build his strength in Benzos, and mercenaries found him generous with gold. He also swore friendship with the Ponans of the north, promising them gold and the return of lands their fathers had lost to Benzos.

Kaldmor the Dark went into the Hills, to seek out new and greater Powers. He found them, for he reached Nem of Toshak, mightiest of evil sorcerers of the Ancient Days. It was given to him to make a *limar* in the form of Nem, through which Nem's Powers flowed forth from the House of Shadows. So mighty were these Powers that when Cragor led his armies forth, he became master over Benzos between one sunset and the next.

But King Nond and Count Arlor fled from Benzos aboard *Red Pearl*, the ship of Captain Thargor, seeking refuge with Baron Delvor and Bertan Wandor in the Viceroyalty of the East.

The Lady Gwynna, wife to Bertan Wandor and wise in sorcery, understood the strength of Kaldmor's new magic. She counseled that help be sought once again among the Khindi. So Wandor and Jos-Pran rode forth into the Blue Forest in search of Cheloth of the Woods and the Helm of Jagnar. In times past Jagnar the Forest King led those the Khindi called forefathers against the Empire of the Blue Forest, and overthrew it with the magical aid of Cheloth of the Woods.

Wandor and Jos-Pran made a bitter journey, for the Blue Forest swarmed with monsters spawned by ancient Beast Magic. In the end they came safely to where Cheloth of the Woods lay, and in that moment Cheloth awoke from his sleep of two thousand years and gave to Bertan Wandor the Helm of Jagnar.

At this time also, Lady Gwynna was taken by servants of the Black Duke and brought before Baron Galkor, chief among those who served Cragor. He would gladly have slain her, yet knew that his master had terrible dreams of giving the Lady Gwynna the hardest of deaths. So he held her fast in the keep of Fors Castle.

Then King Nond and Count Arlor were taken by magic, and brought to Fors Castle and an unhappy meeting with the Lady Gwynna. Yet Nond's hands were left free, so he took up a sword and did battle against Galkor's men. Arlor and Gwynna also fought, then leaped from a high window into the waters of Fors Bay and swam safely to shore. Nond fell, overwhelmed

3

by great numbers, and the Guardian of the Mountain received that part of him which was not flesh.

Count Arlor and the Lady Gwynna rode south. The Khindi took them and wished to make Arlor a sacrifice to Masutl the High Hunter. Cheloth then worked upon the Khindi with his magic, so that they were frightened, yet Count Arlor felt no fear and so earned from the Khindi a Praise Name.

That Praise Name was Fear-No-Devil.

Then Cheloth and Gwynna made a Showing, so that all the Khindi saw Bertan Wandor wearing the Helm of Jagnar. So Wandor at last gained the Khindi to his cause.

Wandor came to the city of Yost in the south of the Viceroyalty with all his war strength, and by a cunning stratagem took the city and its citadel. Now it was winter, and Wandor's enemies forsaw an ending to war in the Viceroyalty for the year. Wandor thought otherwise, gathered his host, and marched north against the city of Fors.

In Fors, that which had the shape of King Nond walked upon the walls at night and slew men in a horrible manner. So Baron Galkor's army was driven out of the city to meet Wandor in battle. The strife was long, but Wandor's war craft exceeded Galkor's, Cheloth's magic surpassed Kaldmor's borrowed Powers, and Galkor was defeated. He fled the field with Kaldmor, and Wandor entered the city of Fors.

In the name of King Nond's daughter Anya, now Queen of Benzos but wed to Duke Cragor and therefore helpless to rule, Count Arlor chose Bertan Wandor to be Viceroy over the East. Now he wore two crowns, and both the Yhangi and the Khindi followed him.

Year one of the reign of Queen Anya:

In the spring the Sea Folk came across the waters of the Ocean to plunder and slay along the shores of the Viceroyalty, for Duke Cragor had given gold to many of them. Others among the Sea Folk had turned toward the Beast Cult of Yand Island and sought favor from its Wizards by taking men and women of the Viceroyalty for sacrifice to the Beasts.

Daraun Son of Hymok, a captain of the Sea Folk and uncle to Berek Strong-Ax, led six seal ships against the Viceroyalty. Among these ships was *Fang of Giyo*, whose Captain was Foyn Son of Thadul, a man noted for ill-luck. With Foyn sailed Telek the Fatherless, who knew the arts of the *mungans* of Chonga.

Duke Cragor sent Baron Galkor with men, ships, and gold to Yand Island to strengthen it, and then to aid his friends among the HaroiLina (as the Sea Folk called themselves). Wandor likewise sent Berek Strong-Ax to Yand Island in the seal ship *Fire of Elya*, to learn what happened there.

Meanwhile Wandor and Gwynna went to a house in the forest north of Fors to seek some days of peace, but did not find it. Telek the Fatherless learned where they lay, and guided the men of Captain Foyn to the house. Wandor and Gwynna were taken and carried north, that they might be sacrificed to the Beasts of Yand Island.

Now there was great fear and anger in the Viceroyalty. The strength of men turned to gathering ships to snatch Wandor and Gwynna free from their captivity among the HaroiLina.

In the land of the HaroiLina, the coming of Wandor and Gwynna was like a stone rolling down a mountainside, loosening other stones until all the mountainside crashes into the valley below. The Keepers of the Hearth of the Mother opposed the sacrifice of Wandor and Gwynna to the Beasts of Yand, without success. Then Daraun Son of Hymok came to a Keeper and promised aid in taking Wandor and Gwynna from the Beasts. At the same time, Baron Galkor spoke to the Beast Wizard Mykto and promised him aid in bearing Wandor and Gwynna safely to Yand.

So when Mykto and Galkor's men took Wandor and Gwynna from their prison, they met Daraun's men and fought a battle on the shore of Stohra Bay. During that battle Wandor entered the House of the *Kym* of Captains of the HaroiLina, took from it the ancient Spear of Valkath the First Speaker, and used it to make good their escape.

However, Mykto used his magic to guide Galkor to Wandor and Gwynna as they crossed Stohra Bay to seek safety among the Hearth Mothers. Galkor slew Daraun, cast Wandor into the waters of the bay, and took Gwynna prisoner aboard his ship.

Wandor came safely to shore, however, and into the care of the Hearth Mothers. That same night Valkath the First Speaker came forth from the House of Shadows and walked among the HaroiLina, cursing those who had served Cragor or the Beast Wizards. Many of the HaroiLina fled in fear, and the others chose to follow Wandor.

Wandor and many of the HaroiLina who followed him came to Fors and the ships and men of the Viceroyalty sailed for Yand Island, where Gwynna now lay a prisoner of the Beast Wizards, destined for sacrifice to the Beasts. Wandor called upon Cheloth of the Woods to raise a wind to speed the fleet's sailing, and Cheloth did so. Then the winds became a fierce storm, so that the fleet of the Viceroyalty was scattered and ships perished. Wandor called on Cheloth to diminish the winds, though he grieved terribly for Gwynna, and the fleet was saved.

The men and ships of the Viceroyalty came to Yand Island on the very day Gwynna was to be sacrificed. In the battle at the landing place Berek and Sir Gilas Lanor slew Foyn Son of Thadul, and Wandor led his men inland. They came in time to see Baron Galkor cast Gwynna into the pit of the Beasts and then flee southward, believing her doomed.

Gwynna faced the Beasts with mighty magic, and they spared her. Then the High Beast Wizard made the pit crumble, freeing the Beasts to battle Wandor's men, while Mykto went to take up the Ax of Yevoda, Slayer of Beasts, the only weapon which might strike down the Beasts after they had done their work.

Wandor followed Mykto, killed him, and took the Ax of Yevoda for himself. Before the coming of night he had slain every Beast, and the Guardian of the Mountain made the earth move to bury the last remnants of the Beast Cult of Yand. Baron Galkor fled in defeat to Benzos, and Yand Island came into Wandor's hands.

Year two of the reign of Queen Anya:
The land of Benzos was troubled by the rule of Duke Cragor and his growing hunger for gold to feed his wars. Telek the Fatherless, who sought to be lord over the *mungans* of Chonga, carried on his plots, and none could be sure whether he was friend or foe. Pirnaush S'Rain, *Bassan* of the City of Dyroka, sought to bring all the Twelve Cities under his rule, but found that he needed new strength for that purpose....

—From THE SHORTER CHRONICLE OF WANDOR

(Second Translation)

ONE

Dehass Ebrun, *Zigbai* or First Counselor to *Bassan* Pirnaush of Dyroka, lay back on the perfumed cushions in the stern of the six-oared boat and shifted his aching left leg into a new position he hoped would ease it. He'd broken the leg when his horse dropped into a pitfall outside the walls of Shimarga, broken it so badly the surgeons had wanted to amputate. He'd fought them off, fought off the infection, and in the end saved himself from having to hobble one-legged to the grave. He hadn't saved himself from ten years of aches, and every time the rainy season came to Chonga the aches became steadily throbbing pain.

He thought of wine, then peered into the damp twilight and decided against it. The landmarks on the bank showed that he was only a few minutes from the palace. Then he could drink all he wanted from Pirnaush's fine cellar, as soon as he no longer needed a clear head for whatever business Pirnaush had in mind. The king drew on his stock of cryptic phrases when he sent messages even to his oldest comrades. Dehass approved the king's caution. No doubt those who couldn't make his kind of well-instructed guesses might think differently, but Dehass had served Pirnaush too long and learned too much.

Tonight they would be talking of either the coming war against Kerhab or future dealings with Wandor and Cragor. The war against Kerhab was so inevitable that Dehass was surprised Pirnaush hadn't set the wheels grinding on it long before. There was no more hope of the city's submitting peacefully to Pirnaush's claim of kingship over Chonga. In fact, there hadn't been any hope for the last three years. If the submission of Timru hadn't persuaded the Fifteen of Kerhab, nothing would.

So Kerhab would have to be beaten, and quickly. If it was allowed to stand defying Pirnaush for as little as two more years, both Shimarga and Timru would start thinking of withdrawing their submissions. The Fifteen of Kerhab would certainly help the other cities' thoughts along these or any other paths which could mean injury to Pirnaush. The price of two years' delay against Kerhab could be ten years' work to do over again, and Pirnaush S'Rain didn't have ten years to live. Dehass expected to outlive his master, but his own life would be worth living only if his master died victorious.

Then there was Cragor, Wandor, and the great duel between them. It was tempting to wish that the two men, the lands they ruled, and the peoples who followed them did not exist, although this might be questioning the wisdom of the Three High Gods—Sundao the River Father, Khoshi Swift in Battle, and Wasra the Mother of Life. The barbarous races of the north might serve some purpose, but generally it was better to ignore them and their wars. Doing so usually was not only possible but easy. Only if the Kingdom of Benzos itself was caught up in a war could Chongan trade be disturbed enough to make the merchants of the Twelve Cities notice.

However, this was precisely what had happened. It wouldn't have happened if Cragor had crushed Wandor and his allies, or if Nond had taken Cragor's head before the Black Duke could strike. As it was, Cragor held Benzos in a firm grip, and Wandor held the eastern shore of the Ocean equally firmly. Above all, he held the allegiance of the HaroiLina and their two hundred seal ships. If Wandor chose to, he could end seaborne trade between Chonga and Benzos. The opportunities for Chongan merchants in the east would not make up a quarter of what might be lost in Benzos.

Several delegations of merchants, including one from Dyroka, had already explained this to Dehass. They'd gone on explaining it until Dehass reminded them that he also could add a column of figures and found their lack of confidence in the king's wisdom disturbing. The merchants knew what could happen to men who disturbed the First Counselor and took their departure with as much haste as their dignity allowed them, but they had a real grievance, and Dehass knew that sooner or later they would be back.

Even if Chongan trade flowed steadily, Dehass was not sure the growing war in the north could be ignored. Wandor could call a hundred thousand fighting men to battle, Cragor probably twice as many. To be sure, many of them lacked both the wisdom and the skills of a proper warrior. Even a Knight of Benzos would be hard-pressed against a Chongan *paizar-han*, let alone a *mungan*, and in siegecraft the northerners were hardly more than children. Yet three hundred thousand fighting men were far too many to be ignored, even if they were now a long way off. It was well to think about them before they came closer.

Dehass looked out from under the silk canopy. The boat was passing the jetty at the foot of the Street of the Pearl Fishers. Dehass picked up his cloak, they were nearing the water gate of the City Palace.

The boat lurched, throwing Dehass to one side hard enough to jar his bad leg. Something grated along one side—probably a raft of timber on its way down from the north. They were hard enough to see, Sundao knew! Then the servants were rolling back the canopy as the river wall of the palace loomed up to starboard. The boat heeled as the helmsman saw the water gate, then swept into the gaping black maw. Damp stone was all around them for a moment, then the boat was gliding across the basin to the palace quay. The rowers tossed their oars, the boat bumped the rope-padded edge of the quay, and Dehass rose to his feet with a groan as his weight came on the bad leg.

Pirnaush's favorite room in the City Palace was on the uppermost floor. It was square, thirty paces on a side, and cooled by a slave-driven fan in the ceiling and by the air blowing through two large windows guarded by blue sea-jade screens. Not a room easily defended—but if an enemy got so far that the upper three floors of the palace were in danger, the battle was already lost.

The windows took up two of the four walls. In the third wall a locked door of polished wood led to spiral stairs. In the fourth a door of gilded bronze latticework led to a shaft running from the roof to the cellar of the palace. An elaborate system of weights and pulleys hauled a metal cage up and down the shaft, one large enough to carry food, wine, scrolls, cushions, weapons, slaves, or anything else anyone using the room might want, all of it delivered without letting in one unwanted eye or ear.

In the center of the room stood a plain reed table, and around it three chairs and a couch. *Zigbai* Dehass lay on the couch, his cane propped against the head and his leg pillowed on cushions stuffed with aromatic seaweed. He sipped fruit juice from a silver cup and looked across the table at the three men seated in the chairs.

In the center was Pirnaush S'Rain himself. His chair was the one he used on campaign, a folding one of plain linen and unpolished wood. It was in harmony with the square-cut gray beard and the dark brown face above the beard, scarred, seamed, wrinkled, squared off and filled out but not softened by good living. It struck a crashing discord with the king's clothing, the plum-colored robe, the white undertunic, the gold lace on hems, sleeves, and sandals, the gold and jewels on the dagger.

On Pirnaush's right his elder son Chiero S'Rain leaned back into the enveloping cushions of a chair large enough to seat two men in comfort. Chiero was clean-shaven and wore robes in a soft shade of blue, like the skies after a heavy rain. He was slimmer than his father, yet somehow his face was softer. He looked—Khoshi preserve him and all who might depend on him!—*gentle*.

On Pirnaush's left was Kobo S'Rain, *Hu-Bassan* of the fleet, second son, and a very different proposition from his elder brother. He sat upright without being rigid, his pigtail bound with a plain brass ring and his beard and mustache trimmed hair by hair. As a *paizar-han* he should have worn two pigtails as well as the short sword and dagger, but in this as in other matters, followed custom only when he chose to. His short robe was black, his sash was a dark red, and under his robe he wore a sailor's white trousers and greased leather sandals with sharkskin soles. Once he'd come to a council meeting with mail under his robe and his helmet under his arm, but that was a breach of etiquette Pirnaush would not allow even to his more gifted son.

His favorite son? Dehass had asked himself that unanswerable question a hundred times. Chiero gave loyalty which would never end, Kobo gave brilliant service with the fleet. Which did Pirnaush value the most? A fascinating question, a vital one for Dehass, and one still as mysterious as the fate of the Dragon Steed of Morkol. Pirnaush had to be taking special care to guard this secret, otherwise he could never have kept it from the man who'd spent twenty-five years fighting, wenching, drinking and scheming at his side.

The bell hanging over the shaft door tinkled softly but insistently. Chiero rose. "Allow me, father." He hurried across the room just a little too quickly to be graceful. He reached the door just as the cage appeared with a tray of wine jugs, plates of fried fish, and drinking cups.

Chiero served the other three, doing the Son's Service as if he were posing for an artist illustrating a book on manners. Indeed, he might prosper as an artist's model or even as an artist. He had real gifts with ink and paint, as he did with a scripting brush, the nine-string harp, the Dances of Kran, the judging of silks, jades, and bronzes, and even the pleasing of his concubines. He had a whole basketful of the gifts needed to win him happiness as a subject of King Pirnaush, and hardly any of the gifts needed in his place as Pirnaush's heir.

Talk died as the king piled fish on his plate and began tearing them apart with his fingers. No one could fault Pirnaush's taste in wines, but when it came to food he still ate like a soldier on campaign. Dehass remembered the early years, when he and Pirnaush had been forced to accept the hospitality of rich merchants and temples whose alliance they sought. Dehass savored each exotic dish, while Pirnaush would look at them as if he expected them to bite him or poison him. Now Pirnaush could eat when and where and what he chose, and it was Dehass's turn to groan at what was set before him.

Even Pirnaush could only eat so much, and the meal finally came to an end. Chiero returned the dishes to the cage, and the king looked at Dehass with one of his deceptively mild grins lurking under his beard.

"Eh, Dehass," he said. "What are we to do about Kerhab, and also about our friends in the north?"

Dehass was used to the king's far-reaching questions and regarded them as a challenge to his wits. He knew he was lucky in being able to do so. He, a few other old comrades, and Pirnaush's sons were the only people asked such questions by the king when he wanted useful ideas and facts. The king always tried to force everyone else to show how much or how little they knew, and showing either too much or too little knowledge had been known to cost men their heads.

Nonetheless, even Dehass was happier when he'd thought beforehand about his answer. He shrugged. "What is there to

11

do about Kerhab, except attack swiftly?" He ran through the line of argument he'd formed in his mind on the way upriver and saw Pirnaush nod.

"I've been thinking so myself. If the Fifteen haven't weakened by now, they won't. I doubt if we could bribe any of them. I know we couldn't assassinate enough of them to make any real difference."

"Not without the help of the *mungans*," said Chiero. "If we had them on—"

Kobo gave a short barking laugh, like the mating call of a river dragon. "We'd get more help and fewer tricks from Morkol's ghost, as long as Telek the Fatherless is among the *mungans*."

"He is not of Chongan blood," said Chiero. "So by the laws and customs of the *mungans*, he cannot—"

Kobo made an obscene suggestion about the laws and customs of the *mungans*. "Take your eyes off your books, brother, and use your ears. Telek can't be chosen *Bassan* of the *mungans*, that's true. But he doesn't need titles to make the *mungans* useless to us. He will certainly hear if we approach any of his comrades to strike at the Fifteen, and then we'll be at the mercy of his whims. Do we want to face what Telek handed out to Galkor and Wandor?"

Everyone in the room knew how Telek had flitted about Galkor and Wandor like a malicious wasp, stinging both sides without fear or favor, maddening both alike. Even Chiero could see the wisdom of letting that particular insect sleep as long as he might wish to, and that the best answer to Kobo's question was silence.

Into the silence Pirnaush thrust himself. "I think we can try dealing with our friends to the north at the same time. We'll need some thought and some gold, but no more than we've used to win less in the past."

Pirnaush drained his cup and refilled it, then lifted it with both hands. "Think. Kerhab's used the years we gave it to strengthen the walls and store everything for a siege. The people stand behind the Fifteen because they've been told Kerhab can now stand a longer siege than we can afford to lay. The Fifteen may be right."

"Father, your strength is such that—"

"It would be stretched to the breaking point if we added a siege of Kerhab to everything else we have to do," said Kobo.

"Manners are all very well, Chiero, but here we deal with the truth."

"Is it the truth, then, that the fleet cannot bring Kerhab to submission alone?"

"It might, if it could get there. But I won't take the fleet up the Pilmau to Kerhab while Zerun lies unsubmitted in my rear. That would be inviting the war against two cities at once. They may eat river dragons in Zerun, but they know how much we need the fleet and how much the city which trapped it might win from our enemies.

"No, the fleet will go up the Pilmau to Kerhab only when we have the city besieged. Then Kerhab's fate will be written in brushwork far clearer than yours. Zerun will not aid doomed men."

Chiero flushed at the sneering reference to his prized script-work. For a moment Dehass thought the meeting was going to fall apart in another contest of jibes and insults between the brothers. Pirnaush often allowed this and sometimes even seemed to encourage it. This time he held up both hands and glared at his sons until Chiero's face returned to normal and Kobo relaxed.

"We have to take Kerhab, even though they're ready for us," he said. "We need help. I suggest we look for it in the north."

Dehass wasn't entirely surprised at the proposal. He'd considered it himself, then set it aside because he could see no practical way of doing it. If Pirnaush asked, "How are we going to win this help?" his blank face would reveal his blank mind.

Fortunately Pirnaush seemed to have been doing all the thinking needed. "Another six thousand fighting men would make the siege of Kerhab safe. Twice that many will make it as easy as something like this ever can be. Cragor could easily send that many, and Wandor wouldn't find it impossible."

Dehass nodded. "Yes, Lord *Bassan*." He hoped he could cover his own rising excitement. "But I cannot imagine either one helping us without some reward. If we reward one, we make an enemy of the other."

"No doubt," said Pirnaush. "But they seem so equally balanced that if one was a friend we wouldn't have to fear the other. What's more, because they're so equally balanced they can't afford to ignore the reward we may offer them."

"They've done well enough balanced this way so far," said Chiero. "Why should they change?"

Pirnaush's smile now made Dehass think of a well-fed cat. With only a little imagination it was possible to hear the king purring. "They can't go on the way they have for more than another year.

"Wandor has to be ready to bring a hundred thousand men into the field. The ones he doesn't have to pay regularly are wild tribesmen, of no use without the others. The others are Royal Army of Benzos, mercenaries, household troops of the Viceroyalty's nobles, the fighters of the HaroiLina. They're the ones to be feared, and they're also the ones who eat Wandor's gold. Why he hasn't been stripped bare long before now, I don't understand.

"Cragor has both less and more than Wandor. He has more trained, civilized men, but also more who have to be paid regularly."

"He also has more to pay them," said Chiero. Dehass fought down an urge to glare. He didn't want Pirnaush interrupted until he'd laid out in plain view all his thoughts on this matter. They grew more interesting almost with each word.

"He's not as well off as you might think, Chiero. He has to defend a long coast against the HaroiLina and a long border against the Ponans. Some lands in Benzos are still ruined from the war against Nond and pay few taxes. Others pay reluctantly, and still others don't pay at all. There's a Count Ferjor who leads five hundred sworn foes of Cragor and holds land two days' ride across. That land's as out of the reach of Cragor's tax gatherers as if it floated in the sky. Cragor loses some gold from Ferjor's holding the land, and more in fighting him.

"To be sure, there's enough gold in the hands of the nobles of Benzos to pay for three armies. But those are the nobles who raised Cragor to power because they wouldn't enrich the kings. Cragor can't pay his armies without taxing the nobles, but what will they say if he does? What will they do? I wonder how Cragor answers those questions.

"So Wandor and Cragor both need gold. We have it. They need ships, Cragor to guard his coast, Wandor to carry his men to Benzos. We have sailing ships and galleys, the best timber in the world, the best shipwrights to work it, sailors, rowers, and captains. They both face castles and walled cities, but don't know siegecraft. We have engines and the men with the skills to work them, passed down from father to son for ten gener-

14

ations. Cragor has a queen, Wandor a lady who should be one. What woman could refuse a crown in sea jade and gold, set with the rubies and pearls of Chonga?"

Pirnaush went on in this high style for some time, gradually slipping into the pure cant of a crier in the Old Market of Dyroka. It reminded Dehass that fifty years ago a small boy named Pirnaush S'Rain had cried the virtues of his father's vegetables. Now a king cried the virtues of all Chonga.

In time Pirnaush fell silent, drank more wine, then went on. "I think we should approach both Cragor and Wandor at the same time. Each should send a trusted man with full powers to Dyroka, so we can compare their offers and choose the best."

"Do we need to spend that much time?" asked Kobo. "Cragor has more wealth and fewer scruples. Wandor has a reputation for virtue which he is said to value highly."

Pirnaush laughed but said nothing. Dehass feared that the king was trying to draw him out but knew he had to speak anyway. "You talk of 'a reputation for virtue.' Wandor has that, indeed, and he may even have the substance. Yet can we be sure his desire for a reputation will stand against his need for gold? Likewise, can we be sure that Cragor will stop at nothing? He may see this alliance as owing his power to—"

Kobo snorted. "To be sure, Dehass. Lecture us all about virtues and scruples. You know the limits of both as well as any of us."

It had been fifteen years since Dehass let himself be nettled by such remarks. Even then, when Pirnaush ruled only Dyroka itself and that precariously, he might have held tongue and temper. Now, too much was at stake. Bringing either Wandor or Cragor into the affairs of Chonga would be a notable victory. Bringing both of them, ignorant of Chongan affairs and too busy watching each other to watch the Chongans around them, would be a gift from all the gods at once.

The Councillor smiled. "Say what you will of me, it does not change Wandor and Cragor. We do not dare cast either aside on the words of other men." He was about to go on, "If I were a sorcerer with the Mind Speech—"; then decided against raising the thought of sorcery. Compared to either Kaldmor the Dark with his Toshakan Powers or Cheloth of the Woods with his own, the few Chongan sorcerers were hardly more than apprentices. Furthermore, the Twelve Cities of Chonga were once colonies of the Old Lands to the south. In the duel between

15

Cheloth and Nem the Old Land had sunk. Now only the waves of the Ocean and the Tok'li Islands lay where the forefathers of all the Chongans had ruled in golden palaces. Fear and hatred of sorcery was born in most Chongans, and few ever outgrew it.

If Pirnaush and his sons were going to forget this, it was hardly Dehass's duty to remind them. Very probably the sorceries of both sides were as equally balanced as the material strength, but Pirnaush might have second thoughts about what would seem to be wagering the whole future of Chonga as well as his own power of this probability.

Pirnaush nodded. "I feel the same as Dehass. These aren't ordinary men, and we'd best take more than ordinary care with them." He turned to Kobo. "Now, Kobo, for our messages we'll need two of the fastest *kulghas*, with captains and crews who . . ."

The discussion turned to the hundred and one details of sending word to Cragor and Wandor. Dehass breathed more easily. If Pirnaush was going to have second thoughts, the time for them was nearly past. When the king came down to details, he was determined to push through to the end, whether in battle, in conspiracy, or in bedding a woman.

The *mungan* Telek the Fatherless also chose a meeting place on a high floor, but there its resemblance to the room in the City Palace ended. It was a closed-off corner of the loft on the eighth floor of one of the great sprawling buildings at the foot of Market Hill. It was as dark and airless and well-hidden as any cellar, but far easier to leave in haste—at least for *mungans*, trained and equipped to leap alleys from roof to roof or to climb any wall offering them a fingerhold.

Telek screwed the hilt-weight back onto his dagger and thrust it into his belt. "So the messengers will be going aboard the ships within a day or two. I think we'd best decide what to do before we leave here tonight."

Hawa shook her head. "That would be deciding too soon, with too little knowledge of what Dehass may be planning." Mitzon frowned, at his suggestion or Hawa's protest Telek could not say.

"Would we?" said Telek. "Pirnaush isn't likely to turn aside from a course which promises so well. Even if he considers it, Dehass can be trusted to turn him back. I think Dehass would bend over backward until his head touched his heels to bring Cragor and Wandor into the affairs of Chonga. Our *Zigbai* would not look as lovely as you do in that pose, Hawa, but he would certainly adopt it if nothing else would advance his plans."

"Perhaps," said Hawa. Flattery had long since ceased to sweeten her. "But Dehass's high hopes may be a double-edged sword blade. He'll push the king indeed, but he may also overreach himself and push too hard. This is always a temptation when an ambitious man sees a chance to bring his dearest dreams to life."

Dehass's hopes weren't the only thing around with two edges, Telek decided. There was also Hawa's tongue. He would leave the matter, since she was prepared to speak this way and might even be right. The next few months would be the greatest test yet of Dehass's varied skills. If Telek rested his own hopes too heavily on Dehass's success—well, his own failure would be less public but nearly as final.

"Perhaps we can leave the decision to our next meeting," he said. "Until then, Hawa should go on with her work at the Inn of the White Plum Tree." She danced there, and a dancer at a soldier's and sailor's tavern is apt to learn a good deal. Dancers were not the only people who revealed themselves at a good tavern.

He turned to Mitzon. "You should stay in the *Haugon Dyrokee*. Seek a post in the River Watch, if you can do this without losing rank." Mitzon commanded a Thirty in the citizens' army raised by Pirnaush, and had hopes of soon rising to command a Ninety. The Shield of Dyroka needed able young captains if it was to hold the balance for its creator against both the old fortress guards of Dyroka and the armies of the allied cities. Pirnaush knew this and made sure the commanders of the *Haugon* knew it too.

Mitzon snorted. "I'm more likely to be raised a step or even two if I move to the River Watch. If Pirnaush is going to move against Kerhab, every man who won't dissolve if he falls into the water will be going to the river troops."

"Good. Do as well there as you've done elsewhere, and I will owe you much." Mitzon knew Hawa too well to risk smiling at Telek's praise, but the older man could tell that he was moved. Mitzon definitely would have to be elevated above Hawa, and swiftly. His wits and steel were no slower, and he would be a far more loyal supporter of Telek's power, whether that power extended only over the *mungans* or far and wide into Chonga.

Telek rose and hooked thumbs in a triangle with the other two. "Farewell, until it is time again." In a moment only another *mungan* could have told that anyone had ever been in the room.

TWO

Jaira the Khind girl was surprised when she heard that a new bannerman was coming to Captain Tagor's company from Benzor. Winter had the north country along the Nifan chained in ice and snow, and Tagor's company was strong. Why send a new man even the two days' ride from the nearest town, let alone all the way from Benzor?

Then she saw the bannerman and thought she understood why he'd come, even before she heard him speaking with Tagor. On a morning which now seemed part of another life, this man had burst into her family's hut waving an ax. Her father had met him with only a log of firewood, and the ax split his skull and face. Her mother screamed, the man lunged at her, and the sixteen-year-old Jaira dashed out the open door.

She should have stayed. She might have fought, and she could certainly have died with her mother instead of fleeing. She'd known this the moment she stepped outside, but two more of Cragor's paid killers were coming at her, and there was no way back. She ran, leaving half her clothing in their hands. They'd have caught her anyway, except that the Duelist Bertan Wandor rode up and killed them. She lived through the day, and none of the surviving Khindi knew how her courage had failed her. So they took her in, and she lived as well as could be hoped until Cragor came to power and ended the lives or freedom of all the Khindi in Benzos.

Now, here before her in Tagor's house was the man. She could not imagine that there was another one like him, with the same height and coloring, the same puckered scar from the

19

corner of his right eye to the base of the right ear, and the same misshapen, doubled-over left thumb. He had a half-healed cut across his forehead and a bruise on his throat as if strong hands had gripped it, but these were not part of the man. He was the same, riding out of her past as he'd ridden out of the forest, sitting on Tagor's stool by Tagor's fire and sipping Tagor's wine that she'd brought him.

Captain Tagor wasn't drinking. "They don't send men up here from Benzos even in the good seasons unless they've put a foot wrong," he said. "What did you do?"

"Not enough to be worth—"

"I'll judge if it's not worth hearing after I hear it. You'll tell me, or you and your men camp outside until you do."

The new man shrugged. "*Hunh*. I was after a damned hedge-sorcerer—"

"I thought the duke's orders were to leave them alone?"

"You want to hear me out or not?"

"Go on."

"This one, they said he was working with a Tree Sister. You know, one of *her* kind o' witches." He jerked the malformed thumb at Jaira. "So it was pretty sure he was up to something. I caught somebody I thought might know where he was." The man held his cup out to Jaira. "How 'bout some more wine, Mudhair?"

The bannerman emptied his cup in three swallows. "Fellow wouldn't talk. I thought I could make him, 'cause I know a lot about that sort o' thing. He didn't talk, and the healers couldn't get him up. Turned out he was nephew to some big-arse merchant in Benzor. Too big to let me stay in the city. So here I am."

"Fair enough, I suppose," said Tagor. "How many men did you say you brought?" The talk now turned to details of war, feeding the new men, and life in Benzor. Jaira saw that the wine jug was empty, snatched it up, and scurried out the door. Tagor's wine and beer was at the other end of the house; perhaps the new man would be gone before she could return. She desperately wanted to get away from him, and not just because he might recognize her.

She'd thought she was utterly cursed and abandoned by Masutl the High Hunter and even the Mother Tree, cast up on the bank of the Life Stream and doomed to rot there like a fallen branch. Now part of the Life Stream was reaching out to her again. How could this be without purpose? And when the man was here because a sorcerer of Benzos was working with a Tree Sister of the Khindi, when she'd been sure there were none alive nearer than the Home Forests—? She had much to think about and no one to guide her thoughts.

After five days of bitter cold the snow was a fine powder swirling around Count Ferjor and the man facing him. It struck the count that if they stayed here long enough they'd both have drifts piled up against their legs as if they were trees.

The man facing the count was immensely broad in skull and shoulders, chest, and belly, and his face would have been as broad if beard and hair hadn't swallowed so much of it. A well-worn leather belt supported a short sword, and a strap held a round shield across his back. His name was Hod ranFedil, and he wanted to be Count Ferjor's ally against the Black Duke.

The count didn't like the man's looks, but looks meant little these days. Knights had sunk to cranking the racks and wielding the hot irons in Cragor's torture chambers, and common whores had slipped steel between the ribs of those Knights. Ferjor's own notion was that Alfod the Judge and Staz the Warrior were both roaring drunk and throwing dice for the fate of the men who served them. Some throws sent a man to serve Cragor, some to serve Nond's memory, some to serve only themselves.

"Are you frozen dumb and deaf, Knight?" shouted ranFedil. "Or shall we do what we came here for?"

Ferjor nodded. "Speak."

"I have three hundred men sworn to me." He stepped closer to Ferjor, pulled a dead branch from under the snow, and began sketching a map on a clear patch of snow in the lee of a thick trunk. "Your hand's on these forests, and mine's on the land here. To the north we reach the Nifan, to the west Lodish. To the east we could reach into the Gailanna Hills, but they're no use to us. To the south we can reach as far as we want, until no farmer north of Behed-Krar will refuse us help.

"I ask that you and I stand equal before our men. We divide all the booty into eight parts, five to you, three to me. When our men fight together, whoever brings more to the fight commands. If our men quarrel we judge together. If blood is shed, there will be gold paid, not more blood."

"What about fighting the Ponans?" asked Ferjor. RanFedil's name, his squat build and hairy face, and his talk of money payment for blood told Ferjor the man was not of Hond blood. He did not look Khind, and the ancient tribes of northern

Benzos were a handful of root-grubbers in the wilderness. Hod ranFedil had to be either Sthi or Ponan.

"We fight them when they fight us," said ranFedil. "Or do you want us to go north of the Nifan, even now?"

Ferjor laughed. "No, not that. But I want you and all your men to understand this. Cragor has neglected fighting Ponan raiders to fight his enemies here in Benzos. With the help of the gods we shall not make the same mistake. When the time comes for us to swear, that will be part of the oath. Priests of Alfod and Staz will be our witnesses, along with our chief captains."

Hod ranFedil seemed to have no objections to swearing oaths by the Five Gods of the Hond. He only grunted. "You won't swear here, now, with the men we brought as witnesses? Don't your men obey you as mine do me?"

"Do your men obey you when they suspect you don't care what they think? I haven't heard that they do, or that you ever fail to ask them. Allow me to do as much. I am a mere Knight and count, but I am not altogether foolish in such matters."

RanFedil stared for a moment, then laughed. "Good. I think we can wait for you. The next full moon, send a messenger. Soon enough?"

"Soon enough, ranFedil."

"Then—honor and farewell, Lord Count." He turned and ploughed his way off into the trees, throwing up a cloud of snow. With cracklings and thuds, outlaws who'd been watching for treachery crawled out from their hiding places. Then there was only the moan of the wind.

The count turned away, calling up his own guards. Hod ranFedil would bear watching even if he became an ally, and still more if Ferjor's captains rejected the alliance. Would they?

Ferjor tossed the question back and forth a few times in his mind, then decided to let it fall. An alliance with ranFedil would nearly double the fighting strength united against Cragor in these lands. He and ranFedil could lead their men into the wide stretch of country lying between their two holds, four days' ride from west to east. That would end the easy times for Cragor's allies and garrisons, rally his enemies, perhaps even make the Ponans think twice about crossing the Nifan. The alliance would also permit the judging of quarrels between the men of the two bands. These quarrels would come as inevitably as the spring thaw, whether the alliance came or not, since Ferjor and ranFedil between them led nearly all the survivors of Cragor's enemies north of Behed-Krar.

Yet what did Hod ranFedil serve, other than his own ambition, which was great, and his hatred of Cragor, which was real enough? A time would come when Cragor was no more, even if Ferjor saw it only from the House of Shadows. Would ranFedil give up the outlaw's life easily, or did he love it so much he'd keep the north country at war until he was hunted down like a wild boar?

There were other worries as well, closer to hand. Did ranFedil have enough captains Ferjor's men would obey? Did he have enough who would obey his orders when it came to dividing the booty, and just what did they count as booty anyway? The alliance would bring the men of each band into the lands of the other, revealing secrets kept long and well. Even if ranFedil and his captains could be trusted, what about the common men? Among three hundred men some would in time think of what they'd learned and how much it might bring them from Cragor. How soon, and what would happen then?

Kaldmor the Dark sipped spiced wine from a silver cup and let the warmth and the fumes rise into his nose. This winter had brought him a clogged, dripping nose and splitting headaches, and no healing spell seemed to have any power against them. Hot wine did some good, particularly if he drank enough of it.

He drained the cup and set it back on the tray. "Very good," he said to the serving girl. "Now go out and get me more. Also have someone throw more perfume on the fire."

The girl smiled, then saw Kaldmor's eyes on her and stopped. The sorcerer knew that, like most of the castle girls, she hoped to find her way to his bed. He also hoped she wouldn't guess the real reason why neither she nor any other girl would be there tonight. Between the wine and his illness, the sorcerer simply didn't trust his manhood.

The girl went out through the tapestry-hung doorway, and Kaldmor lay back on the couch. He wore only purple silk trousers and a ring holding a small *khru*-medallion to aid his personal spells. No vigils in the icy wind or even in dank tower chambers for him! At least not this winter, when the vitalized *limar* of Nem of Toshak could keep watch for any disorders or dangers in the spirit world. It did not have the judgment to decide what to do if it detected any, but Kaldmor had carefully avoided giving it such powers. He wanted a skilled servant, not an equal, and he would turn the *limar* into anything like an equal only if he had to. That need would not come before spring and its new warfare, if it came at all.

The same could be said of his studies of the Powers and spells of Toshak. He'd carried them as far as he needed, and never mind that Wandor had won the battle for the HaroiLina and Yand Island. He'd been far away while that battle was being fought, and if anyone was to blame for the defeat there it was Mykto the Beast Wizard and that stubborn sorcery-hating fool Galkor. Mykto was dead, but Galkor not only lived but enjoyed as much favor with the duke as Kaldmor himself.

That thought seemed to call for more wine. He raised his voice to shout.

"Hurry up, you sows!"

The north wind told the Grand Master of the Duelists that there must already be fresh snow along the Nifan. Here in Tafardos the ground was still bare from the last thaw and the unpaved side streets were knee-deep in mud.

The Grand Master leaned against a fire barrel, to hold himself upright against the wind, and in spite of his fur-lined cloak and layers of woolen tunics, he shivered. When he'd ridden five days along winter roads to Tafardos, and now as he stood in its windy streets, he felt all his seventy years and a few more besides.

Perhaps he'd have felt otherwise if he'd come to Tafardos on some more agreeable errand that closing the Duelists' House there. It had never recovered from the blow he himself had struck it when he had killed its House Master and sent the man's head to Duke Cragor. To be sure, the man had said much and done more than a little to put the whole Order in danger. Nonetheless the death crushed the spirits of the Duelists of Tafardos like flowers trampled by an ox. Without spirit their steel was useless and their loyalty doubtful. Cragor was a man with a very long purse, who would not refuse to buy any man who might do him good service, and Baron Galkor had even fewer scruples.

The Grand Master certainly would not say this out loud. To others he said only that the Tafardos House was now too weak and too poor to be kept alive in the face of the Order's other needs. Then he'd pronounced the fate of the Duelists of Tafardos—their House would be closed and they dispersed among the other seven Houses in the heartland of Benzos—and now he'd come to Tafardos with a band of trusted Duelists to carry out this task himself. It was like stabbing a favorite dog grown old and ill-tempered, or amputating a festering hand—something a wise man will do swiftly, and an honorable man will do himself if he can.

The rear gate of the House creaked open. Eight men came out, four carrying torches and four carrying two brass-bound chests. That was the end of tonight's work, then. When a House was opened the chests for its treasures and secret papers were the first things brought in, and when it was closed they were the last things brought out. In fact and in law the Tafardos House was now an empty shell, with none but the bats, the rats, and the rain having any claim to it.

The Grand Master stepped forward and raised a hand. From the end of the street a two-horse cart rumbled forward. A spatter of rain struck the Grand Master, stinging his cheek like a handful of thrown pebbles. The streets would soon be treacherous with ice. He waved the cart forward more urgently.

"Move, you slowfooted dolts! Do you want to end up frozen solid and decorating the gates like statues?"

Cragor was at the top of the stairs when the woman's cry reached him. He turned, stepping away from the direction of the cry. His guards turned with him, their swords out of their scabbards. Before Cragor could draw, the guards were between him and the woman. Two of them gripped her by the arms and started to pull her back.

"Your Grace! I beg you! For Her Majesty's sake!"

Cragor recognized the voice, and as the woman raised herself on tiptoe he saw her face between the heads of the two guards. It was Lady Helda Odomorna, once Queen Anya's nurse and now first among the Ladies of the Queen's Chamber.

"Stand aside and let her approach," said the duke. He doubted the woman's sanity, but did not despise her influence over his wife. Lady Helda had been with Anya since ten minutes after the queen's birth, and had come closer than anyone else to taking the place of the mother who died bearing her. If there was anyone who could give Anya enough affection to make her less vulnerable to her husband, it was Lady Helda.

On the other hand, she was quite harmless here and now, he had time to spare, and it was never wise to miss what might be a chance to show graciousness to those who depended on him. Cruelty and kindness were both weapons to be aimed precisely, more like bolts from a crossbow than stones hurled at random from a siege engine.

"Yes, my lady? You wish my ear? If so, you have it."

Lady Helda spread her fingers across both cheeks as if her head would fall off without being held on. Her gray hair was tangled and fell down over her hands.

"Honor and greetings, My Lord Duke." She swallowed and was silent for so long the duke began to think her mind was finally gone altogether. "My Lord Duke, you hold a man named Barim Mazor for questioning?"

The duke only nodded. The less he said, the more she might reveal.

"He is innocent, my lord. It is impossible for him to have done any of—what it is said he has done." She repeated this several times in slightly different words while Cragor tried to dig the name "Barim Mazor" out of his memory. Then he remembered, and his face twisted so that Lady Helda went pale, lurched backward, and would have fallen if the guards hadn't gripped her again.

"Damn Barim Mazor!" said the duke under his breath, not much caring whether the woman heard him or not. Would he never hear the end of the affair of the sorcerer and the Tree Sister? He'd already had to send one of his most reliable daggermen north to fight frostbite, Ponans, and outlaws in the forests, because some young fool's uncle ruled the Guild of Carpenters. Barim Mazor was another young fool who'd been caught up in the same net, even though it had caught neither of the two big fish.

"Who is he to you?" said Cragor. "Your lover?" The guards gave him the laughter he wanted. Lady Helda went from pale to red and shook her head.

"He is my grandson. There is no one else in the world I would beg for this way. He cannot have had anything to do with sorcerers. He wanted to be a priest of Alfod, and he hated them. A wise man like you must see this, My Lord Duke. You must."

"I must—" the duke began, then hesitated. He'd been about to say, "I must do nothing of the kind." Then her words about "no one else in the world" started him thinking. There was someone else for whom Lady Helda would probably let herself be torn in pieces by red-hot pincers. Anya. If he offered her the grandson's life, would she agree to abandon Anya?

"I must consider this," the duke said, "But my lady— I have a question for you. If I release your grandson to you, will you retire from the court to your family's estates and return only at my pleasure? I must not neglect the safety of the kingdom. I would certainly be doing that if I released your grandson without being sure he was well watched. I could trust you to do that, if you agree to remove him from the temptations of Benzos."

A rustle of feet and low voices rose from the foot of the stairs, but Cragor could make out no words and ignored the noise. All his attention was on the woman in front of him. He signaled the guards holding her to let her go and stepped toward her. "Well, my lady? Your place here beside the queen or your grandson's life?"

His voice raised echoes in the hall and drew a choked cry from below. Cragor stepped close to Lady Helda, until he had to look down to meet her eyes. As he did, Anya appeared at the foot of the stairs. Lady Helda swallowed, then swayed as if she was only a heartbeat from fainting. Cragor's hand went out to her. He'd meant to grip and hold. Instead, as if his hand had a will of its own, it pushed.

Fifty pairs of eyes widened and fifty mouths gaped. No sound came from any of these open mouths loud enough to drown out Lady Helda's scream as she went over backward, the series of thuds as she rolled down the stairs, or the cry from Queen Anya as the woman reached the bottom.

Three steps brought the queen to Lady Helda's side. It took the duke rather longer to make his way down the stairs, since he refused to run. By the time he reached the bottom, every mouth was closed and every pair of eyes was trying to look anywhere but at the duke or the sprawled form of Lady Helda with the queen bending over her. The spell of silence was unbroken.

Cragor stepped toward his wife, and several of the queen's ladies who'd been moving to join her beside Lady Helda became statues. Anya ignored them all as she moistened a handkerchief with perfume from a crystal vial. As Cragor loomed over her, she pressed the handkerchief to Lady Helda's forehead. The nurse was still visibly breathing, but her eyes showed only the whites and blood was trickling from her nose and mouth.

Cragor reached down to take the handkerchief, and at last Anya seemed to be aware of his presence. "Anya, I shall summon the healers. Best we leave her to them." For once in his life the duke was totally at a loss what tone to use in speaking to his wife, and the words came out flat and lifeless.

Anya jumped as if he'd finally laid the whiplash on her flesh. Slowly she rose, the handkerchief crumpled in one hand. "My lord," she said. She licked her lips and repeated the words twice more. Then:

"My lord, the Lady Helda has been mine. She will be mine. I will see to her care, for I am queen and she is of my household. You—you have done enough with her yourself, without calling in your healers to finish the work."

If he hadn't been keeping himself under iron control, it would have been the duke's turn to start. Anya was as frightened of his anger as she'd ever been. If she'd been an opponent in battle, Cragor would have said she was about to soil herself in sheer terror. Yet a fear which in the past had stopped her mouth and palsied her limbs had this time affected neither. Instead she was setting her will against his, something which seldom happened at all and had never happened before so many witnesses.

She'd even kept enough of her wits about her to put forward an argument he couldn't easily ignore. By law and custom the queen was mistress in her own household. If she claimed her rights over someone in Lady Helda's position, no king or consort might dispute her without questioning her fitness to be queen. Even if Anya submitted, fifty men and women would have seen Cragor set aside the queen's will. That was too many to silence easily.

He would not force battle now, and some good might even come of this affair in the end. The duke had seen enough battle wounds to know that Lady Helda might never leave her bed, and certainly would be an invalid for many weeks. During all that time Anya's attention would be entirely on her old nurse's health, and the duke would not have to lift a finger or speak a word to keep her safely away from affairs of state. And if Lady Helda did die, there would be her influence over the queen gone for good.

"Certainly, Your Majesty," said Cragor. "Lady Helda is in your hands, and may the gods and your own skill speed her recovery." He turned swiftly and began climbing the stairs without another look backward. He felt an odd reluctance to look at his wife's face again.

* * *

Tide, gray swell, and the current of the Avar fought one another, making Baron Galkor's barge lurch and sway, although the snow fell straight from the windless sky. The rowers struggled to keep an even beat, frozen spray turned the thwarts white, and the baron would have been seasick if he hadn't lost that weakness on his voyage to Yand and the HaroiLina.

He'd lost much more on that voyage, but at least he hadn't lost the duke's confidence. Perhaps that proved little, when one considered how few men Cragor could give that confidence to these days, but it would certainly lengthen his days, increase his wealth, and give him at least a better chance to mend his luck and strike a shrewd blow for his master.

Abruptly Galkor's thoughts returned to the present. A ship was looming up in the snow-flecked dimness ahead, where there hadn't been any ship before the snow began. The baron threw his cloak clear of his sword arm. Wandor hadn't yet sent the ships of the HaroiLina against the coasts of Benzos, and he wasn't likely to start during the winter, but—

Before the rowers could ship their oars and pick up bows and pikes, Galkor recognized the ship ahead. She was a large Chongan, the kind they called a *kulgha*. Two masts, with two square sails on the forward mast and a lateen sail on the after one, plus a bowsprit almost long and thick enough to serve as a battering ram. A broad-beamed, slab-sided hull, with high bulwarks and bow and stern well raised. *Kulghas* were a compromise, seaworthy enough to go almost anywhere, deep-keeled enough to sail, shallow enough to navigate the great rivers of Chonga, light enough to row, but with room enough for cargo or fighting men. Like a wandering craftsman, they could do nothing extraordinarily well, but they would do practically everything one way or another.

So the ship wasn't a mystery, but her presence here and now might be. When the Chongans sailed north to Benzos in the winter, they usually sailed in deepwater merchant vessels hardly smaller than the greatships of Benzos. The *kulghas* sailed in spring and summer, except when there was a cargo so valuable it couldn't wait for fine weather and so light a *kulgha* could bear it.

A snow flurry came down. When it passed, Galkor recognized the badge of the fore topsail and the pennant on the mainmast. She was a war *kulgha* in the fleet of Pirnaush of Dyroka. No late-season trader, this one, but that didn't tell him much. Galkor rose, filled his chest, cupped his hands around his mouth, and shouted:

"Ahoy, the Chongan ship! I am Baron Galkor, of Duke Cragor's service! Where are you bound, and on what business?"

In a winter dawn, Zakonta the Red Seer came out to speak to Jos-Pran as he walked on the Wall guarding South Pass. He was bareheaded and barehanded, and wore only a fur jacket over his elkskin breeches and shirt.

He turned to her as she approached and frowned. "Zakonta, you will be cold. There is no need for you out here for hours yet. Get back to bed."

"The bed is not so warm as it was, since you left it," she replied. "And I see nothing out here that calls to you either." She swept her hand along the Wall and the huts and stables of the Yhangi who now held it at the foot.

"It was nothing of that sort calling me."

"What, then? And whatever it is, I cannot imagine either of us being the worse for you saying it."

He whirled to face her so abruptly that for a moment she thought he was angry. "Zakonta, it has long been in my mind to ask you to be my wife and the mother of warriors and Red Seers of the Gray Mares. Yet I now find myself wondering. Can I—can we please ourselves when strength and wisdom are needed for so much else?"

Zakonta wanted to laugh, but knew that really would anger him. If he could think of no other reasons for not marrying her, he could be brought the rest of the way if she only showed a little care.

"Firehair and Wandor have pleased themselves, and when was the last time you heard someone question that?"

"I doubt if they would have been alive for me to hear them if Firehair heard them first," said Jos-Pran with a wry grin. "Indeed, they have pleased themselves. But have they pleased the gods? Where are their children?"

Zakonta was grateful Jos-Pran had no trace of the Mind Speech. She had never been able to ask herself that question with an easy mind, and she knew Gwynna was beginning to find it a real burden. She could, however, conceal her doubts— and suddenly she realized that she could not. She could not bring Jos-Pran the last few steps to the Wedding Circle with

30

a lie or even with a veiling of the truth. That would be riding into a desperate battle on a horse with rot in his hooves.

"Their children are in the hands of the gods, as we all are," she said. "I have my doubts about Firehair and Wandor, but I have seen or heard nothing I would call a sign against them. Nor have I seen or heard anything against us. Your seed is surely sound enough, with two children by your first wife and whatever others you care to acknowledge. You have sown no children in me only because I have used the arts of the Red Seers to prevent it."

"You swear this?"

"Yes, and I will swear it anywhere before any witnesses you ask."

He took both her hands. "I will not ask that."

"It is your right, Jos-Pran. I know what it would be to you to see your children about you again. I know what it would cost you if there was to be a curse on our bed. But I do not see that there will be." He smiled, and Zakonta wanted to shout her thanks to the Earth Voices. He was almost there.

"Yet—I can see doubt still on your face, Jos-Pran. What more is there?"

"Can we—can we make this a fit wedding, at such a time? A feast, a gathering of all the Gray Mares, a giving of gifts —is this the time for such things?"

"Perhaps not. But I do not remember that the feast, the gathering, and the gift-giving are needed. We will need the man, the woman, the lance to jump, the ale to drink, two we trust to bear witness—"

"Do you think Firehair and Wandor would bear witness for us?"

"I think Firehair at least would be angry if we did not ask." *It is done, it is done, it is done,* Zakonta's heart was singing.

Or was it done? A frown replaced Jos-Pran's smile. "All this is true. Certainly I will not ask for much more if I can have you. But—you are highest among the Red Seers. Not by law, but certainly in the eyes of everyone who sees clearly. Am I to marry you as if I were a newly sworn warrior and you were a girl of seventeen, without goods enough to fill one corner of the tent we do not have?"

"Yes."

He laughed. "We are going to have some plain-spoken children, I see. But will the Red Seers let such a wedding pass? I have my doubts, and if they do not let it pass—"

Zakonta sighed. At the moment she would gladly have cast a spell to make all the Red Seers of the Yhangi mute until she was bearing Jos-Pran's child. "You are right to doubt. They may not let it pass. They may speak out. But who will listen? Not I, and you—I remember very well that you once thought the Red Seers a few score tongue-clacking women."

Jos-Pran shifted his grip from her hands to her shoulders and pulled her hard against him. Laughing with his mouth in her hair, he held her and said, "I remember that. I also remember what came of my ignoring the Red Seers when Firehair and Wandor came. But you are right. I will not let the tongues of even the wisest woman stand between us, if you will not."

Zakonta's relief was so great that for a moment she needed Jos-Pran's arms around her to keep her standing. Then she smiled. *The gods keep me from ever lying to him*, she thought. *But may I always have the wisdom to lead him by that terrible pride of his, if I must.*

In Fors, a winter twilight had given way to a winter darkness. This made no difference to those celebrating Baron Oman Delvor's sixtieth birthday in the great hall of the castle. They piled the logs higher in the fireplaces, lit more candles, broached more barrels of wine and ale, and brought in more smoking joints of game and fish pasties breathing spices. One bank of musicians had long since exhausted themselves, but a second seemed ready to go on until dawn.

That was more than Gwynna could do. When the din and the smoke and the wine had numbed everyone's senses, she was able to slip away and make her way up the stairs to the private chambers.

Wandor found her there an hour later. She heard the door open and his footsteps crossing the fur-strewn floor, then felt his arms go around her from behind and his hands rest lightly on her breasts.

"Are you ill?"

"No. Just not as happy as a daughter should be when her father turns sixty after doing so much worth doing." She gently lifted his hands and turned to face him. "I can talk about it with you, but I'd rather no one else knew."

Bertan stiffened slightly. For a moment he looked astonishingly like a small boy waiting to have a splinter dug out of his hand. *He's been told it won't hurt, but he's far from sure he's been told the truth.* It was still this way as often as not when a question of sorcery or her Powers arose, but somehow he always managed to ask the questions.

"Have you seen or been told of any danger to your father?"

"Nothing, or at least nothing which doesn't threaten any man of sixty caught up in a war. He should see enough more years to avenge Nond."

Bertan sat down on a chest and stretched his legs out in front of him. For the first time she noticed he was holding a skin of wine in one hand. Suddenly her thirst returned.

"I sometimes think your father may outlive us all," he said as he handed her the wine. "He isn't called on to hurl himself straight at any enemy who rears his head."

"Neither are you. At least not by anything except your own notions of duty." It was an old question and even a quarrel between them, how Bertan threw himself headlong into each fight. It was so old, in fact, that she'd long since given up hope of doing very much about his habit. She wasn't going to let the matter lie, either. The hardest rock can be worn away by enough drops of water.

"Whatever the rest of us must do," he said, "none of us have ever held back." He took the wine and drank. "We've all charged right up the front stairs of the House of Shadows and knocked on the door. I don't know how we all go on walking the road together, but . . ." He seemed to decide that more wine would help him finish.

As he drank, Gwynna was on the verge of praying he wouldn't finish at all. He'd stumbled onto the same question she'd been facing for several days, in the steadily increasing fear that she knew part of the answer. They would all walk their road together almost to the end, and then their band of comrades would break apart like the ice going out of a river in the spring. She didn't know how many would die, and hoped she would never know who until the time came.

The sound of Bertan's swallowing stopped, and she felt his eyes on her. "You're thinking that our luck's going to turn all at once, just when we're right on the edge of victory."

How did he guess without the Mind Speech? leaped into her thoughts. He handed her the wine, and she drank without tasting it. He looked at her, his head tilted to one side. She realized that he might be drunk already and certainly didn't seem to care if he ended up that way.

When she'd finished drinking, he took the empty skin from her. "No, love, I haven't found a Mind Speech you can't sense.

It's just that we've been looking at the world with the same eyes and hearing it with the same ears for so long. It doesn't surprise me that we're afraid of the same thing."

He gave her a twisted grin. "I don't know much about gods or Powers or sorcery. What I do know, it's mostly been stuffed into me like nuts into a Winter's Day pig. But the Duelists have their own ideas about a fighter's luck. I grew up a Duelist, and what I learned then is telling me something now."

"What?"

"That we can't go back or turn aside. If we try, whatever happens to us will be worse than what happens if we push on. Call it a Seeing or—" he laughed, "—too much wine. But it's what I know."

Gwynna's mouth tightened, and she felt a twisting inside. Now that Bertan had put it into words, she could see it too—either going on without counting the cost or trying to sidestep fate and bringing a curse on themselves. Would the curse be her barrenness continuing, or something even worse?

Bertan looked down at the wineskin, then rose to his feet and stepped toward her. Now there was Mind Speech between them, wordless but carrying a clear message. They'd both danced along the edge of nightmare in the last few moments, and they had to do something to drive away the darkness. His lips brushed hers, then came down on them harder, so that she opened her mouth and reached up to grip the curls of hair above his ears which might have been put there for just that purpose—

Someone knocked on the door. Bertan's fingers stroked her cheek and throat, then moved to the hooks of her gown.

The knock came again, and this time she recognized the rhythm. It was Berek's private knock, the signal for news so urgent that anything could be interrupted to bring it.

Or at least *almost* anything. Bertan's hands fell away, and he turned to the door. "What is it, Berek?"

"A ship from Chonga, Master. A big *kulgha* flying the colors of *Bassan* Pirnaush. They say they have matters of great importance to present to the Viceroy."

"What kind of matters?"

"They would not say more."

"Then they can wait until morning."

"Master—"

"Until morning, Berek. And if they make any noise, drown them in a butt of ale!"

34

She thought she heard the big man laugh. Then his footsteps faded away and silence fell again. She reached up with one hand to unbind her hair, while with the other she guided Bertan's fingers in their urgent work on her gown.

THREE

Three men met in Benzos to judge Pirnaush's proposal and decide how to reply. Between them, Duke Cragor, Baron Galkor, and Kaldmor the Dark had all the knowledge needed for choosing the best course and all the power needed for giving the necessary orders to follow it. Queen Anya could have been present if she'd wished it, but she was now spending all her time on her knees, either beside the bed of Lady Helda or at the palace's shrine to Mother Yeza.

Galkor had heard only garbled tales of Lady Helda's "accident," and not a word about it from the duke. He hated the thought of making inquiries among men and women whose tongues were probably already wagging too much, but what choice did he have if his master's tongue remained still? To leave himself ignorant of what had happened would not be loyalty, but a foolish lack of care and foresight. Now, Kaldmor the Dark was coughing like a consumptive. He had said he'd been trying to cure his various ailments before presenting himself to the duke, but he certainly hadn't succeeded. At least his voice was so feeble that his natural talent for bad manners might be restrained. Galkor was quite happy at the prospect of a quiet Kaldmor, since he'd spent most of last night aboard the Chongan *kulgha*, making friends with her captain by drinking the man under the cabin table. His head and stomach were now paying the usual price for this sort of victory.

The duke sprawled loose-limbed in his chair, cloak trailing on the floor around him, and made a gesture of dismissal with both hands. "We all know the kingdom's dangers and resources. We all know Pirnaush is offering a real opportunity. Unfortunately, he's also offering the same opportunity to Wandor. The Duelist is much weaker than we are. He'll have to sail to Chonga, whether we do or not. Therefore we have no choice either. We must go to Chonga and either outbargain Wandor for Pirnaush's alliance or find some easier method of winning."

Galkor hoped the duke would strike a safe balance between open bargaining and the quiet search for that "easier method." Small mistakes might bring large disasters in Chonga, where not only Wandor and Cheloth but also Pirnaush, the master of intrigue, would be ready to take advantage of them. This whole expedition would be a dangerous gamble, and not much could be said for it except that it was less dangerous than letting Wandor win Pirnaush's alliance unopposed. That would not only increase the Duelist's strength, it would make people wonder if Cragor had grown cautious, uncertain, or even fearful.

Galkor and Kaldmor would go, of course, and the duke himself would come with them for at least the first month or two of the expedition.

"Pirnaush will be honored, and if Wandor does not come we will win a cheap victory. Even if Pirnaush refuses to make the alliance at once, Wandor should be drawn south to Chonga and within our reach. Finally, there will be too much in Chonga that I must see and hear with my own eyes and ears, not yours."

"My lord, you feel that there will be no danger to Benzos from your going?"

"Less danger than from my not going, I think. Don't worry, Galkor. I'm not going to dash off into the forefront of the battle like our gallant opponent Bertan Wandor. I will also take some care about what I leave behind me." Queen Anya would be giving no thought to matters of state until Lady Helda was either healed or buried, he reflected. Most of the affairs of Benzos required no decisions which could not be left to a captain or local lord, at least until spring. For the rest, a seven-man Council of Governance would be chosen from among Cragor's staunchest supporters, their loyalty further assured by a judicious selection of hostages. Sons and nephews would sail with the duke to Chonga, while mothers, wives, and daughters would be guests at Manga Castle until the duke returned.

"Even with the hostages, the Council won't be safe for more than a year or so," said the duke. "But if we're not home from

Chonga in a year, we won't be coming home at all." His voice held a note of weariness Galkor could not dismiss, but fortunately Kaldmor didn't seem to notice it.

When the duke, the baron, and the sorcerer sailed to Chonga they would sail with two hundred thousand gold crowns. They would also sail with two thousand picked fighting men, and as many more as they could find ships to carry. Some of those "easier methods" of dealing with Wandor could be easier still if a stout force of good men was ready at hand.

"Besides," said the duke, "even stone walls in Chonga can suddenly develop cracks large enough to pass a poisoned dagger. We have to reckon with Pirnaush, with Wandor, with Master Besz and his knowledge of Chonga, and probably with Telek the Fatherless and *his* plans."

Galkor's face twisted at the memory of Telek the Fatherless. He was also considering the ships which might be assembled for the expedition to Chonga. On his last expedition the baron had learned that he much preferred to do his fighting on land, but he'd also learned a good deal about ships and the sea.

"Greatships and merchant ships won't help us much once we're bound upriver in Chonga," he said. "They draw too much water, and they're too heavy to row. But we can take the men south aboard greatships, then carry them upriver in galleys and fishing boats. The galleys can make a coastal voyage shorthanded under sail, even in the winter." There were also Chongan *kulghas* wintering at Avarmouth, and Galkor proposed to buy or charter as many of these as they could afford.

When Galkor was finished, Kaldmor took time to blow his nose, cough, spit, and drink some hot wine. Then he frowned and said, "Much depends on whether Cheloth of the Woods comes with Wandor or not. If he does not, his Powers will have little effect in Chonga. Even he cannot easily work across the whole Ocean."

This was something Galkor hadn't heard before, but the sorcerer's tone hinted that it was also a matter where questions would not be welcome. In any case, Galkor knew that even welcome questions about sorcery were apt to bring forth unwelcome answers.

"If Cheloth does come, he will certainly find no opponents worth mentioning among the sorcerers of Chonga," said Kaldmor.

Cragor frowned. "I thought the Chongan temples were wealthy because of the magical skills of the priests."

"Only their healing skills," said Kaldmor. "Men in Chonga are afraid of great sorcery, and would turn against any temple whose priests seriously explored it."

Galkor nodded. "There is a saying in Chonga: 'Men bring offerings to all the temples but their hearts to none.'"

"Yes. By and large the priests of Chonga do not care about the hearts, as long as the offerings come regularly. A priest who did anything to cut them off would have a hard end."

"Apart from the healing, the sorcery which has come down from the Sunken Kingdom is hardly more than street entertainers tricks. There is so much tradition crusted over it and so many errors in the tradition that not even a man with real Powers can learn much from it. No, my lords, the sorcerers of Chonga are as children compared even to what I was once, let alone what I am now."

After that long speech Kaldmor had to blow his nose and cough again, letting Galkor hope the closing boast was the last word from the sorcerer. The hope was vain.

"As for a duel between Cheloth and myself—well, I think I am rather less inferior to him than some people wish to think. However, it would be better for us if such a duel could be avoided.

"I shall play on the Chongan fears of sorcery, letting Pirnaush know that if Cheloth's Powers are unleashed in Chonga new disasters will come to the land. If I were to fight against him, the results would be still worse and still more certain. So I will stand and let Cheloth slay me, rather than put the Chongans in peril by fighting him."

Both Cragor and Baron Galkor laughed. "Is this true?" said the duke. "Or will Pirnaush at least believe it?"

"I think Pirnaush will believe it. It may also be true. Sorcery such as Cheloth and Nem unleashed when they dueled and the Sunken Kingdom met its fate cast a long shadow. Such a shadow might stretch across two thousand years."

"What about the Chongan priests?" said the duke. "Will *they* believe you?"

"Most of them are too ignorant or too frightened of real Powers to question anything I say. Others will not dare speak once I've convinced Pirnaush. As for the rest, they will not be numerous, and gold or steel can stop the mouths of hardier men than Chongan priests."

"Very good," said the duke. "In fact, magnificent. Master Kaldmor, if this trick succeeds in depriving Wandor of Cheloth's aid—" the duke shook his head, "—you can name your own reward."

"I shall think on it, my lord," said the sorcerer. "Do I have your leave?"

"Certainly."

Kaldmor rose and made his way to the door, weaving slightly. The duke motioned Galkor to follow.

"Start work at once on gathering the ships and the men. I will send you my choice of captains tomorrow. We should be ready to sail south within two weeks."

"So soon? We have a shorter voyage than Wandor, and if Pirnaush means to give both sides an opportunity—"

"But what if he doesn't, Galkor? What if the first man to reach Chonga?—" The duke shook his head. "No. I'm letting myself dream, and foolishly. But consider that every day we have in Chonga before Wandor comes is one more day to learn about our battlefield without him watching us."

That was such obvious good sense that Galkor would have apologized except for Cragor's obvious impatience to have him gone. Outside in the cold hall, the baron could look back on the meeting and be pulled both ways. The duke might be uneasy over the queen but his wits seemed hardly slowed. Master Kaldmor's wits, on the other hand, seemed a good deal quicker than before. The trick he'd proposed for dealing with Cheloth was masterly—there was no other word for it. Kaldmor was beginning to think more deeply into affairs of state, and a Kaldmor the Dark who could think like a ruler might eventually be more useful to a desperately beset Cragor than Baron Galkor. Kaldmor could add skill in matters of ruling to his Powers, but Galkor could not hope to do the reverse.

For a moment Galkor felt a chill which did not come from any draft in the hall. Then he shrugged. The danger, if any, was for a future beyond their expedition to Chonga. Meanwhile, Kaldmor's new skills would be a great blessing. When they sailed to Chonga, Galkor would far rather sail with a future rival than with a boastful fool.

FOUR

In the Viceroyalty of the East three people could also have decided what to do about Pirnaush's invitation: Wandor, Gwynna, and Count Arlor—or four, if Cheloth of the Woods condescended to give advice and counsel. Instead, they followed custom and gathered the War Council of the Viceroyalty. If nothing else, this would ease the problem of leaving the affairs of the Viceroyalty in good order when they sailed for Chonga.

"You intend to go yourself?" Gwynna asked Wandor, in private. She raised one eyebrow, giving her face a quirky, misshapen look.

"Of course. If Cragor thinks he can't leave Benzos, I'll be ahead from the moment we reach Chonga. If Cragor risks coming, I'll at least be level with him."

"Then I'm coming too," said Gwynna.

"I never expected you to stay behind," said Wandor, dropping one arm lightly across her shoulders. She curled against him, hair trailing across the pillows.

Neither of us can hold back when there is danger, he thought. *Any more than when there is passion. Perhaps it is another gift from the gods, two-edged like most such gifts. Certainly it is the way we are, and beyond changing.* He laughed.

Gwynna smiled, sharing his amusement without knowing the source. "What is it, Bertan?"

"When we say we're *both* going, who will be willing to stay behind?"

That question and several others were answered—or rather, fought to a conclusion—some days later, when the War Council met.

Everyone summoned was present, although Zakonta and Jos-Pran had ridden all night and looked it. They also had another look about them, one Gwynna hoped she recognized. Had Zakonta knocked Jos-Pran's feet out from under him and sat on his chest long enough to make him agree to marry her? *Please, Mother Yeza, make it so.*

The Council let Wandor get as far as, "Gwynna and I will of course be sailing to Chonga at the head of—" before the arguments began. It was hard to tell if anyone was angry or frightened, since the din reminded Gwynna of a barnyard full of geese. One message was very clear: everyone wanted to go. Bertan was right.

There was no obvious reason for leaving any particular person behind, and neither she nor Bertan could bring themselve to order anyone to stay behind "because it is our pleasure." It would never have been easy, and now it was impossible. Both of them saw the doom-light glowing faintly upon their comrades, and would not strike even the most necessary blows where they might leave scars.

However, the fact remained that the Viceroyalty could not be left entirely without leaders in peace or captains for war. A Cragor whose eyes were turning to Chonga might try nothing against the Viceroyalty this year, and would achieve little if he tried, but still . . .

In time Wandor rose, pounded his fist on the table, and silenced the goose-noises. "Enough bickering. We can't decide who is to go and who is to stay by fighting like children over a rag ball. Gwynna and I must go, also a leader for the ships, a leader for our guards, and perhaps one other. That's no more than five, with a hundred fighting men, a hundred seamen, and however many ships we'll need for them."

"I agree that you two must go, if it is your wish—" began Arlor, hesitated at Gwynna's glare, then went on. "But why so few?"

"Few leaders, or few men?"

"Both," said Arlor. The look he turned on her was almost pleading, and she decided to be silent until he'd finished. Faithful, valiant, and cool-headed (except where his love for Queen Anya was concerned), Arlor would be one of the best men to sail to Chonga. He would also be the best man to leave behind in the Viceroy's seat. The heroic work he'd done when she and Bertan lay captive among the HaroiLina proved that. He desperately wanted to go to Chonga, was desperately afraid of being left behind, would talk himself hoarse trying to avoid it, and deserved to be heard.

Arlor continued. "The reason for more than five going to Chonga is the same as the whole War Council's meeting to decide the matter. We will need all the skill, knowledge, and diplomacy we can muster.

"Consider. I can speak in your place when you are called elsewhere. Master Besz knows the strengths and weaknesses of Chonga's cities and armies. Jos-Pran will lead the Yhangi well, and Zakonta's Powers can explore the sorceries of Chonga's priests. They are said to be weak, but the weak are not always to be despised when one is a stranger in their country."

He continued with the same eloquence, arraying the arguments in favor of the whole War Council's taking ship for Chonga. Most of the arguments weren't new to Gwynna, but she had to admire his skill in forming them into a case as formidable as a bristling wall of pikemen.

Eventually Arlor ran out of arguments and breath. Wandor looked around the table, and Gwynna could see that he saw the same as she did. For the moment at least the others would let Arlor speak for them: he was one strong voice speaking for them all, instead of a goose-chorus.

Except—Master Besz and Captain Thargor were exchanging glances. She would have called them glances of mutual reassurance, even conspiracy, if they hadn't been the two men in the room least likely to be allies. Thargor was a square-framed, square-minded sea captain, knew everything about ships and the Ocean they sailed on, and knew little and cared less about anything else. He distrusted Chongans in general and any Chongan half-blood who'd been a mercenary captain in Cragor's service in particular. Master Besz was a land animal, with an equally complete knowledge of training, ordering, and leading men in war. It was impossible to say what he thought of Captain Thargor, because it was impossible to say what he thought of anyone in the room. He'd shown Wandor complete loyalty since abandoning Cragor's service after the Battle of Fors, but never much warmth.

Besz and Thargor could not be allies. There had to be some other explanation for that look passing between them.

Wandor broke the silence Arlor left behind. "All this is very well," he said quietly. "But you seem to forget that if we all go, we shall all be putting ourselves at Pirnaush's mercy, or even Cragor's."

"That need not be so," said Arlor. "In the first place, Pirnaush will hardly let Cragor move against us in Chonga. Pirnaush allows no plots except his own or those of his most trusted comrades. I think he will try to ride both sides with a very short rein until he decides which deserves his alliance.

"As for Cragor's moving against us on his own—perhaps, but I doubt it. Cragor won't have the knowledge of Chonga he'd need in order to act without Pirnaush's learning of it."

Wandor looked skeptical, and Arlor stubbornly shook his head. "He won't, unless he's got a stronger band of spies and informers in Chonga than Nond ever had. You think he could have that?"

It was Wandor's turn to shake his head. "And if the alliance goes to Cragor?" said Gwynna. "Then he may move against us with Pirnaush's blessing."

"We can guard against that too. Forget about a hundred fighting men and a hundred sailors in a few ships. We should go with a fleet and a good force of our best men, at least two thousand strong. That won't be enough to threaten Pirnaush, and he's soldier enough to see it. He'll also see that it will be very hard for either him or Cragor to get at us easily."

Wandor swooped like a hungry falcon on the flaw in Arlor's argument. "Arlor, do you have any notion how long it would take to gather that many ships? Even the men would need weeks, and the ships would need months. After that we'd have to make an Ocean voyage in deep winter, and how much more time would we lose then? What about storms, short water, leaking seams? It would take more time than we can spare, and it would hardly be worth doing even if we had the time."

Gwynna thought Bertan's anger was more than the occasion called for, but couldn't doubt that it was genuine. She hadn't seen the storm hurled on Wandor's fleet by the water powers, angered at Cheloth's weather-magic which Wandor had hoped would blow the fleet swiftly to Yand. She'd been a captive on Yand, waiting to be sacrificed to the Beasts, yet she'd been in less danger than the fleet and the men aboard it. Wandor had told her of watching the green waves swallow a ship between one breath and the next. He would never gladly send men and ships into the jaws of the Ocean again.

46

Arlor had no ready answer, and in Wandor's mood that meant no answer at all. Wandor spent another minute or so smashing Arlor's protests to dust, then was silent. Gwynna looked around the room. It seemed that the War Council was stunned by the defeat of their champion. Wandor was right—they had no time to spare.

Then another look passed between Captain Thargor and Master Besz. Gwynna stiffened as she realized it *was* a look of complicity. Not only that, but Master Besz was as close to grinning as she'd ever seen him.

"My lords and ladies," said Captain Thargor with elaborate courtliness. "Master Besz and I have thought much upon this matter since the Chongan message came. With all due respect, we believe our Lord Viceroy has not a clear picture of the men and ships we can gather." He turned to his partner. "Master Besz, would you care to speak further?"

Wandor's face was paler than Gwynna liked to see it, and he was obviously holding back his anger with an effort. She felt for him, but she was also biting her lip to keep from bursting out laughing. The precise, courtly speech from Captain Thargor's salt-cracked lips, the elaborate courtesy between him and his fellow conspirator—it was lovely. Those two bastards must have worked this out between them over several nights and much wine, and were now ready to enjoy themselves. Gwynna stretched catlike and got ready to do the same.

Gathering the men would hardly be a problem at all, Besz said. There were three thousand in and around Fors, three thousand more who could reach it within three or four days either by land or across Fors Bay. A little more time spent picking the best, and they would be ready. Wandor and his comrades could sail to Chonga with their backs well-guarded.

As for the ships, that would take somewhat more time, but far less than the Viceroy thought. Twenty-six seal ships and five other Ocean-traveling ships of the HaroiLina lay in Fors Bay or close to it. Their battle captain, Reyget Son of Kurt, said that of these thirty-one, fourteen were ready for sea now and six more could be made ready within two weeks. Each of these ships could carry not less than fifty of the HaroiLina and twenty other fighting men as well. Added together, this was more men than Wandor had taken to Yand.

Other ships which could be ready for sea by the end of the same two weeks included four greatships, nine Ocean trading vessels, and four large coasting vessels or fishermen—seventeen ships in all, each able to carry at least fifty good fighting men and their crews as well. Each of the thirty-seven available ships could carry three months' food and water, as well as her men and their war gear.

To be sure, most of the Viceroyalty's ships drew too much water and were too clumsy under oars to pass up the rivers of Chonga. But that would matter little once they'd crossed the Ocean. For the river voyage seal ships could carry two hundred men—not in much comfort, to be sure, but with little danger. There might also be Chongan fishing vessels, *kulghas*, or galleys for charter from merchants in the seaport cities.

How to get the fleet across the Ocean? They would sail far to the south, hugging the coast until they'd passed at least a week's sailing beyond the southernmost point of the Viceroyalty. Only then would they turn west into the open Ocean. This southern route was largely safe from storms and cold in the winter. It wasn't better known and more used because few people sailed on the Ocean in winter, and in other seasons the southern Ocean was plagued with endless calms.

"What happens if we reach Chonga short of food and water?" asked Arlor. At first he'd been as surprised as Wandor even though these unlikely allies were on his side of the argument. Now he seemed fully recovered, as determined as ever to make sure every side of the question was fully exposed. There were times when Arlor was too honest for his own good.

Both Thargor and Besz laughed. "The merchants will sell us all we can afford to buy and ask us to buy more," said Thargor. "A few will do it because they wish to honor the bond of sailors. Others will do it for the gold. If there's a Chongan merchant who couldn't smell a chance for gold ten leagues upwind, I've yet to hear of him. And Pirnaush won't be able to say a word against it, short of declaring war against us at once."

"But if there is war?" That was Baron Delvor.

"If there is war, we sail to the Tok'li Islands and take what we need there," said Besz. "Few of the islands are held in strength, and none of the garrisons could stand against two or three thousand of our men."

So there were no unreasonable dangers facing the men and ships sailing to Chonga. Neither were there any such dangers facing Wandor's cause through the delay needed to assemble the fleet. Pirnaush was not the man to offer Cragor an alliance simply for coming first. If he said he was determined to give both Cragor and Wandor a chance to win his alliance, he would do so—although he might do many strange things once he had both men in Chonga.

If Wandor sailed with a small band, he still might not arrive quickly. When he did, he would be weak and would look impulsive, perhaps even foolish, if Cragor brought a strong force of his own. Pirnaush would not think well of him, and Cragor would take advantage of any weaknesses. With three thousand men, Wandor would look like a wise and prudent leader in war. He would also have three thousand pairs of eyes to watch Pirnaush and Cragor, three thousand swords and bows to guard his own back or to strike at Cragor's if an opportunity offered itself. A fleet and a strong force of fighting men had to go to Chonga, and in their company all the leaders would be safe. So what purpose was there in leaving behind anyone who could do good service in Chonga? What purpose *could* there be?

Gwynna looked at Wandor as silence fell. The smile left her face as she saw his head bowed in his arms and his shoulders shaking. Then he straightened up, and she saw that instead of weeping he'd been desperately trying to stifle laughter.

He leaned back in his chair, took a deep breath, and smiled. "I am not sure I should thank anyone for any part of this, but what is done is done, and I won't continue a battle already lost. Nonetheless, someone must remain behind. We can hardly put the whole Viceroyalty aboard ships and carry it off to Chonga!"

That drew laughter which blew away the last of the unease. After that matters were settled swiftly. Jos-Pran and Zakonta announced both their betrothal and their willingness to remain behind. After a slight pause for Gwynna to embrace Zakonta, Jos-Pran said:

"We shall move five hundred riders of each tribe of the Yhangi into the Viceroyalty at once, five hundred more if spring comes and you have not returned from Chonga." Last year's harvest had been a rich one, and there would be no trouble feeding so many Yhangi.

Jos-Pran would deal with the war chiefs of the Khindi, while Zakonta taught the Tree Sisters to work with the Red Seers. "The Yhangi and the Khindi have not been brothers, but neither have they been enemies," Jos-Pran explained. "I would also ask that the Hond Lord who has been least a foe of the Khindi stand beside me."

Gwynna's father stiffened for a moment, then shrugged.

"What's there to say? I'll not deny my bones will stand guarding our land here better than being tossed about on the Ocean. I'll stand by the Viceroyalty, Lord Wandor. But by all the gods, I'll not be the horseholder in *all* the battles to come!"

"No one will ask that of you, Father."

While Jos-Pran led the Yhangi and Khindi, Baron Delvor would give orders to the royal troops, the landholders' levies, the mercenary companies, and the militias of Fors and Yost. Reyget would sail with the fleet to Chonga, leaving behind a battle captain to command the remaining seal ships and those which would come south to the Viceroyalty in the spring.

In a winter twilight Wandor stood on the seaward wall of Fors Castle, face to the wind and his great fur cloak thrown around both himself and Gwynna. The waves crashed on the rocks at the foot of the cliff, but the spray leaped high and froze on the wind. The stone underfoot was a finger's-breadth deep in ice, and Wandor's beard was turning as gray as Baron Delvor's, with frost. They used the Mind Speech, since the wind would have snatched words from their lips.

("You're uneasy, Bertan. And it's not just the dangers we face in Chonga.")

("No, although they're part of it. I ask myself—were our friends eager just for the honor of being with us, or do they have the doom-sense in them as well? Do they want to go to Chonga so we all knock on the door of the House of Shadows together?")

Gwynna had nothing easy to say or think about the doom-light and the doom-sense. At least she'd seen no image of defeat in all the blurred images of death—unless they turned back. So they would go forward. At least now that the doom-seeing was with her, she could understand Bertan's sense of being a toy for beings and forces more to be feared than honored. At ease with her own Powers, she'd never before quite understood that fear.

Laughter was still possible, though. ("Berek certainly hasn't seen doom or death,") she said. ("As he left the Council, I asked him where he was going. He said he wasn't sure. Either to throw Reyget Son of Kurt into Fors Bay, or to the temple of Haro Sea Father to give thanks for Reyget's wisdom. He would not have even the kindest plot laid behind his master's back, he said. Neither would he have his master rush into danger with his back poorly guarded.")

("The gods keep Berek, and all like him.")

("Perhaps they will, but let us waste no time with such prayers or wishes.") Cheloth's Mind Speech had a quality they both recognized in a moment, like the taste of garlic or the smell of the sea.

("What word do you have for us?") Gwynna asked.

("That I will be aboard the ships to Chonga.")

She felt Bertan's arm across her shoulders stiffen as if the wind had suddenly frozen it. ("You expect another duel of Powers with Kaldmor?")

("No. The Chongans will not thank either side for unleashing great sorcery among them. Kaldmor understands this as well as I do. He comes to watch me, and I to watch him. What else may be needed in Chonga I cannot say now.")

Gwynna had the feeling that he was telling the truth; for once, "cannot" was no polite substitute for "will not." Cheloth's manner concealed the fact to most, but those who held Mind Speech with him knew that he was slowly coming to honor his human allies.

("We will be glad to have you with us,") from Bertan. Beneath the polite words were others only she could detect: ("Thank all the gods—we can fight for Chonga without another clash of magic.")

Cheloth's Mind Speech faded, and they were alone both in body and mind, as the light failed and the wind rose. The arm across her shoulders moved down to her waist.

("Let's go inside and thaw out.")

Gwynna stepped from under the cloak, shivered, and began picking her way down the ice-glazed stairs to the courtyard.

FIVE

Since dawn there'd been a following wind, strong enough to carry the fleet upstream even against the Mesti's current. Cragor's ships had their sails spread, and for the moment the clunk and clatter of oars and sweeps was ended.

Baron Galkor sat on a bench of planks laid across empty barrels. Even with the sky overcast and the wind blowing, the air was heavy, damp, and stifling. Galkor had been on deck only an hour or so, but already he was slimy with sweat, his hair and beard were tangled like old rope, and his shirt and breeches seemed pasted to his body.

They'd been sailing up the Mesti for five days now, to within a day's travel of Dyroka itself. In that time they'd learned much about living and working in the steamy heat of Chonga. Even those who'd sailed to Chonga before had never been this far inland, away from the sea breezes. By harsh experience they'd learned to dress lightly, move slowly when they had to move, drink much water and little wine, and grease their weapons not only every morning but every night to keep them from showing a brown skin of rust.

Twenty-four hundred men fit to bear arms were now approaching Dyroka, aboard twenty galleys of Benzos, ten chartered *kulghas*, and four large fishing boats. None of the Chongan fevers had struck, the people along the bank were ready to sell food and water, and out in the middle of the river the insects were few. In spite of this, every man in the fleet from the Black Duke down to the youngest ship's boy grew more watchful and less at ease with each passing day.

The whole course of the Mesti from the Ocean northward lay under the rule of Dyroka. Yet they'd come five days up the river with no message from Pirnaush. To be sure, his tax keepers gave the fleet a brief, almost careless inspection as it lay at Bezarakki. Every few hours on the journey north, a galley flying the *Bassan's* banner swept out from the banks and fell into position abreast Galkor's flagship for an exchange which never varied:

"What ships?"

"The fleet of Benzos, bearing the fighting men of Cragor, Duke and Royal Consort."

"Where bound?"

"Dyroka."

"What business?"

"To speak with the Lord *Bassan* Pirnaush, at his command."

"Pass on, under the *Bassan's* peace."

Pirnaush, it seemed, wasn't ready to show either friendship or hostility. Cragor's men began to wonder if they were the mouse lured forward by the cat or the bird charmed witless by the snake. With each passing day there was less chance of a safe retreat if Pirnaush turned against them, and more to remind them that they were in a distant land among a people not their own.

For hours at a time the banks seemed empty of human life. The Chongan forests were the thickest in the world, and in some places a whole city could have squatted invisible half an hour's walk inland. If a northerner could forget the thick heat, the harsh bird-cries, the perfumes of strange flowers and vines from either bank, and the sullen greenish-brown of the river itself, he could almost feel at home. Then they'd pass a town, a village, a fisherman's hut, or a boat on the river, and the frail illusion would vanish.

In places the river flowed naturally between wide mudflats, sloping upward to the trees along the high-water line. Villages nestled among the trees, their boats drawn up at the water's edge several hundred paces away. A few hardy souls built their houses well within the Mesti's reach, perched on stout log pilings, boats tethered like tame oxen to the bracing between the piles, stains on the logs marking the high-water point.

In other places the land was flatter, so that men had to throw up massive dikes if they wanted to live within sight of the river at all. After centuries of labor, some of the dikes had become artificial peninsulas, faced with stone against the current on the north side, guarded elsewhere by logs, and supporting walled towns. From the masthead of his ship Galkor could look beyond the dikes and see the fields—rice, ground nuts, sweetroot, Dead Man's Thumb, and less familiar vines and bushes of Chonga's berries and spices. Some of the fields were flooded, and Galkor saw the ox-driven pumps which controlled the flow of water. Other fields were waist-high in bluish grass or flowers. Through breaks in the dikes, canals with stone locks led off inland.

Galkor remembered the Chongan saying, "In time, one man can move a mountain, although it will not be the same man." Now he could understand that saying, and now he could also understand fully why the Chongans were the world's greatest masters of siegecraft. A people who could build what he saw around him could build an impregnable castle, then devise ways of taking it.

Everywhere there was water to float them were the boats and ships of the Chongans. There were *kulghas* of every possible size and painted every possible color, sailing upstream or rowing down, some empty, some piled high with barrels or sacks, some packed with a human cargo. By now the *kulgha* seemed to Galkor almost a normal part of the world around him.

Other Chongan craft were still strange. There were the squat, bluff-bowed *vibas*, as large as any greatship but built shallow to navigate the river. They moved ponderously along under a dozen slave-manned sweeps on either side. When a *viba* passed close by, Galkor could hear the thud of drums and the cracking of whips, smell the sour reek of the slaves, and every so often watch a limp, naked body dropped off the stern. Fat black arrowfins as long as two tall men followed each *viba*, so none of the bodies floated for long.

There were war galleys churning along, there were fishing boats with latticed square sails and hulls of oxhide stretched over light wooden frames, there were immense rafts of logs bound downstream to the shipyards of Bezarakki, with small huts for the woodcutters perched on top of the logs. There were barges and ferries hauling men, beasts, and goods across the unbridged river. There were small skiffs and dugout canoes, manned by still smaller boys who seemed to delight in swinging under the bows of larger craft, a hand's-breadth from disaster. There were even implausible collections of logs, timbers, and planks, roughly bound together and called *drunos*. Galkor would not have willingly sailed one of them across a duckpond, yet they seemed to be homes for entire families who went bobbing up and down across the river as if they were under Sundao's personal protection.

The Chongas themselves swarmed everywhere—compact, dark-brown people with slightly tilted yellow-gold eyes and hair so black it held a bluish tinge when the sun shone on it. Among the men, slaves were shaved bald, the free common folk wore their hair close-cropped, and the nobles wore it long and drawn out into a pigtail—two pigtails knotted with silver cord if they were of the *paizar-han*.

In the fields and villages, both men and women wore only a strip of cloth wrapped from waist to knees. Among the town dwellers, the respectable women seldom appeared and the men wore baggy trousers, sleeveless tunics, and sometimes armor with a cloak thrown over everything. Galkor was pleased to see that the armored Chongan captains sweated as miserably as any Hond.

At first glance it was hard to believe that there could be so many people in a land noted for floods and fevers, wild beasts and hungry fish. But floods which swept away whole villages also renewed the dark soil. The damp heat spread fevers, and also made crops grow as if bewitched. Three crops of sweetroot or rice each year was not uncommon, and two was the rule in most of Chonga. Some of the beasts and fish ate men, but many others could be eaten. A man with a bow, a few arrows, and a good net could obtain more meat in a week than many peasants of Benzos saw in a year. Chonga took from its children with one hand and gave back threefold with the other.

No great wonder, then, that Chongans were easy in their worship of the gods and saw sorcery with more fear than hope. There was little they needed which might be won by prayers, rituals, and sacrifices, and much which might be lost by powerful magic in the hands of men without honor or judgment.

By noon the river's course ran more east and west than north and south. The maps said it made a bend here, around a great mass of rocky hills which had resisted even its floods, and that the town and naval arsenal of Heidrispon guarded the bend.

An hour after noon, a thunderstorm swept down from the northeast. The fleet stood as if rooted, masts creaked and sails blew out, and the silver-gray sprites of falling raindrops covered the river. Then the storm passed, the fleet moved on, and within another half hour Heidrispon appeared ahead on the right bank.

The town stood on rocks a hundred feet above the river, inside walls five hundred years old. For those same five hundred years it had been the main downriver outpost of Dyroka.

A stout mole at the foot of the cliffs gave a protected anchorage to at least forty galleys, and supported more than a dozen storehouses and sheds. Three broad staircases led up the rocks, and from one tower on the walls a crane on a turntable jutted out into space. Atop the other towers and at either end of the mole were siege engines. Dyroka's galleys guarded the river, but Heidrispon guarded the galleys.

Few of the galleys were rigged and manned, and only three actually had their oars in the water. As Galkor watched, one of the three began pouring out green smoke. More green smoke replied from the crane tower. Finally the galley slipped her anchor and began backing out into the river. As she came into clear view, Galkor saw that she had a dark red hull and a green ornament on her stern, shaped like a peacock's tail.

Galkor heaved a sigh of relief. The peacock's-tail ornament on a galley was the sign of a *Hu-Bassan* of the fleet of Dyroka. They were finally going to hear a message from Pirnaush, or at least from someone more than a galley captain. The baron turned and shouted for his servants to bring him tunic, breastplate, helmet, cloak, and sword.

Kobo S'Rain stood amidships aboard *King's Bounty*, arms folded across his chest, ignoring the men brushing past him to get a better look at the approaching fleet. *King's Bounty* was passing the leading *kulgha*, the one with Baron Galkor's banner flapping listlessly from the fore masthead.

Astern of Galkor's *kulgha* came the rest of the northern fleet, thirty-three vessels. They were a decidedly ragged collection, but apparently all the ships which had started up the Mesti from Bezarakki were still here. A sound piece of river navigation, but Kobo wasn't going to tell them this. His father's orders were strict. "Let them worry about their welcome. Tell them as little as possible. If you see a chance to make them angry, do it. Don't put yourself in danger or risk a fight, but otherwise do your best to insult them. I know that best is good enough."

Kobo shouted an order to the men at the tiller, another to the oarmaster. *King's Bounty* swung sharply toward Galkor's *kulgha*.

* * *

It was a race between the approach of the Chongan galley and Baron Galkor's getting his armor on. The baron won by just enough so that he could also catch his breath and wipe the sweat off his forehead. Then the red galley slid into place only a spear's length from the *kulgha*'s port railing. One of the yellow-painted oars lifted, waved in the air, then thumped down on the *kulgha*'s railing. A man leaped up on the galley's railing, ran lightly across the oar, and jumped down on the *kulgha*'s deck.

He was square-built and bearded, with a *paizar-han*'s array of steel but only a single pigtail, dressed in dark green. The look on his face was that of a man forced to wade through a cesspool to save his life and not liking it any the better for the necessity. Behind him four other men ran across the oar and formed a square around their leader. All of them carried swords and two of them carried decorated crossbows.

Galkor shot a look at his interpreter, then stepped toward the leader and bowed.

"Honor and greetings, my lord *Bassan*."

Before the interpreter could open his mouth, the leader smiled and bowed back, a shallower bow than Galkor's. "Greetings and honor—Baron Galkor, I believe?" His Hond was strongly accented, but quite understandable.

"Yes. If I might ask who—?"

"Of course. You have the honor of meeting Kobo S'Rain. *Bassan* of the Fleet of Pirnaush S'Rain, *Bassan* of Dyroka." Galkor sucked in his breath. Pirnaush's seagoing son! So far he seemed to be living up to his reputation. Galkor decided the best thing to do was to bow a little more deeply than before. There was going to be a battle of etiquette on top of everything else, every minute they were in Chonga. Galkor didn't want to lose even a single skirmish for the duke.

Kobo acknowledged the bow by clasping his hands over his stomach, the sign that the formalities were over. "My father sends his greetings and honor to Duke Cragor, to you, and to all those who come to Dyroka in his service. You are no more than three thousand, I trust?"

Galkor decided the question was not idle curiosity but sought necessary information. "No."

"Good. We did not expect more. Your ships will find a place at Chebdun Quay in Old Dyroka. Your men will be given suitable accomodations in the winemakers' quarter. My brother Chiero will receive the duke in the City Palace."

There was obviously no hope of finding out where Pirnaush was and what he was going to do. Even asking would probably be considered offensive. Galkor stopped himself just in time from bowing again and nodded. "His splendor is most generous. We shall seek to be worthy of his generosity."

"That is not easily done, I warn you." Kobo looked over Galkor's shoulder at the rest of the fleet. "You lost no ships on the voyage from Benzos?"

"One only, and none since we started upriver."

Kobo laughed harshly. "Don't boast of making a safe voyage up the Mesti in this season. It's flowing high enough to cover the sandbars but not fast enough to make the journey real work. Try coming upstream a month from now and you'll be able to boast of those who survive. We shall see you in Dyroka tomorrow."

The red galley slid in close again, the oar came across, and Kobo S'Rain leaped up on the oar again, as agile as a monkey on a branch. His guards followed him, the oar withdrew, and the galley drifted away. Before she was out of hailing distance, Kobo had vanished under the after canopy.

Galkor's anger quickly gave way to laughter. He knew, however, that he would have laughed still harder (and given a year's rent from his estates as well) to see Kobo S'Rain take a false step and tumble into the river.

Kobo S'Rain stayed at Heidrispon while Cragor's fleet crept past, then wrote a letter to his father. The messenger foundered three horses but reached Dyroka by twilight. He found the *Bassan* in the Sea Jade Palace in the hills beyond the Red Wall.

In the hills the winter nights grew cool. Pirnaush read the letter sitting before a charcoal brazier, with a slave girl rubbing his feet and a eunuch boy throwing perfume on the coals. Both were deaf-mutes.

Pirnaush brushed a few words onto the foot of the letter, resealed it, and handed it back to the messenger. "That is my reply. The *Zigbai* Dehass will reward you for your ride and give you a room for the night. You have done well."

The man bowed himself out, and Pirnaush leaned back on his couch, raising one foot so the girl could work on the instep. Kobo had done well, and there would be no more orders for him until Wandor appeared. When would that be, and would he also bring a small army with him?

Cragor's fighting force was somewhat unexpected, but

hardly unwelcome. Its presence merely proved that Cragor was indeed a wise and experienced man of war, and it was certainly no threat to Pirnaush. Since Wandor was also wise and experienced in war, would his wisdom and experience also bring him to Chonga with thirty ships and three thousand men?

Pirnaush felt a sudden racing of breath and heart. Wandor and Cragor together might bring to Chonga nearly all the new strength he needed for moving against Kerhab. The future was suddenly filled with new possibilities. All of them were gambles, but Pirnaush had never held back from gambling as long as he could use his own dice.

SIX

————————◆◇◆————————

Shortly after dawn, they raised the Chongan mainland and
Wandor came on deck. The wind was from the north and
Reyget's *Horned Snake* was heeled well over to starboard as
she beat her way toward the coast. Wandor gripped the railing
to brace himself. His cloak whipped about him and spray coming in over the bow dampened his breeches.

Well astern, barely hull-up from *Snake*'s main deck, the
rest of the fleet was hove-to, waiting. Of the ships which had
sailed from Fors, all but two were still afloat, and most of the
men from one of these still lived. None of the other ships had
all their men alive, however, or their hulls and rigging intact.
Captain Thargor was right about the southern Ocean. It could
be crossed even in the deepest winter, swiftly and with little
danger to ships or men. Reaching southern waters in the first
place was another matter. For days on end, Wandor had relived
the nightmare of the stormy voyage to Yand Island. Smashed
and leaking casks took a toll of the bread, meat, and water.
Some ships were already on reduced rations, the fleet as a
whole had more than three weeks' supplies, and the Chongans
would certainly be waiting for them. A fleet is hard to conceal
even behind a veil of storm, and the weather had been clear
since they entered Chongan waters. Several times in the last
four days they'd been hailed by Chongan ships—greatships,
kulghas, and once a Bezarakkan galley which raced off at a
speed even *Horned Snake*, fastest of the seal ships, couldn't
match.

So Wandor decided to approach the land well ahead of the

rest of the fleet, aboard a fast seal ship carrying twice her normal crew, all of them armed to the teeth. One of the best ways of discouraging treachery was always to show unmistakably that you were ready for it.

The green Chongan shore rose higher above the blue horizon. Coastal craft and fishing boats began to dot the sea, their colored sails rising and falling among the whitecaps. Over the distant hilltops a mass of foamy gray clouds began to swell.

Gwynna came on deck and slipped her arm through Wandor's. The clouds to the north darkened, and the wind held a new coolness as it blew across Wandor's face.

The foremast lookout hailed the deck.

"Harooo! Galley coming down on us, dead ahead! She's red and she's got a *Hu-Bassan*'s feathers!"

That was no surprise. Pirnaush kept most of his Ocean fleet at Bezarakki, over a hundred galleys and *kulghas*—more than enough ships to need several *Hu-Bassans*.

Within a few minutes the red galley was in sight from the deck. She was coming under oars alone, but making good speed. The wind riding before the stormclouds was kicking up the water now, and several times the galley thrust her ram in deep. Captain Reyget ordered the sails lowered but without stowing the yards. They might be able to approach the galley safely under oars, since she was coming out alone, but it would still do no harm to be ready to make sail quickly.

All the small craft Wandor could see were now taking in sail and snugging down for a blow. He gripped the railing more tightly as *Horned Snake*'s men thrust out the oars and went to work. The seal ship came about onto a course matching the red galley's. Her bow split a wave, and for a moment water poured ankle-deep over the foredeck. Then the rowers put their backs into the work, the rest of the crew picked up their weapons, and the galley rapidly grew larger.

As *Horned Snake* came up, the galley backed her oars and Wandor saw a man scramble up on to her lee railing. Behind him four others stood guard at his back. Gwynna let go of Wandor's arm and stepped to the other side of the foredeck, so that one flight of spears or arrows couldn't take both of them. The gap of darkening water between the two ships narrowed rapidly.

The man on the railing wore leg armor and breastplate over a dark green tunic and trousers, and an open-faced helmet with a high crest in the form of a fish's open jaws. He was a *paizar-*

han, with a longsword across his back and a short sword and dagger in his belt. Wandor had to admire his casual grace as he balanced on the railing, one hand loosely gripping the rigging. It was as if the waves boiling between the two ships were his servants who would never dare to harm their ordained master.

Wandor's thoughts ran that far, then he knew the man he faced. Kobo S'Rain, *Bassan* of the fleet of Chonga, son to Pirnaush. One of the most formidable fighting men in Chonga, but also one who could say what he wished and make his own decisions without having to refer to slow-moving superiors.

Wandor's eyes met Kobo's, but neither man bowed. As far as Wandor understood Chongan precedence, the first bow was Kobo's. A man recognized as ruler of three different free peoples and a Viceroy of the East was the superior of a Chongan prince and commander at sea. A moment passed, long enough for a gust of wind to envelop both ships in spray. When he'd blinked the salt water out of his eyes, Wandor saw Kobo bow. It was a shallow, jerky bow, hardly more than a slight bending of his torso.

Wandor's return bow was only a nod and a slumping of his shoulders. Anything more and he would have been acknowledging Kobo's equality. Then he made the gesture of hands crossed on stomach which signaled the end of formal etiquette between them. It was a mark of politeness for Wandor to make the gesture, now that Kobo had conceded his superior rank. Before, it would have been a gesture of weakness or even of ignorance, the ignorance of a "northern barbarian."

Although his perch on the galley's railing was becoming positively foolhardy, Kobo S'Rain still let a moment pass before replying to Wandor's gesture. Then he raised his free hand to the rim of his helmet.

"Honor and greetings, Lord Wandor. You have come to Chonga to wait upon my father, as has Duke Cragor?" Kobo's accent was so strong that he was not easy to understand over the sea sounds.

"I come to speak with your father upon the matter he presented in his message to me. I trust I may hope to do so."

The other bared startlingly white teeth. "Most certainly. My father would give both you and Duke Cragor a full hearing, for he would not decide between you without full knowledge."

"Your father's reputation for wisdom is well-earned," replied Wandor. He wondered how long this exchange of compliments could go on in the face of the mounting storm.

Kobo peered off into the distance, eyes on a horizon rapidly drawing nearer as the stormclouds sucked up the light. Then he shouted to Wandor. "I have heard you came with many more ships than this one. Is that so?"

"Yes. It seemed proper, to be ready to give the Lord *Bassan* whatever aid he might need. So I have come with a fleet and a good bank of fighting men to—"

Wandor broke off as Kobo leaped down to the deck of his ship, then burst into harsh laughter which shook and twisted him until he had to grip the railing with both hands.

Somehow Wandor was able to hear every bark of Kobo's laughter over the wind and waves. It was the most unpleasant laughter he'd ever heard, and having it aimed at him made matters no easier. It also made him wonder what it was that Kobo found so indescribably amusing. Obviously Cragor was already in Chonga, but that in itself could hardly be the jest.

Eventually either Kobo's amusement or his breath was exhausted. He straightened up. "Your worthy enemy Duke Cragor has been among us these past three weeks. He came with Baron Galkor, Kaldmor the Dark, and nearly three thousand fighting men in more than a score of ships. He brought them for the same reasons you have given. Did you perhaps bring—oh, Count Arlor, let us say, and Cheloth of the Woods?"

Telling the truth seemed both polite and wise. "Yes. Likewise my lady wife and others among those who fight beside me."

For a moment Kobo looked ready to burst out laughing again. "By the pubic hairs of the Beloved Hrama and the sword of Khoshi! I'd heard you and Cragor had much in common, but this much? It's as if you are a single mind who happens to be divided against itself, in two separate bodies. Hail, second body!"

His voice turned brisk and sober. "You have charts of the coast?"

"Yes."

"Then steer for Jubon Bay and anchor there. Send a boat ashore when the storm passes, with word for the captain of the fort. Wait, and all your needs will be met."

"Jubon Bay?" Wandor had to shout, to get the words through the howl of the wind.

"Yes. Jubon Bay, and nowhere else! Farewell, Lord Wandor. We shall meet again in my father's house."

Before Kobo's last words flew away on the wind, the galley's oars were thrashing the water. At a shout from Reyget, men hauled up *Horned Snake*'s mainsail. Wind and waves swept the two ships apart, and within minutes the red galley was only a blurred shape behind a gray veil of spray and rain.

Wandor drew Gwynna against him and pulled the hood of her coat over her head. Damp strands of red hair trailed down over a bone-pale face, but a familiar light shone in her green eyes. Separately or together, they would find a way of paying back that laughter of Kobo S'Rain's. Meanwhile it sounded louder in Wandor's mind than the storm.

Kobo S'Rain was a man with a harsh laugh and a cruel wit, but he was also a man of his word. By nightfall Wandor's fleet lay anchor in Jubon Bay under the lee of Cape Sagomara, and weary men fell asleep on the damp decks. Before the morning's sun had dried the planks, boats put out from shore to bring fresh fruit, rice cakes, bales of cordage and sail cloth, and scribes to write down everything else Wandor might need.

For six days the fleet lay at anchor, surrounded by Chongan craft. There were galleys of Pirnaush's fleet, fishing boats, small craft filled with the idly curious, and *kulghas* from Bezarakki bringing the supplies Wandor requested. Day after day the fleet's holds and storerooms grew fuller, and day after day hammers and adzes, fresh lumber, and caulking made good the damage of the passage across the Ocean.

Cragor was not only in Chonga, but had gone upriver to Dyroka weeks ago. He could have been closeted with Pirnaush before Wandor's fleet sighted the Tok'li Islands. However, he could not have won over Pirnaush—not with the welcome the *Bassan*'s men were giving the Viceroyalty's fleet.

To be sure, this hospitality was a trifle double-edged. But was it the Chongans' fault that some men going ashore to fill water casks drank too much wine and drowned in flooded paddies while returning to ships? Was it reasonable to expect the village girls to stop swimming naked along the beaches in plain sight of the ships, even though sailors started deserting?

When the Chongan merchants finally presented their bill for replenishing the fleet, it was surprisingly modest. "I'd like to know how Pirnaush frightened those greedyguts," was Thargor's comment. They were paying barely half what they'd expected to pay, and less than a quarter of what the fleet carried in its strongboxes.

Now that the Viceroyalty's fleet was again ready to cross the Ocean, it began to prepare for the voyage upriver to Dyroka. Besz and Sir Gilas Lanor took the soldiers ashore a company at a time, to harden their muscles and refresh their weapons-craft. Berek and Captain Thargor sailed around to Bezarakki, to charter *kulghas*, hire pilots, and look for an anchorage where the greatships which could not go upriver might be left in safety.

"It's a poor jest, calling any anchorage under the walls of Bezarakki safe," the captain said. "If Pirnaush turns even the least bit against us . . ." He shrugged. "If I could put another two hundred or so able-bodied men aboard the greatships, they'd be safe enough anchored here. We'd not need sailors, either. As it is . . ." Another shrug.

Wandor knew what lay behind the second shrug. There was no chance of finding another two hundred fit men without dangerously reducing the force they could take upriver. With the men they could afford to leave behind, the greatships would be too undermanned to anchor safely in Jubon Bay or anywhere else from which they could get to sea in a hurry.

Thargor and Besz went off to Bezarakki. Two days later a *kulgha* arrived from the city, bearing three hired river pilots and a man named Ikoto Brumm. Ikoto Brumm was high among the slave dealers of Bezarakki, who in Chonga were second only to those of Dyroka itself. He had many hundreds of prime slaves suitable for any purpose which the noble *Bassan* Lord Wandor might conceive. Did the noble *Bassan* wish to buy?

Had Brumm first approached the "noble *Bassan*" Duke Cragor? He had. Did the duke buy any slaves? No. Wandor was about to dismiss the man when a thought sprang to life in the back of his mind. He remembered the money in the strongboxes below. He remembered Captain Thargor's words about needing two hundred more able-bodied men who didn't have to be sailors for the greatships. Above all, he remembered Kobo S'Rain's laughter.

"Yes, I'll buy. What is your price for a man fit for heavy labor, between sixteen and thirty-five years old? I don't need skilled men, just tough ones who aren't half-wits or boys."

"That depends on many considerations, my lord. I can—"

"You can give me an answer at once. What would the price be, delivered at the slave merchants' quay two days from now?"

"Five *quals* of silver a man at most, my lord." Brumm's manner was becoming even more servile, if that was possible. He scented profits.

"Good." Five *quals* was half a *duqual*. At that price he could afford many more slaves than he was likely to need. "I am interested in buying at least two hundred fifty men of the sort I described."

Brumm's face took on the look of a man overpowered by lust. "Two hundred fifty. Yes, my lord. It shall be done. I may have to speak to some of my—"

"Speak to anyone you please," said Wandor. "I want them at the quay the morning of the day after tomorrow. I want them all healthy and free of lice, and I want them at the promised price or lower. I've heard that the price of slaves is lower than usual, because of the number thrown on the market by Pirnaush's wars. Remember that, and do not try anything I would call cheating. If you do, Pirnaush will hear of it."

"Yes, my lord. Certainly, my lord. It shall be done in all ways as you wish." Fear clashed with the lust on Brumm's face as Wandor turned his back and walked away.

Two days later Wandor came to Bezarakki, with a hundred armed men beside him aboard *Horned Snake* and fifty more in a greatship.

The seaport city at the mouth of the Mesti had been one of Pirnaush's first allies, as it had been the ally of Dyroka for most of the last three centuries. Only when Dyroka was too weak to defend it did Bezarakki sail its own course or serve under another banner. It took a great deal to make its merchants give up the wealth to be gained from handling Dyroka's Ocean trade or its priests give up the rich temples those merchants' wealth could build and decorate.

Pirnaush of Dyroka was not a man to trust to mere common interests. Bezarakki lay on an island separated from the mainland by a channel no more than half a mile wide. Pirnaush put Dyrokan garrisons into all the forts controlling the channel and built two new ones. He also drained some of the marshes on the mainland and built a naval arsenal there, with piers, shipyards, barracks, timber yards, and a solid wall around it. More than ten thousand of Pirnaush's men descended on Bezarakki to man the fleet, the arsenal, and the forts. The Bezarakkans paid their taxes to Dyroka by feeding, clothing, and entertaining this horde, and also by turning a blind eye to raped daughters, burned taverns, and fishing boats run down by fast-moving galleys.

The slave merchants' quay and the slave barracks lay in the southern part of Bezarakki, cut off from the rest of the city by a high wall and a canal. Alongside the quay, the water was deep enough even for a greatship.

Wandor and *Horned Snake* reached the quay several hours before the greatship. The wind had died as they rounded Cape Sagomara, and *Horned Snake*'s men promptly broke out the oars. In spite of Wandor's silence about his plans, everyone aboard knew that something unusual would happen when he reached Bezarakki, and no one wanted to delay this a moment.

The rowers' enthusiasm brought *Horned Snake* to the quay even before Ikoto Brumm had the slaves ready. He was abjectly apologetic, and offered to reduce the price half a *qual* per man and also to show Wandor the slave barracks. Wandor accepted both offers.

Slavery was neither illegal nor unknown in Benzos, but it was rare. It was almost impossible to enslave a person of Hond blood, and both the buyers and the sources for slaves of other races were none too abundant.

Chonga was different. Slavery was a normal punishment for a good many crimes, and there had also been twenty years of Pirnaush's wars. There were probably more slaves in the barracks of Bezarakki than in any city of Benzos, and more in the city and its surrounding lands than in the whole northern kingdom.

At last a messenger brought word that Lord Wandor's slaves were ready for his examination. Wandor and Gwynna followed Brumm to the quay. Guards were lined up by the gate to the barracks, while Berek and Captain Thargor stood by at the head of armed men from *Horned Snake*. The greatship was edging in toward the quay, with Sir Gilas standing amidships ready to lead his men ashore.

Berek wore only Chongan trousers. Thunderstone was slung across his back and Greenfoam from one side of his belt. On the other side hung a large leather pouch. If Berek hadn't guessed his master's plan from what was in the pouch, Wandor would be surprised. He'd be even more surprised if Berek had any objections. Alone of Wandor's comrades, the big Sea Folker had been a slave himself, in the household of King Nond. That was an easy slavery, but no slavery was so easy that it did not leave a man with memories no one who'd always been free could hope to understand.

Drums thudded and the head of the line of slaves appeared in the gateway. Chained together in lines of twenty, they filed onto the quay, shuffling from the weight of the chains and leg irons and blinking in the sunlight. Fear of displeasing Pirnaush or the hope of making a large sale seemed to have kept Brumm and his friends reasonably honest. There were a few men whose bodies had obviously been shaved clean to remove gray hair, a certain number of boys not yet at their full strength, a dozen or so missing fingers, and at least one missing hand. That wasn't bad, out of nearly three hundred men. They'd all been oiled, bathed, and given fresh breechclouts, and Wandor could see no reason not to go ahead with his plan.

As the last twenty took their place on the quay, Wandor motioned to four of his men. They staggered forward, carrying a strongbox. A hundred at a time, the silver *quals* were counted out, and twenty at a time the slaves were led forward and turned over to Wandor. The silence was broken only by the clink of coins and chains, the voices of Berek and Brumm's clerk counting, and the splash of water along the quay.

At last Wandor was full owner, without question or limit under Chongan law, of two hundred eighty-six male slaves. He turned to Brumm. "Now, my friend, I ask one thing more. Freeing a slave must be done before a Judge of the First Rank. I want you to send for the nearest one, promise him twenty *duquals*, and tell him to come here at once."

Brumm stared. "A Judge, Lord Wandor? You say—?"

Wandor raised his voice. "I say I want to free all these men. Before today's sunset, all of them will be as free as you or I. It is my wish."

Then Wandor had to stop to keep from bursting out laughing. Ikoto Brumm was staring as if the ground at his feet was pouring out monsters. He took one, two, three awkward steps backward. If he took two more, he would back right off the quay, and Wandor knew he'd be greatly tempted to let the slave dealer drown. Berek was doing a HaroiLina war dance, waving Greenfoam over his head, while Captain Thargor and Gwynna stood with amazement slowly giving way to delight on their faces.

One step short of the quay's edge, Brumm's knees gave way and he sat down on a stone bollard. Gwynna ran up and threw her arms around Wandor, and by the time they got untangled Brumm had recovered enough to speak.

"My Lord Wandor—this is truly your wish? All of them—free? All?"

"Yes," snapped Wandor. "*All.* Are you deaf, or is there some law to say I cannot do this, or what?"

"No, no—no law. But—"

"Then *send for a Judge of the First Rank,*" said Wandor, each word coming like a sword striking armor. "Or would you rather have me carry word to Pirnaush that a slave dealer of Bezarakki will not obey the law and thereby displeases me greatly?"

Brumm nodded, rose, and tottered off toward the gates of the court. The fighting men of both sides watched him go, the barracks guards half-dazed, Wandor's trying hard not to laugh.

"Thargor!" Wandor called. "Translate for me." He faced the slaves and raised his voice.

"Men. I have bought you for my service. I expect that you will serve well. But you will not serve me as slaves. A Judge of the First Rank is coming, and before this day's sun sets you will all be free. Free by the laws of Chonga, free by the laws of Benzos, free by my will and judgment.

"You will bear arms as do the others who serve me. You will eat and drink as they do, face the same dangers, receive the same rewards, stand before me equal to them. Let no one say otherwise, for he who does so lies, and such a lie makes him my enemy as well as yours.

"Now Berek Strong-Ax will pass among you, for it is not fit that free men should wear chains." At Wandor's signal Berek drew a chisel from the leather pouch and stepped toward the slaves. Now Wandor's words finally seemed to penetrate the minds of the men before him. Someone cried out, "Hail, Lord Wandor!" Another shouted, "He is sent by the gods to lead us!" Then even a god couldn't have made out words, as every one of the slaves started cheering. The barracks guards drew back hastily, and Wandor's fighting men, the crew of *Horned Snake*, and even the men aboard the greatship joined in the cheering.

The cheering went on as long as anyone had the breath for it. It drowned out every other sound, even the clash and clang as Berek struck off irons and shattered chains. Above all, it drove out of Wandor's mind the last memory of Kobo S'Rain's laughter.

70

Word of Wandor's freeing the slaves reached Dyroka well ahead of his own arrival.

"To make themselves memorable some men release scorpions at the banquet table, while others release slaves from their chains." So wrote a scribe in the city. Out of discretion he wrote no more, since he served the Five Masters who ruled Dyroka itself in Pirnaush's name. Others could give the matter more thought, and some had to do so.

In the Sea Jade Palace, Pirnaush sent away his servants and meditated all of one evening. It seemed that Wandor might have not merely the appearance of virtue but the true quality. If he continued to show this kind of skill at practicing virtue without giving up power, he would be formidable either as a friend or as an enemy.

It would definitely be better to keep both Cragor and Wandor at a distance for some time. He himself would stay in the Sea Jade Palace, and the northerners could be entertained in the City Palace by Chiero. His eldest son's charm and learning would thus be put to good use. When he wanted to deal with the northerners himself, they could easily be summoned to the hills.

Zigbai Dehass learned not only of Wandor's deed, but of his master's decision. He was not entirely happy about it, either. To be sure, Chiero would give the barbarians a favorable impression of the art and learning of Chonga. Also, Chiero's house was well-watched by his own spies. Unfortunately, nothing important was likely to be done or said in that well-watched house. Most of what would be worth hearing was likely to be said in the Sea Jade Palace, and there Dehass had few people he could really trust.

Keeping watch on Wandor might not be easy no matter where he was. Wandor had come with not two but seven people who might serve as his right arm, and it didn't really matter that one was a sorcerer and another a woman. How to watch all of these well enough to be sure none were doing anything dangerous? *How?*

Cragor was delighted at what he called "Wandor's foolish generosity." It was likely to make Pirnaush suspect that Wandor might be trying to raise the people of Chonga against him. Then the *Bassan* would no longer trust Wandor, and Cragor's battle would already be half-won.

Galkor was less delighted. His master had grasped only a

part of the truth. Pirnaush might become suspicious, but Wandor's appeal to the people could hardly be ignored, no matter what Pirnaush might think of it. Too many Chongans who mourned husbands, wives, fathers, or daughters enslaved in Pirnaush's wars would swiftly hear of Wandor's deed, and few would regard him less kindly because of it.

Mitzon listened to the talk about Wandor, but had little time to spare for thinking about the man. He was too busy learning the names of his new Ninety and getting them settled in the north part of Dyroka. There they would be keeping watch on Wandor's men, when they arrived. In fact, Mitzon's main feeling was one of relief. Wandor's men would be quartered only a few minutes from the White Plum Tree, and at the opposite end of the city from Cragor's men. He and Hawa could work together more easily, and neither of them would have to risk their lives breaking up tavern brawls between the men of the two northern rulers.

Kaldmor the Dark noted Wandor's arrival in much the same way he would have noted a particularly violent thunderstorm. Cheloth was the only one of the company worth fearing, and he'd already sent his proposal for dealing with Cheloth to Dehass. Even if Dehass had doubts about it, Kaldmor could always appeal to Pirnaush, a tough old soldier who saw sorcery in much the same light as poisoning wells. There were times when a hatred of sorcery could be useful even to a sorcerer.

SEVEN

Pirnaush's summons to the Sea Jade Palace came while Wandor was in the bath and Gwynna was doing Duelists' exercises in the same chamber. She did them clothed only in her hair, and Wandor was beginning to think of interrrupting her when the message arrived.

Often she didn't mind being interrupted, and that was one reason they bathed together, without attendants. The other reason was that in Chonga the servants of important people were either spies or at least ready to turn spy at a word from anyone who could reward or punish them adequately.

The problem of spies was made still worse by the fact that many Chongans (perhaps as much as one out of five) had some slight inborn gift of Mind Speech. If they concentrated on a nearby Mind Speech conversation, they could understand more of it than the people conversing might care to have known. So Wandor and Gwynna did their best to arrange times and places where neither the ears of the body nor the ears of the mind could hear them.

Wandor and Gwynna read Pirnaush's message together:

> Lord Wandor,
> Come to the Blue Gate of the gardens of the Sea Jade Palace at the noon hour of the third day from now. Bring with you two whom you trust in all things to hear Our words.
>
> Pirnaush S'Rain
> *Bassan* of Dyroka

"That means you and Master Besz," said Wandor reaching for a towel. "And we're going to meet privately beforehand to agree on tactics and signals."

"Do you trust Master Besz in all things?"

"Yes."

"After Yand Island, so do I," she said. "Also, he and Count Arlor speak the best Chongan."

"Arlor and I will never be in the same place at the same time if we can help it. I won't have too many of us within Pirnaush's easy reach at once."

When they met Pirnaush three days later, Wandor wasn't entirely sure who trusted whom the least. They left their escort at the Blue Gate and followed a man in Dehass's house colors along a snake-twisting gravel path, through a stand of trees so hung with moss and vines that it was like passing through a fog bank. They emerged on rougher ground, which was terraced in places for flowers and herbs, and finally came to the meeting place.

A circular pit yawned in the ground, sixty paces wide and three men deep. A lush tangle of vegetation covered the bottom, but the walls were scraped clean. Nothing which fell in would easily get out again.

A bronze pillar rose from the floor of the pit to the level of the rim. On top of the pillar was a marble platform about twelve paces wide, and on it Pirnaush, his son Chiero, and Dehass the Counselor sat on folding stools. Around the rim of the pit stood fifty of the *Bassan*'s fighting men, most with spears, a few with bows, and four of the largest and ugliest with the armor and two swords of *paizar-hans*. Three walkways of lacquered bamboo led from the rim of the pit to the platform. One obviously served Pirnaush, a second was for Wandor, and the third was for the man standing on the far side of the pit.

Since he'd been set in movement toward his destiny like a stone kicked loose to roll down the hillside, Wandor had seen the Black Duke only once, on the battlefield of Delkum Pass. He'd never been close enough to hear Cragor's voice or see the expression on his face. He stepped forward, found Gwynna's hand resting on his arm, and felt it tremble. While it was also her first meeting with the duke, she'd lived for years with the knowledge of what would happen to her if she fell into his hands. To calm both himself and Gwynna, Wandor began the Duelists' routine of studying an opponent. Face to face like this, he and Cragor were dueling in all but name.

Cragor seemed too thin for his height, and sunken cheeks hinted this might not be his natural state. He still moved with grace, assurance, and the poise of a skilled fighting man. He wore dark red hose and a short unpadded black tunic, black shoes and belt, a sword and dagger, and no cloak or hat. He was hardly sweating at all, since the Sea Jade Palace was two hours' ride uphill from Dyroka on its hot, sodden riverbank.

Galkor wore a less elegant version of Cragor's garb, in dark blue and brown. He moved without the duke's arrogant grace but with the same fighter's poise. Wandor saw mail shining dully at the baron's throat and wrists and a silver-decorated greatsword slung across his back.

Kaldmor brought up the rear, dressed in his usual purple but in the Chongan style, complete to the ivory earrings which were the mark of a scholar. He seemed completely at ease, more so than his master and far more so than Galkor.

Before Wandor could turn his attention to the three Chongans, Pirnaush's blocklike head turned and his eyes widened as they fell on Gwynna. "Heh!" he said. "A woman comes here among us, where she has no place."

Dehass translated for the *Bassan*, while at a signal from Wandor Master Besz was silent. They'd agreed not to spend time and risk showing weakness by having Besz do a second translation, unless Dehass was dangerously inaccurate. Now Pirnaush frowned and pretended to look harder at Gwynna. Both she and Wandor were dressed in a rich version of Duelist's garb, with silk or fine linen where one normally found wool. "Or at least I've heard that Lord Wandor is married to a woman. Did I hear wrong?"

Behind him Wandor heard Besz whisper, "By Chongan law, a woman can take a place in councils if her husband or guardian is present to guide her." Wandor already knew that, but didn't want to use the argument unless he had to, and saving Gwynna's pride was not the only reason. The fewer favors he asked from Pirnaush, the better.

Chiero smiled. "It is said in the Fourth Book of Sundao that only the gods know the strength of a woman."

Dehass's eyebrows rose, and he spoke for himself. "It is also written in the First Book that a proper son will honor his father most by silence in his presence."

Chiero's face twisted, and it seemed to Wandor that both

his protest and his anger were genuine. Was he truly as rumors had him—a charming youth (in spite of being past thirty), who wished everyone well but could do no good for anyone including himself? Regardless, the prince's moment of rebellion gave Wandor his chance.

"Perhaps it is true of many women that they have no place in councils such as this. It may even be true of ninety-nine out of a hundred. My lady is the hundredth." He went on quickly, before Dehass could start translating. "Also, you said only that I should come with two I would trust in all things. You did not say whether they should be male or female, come clothed or naked, have hair or feathers, the skin of men or the fur of animals. I do trust the Lady Gwynna in all things, and to me that seems enough." As he signaled Besz to translate, Wandor felt Gwynna stifling laughter.

Besz not only delivered his translation twice as fast as Dehass, he delivered it in a parade-ground voice audible not only all around the pit but probably all the way to the palace. When Besz finished there was a moment's silence as the echoes died away and Wandor prepared his next set of arguments. Then Pirnaush gave a short bark of laughter and spoke to Dehass.

"We accept the Lady Gwynna here in the company of Lord Wandor," said the Counselor. "Indeed, we have heard much of her, and would take pleasure in seeing more." Then he rose and began delivering what was obviously a well-rehearsed speech setting out Pirnaush's wishes.

Even Dehass's oratorical style couldn't hide the essential simplicity of Pirnaush's scheme, or its formidable cleverness. Wandor and Cragor were both here in Chonga, each with a good body of fighting men. Pirnaush was grateful for such generosity and honorable behavior when they had no obligations toward him. Now he would ask further generosity of them.

Each man should now plan to stay in Chonga with his army until spring. If he had to leave he should put the *man* he most trusted in command. In the spring Pirnaush would march on Kerhab, which defied his claim to rule over all the Twelve Cities of Chonga, and both Cragor's and Wandor's men would march with him. With their strength added to his, Kerhab would be taken swiftly. When it had fallen, Pirnaush would judge whether Wandor or Cragor had done him the best service since coming to Chonga. The man who had done the best service would have Pirnaush and all Chonga as an ally, and the other would be allowed to depart without harm to him or any of his surviving men.

In the silence which followed, Wandor found his eyes reluctantly meeting Cragor's. He sensed two thoughts in both their minds:

If Pirnaush is telling the truth, he's a fool.
If he thinks we believe him, he thinks we're fools.

Before Cragor could speak, Dehass reached into a leather pouch at his feet, drew out a scroll, and held it out to Wandor.

"Lord Wandor, Master Kaldmor sent us this letter. He gave it to us in confidence, and no doubt his motives in doing so were honorable. But it seems to us wiser to bring it into the open. It concerns sorcery, a matter where we cannot risk even the smallest error."

Wandor stepped forward, took the scroll, and handed it to Gwynna. They'd agreed that in matters of sorcery and Powers, she should speak for him when Cheloth wasn't present. Gwynna read the scroll with elaborate care, even studying the handwriting and seals as if they might have magical significance. Then she read it a second time, rolled it up, and returned it to Dehass. By then Kaldmor's face was nearly the same color as his clothing.

Gwynna smiled at the three Chongans. "You were right, my lords, in bringing this to our attention. Master Kaldmor wishes that there be no sorcery used here in Chonga, lest we repeat the disaster which came to the Old Land when Cheloth and Nem fought. Indeed, he has sworn to let Cheloth slay him without a fight, rather than put others in danger through resisting with his Powers.

"A brave offer, my lords, and one which speaks well for Master Kaldmor. Yet I think he makes this offer without need. Master Cheloth and I will not use the smallest spell or the least of our Powers against Master Kaldmor, if he will promise the same toward us. We have no more wish to see the innocent die than he does. Indeed, Cheloth of the Woods has only used his own Powers to defend himself and us from deadly attacks. If Master Kaldmor will let lie the Powers of Toshak he has studied so well, Cheloth and I will be as harmless as stones or tree stumps."

The three Chongans started listening with nearly identical frowns on their faces. Great and terrible sorcery was being discussed here, and by a woman! As Gwynna continued, the frowns gave way to smiles and the smiles to laughter. Cragor remained expressionless, Galkor frowned, and Kaldmor wore an expression for which there were no words in any language Wandor dared to think about. The sorcerer looked as if he might be willing to call up Nem of Toshak himself to be rid of everyone who'd heard his humiliation.

With an effort which drew Wandor's reluctant admiration, the sorcerer made himself capable of speech in a human tongue. "It seems that we have no quarrel. If the Lady Gwynna can speak in this for Cheloth?..."

"I can."

"Good. Then no one need fear a duel of Powers here in Chonga." After that Kaldmor might have been a statue, until Pirnaush's hand was raised in an unmistakable gesture of dismissal to all six of his would-be allies.

Wandor and Gwynna declined Chiero's offer to accompany them back to Dyroka. As soon as they were out of sight from the watchtowers on the palace wall, Besz sent the outriders on ahead and dropped back to guard their rear himself.

"I almost feel sorry for Cragor," said Wandor, barely keeping laughter out of his voice.

"How?" Gwynna's voice was a reminder that she wasn't fond of light remarks about Cragor.

"He's going to be sadly crippled with only Kaldmor to give him aid and advice." Wandor said. "He's going to have to send for reinforcements—"

"Why?"

"Because *we're* going to send for them, and make sure that Cragor and Pirnaush know it. They won't know whether our message is a real order, or has a secret 'Ignore this' in it. Cragor won't be able to take the chance of being weaker than we are when the fighting starts. More important, he doesn't have that many people he can trust in Benzos. He'll have to send—"

Gwynna gave him a slightly altered version of her bedroom smile. "Baron Galkor! Nine chances out of ten, it will be Galkor. No one else can be sure of doing the work properly, and Pirnaush almost certainly knows it. So Cragor won't dare send anyone else, even if it means leaving himself barebacked here. Except for Kaldmor."

"Not completely barebacked," Wandor said. "There are plenty of good fighting men in his company. Some will protect him because their families are hostages in Benzos. The rest will protect him because they know their own lives won't last much longer than his, as long as they're all in Chonga.

"What he won't have is a second mouth to speak for him, a second pair of eyes to watch for him, a second judgment on important matters. All he'll have is Kaldmor, and with your help that street entertainer has just taken himself quite neatly out of the whole game." He smiled. "I wonder how long it will take him to get your knife out of his back." She laughed, and for a moment they rode side by side, holding hands.

A little farther on Gwynna asked, "*Are* we really going to send for reinforcements?"

"I think it would be wise, as long as the Viceroyalty can spare the men and the ships. We may need them simply to help Pirnaush, at Kerhab or in something else which may win him over. If we don't win him over, we'll need the men to cover our retreat."

"You said . . . 'something else which may win him over'?" Gwynna spoke slowly. "What?—"

"I don't know," said Wandor. "I'm going to spend the rest of the winter trying to find it, though. I won't march against Kerhab if there's any way to avoid it."

He was not angry, but it was impossible for him to talk more on the matter now. Gwynna nodded, and as they came around a bend onto a level stretch, she spurred her horse to a canter. Wandor followed her, and the perfumed winds of Chonga blew past them.

EIGHT

———————◆———————

In the main room of the Inn of the White Plum Tree, Hawa was dancing. Mitzon watched both her and the roomful of Wandor's fighting men.

Hawa knew more than a hundred dances, from spear dances for the festivals of Khoshi Swift in Battle to others which explicitly presented activities not at all warlike. She could dance equally well wrapped so thoroughly that nothing but her eyes and toes showed, or dressed only in torchlight and perfume.

Tonight she wore a skirt down to her ankles and a mass of veiling hanging from a brass collar around her throat. As she swayed, the veiling always seemed just about to fly clear but it never did. Mitzon had sewn the fine lead wire into the bottom of the veils himself, and the rest was Hawa's skill. She was an expert at arousing desire without drawing it toward herself. There were many other things she could do with her dancing, but this seemed the best choice tonight. Wandor's men were amazingly well-behaved for soldiers, but they were soldiers. Hawa was doing more than enough to make sure the inn's own girls would have a prosperous night, and in gratitude pass on whatever they might learn from their partners. (That was how Mitzon knew that the ship bearing Wandor's call for reinforcements had sailed downriver three nights ago.) She was not doing enough to cause a riot, which would certainly make her unwelcome at the White Plum Tree.

Hawa swept closer than usual to a large table in one corner, whirling and dipping so that the veils rose as she fell. Mitzon suspected that the two men at the table were getting a special favor, but wasn't worried about them. One of them was Sir Gilas Lanor and the other was Berek Strong-Ax.

They were the other reason besides Hawa's discretion that Wandor's men were doing no more than shouting, stamping, banging their mugs and cups on the tables, and occasionally throwing coins. Somehow the two men had contrived to sit with their backs to most of the room, making an immense meal and several jugs of good wine vanish as if conjured away, and still give the impression that their eyes were on every one of Wandor's men who came through the door. This feat would have drawn Mitzon's attention to them even if tonight hadn't been his first close view of the sworn Brothers to Serve.

They were an ill-matched pair. Berek could have picked up a man the size of Sir Gilas under each arm, and carried another on each shoulder. Yet each seemed more the missing part of the other than most brothers born of the same womb Mitzon had known. They seemed to be able to hand each other dishes and cups as if there were Mind Speech between them. In the din of the room Mitzon couldn't know if they were finishing each other's sentences, but he did know he'd very much like to see them fighting as a team. They'd be more worth watching than any of the other northerners except Wandor and Gwynna themselves.

At first Mitzon had wondered if they were bound as lovers, but Hawa said the inn's girls laughed at the idea, and the love of man for man was also rarer among the northerners than in Chonga. It seemed that each of them had been rarely fortunate in finding a friend he could trust in all that two men might do, whether tumbling an inn-girl or leading a king's fighting men into battle.

Mitzon doubted his own future held such a friendship. His bond with Hawa was that between a man and a woman as well as between battle comrades, and if there'd ever been a hope of equal friendship with Telek it was now gone forever.

The door opened as Hawa finished her dance and vanished, leaving behind a whirlwind of shouting and clapping which blew out half the candles. The sound of the rain outside was lost in the din, but Mitzon welcomed the cool air and the man who came stamping in, shaking himself like a wet dog.

Kiruss Hurn commanded a Ninety quartered in the Street of the Harp Makers, watching over Cragor's men. He'd be a good one to meet, listen to, perhaps get drunk or provide with a woman. Perhaps he could confirm a rumor which had reached

Mitzon only this morning, that the Black Duke was also sending a ship home.

Again Wandor was bathing, but this time Gwynna had finished her exercises when the messenger came from Pirnaush.

As Wandor reached for the sponge he heard in quick succession a brief murmuring in Chongan (which Gwynna now understood better than he did), a gasp of surprise from Gwynna, a number of remarks in Hond from her, none of them complimentary to the messenger, the sound of scurrying feet, the crash of a vase breaking, and then Gwynna's footsteps approaching the door of the bath chamber.

She pushed the door open with one hand and came in holding a shapeless blue bundle under the other arm. Her face was pale enough to make her hair seem even brighter than usual. Wandor could tell she was about to burst, but whether from laughter or from rage he wasn't sure.

She sat down on the couch they'd placed by the bath and started unfolding the bundle. When she'd finished, she held it up and Wandor began to understand what had roused her. It was the clothing of a Chongan woman kept for the pleasure of a wealthy and self-indulgent lord such as Pirnaush. It consisted of a silver-embroidered loinguard, a jeweled, jointed collar, a mass of transparent blue veiling to hang from the collar, bracelets for wrists and ankles with small silver bells on them, and nothing else.

"You're supposed to wear that?" said Wandor.

"Yes. At a private dinner Pirnaush is giving tomorrow night."

Not much time to decide, then. Fortunately Gwynna was very seldom slow to make up her mind, even when the problem would have been totally ludicrous if it hadn't been so delicate. Should she throw away dignity and please Pirnaush by dressing like a pleasure girl, or preserve her dignity, please herself, and give—how much of an advantage?—to Cragor?

She dropped the clothing back on the couch. "The messenger suggested that I put it on—to see if it was suitable, he said." That explained her description of the messenger's ancestors.

Wandor smiled. "You were right to refuse him. You'd look far too good for such a low-born, unappreciative—"

"You!—" she began, taking a step toward the edge of the bath. It was a step too far; Wandor's arm snaked out, caught her by the ankle, and pulled her into the bath. It was waist-deep, and she went completely under, to come up spluttering and applying to him some of the same terms she'd used to the messenger. She sounded genuinely angry, and Wandor was afraid for a moment that she was hurt or at least past seeing the joke. She only stopped when her drenched hair got tangled up in her mouth.

Wandor reached up with one hand to clear her mouth, then kissed her while he undid the belt of her robe with the other hand. The weight of the water dragged the robe off Gwynna's shoulders, and Wandor moved his kisses from her lips to her ear, then the side of her neck, around to her throat, on downward. . . .

Eventually they got up from the couch and Gwynna put the clothes on. The silver bells chimed delicately as she moved about the chamber, turning from side to side, bending forward and backward to try different effects.

Wandor laughed. "Definitely for a select audience." He hesitated. "Is Pirnaush's dinner select enough?"

Gwynna nodded and started pulling the clothes off as she spoke. "I'll wear it, with a cloak over it until we're in Pirnaush's chambers." She grinned. "The uncloaking should come as an interesting surprise."

She pulled on a dry robe and sat down. "Actually I'm not thinking so much of Pirnaush. It will give the old man some harmless pleasure, so why not? It's Cragor who's on my mind."

Her words and her calm both surprised Wandor. "How?"

"I'll keep him from gaining a point with Pirnaush. I may even hurt him. Consider Cragor and—and—what he wants to do to me. How could he have this so much on his mind, unless there was something about me which called to him? I don't know what it is. I don't expect ever to learn, and I'm not sure I really *want* to know. But it's there. I couldn't be more sure if I'd seen it tattooed on his forehead. It's going to be there when he sees me tomorrow night, wearing only a little more than I'd be wearing in his—chambers. Yet he won't dare get within three paces of me or even get drunk to ease himself—not while Pirnaush is watching. Even afterward, he won't have Galkor to talk sense back into him. I don't think the Black Duke will forget tomorrow evening for a long time."

Wandor suspected she was right. He also felt more gratitude than he could put into words now. He wouldn't have dared suggest such a course of action himself. Gwynna was the only one who could say when her pride should be sacrificed. He drew her against him and tried to say with his arms and hands and lips what he couldn't put into words.

It was dawn before Kaldmor dismissed the last of the women and reeled into his bedchamber, to collapse across the sleeping pad. The wine made his head spin in one direction, while the room spun around him in the opposite direction. The effect was unsettling. After a while Kaldmor rolled on to his back and closed his eyes. With the outside world shut out, he found that his mind could start working again.

He'd amused himself all night for the first time in weeks —in fact, for the first time since the night of Pirnaush's memorable dinner. Kaldmor would have laughed at his memories of the dinner if he hadn't known that laughter would hurt his head. There was no doubt that Gwynna had looked magnificent, a queen even in a pleasure-girl's clothing. What spiced the entertainment for Kaldmor was the amount of money he'd won off Chongans who knew of Pirnaush's trick and were quite sure Gwynna would toss the clothing down the privy shaft. He'd have won more if he'd dared bet with the duke himself, or if Baron Galkor wasn't on the way home to Benzos for reinforcements. But then the baron might not have been willing to bet. He also knew Gwynna's qualities better than most.

It was a week after the dinner before Cragor let Kaldmor apply a few light spells against whatever had festered in his mind since he saw Gwynna. Even now the wound from her shrewd blow hadn't entirely healed. Kaldmor hadn't dared use the powerful spells necessary to completely reshape Cragor's memory, and not just because of his agreement with the Chongans. They were too powerful to use on any man whose condition wasn't so desperate that it was acceptable to risk destroying his mind entirely. Cragor would have to purge his memory himself.

He'd also best find other ways of doing it than he'd used during the first week! Kaldmor had heard the screams of the slave girls and afterward seen those who needed healing. Few needed much, and only one would bear scars. This was little enough damage, considering what Kaldmor had seen the duke leave behind in his dungeons in Benzos. Was the duke losing his taste for giving pain, or merely giving it a place behind other, more important matters?

Still, the little the duke had done was enough to set Chongan tongues wagging, and that made it too much. Kaldmor could hardly count on the fingers of his two hands the times he'd heard the whispers of the market place. Wandor's stroke of buying and freeing the slaves in Bezarakki hadn't helped matters either. Time after time the words came: "Cragor kills slaves for his pleasure while Wandor sets them free."

Kaldmor groaned with more than the pain and exhaustion from a wilder night than his aging frame could easily endure. If only Galkor were here! He could say things to the Black Duke that neither Kaldmor nor any of the captains dared, perhaps not undoing the damage from the duke's mad week but at least seeing that no more was done. For years Kaldmor had dreamed of a time when he and no other man would stand at the duke's right hand, and now that the time was here he badly wanted Baron Galkor to return.

Someone knocked on the door, sounding to Kaldmor like the crash and rumble of a collapsing temple. "Go away," he muttered, then repeated it loud enough to be heard. The knocker continued.

"Lord Kaldmor, it demands your attention at once."

Kaldmor rolled off the sleeping pad and remembered that he was naked just in time to snatch up a sheet and wind it around himself. The door opened and two men came in, a servant and a bald man in the robes of a priest of Sundao the River Father.

Kaldmor listened while the priest presented his challenge and the servant tried to make himself invisible. The priests of the Great Temple of Sundao had heard that Kaldmor the Dark knew the magic of Toshak. This they did not believe. If Kaldmor did not wish them to call him a speaker of falsehoods unfit to wear the scholar's earrings, let him present himself at the Great Temple at sunset—this day.

That last detail drew a groan from Kaldmor and made him sit down, head in his hands, ignoring the priest's smile. *Today!* Barely time to sober up and get enough sleep so he wouldn't be a crumbling ruin of a man. No time to make plans for using the *limar* or find a priest at the Great Temple who might be bribed or threatened into revealing some of the plans for the challenge. Of course Cheloth would certainly hear of the challenge, and no doubt he would find a way to watch whatever the priests of Sundao asked Kaldmor to do, without violating the agreement against duels of sorcery.

Kaldmor groaned again. The priest frowned. "Lord and Master Kaldmor—is there sickness in you? Do you wish—?"

"No!" The word came out with a force which surprised Kaldmor himself. He would not beg off from the challenge with an excuse of illness when everyone would know it was only wine. Perhaps the duke would say he was only accepting it out of pride, but Kaldmor found he didn't care. He had the *khru*-medallion, something no more than a legend in Chonga, and very few of the priests would probably know a Toshakan spell from a cartload of pickled vegetables. It could be done.

"At sunset, then," he said, and made a gesture of dismissal that even a priest carrying out the orders of Pirnaush of Dyroka could not ignore.

The "greatness" of this temple of the River Father, Gwynna concluded, must lie in its age, not in its size. The dome was low and narrow-windowed, the side aisles were so low that Count Arlor could not have stood upright in them, and even the main hall was smaller than any she'd seen in the City Palace. The air was thick with the smoke from lamps and herb-burners, every piece of wood and stone she touched left her fingers black, and the floor underfoot was caked with the remains of ooze from ancient floods, long-dead rats, and lamp scrapings. In spite of the lamps she could only see Kaldmor and the four priests at the other end of the main hall when someone cast a light-shedding spell.

Gwynna welcomed the darkness. The temples of the River Father were forbidden to women, and she was disguised as a young soldier. She'd hoped to be able to hide in a crowd of men curious to watch the northern sorcerer at work, but the space for onlookers held less than a score of people.

Light was beginning to glow to the left of the priests again; they were at work on another spell. The sleeve of her leather coat had fallen down over the Watcher Crystal of her left wrist. She tossed the sleeve clear with a jerk of her arm and held the crystal so that it—and thereby Cheloth—had a clear view of the priests' spell.

A globe of pale yellow light grew mushroomlike from the floor, then rose, wobbling uncertainly on the end of a thin stalk of darker yellow. Not a major spell, but so far quite well-executed. Chongans with Powers were seldom learned and still less often ambitious to increase their learning, but they were skilled enough at what they allowed themselves to know. Their healing spells, for example, seemed to work against many of the damp-air fevers of Chonga.

Suddenly the globe of light turned from yellow to blue, then to green. The greenness writhed obscenely, then took shape—the fanged head of an immense serpent, a yard wide, red eyes glowing. Gwynna stiffened. This was no longer a minor spell, and this was no creature out of sorcerous legend but the image of the sort of monster who lived in the deep jungle of Chonga. She'd seen ones as long as four men, and there were tales of ones as long as a seal ship of the HaroiLina.

A sound like an immense cat spitting, and then there was a curved Chongan sword in the air over the snake's head. The sword came down, and the head flew across the hall. Gwynna laughed as the watchers scattered, knowing that the head had no substance. Then she had to jump aside to avoid being splattered by its blood as the head thumped to the floor. It would have broken half her bones if she'd been underneath it. Kaldmor had given the illusion the substance of the snake it represented.

Kaldmor turned, raised his arms, and shouted, "Owiyaaa-ha!" For a moment the snake's head was a semiliquid mass of decay in the middle of a pool of dark ooze, exhaling such an impossible stench that Gwynna gagged and most of the watchers either drew back or vomited where they stood. Then the snake's head sank into the floor, the stain it left behind vanished, and a cool pine-scented wind blew through the temple to drive away the odor.

Gwynna stepped behind a pillar and raised both arms, trying to heighten her awareness of whatever *luor* the last clash of spells had left behind without actually using her own Powers. Through the Watcher Crystal, Cheloth had seen and heard everything here, but he was miles away, too far to read the *luor* with his Powers without violating the agreement against the use of sorcery. Reading the *luor*, though, was one of the most important parts of studying another sorcerer's magic, and it had to be done somehow.

Gwynna even risked a light spell to increase her concentration but found nothing she hadn't already learned from Kaldmor's last four spells. Kaldmor was using his *khru*-medallion, not only more freely but with much greater skill than before. She'd never believed more than half of her own sneers at Kaldmor's incompetence—the other half had been mostly for Bertan's ears.

There was still much of the old Kaldmor in the man, though. She'd seen him come in, red-eyed, slow-footed, like a man risen from his deathbed, and wondered if he was fit to meet the challenge. He met it with a savage enthusiasm that showed more concern with displaying his Powers for the Chongans than anything else, including how much he revealed to watching enemies. Gwynna could have explained only to other sorcerers and not to all of them how she sensed this quality in Kaldmor's spells, but it was there. From this dropping of his guard she might learn much.

Gwynna felt her nose prickling and chest thickening from the dust kicked up by the breeze, but didn't care. As far as she was concerned, Kaldmor could go on proving himself to the Chongan priests all night and well into the next day.

Cragor's dagger sank three fingers into the tough wood of the table in his chamber, pinning the letter from Queen Anya brought by the latest ship from Benzos. He forced himself to finish reading it.

—so Lady Helda has before her no more than a death in life for as long as the gods are cruel enough not to take her to the House of Shadows. She was cast down into this state by your hand, and I shall not forget it. Even if I could, others cannot. I hope you will have no more desire to speak of this when you return victorious from Chonga, for certainly I have none. Doubtless by that time the gods will have been merciful to my old nurse, and there would be nothing to say even if either of us wished it.

Anya

The Black Duke let out the cry of an animal with its leg in a trap. He barely had time to tear the letter to shreds before half a dozen guards stormed into the room, drawn by his cry. He found it easy to curse them roundly without saying why. Even in his rage, he realized that only silence could preserve his dignity.

In the name of all the gods, how much longer would he have to endure this? At least until Galkor returned from Benzos with the reinforcements, and when would that be? The baron's last message said that he might have to bargain with the nobles to get any men other than common mercenaries, and many of those were demanding higher pay.

If he could only deal with one of his enemies—he didn't care which—he could face the other without feeling every moment that he needed extra eyes and ears. Suppose he approached Wandor and proposed that they join forces—if not to strike down Pirnaush and divide Chonga between them, then at least to guard each other against Pirnaush's war of pinpricks and crude jests until spring, the reinforcements, and the campaigning season all arrived?

The duke laughed, worked the dagger free of the table, and sheathed it. That could only be a dream. Wandor could never be trusted to keep such an agreement, even if Gwynna would let him, or even be silent about the duke's approach to him. Pirnaush would learn of Cragor's idea within days, and would probably strike down the duke and all his men without even taking time to denounce their treachery. Then Wandor would have complete victory without having to lift a single sword to win it.

Even if Wandor could be trusted, there were the *mungans*. They would swiftly learn the secret and carry word to Pirnaush even more swiftly, Wandor would *have* to speak to prevent the *mungans* from denouncing him along with Cragor! There was no safe course, but continuing as he'd done seemed the least dangerous one.

Gwynna stood in the gallery which ran around the ship-building shed just below the roof. From below came the whistle of arrows, shouts greeting good shots and laughter and curses greeting bad ones, and sometimes the voice of Master Besz. There weren't many buildings in Dyroka large enough to let archery practice go on through the winter. Besz was determined to get as much use as possible out of this one before Pirnaush found some excuse to take it for his own army.

She turned away from the railing as familiar footsteps sounded on the rickety stairs. For once Bertan was smiling. "I've been talking with Cheloth," he said. "There's no sign of any trouble over your visit to the temple of the River Father."

They could talk more freely here than even in the bath chamber in their quarters. No one else except Berek and Sir Gilas was allowed past the sentries at the foot of the stairs to the gallery.

"I didn't expect there would be. If Cheloth had used a free-flying Watcher, it would have needed an active use of his Powers. Binding a Watcher spell into a crystal and having me take it into the temple on my own two feet is different. I doubt if anyone even noticed the link between Cheloth and the crystal.

The Chongans didn't have the Powers, and Kaldmor was too busy showing off his own."

"They could denounce you as a woman entering a prohibited temple."

"That has nothing to do with magic. Besides, I think Pirnaush might be on our side in that. I think he sees me as a sort of honorary man."

"After the dinner party? His eyesight must be failing." Wandor's smile faded. "If it wasn't for Kerhab, I'd begin to say we were too far ahead of Cragor for him to catch up. We have as many men in Chonga and more and better leaders. We have more loyal men at home, and more powerful sorcery if all else fails. We even have more favor among the Chongans, if they aren't too beaten down to care a bowl of dog piss about anything! Yet we could still lose it all before Kerhab."

She was glad to hear him finally speaking of Kerhab in the light of day. It saved her the need to speak of how many times she'd awakened to hear him say the name in the night, as if it was a curse or an evil spirit he was fighting.

He went on. "Right now we have friends in the cities which may hold out against Pirnaush, and that gives us a freedom Cragor doesn't have. We'll smash it all when we march against Kerhab." He stopped his voice from rising enough to be heard on the floor below. "Even if we win, we'll spend many weeks in a battle against men who will be fighting for their lives and fighting well. There are fifty accidents to make everything useless, and others to . . ."

He shrugged. There was no need to mention the doom-light they saw on their comrades. Gwynna slipped her hand through his arm and for the twentieth time begged the gods to show a way to victory which did not lead through the streets of Kerhab.

NINE

In Benzos, in the Viceroyalty, and in Chonga the remainder of the winter passed. It passed quietly for those who did not listen carefully.

In the north country of Benzos, not even the Ponans cared to face the blizzards. Captain Tagor's men stayed close to cottages and barns they'd stocked and repaired the previous autumn, drank, gambled, told bawdy tales, and occasionally came to blows simply to drive away boredom.

Captain Tragor stayed close to Jaira. Some of the lines she'd grown used to seeing in his face softened during the winter. "Haven't had such a long time at peace since I started soldiering," he said. Sometimes he told her stories of the times before that.

He was the youngest of the three sons of a farmer with enough land to raise them all to healthy manhood, but not to give them all a proper inheritance. So the eldest son got the farm, and the second went to sea, where after seven years he was lost on a voyage to the Viceroyalty. Tagor was stronger than either, sharp-eyed, and quick, so he went to the nearest lord who needed men-at-arms and from there to the mercenary bands which grew so rapidly in the last years of Nond's reign.

Jaira found herself sharing some of the captain's sense of peace. It helped that the Khind-killer whose coming had frightened her so much stayed with his men in a village half a day's ride away. It also helped that Tagor now said things like, "Don't get a taste for this north-country ale, girl. When we go south

I'll give you some proper wine." Was he thinking of taking her with him when his company's work here was done?

Perhaps. She'd seen the coming of the Khind-killer as a sign from Masutl that a great change would soon be upon her. Was becoming Tagor's free concubine instead of a slave such a change? She did not know, and wondered if the High Hunter did. He had not abandoned her after all, but in Benzos he might be as much a stranger as she was.

The hard winter kept Count Ferjor and Hod ranFedil from doing much to make their alliance a living thing. When the blizzards weren't blowing, snow drifts lay as high as the belly of a horse on the iron-hard ground. A dozen of the count's men did spend the last part of the winter with ranFedil's band and fifteen of the bandit chief's men came to Ferjor's camp. They were a closemouthed lot and some of them not too intelligent, but they kept their weapons clean and their weaponscraft sound, did their share of the camp work, and took no more than their share of the food and drink. After a few weeks it could be said that an alliance with such men as these might produce no miracles, but was certainly nothing to be feared.

In any case, Count Ferjor no longer believed in miracles. He did believe that if ranFedil kept his word and his men followed him, spring and summer could weld the two bands into one, end the lives of some of the duke's friends, and break the sleep of many others.

The Grand Master of the Order of Duelists spent the winter in Benzor. It would have been easier to hear tales from Chonga if he'd wintered in Avarmouth, or learn of affairs on the Ponan border if he'd gone north. It would also have been easier for Cragor's spies to learn that the Order of Duelists was interested in these matters. As for spending the winter on the roads, the Grand Master knew age had put that beyond him.

The Grand Master did send out two men, chosen from among those Duelists he could trust to kill themselves rather than yield not just the secrets of the Order but even the knowledge that it *had* secrets. One man went north, to learn what he could of a Count Ferjor, said to be captain of a strong armed band of Cragor's enemies in the north country. If it could be done safely, he should seek out Count Ferjor and learn if the count's band would accept Duelists who might need to flee.

The other man was bound for the Ocean Highlands. There

he could certainly spy out the land, and perhaps speak to one of the Sea Folk ships said to be cruising off the coast in Wandor's service even through the winter storms. In the Ocean Highlands, the Duelists might find refuge if the whole Order ever had to slip away from Cragor's wrath. They would move by night like prowling cats if they could, they would fight their way through by day if they had to, and those who lived would gather by the Ocean. Then they would either build a stronghold among the woods and ridges, or board Wandor's ships and join him beyond the Ocean.

The Duelists would *not* destroy any more of their own people to put off the day of battle with Cragor, as the Grand Master had slain the House Master of Tafardos. That day of battle would come, and when it did they would not shrink from it. The Grand Master was ashamed that he'd ever considered another course, and sometimes wondered what Staz the Warrior might say in judgment to him at the door of the House of Shadows.

He did not go to the House shrine of Staz, however. In this matter he would earn the god's forgiveness on his feet with steel in hand, not on his knees at any shrine.

Queen Anya divided her waking hours into three parts. One part was for her personal needs, one for the temple of Mother Yeza, and much the largest for Lady Helda.

No one seemed to begrudge her the hours spent in Lady Helda's room, doing everything that anyone could have done after it became certain that neither Helda's mind nor her body would ever be whole again. The palace servants did everything which would be needed until Cragor's return, and the small amount of court life which had survived into the last year came to an end. Even after his return from Chonga, Baron Galkor spent little time in Benzor.

In fact, few people spoke to Anya at all during the winter. That she was Cragor's wife set her apart from the duke's enemies, that she was Nond's daughter set her apart from the duke's friends, and that she was Queen of Benzos set her apart from everybody. She found herself much alone, though not more so than she wished.

She had a new bow made—not a lady's hunting crossbow, but as strong a longbow as she could pull. She'd always found a strange peace of mind and clarity of vision shooting at the butts, and hoped she might be able to find it again. Her hopes were not disappointed.

Her thoughts ran back to her girlhood, then forward from there to the ten years of her marriage with Cragor. When she looked at both she could see now how the first had led her to the second. Treated as if she didn't exist by a father who blamed her for her mother's death, she'd come to value any attention at all, without much regard for the form it took. At one point she'd nearly let loneliness and awakening womanhood lead her into running a race from one bed to the next. Yet for all her father's blaming her for his dead queen and her blaming him for years of coldness, she was heir to the throne of Benzos and would not make herself unfit to sit upon it by sacrificing too much to her own pleasure.

So she held back, and Cragor took a virgin princess to be awakened in his bed. For three years she could honestly say that he'd done much to deserve her respect and even in some measure her affection. She could not deny those years of charm, generosity, and virility. Then ambition ran away with him, or perhaps he simply let it off the tight rein he'd been using on it until his position was secure.

She didn't know which was true, and it had long since ceased to matter, because she did know what the other seven years with Cragor had brought her. A weekly beating would have been preferable to much of it. When she was carrying their daughter he gave her a few months' peace, and at the time she let herself hope that he'd had a change of heart. When the child was born, though, he returned to his old ways, and she knew that he'd done no more for her than he would have done for a prize mare about to foal. So his easy manner while she was carrying their son did not deceive her or give her peace, and the prince had been sickly ever since his birth a month before term.

Nonetheless, she endured. She endured because she could not be absolutely sure that Cragor would not reform, because she still could not throw the succession of Benzos into confusion, and because she had no idea where she could go if she fled. Certainly there would have been few willing to help her, with Cragor's power growing and her father still turning a blind eye to his daughter's pain.

Then her father was killed, and she became a queen who decorated the throne of Benzos much as she'd decorated Cragor's palace before. What she might have done, less stunned by events, no longer mattered. What she had done was to think:

If I do as Cragor wishes, I can protect those close to me. He will not strike them down.

She'd been able to think this, and Cragor had been able to rule Benzos until the day Lady Helda came tumbling down the stairs. Now she had to think—something else, certainly.

What? And after she'd finished thinking, what should she *do*? She might have no friends anymore, and certainly there'd be terrible danger to any who helped her. Cragor might be in Chonga for some months, but his friends were still strong in Benzos, and Baron Galkor would be ready to deal with the duke's enemies as thoroughly as a sickle cutting barley. Too many were already crying out to her from the House of Shadows because what she'd done or left undone brought them there. She would do nothing to add to their numbers.

That, she realized, meant doing hardly anything at all for the remainder of the winter, except listening with her new ears and looking with her new eyes. She might hear and see things to her profit, even friends she hadn't known were there.

Baron Galkor did his best in the Black Duke's service, and his best was good enough to send off to his master in Chonga three thousand more fighting men and some ships suitable for river work. He had to dig the men out of a hundred and one obscure corners, but in twenty years of serving Cragor he'd learned not only every obscure corner in Benzos but what each one might hide.

A third of the men were from the households of nobles and the militias of cities, and too many of these were the ones their masters could most easily spare rather than the ones most likely to be useful in Chonga. The rest were mercenaries—three small companies, the scrapings of other companies already in Chonga, and a mob of recruits under captains nearly as raw as the men they led. If they lived long enough, they might at least fill the ditches of Kerhab with their bodies to make a path for better men. Galkor could only hope that meanwhile they would not leave a trail of rape and looting to make Cragor's name stink in Chonga.

Yet there was nothing more that god or man could do to find fighting men in Benzos that winter, and the price of those he'd found did not please Galkor and would please the duke even less. The Council of Governance had voted (with an eagerness Galkor found suspicious) to count the nobles' and cities' levies against their taxes for next year. With less eagerness it dipped into the royal treasury to pay the mercenaries. Galkor's only consolation was sending along with the men a trusted messenger, carrying a list of those men in Benzos who'd been most outrageous in their refusal of aid or the price they asked for it.

In the Viceroyalty of the East, Baron Oman Delvor divided the winter between Fors and Yost, without sleeping a single night at his own castle. He also discovered that paper and parchment were not only alive but could breed. Whenever he left two unanswered letters on his writing table when he went to bed, there would be five more when he returned the next morning.

He'd long ago suspected that this was the case, and it was one reason he'd refused to be Viceroy of the East when Nond asked him, the year before Cragor's marriage to Anya. Looking back on this refusal now he still could not be sure whether he'd been wise or foolish. If he'd taken the Viceroyalty, Cragor would have found it much harder to get a grip on the East. The man who took the seat of office in Fors found it easy to turn a blind eye to Cragor's schemes, even the appointment of Baron Galkor to Yost. Removing Baron Delvor would have taken an open blow, perhaps one sufficient to warn Nond.

On the other hand, King Nond was not much easier to move in his last years than Manga Castle itself. Old friendship could no longer blind Baron Delvor to this fact. Nothing might have changed, and Cragor's blow would almost certainly have struck down not only the baron but Gwynna as well.

As it was, his daughter lived, to know a happiness which must surely be making her mother smile in the House of Shadows. He himself was sound of wind, limb, head, and stomach at sixty, had all the power he'd ever wished for and the chance to use it to good purpose, and knew that Castle Delvor and his lands were safe even in his absence. He was content enough to know that what might have been was a question for the gods.

That winter Castle Delvor was the seat of Jos-Pran and Zakonta, although it saw little enough of the War Chief. He was on the road even more than Baron Delvor, visiting every camp of the Yhangi in the Viceroyalty, guarding against brawls, thefts, and fires which might sour already suspicious farmers.

In spite of this, the plans for the wedding went forward at a good pace.

At first Zakonta wished to delay it until Wandor and Firehair returned from Chonga. She began to think otherwise when the call for reinforcements came, and finally changed her mind when a letter came from Gwynna.

"I am now older than you in some things," said Gwynna's letter, "and I must tell you not to wait for our return. Otherwise Jos-Pran may find new reasons for not doing what both of you wish. Great love speeds the thoughts of women but slows those of men."

Certainly last year's good harvest meant plenty of food and ale, and none of the Yhangi seemed unhappy at the thought of a grand celebration. Indeed, as Jos-Pran said on his return from one journey, most of the Yhang garrisons hardly seemed to know that there was a war going on.

"Some of our people have barely heard of the Ocean," said Zakonta. "Most have not seen it. Even those who have find it hard to believe that a war on the side of the Ocean is any affair of theirs."

"They will have to believe it," said Jos-Pran. "If Wandor and Firehair win in Chonga, the next battle will be fought in Benzos. I will not see the Yhangi hold back from that battle because some are ignorant. I will see about making them learn."

"Yes," said Zakonta. "We shall both teach them. But *after* the wedding."

In Chonga there was work for twice as many leaders as the Viceroyalty had sent.

Wandor and Gwynna went everywhere, but always well-guarded and never with more than two of their comrades. Everyone knew they were being careful not to offer a tempting target; nobody said it out loud.

Count Arlor spent time and gold entertaining the merchants of Benzos in the Chongan cities under Pirnaush's rule. He dealt with both those who openly supported Cragor and those he suspected might still be friends to Nond's cause, and learned much from both. From a merchant named Naram Tekor he got more aid than he would have dared ask, once he promised to carry the man and his family safely away from Chonga when the time came.

Master Besz led his men to attempt the impossible in order to become invincible. The men weren't sure he was succeeding, but most agreed that by spring, storming Kerhab bare-handed would begin to seem easy.

Sir Gilas Lanor and Berek Strong-Ax did everything they could to aid Master Besz, except when they were aiding each other. Sir Gilas nursed Berek through a bout of the blue fever, and Berek nursed Sir Gilas after the Knight got his head cracked breaking up a tavern brawl.

Captain Thargor learned all he could about Chongan ships and Chongan ways of handling them, and traveled ceaselessly up and down the Mesti. It began to be said that one could tell the passage of the weeks by his voyages upriver to Dyroka or downriver to Bezarakki.

Cragor said very little and laughed even less, but left nothing possible undone. His captains did not laugh at all. They wanted to live at least long enough to die honorably in battle before the walls of Kerhab.

Pirnaush S'Rain was probably the happiest man in Chonga that winter. Spring would bring a great victory, and meanwhile he amused himself with small thrusts at Wandor or Cragor.

Dehass the *Zigbai* took great care for his master's interests, but did not neglect his own.

Kobo S'Rain sought the perfection of the Chongan fleet and Chiero S'Rain sought the increase of his own learning. He also sought as much of Gwynna's company as she would allow him.

The two sorcerers found themselves with little work. No one except Wandor and Gwynna saw Cheloth, and even they did not know if he suffered from anything so human as boredom. A great many people saw Kaldmor the Dark, but few of them knew it. He could be bored, and found the duke's company little help in fighting it. He also found that with an undetectably small spell he could alter his face so that in Chongan garb he could explore the city as he chose.

The *mungans* who followed Telek watched everybody, although Mitzon and Hawa began to doubt that there was anything more to be learned. "Without Kerhab thrown into the balance, Pirnaush can hardly avoid choosing Wandor," said Mitzon one night. "With Kerhab, Khoshi alone knows. The only thing left to learn is whether Wandor will march against Kerhab. We'll never learn that unless we can Mind Speak Wandor or Gwynna without their knowing it." He laughed.

100

Hawa didn't. "Don't say that in Telek's hearing."

"Don't worry, Hawa. I won't give Telek any unasked-for help until I'm sure his plans don't go beyond raising up the *mungans* again."

TEN

In time the rains ended and spring came to Chonga. So did the men sent by Baron Galkor from Benzos to strengthen Duke Cragor. They arrived less some five hundred of their number and most of the discipline Galkor and their captains had been able to hammer into them before they boarded the ships for Chonga. Berek brought word of their arrival and their quality.

Two days later Pirnaush called both Wandor and Cragor back to the pit in the garden of the Sea Jade Palace. Galkor was still in Benzos (and Wandor prayed he would stay there), so the duke came with Kaldmor and an unknown Knight. Wandor and Gwynna came with Besz again. They both knew Chongan well enough now to manage ordinary conversation, but not to catch fine points and subtle meanings.

The distant hills which had lurked in the mists now stood out under a blazing sun, and the two hours' climb from Dyroka no longer left so much of the heat behind. Pirnaush himself seemed happier, even excited. His robe was black and only his sandals bore any ornaments. He gave Dehass no elaborate greetings or compliments to translate, only a bald message:

"Tomorrow at dawn, the horns sound, to declare that we are at war with Kerhab. By noon I shall be at the City Palace. At sunset you and your most trusted captains shall come to me. We have gathered our men and our ships for the war with Kerhab. Now we must gather our thoughts.

"Lord Wandor. Your men will be no more than half the number of Cragor's. Is that not so?"

"They are."

"You have summoned more from Benzos?"

"Yes."

"It is a long voyage, to be sure."

"As you said, Honored Father, it is a long voyage," said Chiero. "Also, Wandor's men are so perfect in battle that they are surely worth far more than their numbers. I have watched Master Besz and his captains at work. Khoshi himself could not have taught more!"

Instead of Dehass rebuking the prince, the *Bassan* looked at his son, smiled faintly, and nodded. Apparently Chiero S'Rain, endlessly seeking to be gracious to his father's guests, had accidently said the right thing. Wandor felt sorry for Chiero. If not fit for the place he held, he was certainly worthy of a better fate than he was likely to meet, caught up in his father's battles and schemes, like a river-pig in the coils of a snake.

Now it was Cragor's turn. "Lord Cragor. Your new men are still at Bezarakki. It seems wisest to have them sail with the fleet and join us before Kerhab."

Cragor shook his head. "With all respect, Lord *Bassan*, I disagree. They have come to serve you after a long, hard voyage. If they remain aboard ship for another month, I fear they will not be at their best when you need them. Let them come up the river and put land under their feet."

Wandor found himself nodding. Cragor's reinforcements could best be kept in order if the duke kept them under his eye and hand, and he'd stated strong arguments to make Pirnaush let him do so. Cragor's men might have only one head to lead them rather than several, but that one head was well furnished with knowledge of war.

Pirnaush smiled. "Certainly, friend Cragor. I would not have anyone held back from the battle and the rewards of our victory." He looked from Cragor to Wandor and back again. "At least we would have no common men held back. We would ask that Lord Wandor leave in Dyroka one trusted captain, to greet and send on his new men when they reach us.

"I will also ask that both Kaldmor the Dark and Cheloth of the Woods remain in Dyroka during the war. It will not be so easy for them to remain unseen and rouse no fear in the camps as it has been in Dyroka."

"You do not expect we shall face any Powers from Kerhab?" asked Gwynna.

Pirnaush's laugh was a short harsh bark, and he spoke directly to the northerners. "The Fifteen are fools, to fight this long against us and risk their city for no reason. They aren't foolish enough to think they have any sorcery worth using against us."

The duke understood enough to nod. Gwynna's fingers played a message of doubt on Wandor's sleeve, but he found himself desperately wanting to believe there would be no sorcery involved in the war against Kerhab. It would be bad enough without that.

That evening, Cragor was smiling broadly as he watched Hawa dance. He watched her surrounded by a litter of girls, cushions, empty plates and bowls, wine jugs, and discarded clothing. At the other end of the lacquered table, Kaldmor the Dark did the same.

"We're going out of here, and wherever we go it can't be as bad," said the duke to a surprised and pleased Kaldmor the Dark, when the sorcerer found himself the duke's only guest. "Prisoners drink when they go free, so why not us?"

The duke called up the best of food and wine, ordered girls from the finest pleasure houses, and even sent word to the White Plum Tree that if the dancer Hawa came tonight she would be well rewarded. Hawa had to fight down not only Mitzon's fears but her own before she could decide. What the Black Duke did in his blackest moods they both knew. On the other hand, such a good chance to watch the duke with his guard down would not come often.

In the end Hawa came, and knew almost from the moment she whirled into the chamber that she'd been right to do so. These two unlikely drinking companions, duke and sorcerer, were far too happy and wine-flown to be dangerous. So she signaled the flute girl to play faster tunes, and set out to give Cragor and Kaldmor her very best, except for a few ornaments she now saved for Mitzon and a handful of his most appreciative friends. A generous purse from the duke would do no harm, and being in his good graces would do even less. Apart from that she had pride in her dancing, and in that pride she would not hold back her best from any man who might be going into his last battle. Khoshi's judgments fell alike on the virtuous and the evil, and arrows or swords could not tell between dukes and spearmen.

Hawa left behind her a flute girl who couldn't blow another note, several more empty wine jugs, and two men completely at peace with the world. She carried in her left hand what was left of her clothing, and in her right a purse with the duke's crest on it. If that purse held only copper it was still generous; if it held silver she was near to being a wealthy woman.

As the door closed behind Hawa, Kaldmor pushed an unknown number of perfumed arms from around his neck and sat up. At the other end of the table the duke was waving, all three of him. Kaldmor blinked, and the number of dukes shrank to two. He didn't think it was worth the trouble to get them down to one. He *knew* how many Cragors there were. The duke had no Powers to turn himself into twins, and anyway he was Kaldmor's friend and would never play a trick like that even if he could.

"Master—Kaldmor—" said the duke slowly. He never slurred his words, no matter how much he drank, until he could no longer speak at all. However, his heroic efforts not to slur his words made them come out one at a time, as if they were coming out of a narrow-necked jug.

Kaldmor sat up straighter and found his vision improving. Now there was only one Cragor, slowly rising to his feet. One hand held a wine cup, the other kept his breeches from falling down and tangling his feet, and two girls flanked him, arms around his waist and heads against his thighs. It was hard to tell who was holding up whom.

"Yes, lord?"

"Your—friend—your—thin friend—"

After a moment Kaldmor realized the duke was talking about the *limar* of Nem of Toshak. They called it, "the thin friend," and carefully avoided speaking of it or doing anything with it which might let anyone suspect its true nature. *Limars* were a lost art in Chonga, and the few Chongans who'd seen it were convinced it was no more than Kaldmor's apprentice or perhaps even a body servant without Powers.

"Yes, lord. Our friend?"

"Want—him—with me—at Kerhab. *Need* him. Gwynna—there."

This was a more complex idea than the first one, and it took Kaldmor longer to grasp. When he did, he was delighted. He'd thought of sending the *limar* with the duke, to balance Gwynna, since it could maintain its own disguise. But that would mean the duke's having it near him during the campaign, and Kaldmor knew how much the duke disliked the *limar's* presence. He hadn't dared suggest it himself, but if the duke's distaste was this much under control . . .

"I'll ashk—ask—the friend," said Kaldmor. He was embarrassed to discover that his words were now coming out as slowly as the duke's without being as clear.

"Haaaya!" shouted the duke, flinging his arms over his head. This caused his breeches to fall down and overthrew his balance. He fell backward, and the two girls holding him barely managed to keep him from flattening a third girl who'd gone to sleep directly behind him. She squealed and wriggled out from under Cragor, who muttered a few things which might have been words, then started snoring.

Kaldmor lurched upright, putting one foot into a half-empty bowl of spiced eels with rice. *Tonight—I am Cragor's body squire*, he thought. *I must get him to bed.*

With the help of all the girls—the number kept changing—Kaldmor did his duty for Cragor. He left the duke asleep, with one of the last two corked wine jugs propped on his chest. With two girls holding him up, the sorcerer followed a serpentine path back through the dining chamber toward the guest quarters.

As he passed the table he saw the flute girl sitting cross-legged beside it, eyes on the floor. He hadn't noticed her while she was playing for Hawa's dancing, but now that he saw her more clearly he realized she was quite pretty. He grabbed her by the hair and she squealed, more in surprise than in pain. Then she smiled and rose easily. Kaldmor put an arm around her waist, and sorcerer and girls lurched off.

Wandor and Gwynna lay on their wide gauze-screened bed, only their fingertips touching. Sleep seemed as far away as ever. It wasn't just the heat, Gwynna realized as she raised herself on one elbow and for the twentieth time tried to get Bertan to meet her eyes. The heat was bad enough, to be sure—she wished she could strip off not just her clothes but her skin as well, and let whatever breeze might reach this chamber blow across her bones.

Bertan lay rigid, spread-eagled like a man tied down and waiting for the executioners to go to work. His face held as much pain as if they'd already started, and much of that pain was reaching her even without Mind Speech. She decided that if Bertan didn't find some relief on his own before long she would use the Mind Speech to ease him, and never mind the danger of being overheard. It could hardly be a secret any-more, that they took little pleasure in the march on Kerhab. First she had to calm herself, though. She'd already used all the light, undetectable spells she dared. What else was there? In a whisper she began reciting the list of men in Wandor's strength and the supplies for them, then what they'd learned of Cragor's force. By the time she'd reached the muster of the *Haugon Dyrokee*, her mind was so completely concentrated on lists of men and war gear that Wandor's sitting up made her start and roll toward the edge of the bed by sheer reflex. She brushed the hair out of her eyes and rolled back toward him as he sat cross-legged, eyes still blank but the pain—praise Mother Yeza!—gone from them.

"I think that Count Arlor—" His voice was a dry-throated croak, and he paused to pour half the water jug into himself. "I think Count Arlor and a hundred or so picked men will be enough to leave behind. He can bring the new men north when they come."

"He'll be the best," said Gwynna. Reciting the arrays of fighting men must be nearly as powerful as an actual spell; her voice had stopped shaking, with relief. "He can speak to more Chongans, and no one who comes with the new men will object to being under his command." Then she rested a hand on his knee and formed the Mind Speech link.

("Was there any other choice?")

("I couldn't see any. I owe Kerhab more justice than they'll be getting from me. They've done me no harm by standing out against Pirnaush. On the other hand, they haven't thrown their lives, wealth, and hopes into the balance for Nond or me and against Cragor. There are too many who already have, and I won't buy a clean conscience with their blood and hopes. My own, perhaps, but not theirs.")

Was he going to risk and perhaps throw away his life to ease his conscience? Gwynna started, thinking the blunt ques-tion, but as soon as he recognized it she saw him smile.

("No, I'll take as much care of myself as I can. And don't throw stones at me for taking risks until you've stopped taking them yourself.")

Her hand crept over Bertan's body. After a moment she realized he wasn't going to be stirred, and found herself neither surprised nor particularly disappointed. Sleep was beginning to seem possible.

They lay down again, and sleep did come for an hour or so, until dawn brought the horns and drums crying out all across Dyroka, that the *Bassan* was going to war.

ELEVEN

From maps, Wandor knew the lands and waters which would
shape the coming campaign. It would take place in the valley
of the Hiyako, which joined the Trinopo at Zerun to form the
Pilmau, the second largest of Chonga's rivers. Kerhab lay north
of Zerun, about halfway to the head of navigation on the Hiyako. Several ranges of heavily-wooded hills stretched southward from the mountains of Kalgamm, dividing the upper valley of the Hiyako from the upper valley of Dyroka's own Mesti.

Kerhab shared the combined valleys of the Trinopo, Hiyako,
and Pilmau with three more of the Twelve Cities. At the mouth
of the Pilmau, Aikhon had been a Dyrokan ally during most
of Pirnaush's rule. It certainly would not resist the passage of
Kobo S'Rain's ships upriver.

At the junction of the Hiyako and the Trinopo stood Zerun.
It still would not admit Pirnaush's armies or even his envoys,
but it was an enemy more in name and by law than in fact. Its
own lands and wealth were modest, its leaders and fighting
men less than bold, its walls ancient and low. Once, its rulers
had hoped to cure these weaknesses with aid from other cities,
but that hope was gone. The great cities of Shimarga and Timru
both acknowledged Pirnaush's rule, and Kerhab could not spare
a man, an arrow, or a *qual* for any other city.

Still, it was not a city Pirnaush could trust. So Kobo S'Rain's
two hundred twenty ships would come up the Pilmau to just
below Zerun, and watch it as Pirnaush's army moved on Kerhab. When Kerhab was safely besieged, the fleet would come
north, to join Pirnaush under the walls of Kerhab. Once Kerhab

had fallen, Zerun would hardly dare refuse Pirnaush's envoys, let alone fight off his armies.

To the northwest, well up the Trinopo, stood Shimarga, for many centuries the third city of Chonga. Shimarga had sworn oaths to Pirnaush, and he called it "friend." Perhaps some men in it deserved that name. But there were enough others to be a second reason for keeping the fleet below Zerun until it could meet the army at Kerhab. Even the most hot-headed Shimargan would think twice about trying to aid Kerhab in the face of the united power of Dyroka.

Then there was Kerhab itself, squatting on the east bank of the Hiyako. Eighty thousand people lived within its walls, and eight or ten times as many in the lands it claimed when anyone asked who ruled what. Its people averaged a trifle darker than most Chongans, and it was said they were shrewder in trading foodstuffs and more adept in brass-working. Otherwise there was little to be said of Kerhab which could not be said of any other of the Twelve Cities. Its people fought best from behind their walls, the people of its outlying towns and villages loved the city folk no better, power lay first in the hands of the great merchants and only second in the hands of such fighting men as the merchants favored.

The Fifteen who ruled in Kerhab had won more obedience and respect than many who ruled in Chonga, if no more love. They had worked long and hard to prepare their city for the war, with much knowledge of war and such honesty that even Pirnaush saw no hope of spreading tales of their corruption.

Wandor did not find himself loving the war against Kerhab more than before, or feeling more at ease about leading his men into it. He would admit that Kerhab might be nearly as dangerous as Pirnaush and Dehass thought, and that in their position he himself might have found it hard to think of any peaceful solution.

Daily I learn more of ruling, and each day at the hands of stranger teachers.

The great map embroidered on silk which covered one whole wall of the council chamber made the inevitable course of the war clear at once. Send an army up the Mesti and the fleet up the Pilmau. Have the army march from the valley of the Mesti into the valley of the Hiyako through a pass in the hills used by armies and merchants for at least six hundred years. Bring the army and the fleet together before Kerhab and lay siege to it, with all the Chongan skill in siegecraft. Push the siege even more vigorously than usual—with the men of his northern allies and friendly cities, Pirnaush would have something like fifty-five thousand men before Kerhab, more than enough to permit trading lives for time. Force Kerhab to submit, if necessary by storming it. Treat it harshly or gently, as circumstances dictated, but disarm its fighting men, garrison its forts and walls, carry off its ships, and generally make it at least impotent if not friendly.

At first Pirnaush's plan of campaign held so few surprises that Wandor nearly fell asleep. He was tired, the chamber was hot, and Pirnaush kept passing the wine around at intervals. About all that kept Wandor awake were Pirnaush's occasional bawdy jokes or tales of old campaigns.

Pirnaush was using his son Kobo as a translator. Wandor, Gwynna, Arlor, and Besz faced Cragor and two of his captains. Arlor had to know all the secrets of the coming war, and there seemed no danger at this late hour in having him and Wandor in the same place. Neither Cragor nor Pirnaush would care to open a bag of serpents by open violence.

At last Pirnaush stood up, drew his sword, and began to describe the surprise he intended for the Kerhabans. Until Kobo brought his ships up the river, the army before Kerhab would have no way to move on the water. This would cost lives and time, and leave the riverside walls of the city free from attack for too long. Unfortunately there was no way to bring boats overland from the Mesti, and the Kerhabans would take most of their own craft upriver out of Pirnaush's reach and scuttle or hide the rest, as they'd done three times before in wars with Dyroka.

There was another pass through the hills between the Mesti and the Hiyako, far to the north, little used, and unlikely to be guarded. If a strong force of mounted men could be pushed through that pass, they would come out at its western end only a day's ride from the head of navigation on the Hiyako and the usual refuge of Kerhab's ships. With luck, the riders could surprise and capture the whole fleet, or at worst force the Kerhabans to destroy the ships.

A *mounted* force? Wandor wasn't sure he'd heard the *Bassan* correctly. Most of Chonga's land would not grow proper horse fodder, so horses were rare and generally too valuable to expose to the insects, snakes, and fever mists of the river valleys where most of Chonga's wars were fought. Then Wandor remembered that Pirnaush was trying to change this, with a horse-breeding

113

town in the upper Mesti valley. He'd found good pasture and also started oat-growing; there were also rumors he was trying to breed fever-resistant lines of horses.

"We have six thousand horses up here—" Pirnaush's sword struck the map near where Wandor expected "—all of them broken to riding. The North Riders will be four thousand men under *Hu-Bassan* Meergon. Two thousand will be Dyrokans, half riding, half walking. I'm sure it's no secret that not many Chongans know which end of a horse bites and which end kicks." Pirnaush seemed to look at Wandor and Cragor simultaneously without turning his head toward either. "The other two thousand will be northerners, half from each."

Wandor found himself speaking calmly and keeping a straight face as he did so. "Many of my thousand will be from people who are most strongly bound to me. So I will lead the Viceroyalty's thousand into the north myself." Beside him he heard Gwynna stifle a gasp, then a giggle.

The Black Duke looked as if red-hot needles were sticking into tender parts of his body. His breathing reminded Wandor of a blown horse. As if he'd had a Mind Speech link with his enemy, Wandor entered Cragor's thoughts.

I have to do the same as that damned Wandor. Otherwise Pirnaush will think I'm holding back from helping what has to be his favorite part of the campaign. But if I go north, can anyone else lead those gutter mongrels Galkor sent me?

And can Wandor be thinking of "accidents" in the north? At least his bitch queen won't be handing him poisoned daggers to put into me.

"Your Splendor, why not?" said Cragor, breathing like a man again. "Indeed, I shall be happy to join Lord Wandor in making your blow in the north a success."

Wandor didn't remember much else about the evening. He remembered that Pirnaush's look of triumph was almost obscene, that Cragor started cursing in low-voiced Hond as he left the chamber, and that he himself didn't dare laugh until he and Gwynna were alone. Then he laughed until he was sprawled helpless on the bed with Gwynna standing over him, holding the water jug.

When he'd caught his breath, he said, "I think—I think if I went to Cragor tonight, suggesting we join together against Pirnaush, I'd have him with me."

Gwynna set the jug down and nodded slowly. "And I almost

think we could trust him to hold to the bargain. But the *mungans* would certainly put their knife in."

"Yes, and even without the *mungans* I wouldn't wager on either Cragor or myself against Pirnaush." Wandor raised his voice to make sure any eavesdroppers heard him plainly. "The gods know I'm far from loving the man, but I'd be a fool to deny he knows both kingship and warcraft."

TWELVE

Wandor took the initiative by putting himself at the head of his North Riders and kept it by a wise choice of men. It also helped that four hundred of the men he'd brought to Chonga were Yhangi and an equal number were Khindi.

All the Yhangi and half the Khindi went north with him. The Yhangi of the Plains knew horses as few other peoples did; if a horse could be ridden they could ride it. Also, they were horse archers, deadly opponents on horseback even when they couldn't press home a charge with lance and sword. The Khindi were not horsemen, although most of those who'd followed Wandor to Chonga could get on a horse and some of them could actually stay on it. They were archers, and they were also woodsmen. Stalking their prey in forests was a high art with them, whether the prey had four legs or two.

The rest of Wandor's men were a mercenary company, levies from the Viceroyalty's barons, and a personal guard of exiles from Benzos. He took no other captains north with him. Arlor would be staying in Dyroka, and Captain Thargor would remain with the ships on the Mesti when the army marched overland. Gwynna, Besz, Sir Gilas, and Berek would be needed to lead the men to Kerhab.

The North Riders went aboard their ships as soon as the captains had the men picked. Twenty *kulghas* and five galleys carried them upriver to the ambitiously-named Rok-Vagai—"City of the Horses"—then headed south again. A day's march north of Rok-Vagai the Mesti was shallow enough for mounted men to ford.

If they could be mounted in the first place. The reports that the six thousand horses of Rok-Vagai were all saddle-broken turned out to be optimistic. Judging from *Hu-Bassan* Meergon's fury, this wasn't another of Pirnaush's jokes on Wandor and Cragor. All three chiefs were victims of an ancient form of the gods' ill-will, the servant who promises the impossible to please his master, then says he's done it to avoid punishment. Several of the horsemasters of Rok-Vagai were beheaded on the bank of the Mesti, but this did nothing to tame half-wild horses.

Wandor's Yhangi saved the North Riders. Each of them quickly tamed a mount for himself, then went to work with all their skill on taming more. It didn't help Cragor's temper to see Wandor's men doing this work, but he found a way to at least avoid looking foolish. The two hundred or so of his own men he could mount were set to riding night and day patrols around Rok-Vagai. If any Kerhaban spy got in to learn what was happening or got back out with the news, it was not the fault of the duke or any of his men.

The training of the horses was not done without many casualties among the animals and a few among the trainers. Wandor chartered a *kulgha* to take the injured downstream to Dyroka. On the morning the *kulgha* dropped downstream, the North Riders left Rok-Vagai in the opposite direction.

The fording of the Mesti cost fewer men and horses than Wandor had expected. Then the North Riders advanced westward in three separate columns. By mutual agreement only the three leaders met, and that only for a daily council of war. Perhaps this was guarding against shadows. Most of Cragor's men were mercenaries, whose swords remained sheathed or struck at the orders of the man who paid them. Among Wandor's men the Yhangi would not avenge Cragor's slave raids on his men if Wandor so ordered, the Khindi had barely heard of the Black Duke, and the mercenaries followed the same law as Cragor's. Nonetheless, all three leaders agreed that even one incident would be too many.

During the three days it took to cross the actual pass, the North Riders moved with half the Chongans in the lead, Cragor next, the rest of the Chongans after him, and Wandor bringing up the rear. Apart from making sure that the men on foot kept up and guarding the horses from brushtail cats and wolves, Wandor had little work during those three days. He was able to enjoy the crisp weather, drink from clear mountain streams, smell firebloom and the smoke of cooking fires. He could see slopes tinged with blue and gray close at hand, and beyond them mountain peaks blazing white with snowfields flung aloft against the sky. Some of the mountains reminded Wandor of pillars holding up the sky, while others looked more like the claws of giant beasts trying to drag the sky down to earth. These were the southern peaks of the mountains of Kalgamm, and it was toward the mountains that the Dragon Steed of Morkol had been flying when men last saw it.

Wandor didn't think very often about the legendary Dragon Steed of the wizard-prince who founded Chonga after Nem and Cheloth sank the Old Lands. It broke his pleasure at being in a land where the native sorcery was feeble and the Powers of the northerners might not be called into use.

Then the North Riders were through the pass and on their way down into the valley of the Hiyako. For two days they stopped while the thin and now fairly tractable horses grazed on a hillside of lush grass and the scouts moved out ahead. Most of the scouts were Yhangi or mounted mercenaries from Benzos, the rest were Khindi.

Two days after the march resumed, the scouts returned to report that they'd found the ships of Kerhab. Even more important, they'd found a route which would bring the North Riders down upon the ships like a flash flood. A night march, followed by a dawn attack, and the North Riders' work should be done.

Wandor dismounted, handed the reins to a Yhangi horse-holder, and slipped forward into the belt of trees along the riverbank. The scouts on the other side led him to the best point for viewing the river and the Kerhaban ships.

The ships lay in the mouth of a channel behind a long narrow island which screened them with rank, second-growth forest. Most of the ships also had branches tied in their masts and to their railings, so it was hard to tell how many there were. Kerhab was said to have more than a hundred ships, and it looked as if most of them could be here. Between Wandor and the water lay two hundred paces of slope, gentle and bush-grown at first, then steepening as it dropped toward the river, but almost bare enough to let a horse gallop. At the water's edge was a narrow sand beach, where Kerhabans sat around campfires and open-fronted leather tents. Smoke rising in several places from the ships and the island told of more guards.

Wandor heard twigs crack and bushes rustle behind him,

and saw fifty Khindi and mercenaries creeping up to join the scouts. The new arrivals were just settling into place when suddenly two Kerhaban soldiers broke out from the woods to Wandor's right. One stumbled along, leaning on the other. As they ran, they shouted words which hardly needed to be understood. Wandor jumped up, and as the Kerhabans around the campfires started reaching for their weapons he shouted to the men behind him.

"Follow me!"

They ran boldly, knowing that safety lay in covering as much ground as possible before the Kerhaban archers went to work. As they ran, the smoke from the ships and the island turned blue, then more smoke began curling up from other ships. As Wandor reached open ground he saw the Kerhabans on the shore picking up arrows and thrusting the heads into the campfires. The heads flared up, the archers nocked the arrows and shot, and where the arrows came down on the decks of the ships smoke began to rise. The Kerhabans hadn't sent enough men north to defend their ships against any sort of attack; they did not have the men to spare. At the same time, they had not left the men they did send unprepared to deny the fleet of Kerhab to any enemy who did attack. If they'd followed custom, there were tar barrels and brushwood piled on the deck of each ship.

Wandor wasted no time or breath turning to shout orders. He plunged forward, aware only of the men close on either hand, until suddenly the heavy breathing and footfalls were joined by a blaring trumpet and the swelling thud of hooves. Cragor himself swept down from the left at a canter, leading half a dozen mounted men of his personal guard. They cut in behind Wandor and the men flanking him. One horse shied and spilled his rider. The duke ignored the fallen man, spurring his mount ahead and drawing his sword in the same moment.

The brief check to the other riders gave the Kerhabans time to nock regular arrows, take aim, and shoot. Three saddles were emptied, all the horses went down or bolted, and the Black Duke himself vanished as if by magic. Wandor and the two mercenaries still beside him reached the riverbank, sprang down a man-high drop to the beach, and found Cragor.

He'd gone over the bank where it was nearly twice as high as a man, landing unhurt. But he'd lost his sword, and with only a dagger he was facing a dozen Kerhabans less than ten paces away. As they realized they had choice prey within easy reach, bows went down and short swords and axes came out.

Wandor could never remember if he had any doubts about what he ought to do. All the thoughts he remembered were of how to do it. He saw that he and the two mercenaries had more armor and longer swords than the Kerhabans, and that none of the archers had a clear shot. He sounded his war cry and ran toward the duke. The two mercenaries ran with him as if he'd gripped them and dragged them along.

Three Kerhabans had their eyes on the duke and their backs to Wandor. The first went down from a mercenary's thrust, the second turned in time to meet Wandor's dagger, the third had his ax raised over Cragor's head when Wandor's sword came down. The axman screamed and reeled back, clawing at his ruined face and forcing a comrade within reach of the second mercenary. A Kerhaban swung wildly at the duke as Wandor came at him, but only knocked the duke's open-faced helm askew on his head. The duke's vision was still clear on his engaged side, and he kicked one opponent in the belly and parried another's short sword with his dagger as Wandor drew the last man away.

The man was all attack, but fast enough to be dangerous. Wandor had to keep his distance until he could slow the man with a cut to the arm, then get in under the next swing with a dagger slash to the throat. Then there was another trumpet blast, which faded into a dying-bird squawk as the trumpeter fell off his horse, and more of Cragor's men were riding up to join the battle. Wandor's men were also reaching the bank and playing archery on the ships. He saw Yhangi among them, and decided to stay by the duke to guard the man against "stray" arrows from some Yhang who might remember the slave raids too well.

Cragor was now struggling to pull his helmet straight with one hand. Wandor reached out to help him, and found his arm suddenly stiffening. It was as if he knew his hand would catch fire or rot off if he touched the duke, and though he knew everyone except Gwynna would laugh if he mentioned it, the feeling was much too real. Then the helmet slid around into position, and the duke was staring at Wandor with more bewilderment than the human face is made to show.

"Thank you, Lord Wandor," said Cragor at last. "We shall speak more of this, I think." Then he turned and ran with long strides down the beach to where the bank was low enough for his men to help him up it. By a great effort of will, Wandor stopped staring after him and turned back to order some of his men to take the Kerhaban guards' boat, others to examine the tents and the bodies.

Between two and three hundred Kerhabans had been guarding the fleet. By noon half were dead, a few more on their way downriver, and the rest were in the hands of the North Riders, along with more than fifty of their ships. Meergon had ridden up in time to see the burning ships and promise that all the prisoners would be bound and put aboard the next ship set on fire. This saved half the fleet, and also saved Wandor any need to give the order himself to keep Cragor from winning that dubious honor.

Before nightfall, the North Riders were spread out in three camps along the riverbank, the island was garrisoned, and the men on foot had come up. From the door of his tent, Wandor could see the lanterns of the men working on the ships twinkling like overgrown fireflies.

He knelt by a basin of water, sponging his chest and shoulders and greatly wishing he had Gwynna here, if only to apply her skilled hands to all the muscles he seemed to have twisted or tightened beyond nature's limits. He'd been in bloodier, longer, and closer fights, but none which had left him at once so drained and so little at ease.

A sentry called out a challenge, there was an incomprehensible reply, then:

"Holy Mother Yeza, it's the Black Duke!"

Wandor knocked over the basin reaching for his sword, dropped the sponge, and stood up. A voice came out of the darkness beyond the campfire:

"Lord Wandor. May I enter and speak with you?"

"If you come alone, yes." Wandor stepped to the door as the duke appeared out of the darkness, with what seemed like half of Wandor's men crowding behind him. Wandor raised his voice. "Surround the tent, but keep well back. The duke has my sworn word for his safety." Wandor still did not sit down and put his sword aside until Cragor had seated and disarmed himself. Even then the duke carefully avoided turning his back to the tent door.

"Honor and greetings, my lord duke," said Wandor. For the moment they were two men of Benzos, and a duke and Royal Consort was the superior of a Viceroy without noble rank.

122

After saving the man's life, Wandor could hardly see much purpose in simple rudeness.

"Greetings and honor," said the duke. He sounded even more tired than Wandor. "It seems that what happened on the shore this morning is no secret in the camps."

"Did you expect anything else?"

"No. And even if it was only between us . . . I want to reward the two men who fought at your side as they deserve. And you . . ." Cragor sighed. "Lord Wandor, did you save me just so I would be altogether lost for a proper way to reward you?"

In spite of the light tone he was forcing into his voice, Cragor was obviously in no mood for mockery or laughter. Wandor's mind slipped into a familiar pattern. He'd won this Duel by so many hits; what should be the price paid by his opponent's patron? After a moment, the answer emerged.

"First, there is the matter of my comrades, above all my lady." Wandor's voice hardened suddenly, and the duke started as if he'd drawn a knife. "It's no secret what you've dreamed of doing to her if you took her. These dreams will come to an end. I think your—*pleasures*—are those of a man the gods did not make quite whole. But if you do not feed those pleasures on my lady, they can remain a matter between you and the gods. If you take her, give her a quick and honorable end."

Cragor stared at Wandor as he'd stared after the fight on the shore. Doubtless he'd been expecting to hear Wandor ask that Gwynna be held inviolate, and was now even more certain that he was in the presence of a madman. Wandor had his reasons, but they were not for Cragor's ears, and perhaps he would not understand them even if he heard.

Gwynna had followed a warrior's way, and faced its dangers with open eyes. To ask that she be forever shielded from some of those dangers would be to shame her in a way she would not forgive. He might do it for the best and truest of reasons—that too much of him would die with her—but that would not make any difference. Gwynna was too proud to accept that there could be any reason to treat her as woman rather than war comrade.

"I can do this," said the duke at last.

"You will swear it," said Wandor, in the same tones he would have used to state that the sun rises in the morning and sets in the evening. "You will swear it before witnesses, so that if Gwynna ever does go to your executioners, gods and men will call you not only an animal but an oath-breaker."

123

There was a jug of half-sour wine beside Wandor. He poured a cupful and handed it to Cragor. The duke drank, and slowly the color returned to his face.

"This also can be done."

"It will be done, when we join the army before Kerhab. The other thing you can do is sit and listen to me explain why I saved you. Believe it or not as you choose, but listen."

The duke swallowed more wine, and his mouth twisted. He was now clear-headed enough to notice the sourness. "I will listen."

"I didn't know if I could save you by going forward. I did know that if I held back, I'd be killing you as surely as if I split your skull myself. There'd have been witnesses too, some of them your men. I might not have lived many minutes longer myself. Some of your men must follow you for love, and many would call it a matter of honor to avenge you.

"Even if your men didn't take vengeance, there was still Pirnaush. He would have been a danger to me, and he'll be a danger to you if I die from anything you do or leave undone.

"Consider it. One of us kills the other. Pirnaush thinks he can win over the dead man's followers by avenging their fallen leader. He does so. Now both of us are dead. My people have less to lose than yours, because Arlor and Gwynna and the rest could and would step forward. You have no one, at least no one who can hold Benzos together against nobles who are already growing restless."

After a moment the duke found his voice. "Yes. And even if Pirnaush struck down all your people in avenging me— gods, then both our lands would fall apart. Pirnaush would be the best master left in all the world."

"At least for our mercenaries," put in Wandor.

"Even they would be enough to give him absolute rule in Chonga. And with Chonga united under him, and no ruler elsewhere fit to stand against him . . ."

"I doubt that Pirnaush aims at the throne of the world." said Wandor. "He's too old."

"*He* is, but what about Prince Kobo? If his father lives long enough to give him a united Chonga and more ships and men than anyone else . . ." This time the duke did not finish because he'd seen the agreement in Wandor's eyes. Kobo S'Rain was a man whose ambitions would grow as fast as his chances of realizing them.

"Shall we agree, then, to keep each other alive long enough for Pirnaush to judge between us?"

"Yes," said the duke. "I will not swear it, and I will not pray that you be spared from fevers, snakes, and other people's steel. But you are safe from me."

"And likewise you from me."

Cragor reached out to take Wandor's hand, then stopped as his arm stiffened in a gesture so like Wandor's after the morning's battle that Wandor laughed out loud. For a moment the duke joined in the laughter, then stepped out into the night. It was some time before Wandor even had the strength to pick up the wine jug and pour himself a cup.

THIRTEEN

———◆———

Even this far north the valley of the Hiyako could be unhealthy
for horses. Meergon ordered three Nineties of Chongans to
drive them off to high pasture and guard them until Pirnaush
could send enough men to lead them back to Rok-Vagai. The
rest of the North-Riders started boarding the Kerhaban ships.

When the improvised fleet was ready, Meergon gathered
the leaders aboard his ship to celebrate. Over captured wine,
the *Hu-Bassan* grew warm enough to admit they'd won a victory he really hadn't expected. He'd thought he was being sent
north as punishment, to command a witless and foredoomed
enterprise which could only end in failure for everyone, death
for many, and disgrace for him.

"But this was not so. All fought as if they fought for love
of me, and this fighting was enough to bring victory. I will not
forget this. I will never forget the gratitude I owe to Lord
Cragor—" he drank, "—and to Lord Wandor—" He drank,
coughed, and dropped his cup to the deck with a clang.

There was far more wine than food at the party, so that not
even Wandor remained entirely clear-headed. Meergon drank
so much that he had to be carried to bed, but said nothing more
against Pirnaush and never failed to praise Wandor and Cragor
with scrupulous equality. He was also on his feet the next
morning, to give the orders which started the fleet on its way
downriver to Kerhab.

Meergon didn't let his eagerness to complete the victory
make him careless. The fleet moved by day and anchored by

night, with sentries alert and everyone with his weapon close to hand. Kerhab's squadron of light river galleys hadn't been found with the ships in the north, and with surprise on their side even two or three of the galleys could do far too much damage. The fleet also had no pilots for this stretch of the Hiyako, and as it dropped toward its summer low the river was certain to sprout sandbars and ship-gutting submerged trees.

On the second night Cragor came to Wandor's ship and asked for another private conversation. This time the duke had nothing on his mind but war. The North Riders had fifty ships of Kerhab, he said, and it wasn't at all certain the Kerhabans knew they had them. Those guards who survived had fled before they could tell how many ships had been captured. The Kerhabans' eyes would be on Kobo and the fleet, and they might not be thinking of danger from the river before he arrived.

Now suppose the North Riders launched their own attack? They already had fifty ships and more than three thousand men. Among the men were certainly many who could erect siege towers on the ships' decks, forge grappling hooks, assemble scaling ladders as the fleet sailed south. A day north of Kerhab, it could put in to shore and take aboard as many men from Pirnaush's main army as the *Bassan* would spare or the ships would hold.

Wandor did a few sums in his head. "For a few days, we can hold another three thousand."

"Yes. That should be enough for storming the riverside walls of Kerhab."

"Not for taking the city, though. They had more than fifteen thousand men under arms when we left Dyroka. They may have even more now."

The duke didn't expect to storm Kerhab with only six thousand men. He merely expected to hack out a foothold along the waterfront. Then Pirnaush could pour more men into the city through the captured water gates, ferried there by the captured ships.

"Pirnaush will certainly have at least twenty thousand men before Kerhab by the time we can strike," Cragor explained. "The city has no more than five thousand fit to take the field outside the walls. The *Bassan* can surely send half his men aboard ships and into Kerhab to finish the work we've begun. With the enemy at their front door and their back door broken down, the Kerhabans will have no hope."

The duke was proposing a gamble, but one which might

succeed by throwing surprise, speed, and sheer ferocity against perhaps unprepared and undermanned defenses. To be sure, Cragor would win much honor with Pirnaush for suggesting the attack, but Wandor would not be far behind if he led his men up the walls beside Cragor.

There was also an aspect to this attack Cragor hadn't mentioned. Ending the war against Kerhab with such a swift stroke would spare everyone death and danger, starting with the Kerhabans themselves. If they yielded now, Pirnaush might consider easy terms for them as long as they acknowledged his rule. If they fell only to an assault launched after a long and bloody siege, Pirnaush might order the city sacked both as an example and as a punishment, even if his men didn't take matters into their own hands.

If Kerhab did not fall to assault, Pirnaush would never relax the siege unless he was forced to by revolts or plots elsewhere in Chonga. These might well come, and then Wandor and Cragor would be caught deep inside Chonga as the whole land flared into war, with no certainty of finding allies or even a safe journey home. Otherwise, the siege would go on until Kerhab's defenders were no more than a handful of fever-ridden skeletons, shambling through streets choked with rubble and rotting bodies, living on rice hulls and rat's flesh, barely able to cock a bow or lift a sword. No Chongan army in such a long siege had ever escaped a murderous toll from disease, and the northern men would go down even faster than the Chongans. The leaders themselves might not be spared, and neither the gods of Benzos nor the gods of Chonga could say what might come of *that*.

"No one will gain from a long siege, that is certain," said Wandor aloud. The duke nodded. "So let us put this before Meergon."

The *Hu-Bassan* was delighted, and not just because the duke's plan offered him the chance to be associated with another unexpected victory. He saw the advantages of a quick assault and all the dangers of a long siege as clearly as Wandor. Meergon added a few details of his own and sent a heavily-manned *kulgha* downstream with word to Pirnaush. Meanwhile the North Riders' fleet anchored in the mouth of a tributary of the Hiyako and started assembling what they'd need for the assault.

The work went on from first light to nightfall and sometimes by torchlight into the darkness. Cragor's men and Wandor's worked closer together than before, but also too hard to have the strength to quarrel even if they'd had the will. Few did. The two armies had now seen each other fight and had not found each other wanting. By his orders, Wandor's men spoke softly of his saving Cragor. Also, while the storming of Kerhab would be bloody even if it ended in victory, both the blood and the victory would be shared equally if no one held back, and both the duke and the Viceroy made it very clear that no one would, themselves least of all. By the time the *kulgha* returned with Pirnaush's approval of the plan, Wandor knew he had nothing to fear from Cragor's men nor they from him. The soldiers were still two armies rather than one, and would do best fighting well separated—but that would make little difference to Pirnaush, and still less to the defenders of Kerhab.

The night was clear, except for a light haze on the water. If the attackers had lost surprise, they weren't going to get it back now. Mitzon was sure surprise was gone, perhaps through the work of Telek or *mungans* serving Kerhab, perhaps only because the eyes and ears of desperate men grow sharp. Mitzon was very glad his own Ninety would go in through whichever water gate fell first and fight to hold ground in the city itself. They'd have a fight of cat against rat in the narrow streets, to be sure, and they'd be fighting women with spears and children hurling pots and furniture from high windows, but it would not be what the men fighting on the walls would face.

Mitzon climbed onto the railing, then into the rigging. As he climbed toward the foretop, he began thinking what he would have ready to defend the walls of Kehab if the task were his. Catapults in the towers and archers behind every arrow slit. The Turtles of Kerhab and lighter men on the battlements with axes and spears to use against ladders. Pots of warfire ready to hand, at least one for every man on the walls, and everything needed for lighting the fuses and relighting them until they stayed lit. Torchballs and torchspears, pots of ash-water to burn out eyes, and plain stones to crack the skulls of men or the planks of ships. Stone throwers in the streets behind the wall on the landward side, with armed men waiting beside them, ready to go wherever the attackers were pressing hardest. Messengers to carry word of victory or defeat, women with herb-boiled bandages for the wounded. . . .

By the time he'd reached the foretop, Mitzon was above the haze, nearly on a level with the tower tops of the city. The ships all around him seemed dream shapes, and the night twisted the little sounds from them. A bucket dropped on deck sounded like a sword blow, the squeak of oars in locks was a man's death cry, a low-voiced order for silence was a serpent's hiss.

Mitzon did not know when the oarsmen of the leading ships began their battle stroke, or when the alarm sounded on the walls of Kerhab. He only knew that in one moment there was darkness, and in the next moment battle flared all along the walls, from the tops of the thirteen towers to the decks of the ships now crowding up against these towers.

The battle din was confused; it was easier to distinguish lights and colors. There was the blue of Kerhab's warfire, torchballs in gold and green, orange snakes in the air as fuses trailed sparks, the dance of reflections on the armor of the men on the walls and the men climbing up toward them.

Mitzon had heard of "the terrible beauty" in a battle by night; he now saw more terror than beauty.

Close to the wall, there was practically nothing but terror and very little beauty even for those men who lived long enough after the Kerhabans went to work to notice anything.

Wandor had most of his own storming party—his personal guards plus twenty Khindi—drawn up in the stern of the *kulgha*. There they'd be clear of anything dropped onto the bow and partly shielded by the siege tower amidships from spears and arrows.

This was sound reasoning as far as it went, but it made no allowance for eager men at the sweeps below. The *kulgha* swept up to the wall well ahead of the vessels on either side of her, giving the Kerhabans a disastrously long moment of undisturbed practice against her. Everything they could send into the air or over the walls rained down on Wandor's ship.

A sailor waiting on top of the siege tower to lower the gangplank on to the walls came hurtling down, two arrows in him. A Khind clutched at his thigh, staggered a few steps, and fell down the aft hatch. A mercenary's sword clanged on the deck, fallen from suddenly limp and bloody fingers. A torchball landed on the foredeck, throwing light and also setting fire to the trousers of a man waiting to drop anchor. He beat at the fire, dancing wildly. Wandor shouted at him to lie down and roll, then a stone from the wall crushed both the flaming trousers and the leg inside them.

A clay pot of warfire landed with a thud on a stack of matting thick enough to break its fall. It rolled to the deck with a sound lost in the din all around, and Wandor pressed the flat of his sword against the fuse until the sparks died. With one hand he lifted the pot and pitched it over the side; with the other he sheathed his sword.

"Come on!" he shouted, and managed to grin. "It's safer up on the wall!"

The siege towers built on seven *kulghas* were improvised open-sided affairs, with four legs and only enough crossbracing to keep them erect until their work was done. Wandor climbed up inside this one on a roughly dressed tree trunk with lengths of branch nailed across it. As he reached the platform on top, the gangplank crashed down, creaking ominously but not breaking. One of the sailors who'd lowered it was sitting glaze-eyed on the platform, trying to pluck a bolt out of his groin. Another was scrambling down one of the tower's legs, until a spear from a catapult pinned him like a doll halfway down.

The sleet of bolts and arrows slackened as Wandor stood up. To starboard other ships were now against the wall and raising scaling ladders. He drew his sword and dashed across the gangplank onto the walls of Kerhab. To his left was the flank of a tower, with an iron-braced door staring at him. To his right were the scaling ladders and men from the other ships. Behind him three more men crossed to the wall, but as a fourth set foot on the gangplank it cracked and sagged, then slid clear. The man's scream as he fell was the first human sound Wandor's ears had picked out clearly in quite some time.

From the top of the tower and the arrow slits on either side of the door crossbows let fly. Two of the three men behind Wandor went down. The third staggered from a glancing blow. Wandor felt a red-hot club laid across his ankle. At this close range even the lightest Chongan crossbows could pierce armor, and the big fortress bows could put a bolt clear through a man.

A monstrous armored shape loomed up, one which had to be human but could not be. It was one of the Turtles of Kerhab, tall, massive men, trained and equipped for this sort of fighting. They wore armor so heavy even they could barely move in it, but they weren't supposed to be lightfooted. While the armor turned aside all attacks, they stood atop walls and barricades, thrusting, hacking, or slashing at whoever came within reach.

This Turtle's armor was reddish-black, and he wielded an eight-foot pole with hooked crosspieces and a yard-long curved blade on the end. The blade came down on the helmet of the topmost man on a scaling ladder. The man seemed to turn boneless all over and fell back on the man behind him. Their combined weight overbalanced the ladder. Wandor didn't watch it fall; he was charging the Turtle, sword raised for a thrust at the man's eyeslit.

The Turtle lowered his head so that Wandor's thrust missed, then brought his weapon hard across Wandor's ribs. Fortunately only the pole struck Wandor; the blade would have split him as thoroughly if not as neatly as an eel sliced up by a fishmonger. He lost his sword, then his balance. As he went over the edge he kicked himself desperately out into space, missed the ships and the outward curve of the base of the wall, and plunged into the Hiyako. He went under with eyes closed and mouth open, fought his way to the surface and came up next to a floating body with only one eye left to stare at him. He spat and coughed out water, then both he and the body went under again in the wave which rose as the Turtle struck the water.

Wandor and the dead man rose to the surface again; the Turtle did not. Wearing two-thirds their own weight in armor, the Turtles floated like anvils. Wandor coughed out more water, struck out toward the ship, and found his knuckles scraping weed-slimed planking. Almost by instinct he moved aft, toward the *kulgha*'s waist. Voices shouted recognition above him, and a rope splashed into the water beside him. It was one of the ropes he'd had made ready for just this purpose, with a loop on the end.

As he gripped the loop, something cracked like a huge tree going over, and shouts changed from recognition to warning. Wandor pressed himself against the *kulgha*'s planks like a baby to its mother's breast as the siege tower came down with a terrific crackling and crashing, shedding pieces of timber large enough to crush a man.

Wandor was so close under the curve of the *kulgha*'s side that none of the pieces touched him, although he was forced underwater as the ship rolled violently. Then he finally got a firm hold on the rope. The men on deck heaved, his battered ankle seemed to scream in protest as it struck the railing, and as the pain ebbed he found himself kneeling on the ship's scarred deck. Without rising to his feet, he gave up his last meal and a bellyful of the Hiyako's water. Then with a hand on the railing and other men's hands under his arms he stood up.

He quickly learned that no one knew for certain what was happening but everyone suspected the attack was making little progress. With her siege tower gone, this *kulgha* was certainly doing more harm than good where she was, blocking off the wall from better-equipped ships and killing her own men. Wandor leaned against the stump of one leg of the tower and ordered the rowers back to their benches.

As he did, two pots of warfire crashed down on to the deck near the stern. One fuse was out, but both pots cracked open and the other fuse was enough to ignite everything. The thick, sharp-smelling oil spread across the deck, spewing up smokeless blue flame as it went, swallowing two men so quickly they barely had time to scream.

The warfire spread farther, toward the after hatch. More cries from below jerked Wandor into movement. The *kulgha*'s forward hatch was nailed shut to provide a solid base for the now-vanished siege tower. The after hatch was the only escape route from below, and if the flames blocked it the men below were doomed.

Wandor ran aft and a sailor ran beside him, water slopping from the bucket he was carrying. Wandor kicked at the bucket, spilling it on the deck. "You fool!" he screamed. "Water on warfire spreads it! Sand, you hear me? Sand!" He'd seen to it that bags of sand were piled ready along the railing. He picked up one and swung it toward the flames, felt the sacking tear like rice paper, and saw the sand scatter uselessly.

Now Wandor picked up a sandbag under each arm and ran toward the flames. He would have run into them if two men hadn't scrambled out of the hatch almost at his feet. They took one sandbag; he clawed the other open and emptied it at the edge of the flames. "More sand!" he shouted. More men climbed out of the hatch, then there was a soft thud and the hiss and purr of more flames behind him. He ignored them. "More sand!" he shouted again.

"Lord Wandor—"

"More sand!"

He was reaching for the sandbags he knew must be somewhere close, and other men were reaching for him, gripping his arms. What were they doing, slowing him this way?

"More sand!"

Instead there were more arms, except that some of them

134

weren't arms of flesh and blood. They looked more like the arms of fire sprites, blue and flickering as they reached up for his legs. A sudden rush of dark human shapes, and this time all the arms were solid, lifting him clear of the reach of the fire sprites, lifting him clear of the deck. Was he going to fly, like the Dragon Steed of Morkol?

He was not. He was going overboard, as the flames swept for and aft along the deck of the *kulgha* and the last few men off leaped with clothes and hair smoking. He was also slowly regaining a human's reasoning power, and held on to it even when the waters of the Hiyako clawed at his burned legs.

He listened, waiting for the screams of the men who had to be dying below, letting the men on either side of him hold him up. He waited, heard the continued din of battle and other screams and cries from farther away, but heard no screams from the *kulgha*. After a while he began to understand that they weren't going to come, that the men who'd been below were safely in the water with him. When he knew this, he found that he could start swimming.

Mitzon strode aft along the port side of the *kulgha*, stopping almost in the shadow of the aftercastle. The man leaning back into the corner formed by the railing and the aftercastle *was* Lord Wandor—the men from the burned *kulgha* hadn't lied. Mitzon recognized the misshapen nose, the scar over the left eye, the short beard now too drenched to curl, the long Hond bones and the dark coloring so different from the Hond.

Blank dark eyes rose to meet Mitzon's. The *mungan* swallowed. "Lord Wandor, I am Mitzon, *Ki-Bassan* of—"

"You'll get your reward." A blank voice too. Mitzon shrugged, not resenting the words. Too many men could only think of pushing themselves forward when they had a great lord in their debt.

Wandor straightened himself and looked at Mitzon. "The attack has failed."

"Yes. Word came a short time ago. Cragor saw we could not break through into the city, and sounded the retreat."

"How far did we go?"

"I heard we took two towers, but the Kerhabans blocked the stairs and the doors. I know we took a water gate, but they came back at once. Over a hundred fell before they drove us out."

"Cragor is no fool. Let no one ever say that in my hearing."

"I understand, Lord Wandor. There is a healer within hail, I think. I can have him—"

"No." The dark face bowed into the shelter of the charred sleeves. After a moment the shoulders began shaking. Mitzon turned away. In this moment Lord Wandor would be alone even with a hundred sworn friends at hand. The best gift a stranger could give him was to look elsewhere.

FOURTEEN

The wounds on Wandor's body healed swiftly, because Gwynna and Berek saw to it that he got the best possible care. The wounds within healed less swiftly. It did not help as much as Gwynna had hoped, for him to learn that the night's attack had not been a complete disaster after all. A defeat, yes, and one which made a long siege of Kerhab with all its dangers inevitable, but far less costly than might have been the case.

The dead and wounded numbered no more than a thousand, with less than a score of ships burned or sunk. The Kerhaban had lost nearly as many people, including more than half the Turtles, and shot off more arrows and much more warfire than they could afford. Their courage was unshaken, but so was that of Pirnaush's army, and all through the siege camp, men praised both Wandor and Cragor.

The Black Duke was honored for conceiving the attack from the river and also for seeing the moment of defeat and ending the attack. "You'd think he'd been war-taught in Chonga," was a common way of praising him. (The Chongans honored skill and subtlety in war; a man who would die rather than retreat a pace was perhaps a child, perhaps a halfwit, certainly not fit to command in battle.) On the other hand, Wandor had been first on the walls, deeper into the close fighting, and rather more seriously wounded. (Cragor had only lamed a shoulder when a ladder gave way beneath him.) Nor did the tale of his standing amid the flames until the men below were clear lose anything in the telling and retelling.

Between the deeds of Wandor's men and Cragor's, there

137

was absolutely no difference the keenest eyes or the most persistent questioners could discover. While Wandor's men had done more on the walls, Cragor's men had done more at the water gate, at times against odds of four to one. Even Cragor's household levies and Wandor's Yhangi took to greeting each other in the camp streets, and the mercenaries were more likely to raise drinking cups than swords to each other.

"All of this should make me happier than it does," said Wandor as he lay one afternoon with Gwynna sponging his burns with oil. "Kings have been called great after losing ten times as many men and doing less."

"But you still can't see yourself as a king?"

"Oh, I can," he said. The sponge pressed too hard on a half-healed spot, and he stiffened for a moment. "I can," he repeated. "But when I do, I'm looking through the eyes of the Duelist who would put himself in danger for silver and honor but shed no other man's blood if he could. The Duelist stands beside King Wandor, looks at him, often doesn't like what he sees, and sometimes can't remain silent."

"As long as I know which one is in my bed, I'll not say a word against either."

Wandor sighed. She would try to take away his unease with light words, and with more when he was further healed. She would not succeed, and he couldn't even know if he wanted her to.

What healed Wandor's invisible wounds was Cragor's oath-taking. Whether the Black Duke kept his promise to Wandor out of mere gratitude, or because he saw the defeat as a judgment of the gods, he swore honorable treatment for Gwynna not just once but twice.

The first time, he took the oath before Pirnaush and his two sons, four of his own captains, Wandor, Gwynna, Berek, Sir Gilas, and Master Besz, as well as priests of Staz the Warrior and Khoshi Swift in Battle. No one else witnessed the oath, or was even permitted within hearing. With a grave face the duke described what he was foreswearing in sufficent detail to make Gwynna turn pale. Then he swore by a list of gods which almost exhausted his breath that Lady Gwynna would receive at his hands only "ransom, honorable captivity, or clean death." She would receive nothing else by anything he did or left undone, or by anything done or left undone by any man owing him any form of obedience recognized under any land's laws.

The second oath was sworn in the open air and the open daylight, before anyone who cared to stop within earshot—and as Cragor's words were repeated by Master Besz, that meant half the camp. Cragor swore to give all men and women in Lord Wandor's service honorable treatment according to the custom of war among the Hond and the laws of the Kingdom of Benzos. (Wandor and Gwynna insisted on this phrase; they knew that the Khindi, Yhangi, and Chongans all admitted torture as a custom of war.) After that Wandor and Gwynna made matters equal by swearing to give Cragor's people the same treatment. Again Master Besz brought the words to half Pirnaush's army and some of the Kerhabans as well. Then Wandor and Gwynna went back to their tent.

Gwynna turned even paler during the second oath-taking than during the first. As they entered the tent, she started shaking so violently Wandor touched her forehead. No chills, no fever. Then she clutched his shoulders until her nails penetrated both cloth and skin and pressed herself against him.

"Bertan, that—oh, gods, that you've put *that* behind me— what can I do or say? *What*?" The last word was a choked cry, as if she felt the hot irons on her flesh. He held her, sensing that when she didn't have words she didn't expect any from him either.

At last she stopped shaking, and with her mouth muffled against his chest said, "Death—I was afraid of it, in one way or another. From when I was fourteen, I knew it would keep me from doing work I was called to do. Then we met, and I knew it would—carry us apart. But—Cragor's tortures—to have an animal watch me turn into something less than an animal, to feel not just my body but my spirit being torn until— until—until—" She wept in relief then, as he'd never heard her weep in pain or fear or grief.

A week after the river attack, Count Arlor arrived with the reinforcements from the Viceroyalty, and Wandor felt even better. Without the count he felt as if his right arm was, if not cut off, at least dangling useless. Of the reinforcements, the count had left behind in Bezarakki two hundred warriors of the HaroiLina and five experienced Captains under Reyget Son of Kurt. The freed slaves aboard the greatships were also turning into tolerable soldiers, so all the ships left behind were now adequately manned.

"The greatships and the seal ships can now reach the

Tok'lis," said the count. "Once Reyget finishes loading fresh water and stores, they could sail all the way home any time they had to." Wandor hoped such a headlong retreat wouldn't become necessary, but appreciated having the route for it kept in good order. It gave him an advantage over Cragor, who still had more men before Kerhab but many fewer guarding his line of retreat.

In Dyroka itself, the count had left a hundred men to guard the barracks for the third fleet from the Viceroyalty that was due before winter, and also to keep their eyes and ears open. "I do not know how well Cheloth can listen without using his Powers."

"And he won't tell you?"

"Do horses fly?"

The count had also left behind in Dyroka a reliable spy, the son of a Benzos merchant—in fact, son of one of Cragor's allies on the Civic Council of Benzor. "He's one of the last men Cragor would suspect, although he hates the duke's usurpation. His wife had much influence there, I know."

"I hope they both realize there is danger, if not from Cragor then from the *mungans* and Dehass?"

"Before he would agree to work for us, he insisted that we carry him and his family back to the Viceroyalty when we leave. He knows. I can't imagine anyone who's lived in Dyroka and learned anything about Dehass not knowing the danger of crossing the man."

"Pirnaush seems to trust Dehass."

"He's right to do so. Dehass will serve Pirnaush faithfully, as long as that service earns him all he wants. But he's no Baron Galkor. He keeps his own friends and his own purse at the best of times, and he's not the man to go down with his master. At the moment he's nobody's enemy, but neither is he a man I care to leave unwatched."

A more immediate problem than Dehass was the reinforcements. There were four hundred of the HaroiLina, and as many sailors and craftsmen from the Viceroyalty. There were also two thousand infantry of the Royal Army of Benzos, under a baron who plainly stated his thoughts to Wandor.

"My son was slain fighting against Cragor, likewise my daughter's husband. My daughter miscarried from grief, and both she and my wife are now held by my wife's father, who serves Cragor. There is too much blood between me and the

140

Black Duke for me to serve beside him. I am not the only man among the royal army with such a tale, either."

Yet the royal infantry were the best of Wandor's fighting men. If they held back, his fighting power would be weakened much more than he could afford, and also his reputation as a man who was obeyed. Pirnaush would not overlook this, particularly if the Royals' hatred for Cragor led to brawling and bloodshed.

The solution came from Arlor, and it was so simple that Wandor called himself a fool for not thinking of it himself. The royal army assembled by the riverbank, and swore the Oath of the King's Soldier, to obey the king or the lawful captain placed over them by the king, and:

> When through weakness of mind or body the king shall give no fit orders, or through usurpation the power of the king lies in the hands of a despot unfit in the eyes of gods and men to rule, the soldier shall obey the orders of those sworn to act under law until the true mind of the king or the true king himself shall be restored upon the throne of Benzos.

This oath-taking was not quite as well-attended as Cragor's. No one expected the Black Duke to appear to hear himself called a usurper and "a despot unfit in the eyes of gods and men to rule," or his captains to appear to hear themselves called the servants of such a man. Pirnaush was inland, settling a force of the *Haugon Dyrokee* into camps along the road they were building between the valleys of the Mesti and the Hiyako. Kobo was north of Kerhab, at work on two proper siege towers, each mounted on the hulls of two *kulghas*. Meergon and several other *Hu-Bassans* did appear, and so did Chiero S'Rain.

Indeed, Chiero took a great interest in the whole oath-taking, and afterward discussed it with Wandor, Gwynna, and Arlor, showing charm, wit, and a considerable knowledge of the forms of oaths in various cities of Chonga and in other lands as well. When he left, he gave Gwynna a vial of rare scent, and everyone agreed that the gods had not really mismade Chiero S'Rain, although they had certainly misplaced him.

Count Arlor watched the whole oath-taking with an expression which had to be called a smile, although Wandor knew he would not have cared to see such a smile if he'd been the count's enemy.

The siege of Kerhab settled down to steady, inexorable preparation for the storming of the city. Pirnaush obviously had no intention of trying another assault before he was thoroughly prepared; just as obviously he had no intention of waiting for hunger, disease, or fear to break the defenders. In spite of the hard work and monotony, the hot weather, and the not-infrequent casualties, the northerners found much to interest them. They were seeing the famous Chongan siegecraft at work against a worthy opponent.

As the days passed, Wandor realized that the Chongans were not workers of miracles. They had no marvelous secrets for building or attacking fortifications, and except for the warfire, no weapons unknown in the north. What they did have was leadership, skill, and discipline in their efforts. Pirnaush had in his service five hundred men who did nothing but study and practice siegecraft, and every soldier in his army was given skill with ax, hammer, or spade, as well as spear, bow, or sword. Chongan siege engines were better built than those of the north, more numerous, and used with more skill. Finally, Pirnaush had brought to Kerhab three thousand slaves, who did most of the work too dangerous or too filthy for even the lowest of free soldiers.

Kerhab had reinforced its walls on both the inner and outer faces over the last two years. In many places they were now too solid to be breached by anything short of the very largest stone throwers, and Pirnaush had too few of those to rely on them completely. He gathered those he did have in two places under heavy guard and kept them busy night and day, hammering away with a steady stream of three- and four-hundred pound stones.

In other places, smaller engines went to work, trying to destroy the walkways on top of the walls and the upper levels of the towers, or at least to keep them free of archers while the ditches below were filled in. The ditch-fillers worked under the cover of large shields of reeds covered with leather soaked in urine to resist warfire. Stones, timbers, and buckets of earth were piled up just out of bowshot of the walls, then passed forward from hand to hand under the cover of more shields to the men on the edge of the ditch.

The heavy stone throwers hammered at the walls where they were protected by a water-filled moat; the shielded men worked where there was only a dry ditch. At one point along the ditch, a wheeled siege tower was rising, ready to be pushed forward across the filled-in ditch for the assault. On the river the two shipborne siege towers also rose steadily higher. Everywhere men were hammering together scaling ladders, tying hooks on the ends of ropes, and piling up torchballs for night fighting.

The work did not go forward without occasional mishaps and a steady toll of men, struck down by arrows or spears, crushed by stones, burned by warfire, blinded by ash-water, maimed in accidents, collapsing from the heat or the exertion. Most of the casualties came in ones and twos and half-dozens; the Kerhabans seemed to be frugal with both their weapons and their men. They certainly made no effort to attack the siege engines on the ground, and Wandor couldn't tell if this was a calculated decision or the paralysis of the bird charmed by the approaching snake.

There was no sign of sorcery, or at least none that Gwynna could detect; if Cheloth did any better he held his own counsel. Wandor lost no sleep over this. The only man in Kerhab of whom anything magical had ever been whispered was a scholar named Beon-Kagri. While he was descended from Shimargan miners (who often had some crude Earth magic), he also was one of the Fifteen who ruled the city and an unlikely candidate for secret delvings into unlawful matters.

Also, there was little trouble between Wandor's men and Cragor's. Even if the two forces had been more hostile and the leaders less careful, they were so far apart that occasions for quarrels would have been rare. Cragor's men were camped on the riverbank at the far northern end of the siege lines. Wandor's held a section of the southern half of the lines, facing one of the breaches which gaped wider each day, spilling tons of stone into the moat.

So the weeks followed one another with the monotonous persistence of the buckets of earth moving forward to fill in the ditch. The walls of Kerhab began to show damage, and the siege camp began to take on the look of a city.

At the end of the tenth week, Pirnaush announced the assault for the second day following. Late the next afternoon, Wandor and Gwynna found themselves faced by their comrades— Berek and Sir Gilas, Master Besz, and Captain Thargor, with Count Arlor speaking for all.

"Lord Wandor, Lady Gwynna—there will be no need for you to lead our people into the city tomorrow."

"If we don't, who will?" said Gwynna.

"Berek and I will be at the head of the men," said Sir Gilas. The huge Sea Folker and the small Knight exchanged grins. "We've always wanted to fight as a pair. This seems as good a chance as we can hope to find."

"Also a good chance to be killed," said Wandor.

"No more for us than for you, Master," said Berek.

Wandor looked at Gwynna, knowing that if she'd arranged this he was going to be angry with her, no matter how unjust it might be. Her eyes met his steadily. Without Mind Speech he could not be certain, but other signs he'd come to recognize told him that this was as much of a surprise to her as to him. From her smile, though, he saw that she was quite prepared to welcome it.

King Wandor and Master Duelist Wandor exchanged looks, then the one body they shared shrugged and laughed. "Very well. Gwynna and I will be well to the front, but we won't fight you two for the first place."

Then they were all gathering around him and Gwynna, and he saw the doom-light on them. It did not shine brightly; perhaps there was no doom close in time or space. But it shone with a steadiness he'd never seen before. They might live long years or short days before it came, but the doom would not pass them by. He looked at Gwynna, and saw in her eyes the same knowledge which must be in his.

FIFTEEN

———————◆———————

Dawn came to the army in the siege camp, to the ships on the Hiyako, and to the city of Kerhab trapped between the two.

Creak of sweeps, splash as their blades cut the oily surface, curl of water at the *kulgha*'s bow, clink of chains as the slaves strained back and forth. For the first time in days, Mitzon found himself with nothing to do. He had to stay on deck to give the signal to the men below, but otherwise he could be asleep until the *kulgha* drew alongside the floating siege tower.

Two hundred paces away the tower rose from the two *kulghas* supporting it, swaying gently as the two galleys pushing it toward the wall thrust unevenly. Compared to the improvised towers used in the first river attack, this one was awesome. It was hardly smaller than the tower of a fortress, closed in on all sides with overlapping shields like the scales of a snake's belly and then covered with urine-soaked leather against warfire. There was room on top for twenty men to stand and shoot, while others climbed up ladders inside and ran past them on to the walls across a gangplank wide enough to take three abreast. The two *kulghas* carrying the tower were among the largest in Kobo's fleet, yet they rode lower in the water than any sailor would call safe. That was why the building of the second floating tower had been stopped; there really weren't two other *kulghas* big enough to carry one safely. The duke hadn't been happy about throwing all his men onto the walls through the one tower. Apart from the danger if the tower sank or burned, his men would now be taking a much smaller part in the storming of Kerhab than Wandor's.

The morning was clear, with no haze to confuse sight or sound. Along the walls of Kerhab, Mitzon could now tell which towers were too battered to support archers. He pulled off his helmet and the already sweat-sodden hood under it. He'd have to put it back on soon enough, then lead his men aboard the siege tower and up the walls. No doubt a place so far forward was an honor to him and his men, and it was certainly proof that his identity as a *mungan* was still a secret, but the fact remained that he was going to be where the judgments of Khoshi fell the thickest.

However, he'd said his farewells to both Telek and Hawa. He parted from Telek with easy words, out of respect for the man's past achievements if not for his future ambitions. He parted from Hawa with—he would not let all those memories pour in and weaken him. Not now.

Khoshi, the judgment is yours. Mitzon undid his sash and mopped his face with it, then settled his helmet back in place and tied the thongs under his chin and through the hooks on his breastplate.

A stone rose black against the sky over Kerhab, then plunged toward the river. Water spouted as high as the mast of a small ship no more than twenty paces from the siege tower. From two towers on the wall, spears suddenly bristled like the spines of a thornfruit. *Good shooting, but poor men on the towers*, thought Mitzon. Standing up to cheer, they'd revealed themselves too soon.

Another stone came across the wall from a different direction, but fell only a little farther away from the siege tower. Two sailors opened the hatch behind Mitzon. As they did, Mitzon heard the distant rumble of many fast-beaten drums and a sharper chorus of trumpet calls. On the inland side of Kerhab, the storming parties were going in.

Arlor stood on a rise of ground and watched the storming column advance toward the southern breach in the walls of Kerhab. He was high enough to see all the way forward to where Sir Gilas and Berek would lead their men into the breach, and all the way back to where he hoped Wandor and Gwynna would stay until he gave them the signal. Toward the city, all the way to the moat, was the "dead belt" around Kerhab—earth burned, trampled, and gouged clean of life, then littered with stones and shards of clay, discarded weapons and clothing, bodies so charred they'd barely started decaying and others which even hardened soldiers could not approach.

The leading men of the storming column moved forward into the dead belt at a trot. They moved in pairs, each pair carrying one of the reed and leather shields used to protect the ditch-filling parties. Carried vertically, these shields now protected the head of the column from the archers on the wall.

As the head of the column approached the breach, the shields offered less protection, but meanwhile slingers and Khind archers went to work on either flank. They threw and shot on the move, not accurately but faster than the crossbows. Stones and arrows whizzed down about Kerhaban ears, disturbing the aim of many though probably hurting few.

Still closer. Now when a bolt drove through a shield and one of the men carrying it, the survivor could stagger to the edge of the moat. Some shields fell flat, making paths across the rubble half-choking the moat, others were set in place vertically. Most of the shields now bristled with bolts and arrows and shone dark with blood. Crossbowmen took places behind the standing shields, dueling with the men on the wall at close range and ducking behind the shields to recock and reload. The archery from the wall began to slacken.

The slingers and the Khindi on the flanks scattered as the main body of the storming column came up, half of them levies from the Viceroyalty under Sir Gilas, half from HaroiLina under Berek. They flowed around either side of the shieldmen and archers like a river flowing around a fallen boulder, then met at the edge of the moat and pushed forward across the bridge of shields and fallen rubble.

Perhaps it was just Arlor's imagination, but each part of the column seemed to have something of its leader in the way it moved. The Viceroyalty men seemed to dance over the ground, as light-footed and eager as the small slim figure in armor waving his sword at their head. The HaroiLina marched with a steady, oxlike tread, most of them carrying their axes and swords over their shoulders as Berek carried Thunderstone. Side by side the two bands crossed the moat, men falling now as Kerhaban archers found targets they could not miss, and side by side they rose up the rubble.

Arlor had to force his arms not to raise sword and shield and his legs not to hurl him forward to the breach. But when Sir Gilas and Berek swore to lead the storming column, they also made him swear to stay safely clear—to guide the others forward, they said, and also to make sure the Viceroy and his lady stayed where they were supposed to. Arlor vowed to Alfod and Staz to keep his oath, and never to swear one like it again.

Berek and Sir Gilas vanished side by side through the breach, carried forward by their men like two pieces of driftwood hurled high on a rocky shore by a storm wave. Arlor turned away from the wall and saw the royal infantry standing with their backs to the battle. Wandor was keeping them close under his hand and eye.

Arlor also saw a flash of gold above a green helmet among the royal troops. Gwynna couldn't wear her favorite green leather hat over a helmet, so she'd bound the feather to its crest. Friend or enemy could pick her out as easily as usual.

Master Besz came up, and Arlor turned his attention to the wall again. The men of the storming column were scrambling up the rubble and vanishing into the breach by the score. There was little to be seen except their backs, an occasional man falling, and a swelling cloud of dust and smoke from inside the wall.

Berek and Sir Gilas found the breach in the wall like a dust-shrouded valley, with ragged slopes of stone, brick, and timber looming on either side and a rubble-strewn floor making footing precarious. On the other side of the wall and the dust cloud was exactly what they'd expected to find—a second wall, of rubble and stones braced with heavy timbers. It formed a half circle around the breach, and the top was lined with archers, spearmen, and a few of the Turtles.

The lower part of the inner wall was at a slope, and the two men ran at it, ignoring a stickiness under their feet. As they reached the foot of the upper, vertical part, a Kerhaban above hurled a lighted torch on to the stones behind them. The whole space between the inner and outer walls blazed up in the blue flames of warfire.

The two men were so far clear of the flames that not even the warfire clinging to their boots ignited, and so far ahead of their own men that not many of these were caught by the trap. The unlucky ones died screaming, while the archers on the inner wall tried to get a glimpse of the attackers in the breach through the curtain of blue flames and thick gray smoke. They didn't see the two men practically at their feet.

Berek dropped his ax and bent down, Sir Gilas climbed on to his shoulders, Berek rose to his feet, and the Knight leaped high. He easily reached the top of the wall, and the first man he faced fell off in sheer surprise as an enemy seemed to drop from the sky. Meanwhile Berek started pulling at every timber he could reach, using his vast strength steadily and without haste.

Sir Gilas killed the next three men he faced with hardly more trouble then he'd had with the first one. The men on top of the wall either had spears he could duck under or crossbows nearly useless in a tangled fight at sword's point. Other men were running up toward the inner wall along the street behind it, but he knew he'd have the advantage of height if he could clear the top of the wall before the newcomers reached the base.

He'd dealt with seven opponents before Berek found a vital timber, heaved it loose, and brought half of the inner wall's vertical portion down with a crash like the skies falling. Sir Gilas found himself with no opponents and very nearly with no footing. He leaped free in time to avoid falling helplessly, came down on hands and knees, retrieved his sword, then turned and shouted through the flames behind him.

"Throw stones, you fools! Throw stones into the fire! They won't burn! Throw stones and make a path!"

Then he and Berek had to face the Kerhabans from the street scrambling toward them over splintered timbers and the bodies of their comrades. Fortunately Berek not only had Thunderstone in his hands but room to use it, while Sir Gilas was ideally fitted to strike down anyone who got in under the murderous swing of the great ax. After the first collision not even Kerhabans fighting their last battle for homes and city cared to face the Knight and the Sea Folker.

A few had the wit to scramble up the remaining vertical portion of the wall, but by the time they did this the warfire was dying out and Khind archers were on top of the outer wall. Shooting through the thinning smoke, they easily kept the top of the inner wall clear. Meanwhile everyone in the breach who could lift a stone was heaving it into the warfire, and gradually something like a line of stepping-stones across a stream crept toward the two captains.

The first men to make their way across the stones had to hold their breaths to keep out the smoke and still felt the heat clawing at hair and skin. They still came on behind their captains and forced the breach of the inner wall. As the warfire burned out, all the surviving men of the storming column poured into Kerhab.

Beyond the inner wall was a narrow street and at the end a third wall, a makeshift affair of stone-filled barrels and loose timbers. From somewhere out of sight a stone thrower had the range of the street, and as the attackers advanced, a stone the size of a sheep crashed down on them. It struck down five men, but their bodies kept it from shattering into pieces to kill more. The men who survived were only enraged further, and they rushed the third wall so furiously they might have swept it clear with nothing but lengths of firewood in their hands. As it was, not a man of the wall's defenders lived more than a minute.

Berek shouldered Thunderstone, its blade and handle now completely red, and seemed about to start exploring the side alleys for fugitives. Sir Gilas tapped him on the shoulder with the flat of his sword.

"Ho, brother. One of us should stay here, and send a message back to Arlor. We have the breach, but we'll need more men to hold it before long."

"Wise." Berek reached into the purse at his belt with a hand as red as his ax. "Toss for who goes and who stays?"

"Toss it shall be."

A stone fell close aboard, tons of water rose into the air, and most of it seemed to fall back on Cragor. He spat out mud and curses, then felt the deck under his feet shiver as the galleys astern of the siege tower butted hard into the *kulghas*. Rattle, squeal, *crash*, and the gangplank on top of the tower went down onto the wall. Cragor tore open the door at the base of the tower and dashed inside as his men swarmed up the ladders.

Before the duke was halfway to the top he found a Chongan *Ki-Bassan*—that damned Mitzon who'd saved Wandor!—also bringing his men up. For a moment half again as many men were packed inside the tower as it could hold; there was a not altogether good-natured shoving match on the ladders. Cragor had curses flung at him and elbows shoved into his armored ribs, returned the favors, breathed in air thick with the smells of wood, tar, human sweat, leather, and ripe urine. Finally enough of the men ahead of the duke reached the gangplank to release those behind them. The duke raced up the ladders as fast as he could move in his armor, outstripped the two knights-sworn to stay with him, and reached the wall of Kerhab before they'd got clear of the ladders.

As the duke looked back at the tower he saw it was leaning noticeably to the left. A look downward showed a hole gaping in the foredeck of the port *kulgha*. One of the stone throwers had finally made a hit. The tower wouldn't last much longer.

Mitzon's men swarmed onto the wall, then a *kulgha* with more of Cragor's mercenaries slid alongside the tower and its men started leaping aboard. By now the tower's damaged *kulgha* was noticeably lower in the water. Cragor did his best to ignore the bolts and arrows whistling about him and looked both ways along the wall.

Everywhere *kulghas*, galleys, and smaller craft were nuzzling up to the wall like nursing puppies. Scaling ladders were going up and men climbing them, or were falling back along with their ladders, but more were getting on the walls and even down into the city.

Cragor cupped both hands and shouted down to the mercenaries on the deck of the siege tower. "Get back aboard your ship and go up the ladders! The tower's sinking, and you'll be drowned when it does. Don't stand there gaping! Hurry!"

As if to enforce the duke's orders, the tower tilted even more sharply. The greenish-brown waters of the Hiyako were lapping at the *kulgha*'s foredeck. Some of the mercenaries scrambled back to their own ship, then the tower began the steady swing to the left which told the duke it was going over.

Men inside the tower screamed and clawed their way into the open from top and bottom. On the deck below, the mercenaries were leaping over the side, then the gangplank to the wall slid sideways and away. Cragor gripped the outstretched arm of a mercenary as the gangplank dropped out from under the man, though he struggled so frantically that he nearly pulled Cragor off the wall and howled in fear until the duke was tempted to let him drop. Somehow they both survived until a bolt from a Kerhaban rooftop took the mercenary in the face.

Although the attackers now held nearly half the river wall, they faced steadily increasing archery. There were mostly dead Kerhabans on the wall now, but plenty of live ones lurking in every door and window and on every rooftop with a clear view of the wall. Cragor saw four men go down as he trotted along the wall, but apart from keeping his shield turned toward the city he ignored the bolts and arrows as he would have ignored a shower of rain. He was wearing the heaviest armor he could bear on foot, and although the armor was gathering new scars today, so far the man inside it had not. Most of the heavy bows had been on the walls; the lighter ones left to the men inside the city could not pierce Cragor's armor at this range.

At last the duke saw his banner bearer scrambling up a ladder from the deck of a galley, the short battle staff under his arm and the banner itself tied around his waist like a sash. He bowed as the duke came up. "My lord, word's come from the land side. Wandor's through one breach, and Pirnaush's through another."

Cragor looked back toward the river. The siege tower was half-submerged, with loose planks floating around it and bubbles of air and faint screams escaping from it. The galleys were hauling sodden mercenaries out of the river. Men seemed to be climbing ladders almost everywhere, and where they weren't, ships with stone throwers on their decks were shooting over the walls. A house collapsed in such a thick cloud of dust that for a moment Cragor was afraid some fool was using firepots. A few of them in the wrong place could burn half the city, something Pirnaush would not care to see done without his orders.

Along the wall, some men were now pulling up the ladders and lowering them down the inside of the wall. One of Cragor's knights came limping up, to tell him that the other was dead.

"A good and honorable fighter," said the duke. Every man who didn't survive the fighting in Kerhab was one less he'd have to face Wandor when they tried conclusions again. "He should have some company on the way to the House of Shadows."

Cragor slung his shield, hefted his battle ax, and stepped onto the nearest ladder leading down inside the wall. "Raise that banner and follow me, friends. It's time for Wandor to receive a message that we also are inside Kerhab."

About the time Cragor set foot on the ladder, the royal infantry of Benzos marched up to a gate now held by Berek's and Sir Gilas's men, and Count Arlor led them through. He also took along Wandor and Gwynna, well to the rear of the Royals but glad to be moving again.

The Royals marched up the two widest streets they could find, and along a third went Sir Gilas and Berek at the head of their remaining men. All three streets led into the main square of Kerhab, before the House of the Fifteen. Along the march, the advancing men endured occasional stones and bolts from above. When they reached the square, they found at least five thousand of Kerhab's fighting men drawn up, ready for a straight fight. The men were supported by archers and women and children with stones, perched in every possible place around the square.

The Royals dressed their lines, tightened helmet straps, checked the edges of halberds and the points of pikes. Sir Gilas called up some Khindi to deal with the Kerhaban archers. Arlor sent back word that Wandor and Gwynna should come forward to join him. The drums rolled on both sides, and the trumpets of the Royals sounded for the advance.

Then more drums and very badly played trumpets sounded, and up the streets into Wandor's rear flowed a mass of the *Haugon Dyrokee*, eager to join in the battle. They came at a trot, crashed into the rear ranks of the Viceroyalty men, and got hopelessly tangled with them. The shoving match here was not good-tempered at all, and it very nearly turned bloody when Baron Haagabor of the Royals ordered his rear ranks to face about and meet the Dyrokans with leveled pikes.

Then Chiero S'Rain rode up through the press of his father's men, helmetless, splendidly armored, and nearly without an escort. A hundred hostile eyes picked him out, and fifty arrows and bolts flew at him. None of them hit him but most hit some human target among the *Haugon Dyrokee*. Their own archers promptly returned the Kerhaban fire, and for the next few minutes Wandor and Gwynna had as much work and as much danger as they could have found in the forefront of a battle. The *Haugon Dyrokee* were ready to turn into a panicky mob, arrows from both sides were flying in all directions, the horses of Chiero's escort were trampling everything within reach, and the Dyrokan captains seemed to have sunk into the stones of the square.

Eventually Wandor found the commander of the *Haugon Dyrokee*, an elderly *Hu-Bassan* recently arrived from Kerhab, who'd taken command from those who'd served through the siege by virtue of his high rank in the old nobility of Dyroka. He'd never seen Wandor, and refused to believe that this sweating, dark-faced northerner in improbable armor was anyone from whom he had to take orders.

Then Gwynna almost literally fought her way through the ranks of the Dyrokans and gave Chiero S'Rain a tongue-lashing no one who heard it ever forgot. She told him that since he had rank above everyone else here, he should use it to bring some order out of chaos and prevent death and dishonor among both his father's men and his father's friends. Without lowering her voice, she went on to tell him that if he *did* insist on riding up to a battle, he should at least put on a helmet and some less conspicuous armor. It was no honor to be the biggest and easiest target on any battlefield!

Chiero smiled, then laughed as Gwynna gave him his orders, and after that started giving his own. The *Hu-Bassan*, seeing the northern woman treating Pirnaush's heir like a small boy who'd forgotten to wash behind his ears, concluded that these northerners did have a right to command and he had a duty to obey. Between Chiero, the *Hu-Bassan*, Wandor, and Gwynna, the *Haugon Dyrokee* were put in order or sent on their way with surprising speed.

By then the main battle in the square was over. Berek's and Sir Gilas's men had their blood up and comrades to avenge, but no one could ever say for certain what made the Royals fight like men possessed. Perhaps they saw that the road to vengeance and home lay through the ranks of the Kerhabans. Perhaps they fought for the honor of the army which a murdered king had raised high. Perhaps they fought for their own honor and reputation, to show that exile under the strange Viceroy hadn't blunted their skills. Perhaps they fought, as one captain said, simply because they knew that the *Haugon Dyrokee* behind them were going to panic, and they needed to clear a safe path out of the square for themselves.

However it was, they attacked as if each man in their ranks faced his deadliest enemy. In the time it takes to serve one course of a banquet, three out of four Kerhabans in the square were dead and the unwounded survivors were scattering through the city, leaving behind them weapons, armor, and footgear. Half the square was carpeted with bodies, and hardly a finger's-breadth of stone showed free of bloody or still uglier substances. More bodies hung out of windows or sprawled on the front steps of the House of the Fifteen, more blood was spattered on walls, and from all sides came faint shouts, war cries, and screams as the last archers were hunted down.

For once both King Wandor and Duelist Wandor looked with the same bleak thoughts at the bodies and heard with the same ears the carrion birds crying above the rooftops and the drone of gathering flies.

SIXTEEN

When the fighting in what came to be called the Square of Blood was over, Kerhab was defeated. What little chance there'd been of driving the attackers back beyond the walls died with the defenders of the square. Now Pirnaush's men in the city outnumbered the scattered defenders nearly three to one. The only question left was how long before these men died or yielded, and what would happen to their city afterward.

Wandor and Gwynna quickly discovered that most of the remaining defenders were not men at all, but women, children, and the sick or aged who died because they didn't know how to either fight or yield. The worst was over by midafternoon, leaving Wandor and Gwynna slumped on a bench in a captured tavern. Some of their men searched it for food and wine, and others carried out the bodies of the landlord and his wife.

They'd also taken out the landlord's son, a boy of three. "Mother Yeza's been merciful," said Gwynna wearily. She sounded doubtful of the mercy or even the existence of Mother Yeza. "He knows something's happened, but not exactly what. Young as he is, he should be safe now."

"From our men, yes, and probably from Cragor's," said Wandor. "But what if Pirnaush orders the city sacked?"

Would Pirnaush order Kerhab ruined as a lesson to his enemies? He was certainly capable of it, and (King Wandor whispered) might even have good reason for it. But being here, commanding men who'd have to carry out Pirnaush's orders, and above all seeing the stunned faces of Kerhabans who might have received only a reprieve, not a pardon, made King Wandor's whisperings not very pleasant hearing for the Duelist.

Before Gwynna could reply, some of the men emerged from the cellar with beer, salt fish, and pickles. After eating, Wandor and Gwynna sought the privacy of the kitchen, but before they could consider the matter of the sacking any further, the door opened and Chiero S'Rain walked in. Gwynna's expression changed from grim foreboding to charm with a speed which compelled Wandor's admiration, and they both bowed.

Chiero returned the bow. He still wore an elaborately decorated breastplate, but his gauntlets and arm and leg armor were now as plain as the poorest *paizar-han*'s. A green cloak flowed from his shoulders, and under one arm was a high-crested, open-faced helmet. Wandor realized with a faint surprise that for the first time, Chiero was wearing armor without looking like an actor in a pageant.

The prince put his helmet on the kitchen table and helped himself to a cup of beer. "I cannot give you gratitude with the—ah, *weight*—behind it that my father can," he said. "But I give you all I can, both for myself and for the Shield of Dyroka."

"We had our duty to them, as we had to our own men," said Wandor, and Gwynna added:

"It was no fault of theirs or yours that they were brought forward at the wrong time and into the wrong place."

Chiero's eyebrows rose. "I hear hints against the *Hu-Bassan*."

"You do," said Gwynna, and Wandor nodded.

"Perhaps something shall be said to the *Hu-Bassan* when the war is over," said Chiero. "For myself, I would rather speak to both of you, and not on war."

"If your father so arranges matters, we would share that pleasure," said Gwynna. Another exchange of bows, and she and Wandor were alone in the kitchen.

"Are you trying to charm Prince Chiero into being more of a man?" he asked.

She smiled. "Making him more of a man is certainly better than making him a eunuch, isn't it?"

Cragor's men and the Chongans beside them fought through the houses along the riverfront against resistance as determined as anyone met that day in Kerhab. After the battle of the Square of Blood, however, the fighting in Cragor's part of the city quickly sank to the level of a tavern brawl. The duke sent out scouts to reach Wandor's advancing men and drew everyone else back into formed bodies close under his captains' eyes. Galkor's reinforcements had fought well, but he would not trust their discipline in a newly taken city. While Pirnaush might in the end want Kerhab reduced to ashes and rubble, it would be by his orders and not by his riotous allies.

The merchant who played involuntary host to Cragor had hoarded a liberal stock of food and wine, which his servants were in due course persuaded to bring out. Cragor sipped pale green wine and ate soup and melon, while his guards tossed coins to divide up the rooms of the house, their portable furnishings, and the female servants.

Cragor was scraping the last flesh out of a melon rind with a silver knife when a shadow fell across his table. He looked up and saw the *limar* standing beside it.

That damned thing looks more human each day. Now it can look uneasy at approaching me. Is this Kaldmor's doing or is something human really creeping into it?

Cragor pulled his thoughts back from that last question like a horse from the edge of a chasm. "Something human" entering the *limar* from outside the world might easily come from Nem of Toshak himself, or at least from the House of Shadows.

"Yes, Narl?"

"A message, my lord. For your ears only." The *limar* nodded toward the stairway, and Cragor saw in its wide dark eyes a hint of the bluish light of Toshakan Powers! The message would be from Kaldmor in Dyroka, and it would be too long for the *limar* to pass into the duke's mind with a touch of its fingers. Cragor welcomed that, even if the message was bad news. He'd never been at ease being touched by the *limar*.

At the top of the stairs was the merchant's bedchamber. The duke led the *limar* in, stuffed a scrap of cloth in the keyhole, pulled the door shut, locked it, piled furniture against it, then led the *limar* to the corner of the room farthest from both the door and the window. It stood silently as he crossed his arms on his chest.

"Yes, Master Kaldmor?"

The blue light in the *limar*'s eyes brightened, and Kaldmor's words came out in its own thin voice. "My Lord Duke. Cheloth of the Woods seems unable or unwilling to listen to us, or attack any link I form with the *limar*. I do not know why this is so or how long it may last, but I am sure that it is so. I have tested it, and if I have not drawn Cheloth's attention by now—"

"Yes, I see. Since time is short, forget telling me *why* and only tell me *what*."

"Eh?"

"*What* do you want to do with this link, you—"

"Ah, my apologies, my lord." The *limar*'s voice could not convey most of Kaldmor's supercilious blandness, which was just as well for the duke's patience. "If Cheloth cannot detect or attack my link with the *limar*, I can use it to give the *limar* control of several of my most useful spells."

"Give the *limar* control?" Cragor knew just enough about what this meant to have his doubts about it. "To use the spells at its discretion?"

"You understand clearly, my lord. Your understanding of the world of Powers grows—"

"My temper grows short. You cannot use these spells yourself, either directly or through the *limar*?"

"Not if Cheloth becomes watchful again, which he may do at any time. Or at least not without great danger. Cheloth could not only break the link, he could attack the *limar* itself. Even the Lady Gwynna might be able to launch such an attack, if Cheloth warned her. She has Powers of her own, and since she worked against the Beasts of Yand they have—"

"Kaldmor, I know of Gwynna's Powers. I also know fire-tongs from swords. *Be brief.*"

"Yes, my lord. Even if nothing else happened, we would be caught red-handed breaking the agreement against sorcery which we ourselves proposed. Pirnaush would take that most ill."

Kaldmor was certainly developing one of the skills of state-craft, a gift for understatement. Pirnaush would be furious, and if half of what Cragor had heard about the day's fighting was true, making Pirnaush furious would be the end of the duke's hopes in Chonga. The taking of the first breach and the battle in the Square of Blood were on everyone's lips. So were the names of Wandor, Gwynna, and all the Viceroyalty's captains except Master Besz, who was not talked of only because he'd done his work so quietly and so well that no one saw him doing it.

The duke had to walk softly in any matter where Pirnaush might take offense. He also could not afford to be without any weapon he could safely acquire. The battle for Pirnaush's favor might already be lost, but he would still have to fight the battle to leave Chonga alive. Yet—putting Toshakan Powers into the *limar*, completely under control of whatever it used in place of human judgment—unnatural, unwise—the duke clenched his fists until his nails would have drawn blood if he hadn't been wearing gloves—*unavoidable*.

He sighed. "Can you at least tell me what spells you will be putting into the *limar*?"

"I must put them into it first, and tell you afterward if I have time." Then, before Cragor could say more, the dusty room blazed up with the searing blue fire of Toshakan Powers. The duke clapped his hands over his eyes. He heard a strangely human grunt from the *limar*, like a man lifting a weight he's finding too heavy for comfort, and a faint dry-leaf crackling. A wind blew through the room, kicking up enough dust to make Cragor sneeze. When the sounds died and he opened his eyes, it was to find the *limar* sitting cross-legged on the floor, its eyes blank.

"Master Kaldmor—"

The *limar*'s eyes flickered. "His work is done and the link broken. The spells are mine."

"What are they?"

"I may tell you only when they are to be used."

Not being human, the *limar* had no real sense of how close it came to having its head lopped off. Cragor's hand was actually on his sword hilt before he could stop himself. Then he laughed. Kaldmor hadn't changed, would never change. He would still use every shift and stratagem he could think of to avoid answering questions about the use of his Powers. It was always maddening, and at times like this it could be dangerous. The *limar* was now a deadly weapon of Power, but it was hardly under Kaldmor's control and not at all under the duke's.

Still—was it a mere matter of Kaldmor's vanity, or could there be good reasons for hiding the paths along which he walked in search of the Powers of Toshak? The Powers of Toshak and above all of Nem were unlike most sorcery which had ever existed, unlike any since the fall of the Sorcerers' City. Kaldmor was marching steadily deeper into this unknown land. If his steps were guided by something more than mere chance (and the duke rather hoped they were), he might have good reason for his silence.

* * *

Wandor and Gwynna had nearly decided Pirnaush would give no order to sack Kerhab when Master Besz brought the *Bassan*'s order to them.

"We are to take all weapons, jewels, gold, and silver from Kerhab. Nothing else is to be touched, nothing burned. The Kerhabans are to be left in peace, unless they try to resist or hide anything of value."

Wandor shrugged. It was about what he'd expected—orders which would let Pirnaush deny responsibility for any real outrages, while practically ensuring there would be some the Kerhabans would not soon forget. Gwynna looked as if she wanted to either throw up her hands in despair or spit on the floor in contempt, and Besz's face was as close to a frown as Wandor had ever seen.

"Fortunately, there is a temple of Murorin within the quarter given to our men. The temple should give us all Pirnaush can expect us to bring him, without taking much from Kerhabans who might be driven to fight. The temples of Murorin take in as much as those of the Great Gods and give out far less."

Besz went on to describe the plan he'd settled with Count Arlor. The mercenaries and tribesmen would surround the quarter, blocking every street. The Royals would guard the area around the temple itself, and also make a perfunctory search of the houses. Picked men under Wandor and Gwynna would strip the temple. Their presence would clothe the affair in as much dignity as could be hoped for, and reassure Pirnaush of their zeal. Gwynna's Powers could deal with any minor uses of sorcery by the priests of Murorin.

"Well done," Wandor said. "That should keep the Royals away from Cragor's men and the mercenaries and tribes away from the Kerhabans. Beyond that—we can hope for the gods' protection." He rose, and with Gwynna followed Besz out into the fast-darkening streets.

SEVENTEEN

Kerhab's temple of Murorin was about the same size as the Great Temple of Sundao in Dyroka, but there the resemblance ended. It was immaculately clean, every bit of wall, floor, and ceiling was decorated, and there were a dozen statues of the god, each in a niche of mosaic, patterned marble, or gilded bronze with a massive jade offering table before it. Gwynna stood by a pillar encrusted with jade masks and silver-gilt serpents, and watched the men go to work with hammers, prybars, and axes. The torchlight showed no beauty one could regret seeing destroyed, only the wealth the god had gained from the merchants who sought his favor.

Over her Duelist's clothing Gwynna wore only a sword and dagger to ease the work of using her Powers. Now she rested forehead and one hand against the nearest pillar and tried to search within it for any signs of binding sorcery worked into the fabric of the building. Simple versions of such spells were known in Chonga and used for protecting strongboxes and the like. They were seldom dangerous, but any spell was always best sought out beforehand rather then merely stumbled upon.

As she deepened her search, she heard a faint sound from the side aisles behind her. She ignored it, heard it again, then recognized it as it came a third time. It was a child crying.

She waved to Bertan, standing two pillars farther up toward the dome. He came, and as she heard the sound a fourth time he stiffened.

"You hear it too?"

"Yes. Shall we—"

"It could be a trick."

"Sorcery?"

"I haven't found any yet. But there could be natural traps." Wandor turned, drew his sword, and waved it to bring three men across the temple to them. "Follow us."

This temple had four side aisles, two on each side, and each pair separated by a solid mosaic-encrusted wall with bronze doors at each end. The doors were the only access to the second aisle, and Gwynna wondered what it was used for. *Probably to display more ugly offerings,* she thought.

The door at the dome end of the aisle was nearest. A light reading with her fingertips told her only that the door was unlocked. She hesitated, remembering her own words to the men, "Don't unlock any door without me watching, and don't trust any unlocked door." Should she ignore her own advice? Then the child's cry—it couldn't be anything else—came again. As Wandor stepped up close behind her, she drew her sword, rested the point in the door's keyhole, and thrust hard.

The door swung open, and it seemed to her that a blast of cold damp wind laden with grave-stenches poured out of it. All her awareness of Powers at work came awake, and she raised one hand to start a light shielding spell while she clawed at the buttons of her tunic with the other. A cry not in her own voice forced its way out of her throat. Then she felt a twisting and hammering of all the senses of her body—the floor tilting under her with a terrible squeal and grinding, Bertan's hand clutching her shoulder, his own cry telling her that he also felt void under him—at last air rushing past her as she plunged down into darkness.

No creature of flesh and blood can run faster than bad news; news as bad as Wandor's and Gwynna's disappearance seemed to fly on magical wings. Before Master Besz could run from the front door to the black pit gaping in the side aisle, two of the men who'd seen the pit open ran screaming the length of the temple.

"They're lost, they're gone, the earth took them! Sorcery's loose on us! The temple is cursed!"

Then Besz was too busy preventing panic among the men still in the temple to follow the fugitives. By the time he'd succeeded, the news was out past all hope of recall. Besz could only leave the men in the temple crowding as close to the door as they could and dash out into the darkness to try replacing rumor with knowledge.

He was lucky in meeting a grim-faced Count Arlor almost as he left the temple. He asked the count to explain matters to the Royals and to summon Berek and Sir Gilas, then hurried off toward the mercenaries and the tribesmen posted around the quarter. He reached them after they'd learned something terrible had happened but before they knew what it was. He was in time to tell as much of the truth as could be told and deny that Cragor could have done it.

Besz prevented incidents with Cragor's men, but word still reached the Black Duke. Within an hour, Cragor knew clearly what had happened. He stepped aside into an alley and considered what use to make of this gift from the gods, if indeed it was that. Should he assume that Wandor and Gwynna were already dead or doomed, and remain at the head of his men? The fighting had shaken their discipline, and leaving them would be a gamble.

It would not, however, be as much of a gamble as assuming that Wandor and Gwynna were dead. Everyone seemed to fear the worst, but no one had seen anything but the black pit in the temple floor. That was not enough for Cragor. If they'd vanished through sorcery, Gwynna could meet it with her own Powers, and also call on Cheloth. Nothing in the agreement on sorcery prohibited its use against Kerhab. And if the trap was purely natural, those who'd set it might learn they'd sought foxes and caught bears.

He had to *know* they were dead, kill them if they weren't and do it now, before their surviving comrades recovered their wits. He didn't fear much from the Chongans. None of them knew anything about northern sorcery, Kobo was still out on the river, Pirnaush was drinking in his tent, and though Chiero might still be in the city, he was a fool.

One gamble he'd already taken was now about to pay. He'd kept the *limar* close at hand, even at the risk of sharp eyes penetrating the disguise. He now called the *limar* into an alley.

"Is there a spell you can use to find Wandor and Gwynna and then kill them if you find them alive?" The *limar* seemed to hesitate. The duke damned Kaldmor's command to it and added, "You only need to say 'Yes' or 'No'."

"Yes," the *limar* said. After a moment it added, "I can also use a second spell parallel to the first one. This second light spell will disguise the first great one, so that no one in Chonga save my master—"

"And Cheloth," put in the duke. He would endure Kaldmor's arrogance from the sorcerer himself, but not from the man's creation.

"Cheloth, of course."

"Can you know if he's watching?"

"Only by taking time to link with my master. That might draw the attention we fear."

Unfortunately this made too much sense. "Very well. Stay here until I come for you. I will bring a Healer's robe and pouch for you. Will you need anything else?"

"No."

Cragor backed out into the open street, unwilling to turn his back on the *limar*.

Count Arlor hadn't slept since this time last night, or taken off his armor since well before dawn. Now he stood in the square before the Temple of Murorin, leaning on his greatsword and waiting for—what? At least leaning on his sword made a fine valiant picture and kept him from toppling forward on his face. He badly wanted to take off his armor, now that it seemed to be protecting only itches, bruises, and sore spots.

Hooves clattered, and Chiero S'Rain rode into the square. Behind him tramped a dozen armed men in Cragor's colors, and behind them the Black Duke himself and a tall man in robes. Arlor suddenly found his armor more bearable. He raised his sword in salute, thereby alerting all his archers watching from the rooftops, then slid it into the sling across his back and stood waiting for the prince and his friends.

Chiero reined in and waved at the men behind him. "Greetings and honor, Count. I took the liberty of assuming that my presence with these men would serve as adequate safe-conduct. I trust your sentries disobeyed no order of yours in letting us pass?"

"They did not. Any man in your company is welcome here." Arlor suspected that the formal courtesies hid Chiero's uneasiness, and knew that his short replies revealed his own.

Chiero cleared his throat. "Duke Cragor has made a most honorable offer. He offers the assistance of this Healer—" pointing at the man beside the duke "—in finding Wandor and Gwynna."

"Or at least in discovering their fate," said the Healer. "You must understand, I cannot reach out and restore life to bodies which may no longer be—"

"Yes, I understand," said Arlor.

"Very good. I took the liberty of giving the man two objects which I knew had been linked with Lord Wandor and Lady Gwynna. Through these, the Healer will send a spell to search out their life force."

"They cannot have gone beyond the reach of this spell," said the Healer. "If they live, I shall find them."

"Isn't this a use of Powers against the agreement we made last winter?"

Chiero shook his head. "The duke himself also asked that question. I think not. The agreement bound Kaldmor and Cheloth not to strike at each other or their allies. It did not bind either to leave himself defenseless if men of Chonga chose to use sorcery."

Arlor had to agree, but found it hard to put his agreement into words. "Come, my Lord Count," said Cragor. "I know your men have done all that men can do, searching the temple of Murorin. We must go beyond human means now, or risk leaving Wandor and Gwynna to a fate I would not see fall upon honorable foes."

This time courtly language was concealing unmistakable eagerness. Arlor frowned as he looked at Cragor, seeming blacker than the night in his battered armor. The only thing the duke could be eager for was treachery, but that was not an accusation to make here and now.

"Very well," Arlor said. "Does the Healer wish to enter the temple?"

"Yes," said the duke, and followed the robed man who was already moving toward the door.

The Healer spent some time on the very edge of the pit which yawned where the door between the aisles had stood, with Cragor looking over his shoulder. Arlor had to admit the duke's courage. He himself would rather have stormed the walls of Kerhab again than stand by the pit and see the brightest torches show nothing but a rock shaft plunging away into what might be the House of Shadows itself. Fortunately he was able to stand halfway to the door, trying to look in all directions at once. By the time they came out, Berek had arrived with fifty of the HaroiLina, while forty Chongans now made a circle around Chiero.

Berek slipped across the square to Arlor and whispered in his ear. "The Healer. Is he what he seems?"

"I wish I knew."

"I have seen a man very much like him with Kaldmor sometimes. I hear in the taverns that man is Kaldmor's servant."

"Without Powers?"

"Yes. But this Healer is working a spell, so—"

"I know." Arlor shrugged. "But I can't imagine a sorcerer like Kaldmor having a servant without some Powers. Perhaps this searching out life forces is his only one."

Berek nodded, but stared at Arlor as he did. Arlor remembered how he'd faced Berek after Wandor and Gwynna were taken by the HaroiLina. The big man had been ready to distrust and even fight anyone he thought might have failed in duty toward his Master. Berek wore much the same expression now.

He doesn't believe that Healer is real, and he's not far from putting the matter to the test. If he does that, he'll die for doing what is my task, now that I lead here. As he stepped from behind Berek and loosened the throwing knife in its wrist sheath, Arlor had the feeling Wandor stood beside him, smiling at Arlor's thrusting himself forward where he'd forbidden Wandor to go. *I cannot do otherwise*, he replied to the smile.

And neither can I, said Wandor, and then mercifully was gone.

The Healer stepped to the door of the temple, and Cragor stood guard with drawn sword. The rest of the watchers drew into a smaller circle, the Chongans moving with obvious reluctance. The only one among them who didn't seem frightened was Chiero. *If the gods spare him, we may yet seem him leading armies into battle.*

The Healer stripped off his clothes, opened his pouch, and drew out a scarf and a pair of spurs. Arlor didn't recognize them, but swore he was going to learn how they'd reach a servant of the Black Duke. Cragor stepped to one side, the Healer bent down and placed the scarf and spurs on the temple steps, and everyone in the circle except Arlor and Chiero took one step backward. Then the Healer drew himself straight, the count's arm snapped up, and the throwing knife flew at the Healer's back.

Before any of the watchers could respond to the sight of the flying knife, blue witch-fire flared around the Healer, forming a globe which met the knife and knocked it harmlessly to the ground. A thin curl of smoke rose from the blackened metal.

The Healer whirled, eyes blazing blue; then to the men on the rooftops it seemed as if the battle for Kerhab was being fought again.

Berek raised Thunderstone, Arlor drew his greatsword, and both charged Cragor. Berek moved ahead, swung Thunderstone, and met another globe of blue fire which not only knocked the ax out of his hands but knocked the duke down the stairs. Cragor would have died in the next moment under Arlor's sword if six of his own men hadn't leaped forward. Three dragged him to safety by his feet, while the others faced Arlor and Berek and died for it.

Now Arlor knew what the Healer had to be—Kaldmor's *limar* of Nem. It was turning back to its original spell, holding a *khru*-medallion over the scarf and spurs. They began to smoke, Arlor braced himself for a desperate lunge and grapple —then green fire flared up almost in the *limar*'s face, knocking it over backward and tossing both objects so high Arlor lost sight of them in the glare. The *khru*-medallion flared white and became a black patch on the stone, pouring out blue smoke.

The *limar* rose, blueness pulsing around it more savagely than before as Kaldmor linked with it and fought Cheloth. In the moment of balance there was a wild scramble for the safety of the streets leading out of the square. The Chongans ran the fastest, carrying with them their frantic prince on a half-mad horse. In three deep breaths, the square held only Arlor and Berek, Cragor, and the men who seemed willing to die with him if that was to be their fate, the *limar*, and the warring Powers of the two sorcerers.

Green and blue pressed against each other for an hour-long moment, until Arlor saw sparks and felt heat like a blacksmith's forge pouring out from where they met. Then the *limar* leaped into the air, arms outstretched as if it was going to fly—

"It *is* flying!" Arlor screamed. The *limar* soared until it was higher than the rooftops, and the green flames of Cheloth soared after it. They licked at it—and then the *limar* was gone in a thunderclap which knocked Arlor and Berek to the ground and several archers from their rooftop perches. A moment later the green fire flowed into the temple of Murorin. The temple shook all over, the windows fell out, tiles cascaded from the roof, and all at once green fire was shining through a thousand cracks in the walls. Another moment long enough to let a man grow old, then the green fire went out and the temple of Murorin collapsed upon itself with a roar.

As the roar died away, Arlor heard approaching hooves. He turned, coughing at the smoke and dust filling the air, and found himself facing Pirnaush S'Rain. The *Bassan* leaped down from his horse like a sky-stone falling, and landed with a youth's lightness. He wore only baggy trousers and the sash of a *paizar-han*. His feet were bare, and so was the two-handed sword he carried. Arlor held his ground and his own weapon only by a gigantic effort of will. He'd seen friendlier looks than the *Bassan*'s on the faces of men he'd fought to the death.

Pirnaush's sword came down. The legendary steel of Chonga's *paizar-han* blades hacked more than halfway through Arlor's greatsword. Then Pirnaush whirled, to see an unarmed Cragor staggering to his feet. A quick look told the *Bassan* that Cragor's sword was the one lying blackened and twisted on the temple steps. He backed away until he could face both men. Then he roared:

"Who started this hog-raped dung-spattered game?"

Chiero S'Rain came forward, bowed, then went down on one knee before his father. He looked up at the sword waving over his head, then at his father's sweat-gleaming face.

"Honored Father, if there is anyone who can be said to have started this—"

"Speak short, damn you!"

"—it is your unworthy son."

The sword trembled, then Pirnaush lowered the point to the ground. "Sssso."

"Yes." Chiero told the story briefly, in fact so briefly that his father asked him to go back and fill in some details. When it was done, Pirnaush looked at his son, shaking his head. Then Arlor saw the king smile and heard him speak.

"Well, great kings have made bigger mistakes wanting to do good. You're just learning." He looked back over the square. "No hurt done either, except to the ones who started it all." He looked at Cragor and his smile faded. "Anything I want to say to you, I'll say later. For now—" He jerked his sword toward the nearest street. The duke managed to keep more dignity than Arlor would have expected as his men nearly dragged him out of the square.

By now Arlor again commanded his wits and his tongue. "Lord *Bassan*—?"

"Yes, Count?"

"Now that the sorcerers' truce is broken—I would like to call Cheloth to Kerhab—have him examine the ruins, seek out

168

Wandor and Gwynna...." His voice trailed off as Pirnaush turned to where two shaking Chongan soldiers were leading up his horse. "Lord *Bassan*, I beg you." Arlor was ready to go down on his knees, partly because they would barely support him anymore.

Pirnaush stopped with one hand on the saddle. Arlor saw that hand was trembling and Pirnaush's sweating face was as pale as a Chongan's could be. He knew the answer even before Pirnaush shook his head.

"Count Arlor—I can't. I'm not sure I even wish I could. Kaldmor was treacherous, I know. But Cheloth smashed the temple like a boy kicking a dog. Bring him up here, and Kaldmor's going to fight him again. More and more sorcery, running loose in Chonga. No! And that's a no for me, and for my people. How long could I rule, them knowing I'd let all that sorcery loose?"

How long indeed? Arlor asked himself. *And do I really believe Wandor and Gwynna can still be alive?*

Yes.

Can I convince Pirnaush there's any reason for this belief?

No.

Pirnaush swung himself up into the saddle. "Don't worry, Count," he said with a faint smile. "The matter of alliance isn't closed yet." The smile broadened. "Certainly you kept your promise about the temple."

"Promise?"

"Oh, Master Besz sent the message? He said you would make the temple of Murorin forever useless to the men of Kerhab. You certainly did that." He chuckled, and the chuckle turned into a laugh as he rode off.

Arlor suddenly felt as if his head weighed three times as much as usual. He staggered, and might have fallen if Berek hadn't been there to hold him up.

EIGHTEEN

Wandor awoke in darkness. The grave-stench was gone, replaced by the subtler odors of earth, mold, and stone. There was smooth, hard wood under him. No bones seemed to be broken, but he ached as if he'd been beaten by three or four men with clubs, and a spear shaft of pain drove down through shoulder and chest as he sat up. He gasped, and heard an answer from the darkness.

"Bertan?"

"Gwynna?"

They groped toward each other by sound and by touch. His hand reached her hair, moved down to her shoulder, and drew her to him. For a moment they clung to each other. Then Wandor followed the urgent promptings of his muscles and lay down, Gwynna curled up against him.

"Where do you think we are?" she whispered at last.

"Somewhere under Kerhab—*far* under Kerhab. What I want to know more is how did we get here. A physical trap, or sorcery?"

Gwynna was silent for a moment, then said, "I can explore. If anyone—interferes—I should be able to withdraw in time."

In a few minutes, Gwynna sat up and took off her clothes. Wandor heard her breathing slow to the controlled rhythm she used when preparing to work with her Powers. He stood up and stepped back as her hair began to glow. It revealed her sitting cross-legged on a floor of wooden squares, her skin unblemished except for a few patches of dirt and dust. Looking down at himself, Wandor saw that he also had no bruises or injuries to justify the pain he'd felt.

As Gwynna worked, Wandor studied as much of their prison as the light from her hair revealed. It seemed to be square, about twenty paces on a side, with stone walls and a ceiling too high to be visible now. In one corner was a simple hole in the floor, in another a bucket of water. Nothing else to show this prison wasn't in a place beyond the world where he and Gwynna were the only life.

Finally Gwynna pressed both hands to her temples and bowed her head forward. Before the glow died from her hair, Wandor was beside her, fingers kneading the shoulder and back muscles which always knotted themselves during her work. Slowly her breathing quickened to its usual pace. When she spoke, it was mind to mind.

("They have to listen with their ears now.")

("Why?") He believed her, but this made the mystery deeper.

("There is a spell bound into this chamber. No Power can reach into it, or get out of it either.")

("Not even Cheloth's?")

("No.")

Knowing the truth wasn't always encouraging, even if it was better than ignorance. ("Is this Kaldmor's work?")

("I can't imagine how it could be. This is pure Earth magic, and Toshakan Powers come mostly from the Air. Also, it has some original aspects, the sort you'd expect from a scholar of magic. Kaldmor has always been able to learn what somebody else can teach, but he's not a creator of original sorcery.")

("Thank the gods for small blessings.")

Slightly amused agreement.

("So—the Chongans do have some great sorcery?")

("Yes, or at least Earth Powers.")

("Beon-Kagri of the Fifteen?")

Mental shrug. ("Perhaps.")

At least they were not in the grip of Toshakan magic, and beyond that there seemed to be nothing they could do for now. They could use the Mind Speech, and Wandor only now realized how much he'd missed it during all the months they'd feared listening spies. Gwynna also had her Powers intact, and when this strange magical barrier no longer stood between her and their captors, much might happen.

Meanwhile, they were both exhausted from the day's fighting and from whatever had been done to capture them. Wandor took Gwynna in his arms and she wrapped herself as tightly as she could around him. Clinging close, they let sleep take them.

They awoke to the sound of booted feet, clanging metal, and a harsh voice.

"Up! Up, curse you!"

Wandor blinked himself awake and shapes slowly formed around him—a dozen armored men, two with *paizar-hans'* swords, the others with crossbows or throwing spears. One of the *paizar-hans* was standing over Gwynna, prodding her none too gently in the small of the back with his sword, but also standing so that his archers had clear shots at Wandor.

Wandor stood up, his thoughts grim. These guards were too alert and well-armed to justify any attempt at escaping or even finding a quick death—and from the expressions on their faces the death planned for the prisoners was anything but quick. Well, he and Gwynna had made themselves enemies to Kerhab of their own free will, even if they'd made their choice out of duty to those who followed them.

The guards marched their prisoners a surprisingly long distance down a low, brick-walled passage. The passage looked new and ended in a door of solid bronze, scarred with swordcuts and green with age. One of the *paizar-hans* stood by the door and shouted an announcement of their arrival.

With a rumble and a squeal, the bronze door slid into the wall. Wandor and Gwynna were pushed violently forward, and as they struggled for their footing on an ice-slick stone floor, the door slid shut behind them. Gwynna went to her knees, but Wandor pulled her up and then both stood facing their judges. Gwynna stood as if she were about to be crowned rather than condemned to death. Wandor crossed his arms on his chest, and by a fierce effort of will met the judges' eyes.

There were three judges. The one on the left was a small, broad-skulled, white-bearded man in smoke-soiled gray robes. The dark man in the middle also wore a robe. The man on the right wore armor, and a bandage hid half his face. In front of the small man was a carved ivory staff, in front of the middle one a scroll, and in front of the wounded warrior a sword. This was according to the customs in dealing justice common to all the Twelve Cities of Chonga.

The small man in gray seemed to be the chief judge. He

173

folded his hands on the table. "We are three of the Fifteen of Kerhab. You come before us to be judged for your crimes against the city. Will you speak for yourselves?"

Wandor looked at Gwynna, and as he did the small man made a curious gesture, touching one end of the ivory staff lightly with two fingers. Gwynna nodded, and Wandor spoke.

"My lords of the Fifteen, you have the power and the right to judge. I am not going to argue against that. I will only say that we came to Kerhab not out of hate for it—"

The armored man spat, hitting the floor neatly between Wandor and Gwynna. The other two looked sharply at him. Wandor continued.

"Not in hate for it, but in doing what we thought best for us and those who followed us. They had more right than Kerhab to ask of us our best, and we gave it to them. The cost to Kerhab was great, and if you choose to ask our lives in payment, so be it." Wandor did not feel nearly so resigned to his fate as those words suggested, but he knew that here anger would be as useless as fear.

"It will hardly be just your lives," said the man in the middle, and the armored man nodded. The small man looked at the door, then at his fellow judge, and silenced him with a shake of his head.

"It will be as you decide," said Wandor, with a shrug. "But decide wisely. You think to take vengeance for your dead, but our comrades will take vengeance for us, instead of leaving Kerhab in peace."

"Pirnaush's peace!" said the armored man, not quite spitting again.

"If you think you do Pirnaush much harm by killing us, think again," said Gwynna. "He can still avoid an alliance with the Black Duke by turning to Arlor and our other comrades. They will give him as good service as we might have. Our deaths may be a vengeance for Kerhab's dead, but they will bring the city no good that I can see."

"You seem vain enough to expect an easy death," said the man in the middle. He spoke as if the prisoners' refusal to cringe was a personal insult. "Perhaps I should teach you otherwise." The small man looked at him, but this time did not shake his head. Instead he looked toward the door while his fellow was "teaching" the prisoners. He did this in such detail that Gwynna turned pale, and Wandor found his stomach twisting.

The small man seemed to be ignoring both his friend and his prisoners. A thought crept into Wandor's mind. *He doesn't seem to care whether our courage breaks or not. Is he trying to gain time, and if so, why?*

When the man in the middle finished, the man in armor took up the abuse, still without protest from the small man. When the armored man finished, however, he turned to the others and said sharply, "No more time for you, Beon-Kagri. None. We vote."

The small man spread his hands, carefully not touching the ivory staff, then nodded. "Very well. You first."

"Death," said the armored man.

"Death," echoed the man in the middle. "The death we have promised them."

A long silence. Wandor reached for Gwynna's hand. The armored man laughed coarsely.

"Not death," said Beon-Kagri.

The others turned in their chairs and glared at him. The armored man drew his sword, while the man in the middle picked up the scroll, tore it in two, then tore each half into smaller pieces.

"They have done *this* to Kerhab, Beon-Kagri. They still should not die?"

"They did it with Cragor."

"We do not have Cragor," said the armored man.

"If we did—" began Beon-Kagri, then broke off as both the others began talking at once. Voices rose, until Beon-Kagri was as loud and seemed to be as angry as the others, and words came so swiftly that Wandor began to lose his grasp of what was being said. Then as if they were a single mind, all three shifted to a language which Wandor could recognize as a form of Chongan but no more. He heard what might have been the word "Merkahl" twice, then gave up the struggle. Gwynna seemed unable to do any better.

Wandor knew that any three of the Fifteen of Kerhab could pass judgments in the name of the whole body, but only if all three agreed. Beon-Kagri not only didn't agree that he and Gwynna should die, but seemed determined to resist his fellow judges until they accepted his own judgment. Wandor could hardly believe Beon-Kagri was doing this from compassion, and he could no more than guess at other reasons the man might have.

Then Beon-Kagri stiffened, rested both hands on his staff,

seemed to be listening, then nodded. The door behind Wandor slid open, then a figure passed between him and Gwynna who made Wandor doubt both his eyes and his wits.

Telek the Fatherless. Telek, here beneath Kerhab, in a chamber where three of the Fifteen sat in judgment, wearing *mungan*'s black, two swords, and a face which gave away no more secrets than usual. Telek, entering this chamber as if he was an invited, even honored guest.

Desperation drove Wandor to Mind Speech.

("How?")

("We'll—") She got no farther before Beon-Kagri's hands tightened on the staff, then twisted. Wandor felt Gwynna not only breaking the link but shielding her mind against a close, and powerful listener. In that moment he knew the answer to the question of Beon-Kagri's being a sorcerer, and wondered what part the man's Powers had played here.

Telek was speaking now. "—vengeance, indeed. Not only by the swords of comrades left behind, but by the Powers of Cheloth of the Woods. His anger at what Cragor and Kaldmor tried to do is great. If he strikes at Kaldmor, what may come to Chonga?"

"Curse Chonga," said the armored man, but his voice seemed less harsh.

"You may indeed be cursing Chonga," said Telek. "Remember that Kaldmor now wields many of the Powers of Toshak, and Cheloth wields all those he ever had. Remember what came of the last such duel."

"What difference will it make, whether these two live or die?" said the middle man.

"Who knows?" said Telek. "Perhaps much. If they die, and Pirnaush turns to Cragor, why should Cheloth hold back in his next duel with Kaldmor? Why should Wandor's comrades ask him to do so?"

That reached the two judges who wanted the prisoners dead. Telek saw this and pressed his advantage. "Even if Chonga does not come down in ruins, what about Kerhab? Is everything so utterly lost that you no longer care what happens to the city?

"If they die at your hands, Kerhab is doomed, because Cheloth will know exactly what happened to them. Remember what happened to the temple of Murorin, and ask yourselves if you want to bring the same fate on all of Kerhab, even if Pirnaush spares it."

Gwynna's fingers gave Wandor the simple message that

Telek was lying. Cheloth could not do this, as far as she knew. The other two Chongans seemed as ignorant and afraid of sorcery as most of their countrymen, but Beon-Kagri was another matter. Would he want the prisoners alive badly enough to join Telek against his fellows? Wandor shifted his gaze to the sword in the armored man's hands. He might just be able to move in and take it, and if Gwynna could strike at Telek while Beon-Kagri was holding his attention, they might find at least—

— a clean death. No more. Wandor cautiously shifted his feet for a better stance and started to recite the Duelist's Oath to himself.

Then Beon-Kagri nodded, Telek stepped out of Gwynna's reach, and the spectre of blood shed in either desperate battle or torture chamber lifted. Beon-Kagri thrust his staff into his sash and smiled. "Then it shall be as I wish? They shall go north and seek the Dragon Steed of Morkol?"

The armored man's agreement was a growl, the middle man's a nod. They seemed to have no voices left. Then the door opened and the guards' hands drew Wandor and Gwynna out of the chamber.

In the darkness of their prison, they formed a Mind Speech link.

("We've found our sorcerer, at least,") said Gwynna.

("I know. Beon-Kagri.")

("Yes. How did you learn?")

("The staff, for one thing. The way he seemed to be in command. Then, when I felt you shielding your mind against Powers close at hand. . . . He felt like the right one.")

("You're much farther from being afraid of magic than you once were.")

("It's the strange company I keep. Don't throw stones at the Chongans' fears, either. Those fears saved our lives. If they'd all known that Telek was lying—")

("He was lying about Cheloth's learning how we died. I don't know about the rest.")

Wandor felt a warm caress, both on his skin and in his mind, then the link faded.

NINETEEN

More by accident than by intent, the duel of sorcery at the temple of Murorin saved Kerhab from the worst of Pirnaush's planned sack. Most of the Chongan soldiers were too frightened to steal anything except wine and ale to drive out their fear. Most of the Kerhabans huddled in corners well out of the soldiers' way.

This did not make Pirnaush any friendlier toward Cragor. He summoned the Black Duke the next morning and apparently addressed him in words neither flattering to his character nor suitable to his rank. No one else heard what Pirnaush said, but those who saw the duke leave knew they were seeing a man who would not forget and might not forgive.

Kerhab might still have suffered heavily from Wandor's men, but Arlor and the other captains kept order until morning, when Pirnaush came to their aid. Cragor's men were ordered to a camp along the now-completed road between the valleys of the Hiyako and the Mesti, a full day's march from Kerhab. Most of Wandor's men were put on the march all the way back to the Mesti and Dyroka, escorting a train of slaves, prisoners, wounded, and the hastily-embalmed bodies of high-born Dyrokans homeward bound for cremation.

Five hundred of the Viceroyalty's soldiers remained in Kerhab, picked men under Sir Gilas Lanor and Berek Strong-Ax. The only thing which reconciled Count Arlor to losing their services was that the two would leave nothing undone in Kerhab to solve the mystery. They could not bring Wandor and Gwynna back from the dead—if they *were* dead, an idea Arlor still denied so resolutely and on so little evidence that he kept silent for fear of being called mad. The Brothers to Serve would certainly invade the House of Shadows itself if they thought the answer to the mystery lay there, and their men would follow them.

Shortly after noon, Count Arlor was standing by his tent, when Chiero S'Rain rode up with a small escort. He greeted Arlor without dismounting, and asked him to walk aside for a moment. On the bank of the river, Chiero dismounted.

"I must tell you, Count, that I grieve almost more for Gwynna than for Wandor."

"She would never have come to your bed," said Arlor. Chiero's face twisted so that the count immediately regretted those words. Pirnaush was right. Chiero had been foolish, but only out of regard for those his folly had put in danger.

"I know this as well as you do," said Chiero. "I would gladly have such a woman when I take a lawful wife, but I think there is only one Gwynna."

"You can be sure of that, my lord."

"If it would not go against your wishes, I would like to do an honor service to the lady's memory. You are first among those Wandor and Gwynna left behind, so I come to you for permission."

Arlor was familiar with this Chongan custom. An honor service could be anything from marrying the widow of the person you wished to honor, to donating a cheap brass mask to some moldering temple. He wanted desperately to ask Chiero to intercede with his father and persuade Pirnaush to order Cragor not only out of Kerhab but out of Chonga. Unfortunately matters of statecraft and war were not lawful subjects for honor services. There'd been too many assassinations and blood feuds before this became the law.

"We can speak more of this when we return to Dyroka. But there is one service you can do us now."

"Name it."

"How did the scarf and spurs the *limar* used come into your hands?"

Chiero looked confused, then suddenly his understanding awoke. "Ah. You thought they might have been stolen and given to me as part of a plot?"

"Yes."

"Not at all, Count. They were gifts from me, the last gifts

180

I gave them, the day before we stormed Kerhab. I knew where they could be found, and sent men to bring them."

"In that case, my lord, you can be sure that the *limar* couldn't have done much harm to Wandor and Gwynna. Such gifts couldn't have been linked to them long enough to support its Powers." He smiled. "Of course they couldn't have done much good either, even if the *limar* had been an honest Healer. Perhaps you should study a little northern sorcery before the next time comes when you want to use it to help friends."

"I may do that," said Chiero soberly. "But I would have learned the most from *her*, and she is gone."

Wandor awoke, knowing even before he opened his eyes that the journey north in search of the Dragon Steed had begun. Under him was prickly grass, overhead the damp hot stillness of the Chongan forests. When he did open his eyes he saw a pattern of leafy branches against a red-tinged sky. He sat up, and saw Gwynna lying half under the drooping leaves of a huge fern, apparently unhurt. Someone, however, had odd notions about proper clothing and equipment for a journey through the Chongan forests.

Both of them were barefoot and wore only Chongan trousers and their own shirts. Gwynna's trousers were too large and Wandor's too small. Two spears lay beside Gwynna, and between the spears a small leather sack and a water bottle. This was either a rough joke at their expense or an attempt at killing them in a way for which no one in Kerhab could be made to bear the blame.

In her turn Gwynna sat up and looked around. "We're going back to Kerhab and ask a few questions."

"I hope Telek will answer them peacefully. I doubt if Beon-Kagri will, but with him we can ask Cheloth for help."

"Yes, although I hope we won't need to press Beon-Kagri too hard. He may have decided to use the story of sending us north as an excuse for getting us out of reach of the other Kerhabans."

"I'm not so ready to call him innocent. If he didn't want to hurt us, why did he use his Powers to take us in the first place?"

"Perhaps Telek made him think again. Or perhaps he's afraid of Cheloth. I wish we knew what happened around the temple of Murorin!"

Wandor reached for one of the spears, and got to his feet. "We might do well to camp here."

She shook her head. "We'd do better finding a pond or a stream. Something to guard our backs while I call Cheloth, to give us water, and to guide us in the morning."

That was woods wisdom. Any barrier which guarded their backs from the jungle life was worth seeking. Unless they were outside the valley of the Hiyako, any stream would eventually lead them to its bank. Kerhaban fugitives might roam the jungle, but the river belonged to Pirnaush and his allies.

Before they'd gone a hundred paces west they had to push through a broad patch of thornroot which clawed at their feet and ankles. Insects nipped and nibbled at every bit of exposed skin, and Wandor suspected he'd been drugged in the prison. At irregular intervals he felt vague aches in his joints, like the pain he sometimes felt in old wound scars in bad weather. The light was nearly gone when they came out on the bank of a stream leading south. About sixty paces downstream, Wandor saw a clearing on the bank, roughly the size of a cottage garden. He looked at Gwynna and she nodded.

After the first few steps along the bank, Wandor felt the aches and pains return sharper than ever, until he had to grip a vine with one hand to keep from stumbling into the water. He managed to stay on his feet, taking one step at a time, until he'd covered most of the distance to the clearing. Then waves of pain crashed over him until he had to grip another vine and dig his spearpoint into the ground to keep from falling.

"Bertan?" There was something unnatural in her voice too.

"Pain. Pain like—fire around my bones—tearing the flesh off—can't move—"

She gasped. "In me—too." Her hand gripped his shoulder, and she gasped again. Then he felt the pains fade, and coolness where there'd been fire. "Forward—quick!"

He lurched toward the clearing, as fast as he could without pulling free of Gwynna's hand. Something told him that the pain would flow through him again the moment she let go. He also had the sick feeling she was adding to her own pain by taking away most of his.

They reached the clearing without another word spoken, both of them moving like people twisted and torn on the rack. Then Wandor's legs turned to water, Gwynna's hands slipped from his shoulder, and for a moment he completely lost his senses.

When they returned, Gwynna was holding his head on her lap and wiping his lips with the dampened sleeve of her shirt. He still felt as if he'd been on the rack, but no longer as if he was actually on it with the executioners hard at work.

They both drank from the water bottle.

"Sorcery?"

Gwynna nodded. "Beon-Kagri, I think."

"You're not sure?"

"It's a powerful Earth spell. I doubt Kaldmor could have gained that much Earth Power without either me or Cheloth learning of it. Remember, Nem was an Air sorcerer. Beon-Kagri is more of the Earth."

"Do you know what the spell does?"

She'd pulled off her shirt to wipe his face. Now she started unlacing the trousers. "I think I can learn."

"Without danger to yourself?"

She bristled like a cat with its tail stepped on. "You *will* go on holding me back."

"Yes," he said bluntly. "And you can't stop me, either. You rush into affairs of Power the way I rush into battles. Certainly you've never held your tongue about what I do."

Gwynna's face set even harder, then Wandor's thoughts caught up with his tongue. "Besides, I'll find it hard to reach Cheloth without you. If you're not able to work, I'll have to wait for him to decide to come looking for me. You know how long that could be."

The mask thawed. "Too long."

"Yes. Now—let's eat before we even talk more about magic, let alone try to do it."

She shook her head and stood up. "I won't be doing real work now. I'll just make myself sensitive to the effects of the spell and let it work in me until I can read it."

Gwynna flowed into her cross-legged pose and began breathing slowly and deeply. Her eyes took on the remote look Wandor knew too well, but her hair didn't glow. She was using her Powers at a very low level. At last she stood up and walked away from the bank of the stream. She changed direction every few steps, until she seemed like a compass needle hunting the north. Then like the needle finding the north, she steadied in one direction and walked briskly toward the forest thirty paces away. Two steps, three, four, five, six—

As she finished the sixth step she quivered all over like an ox when the drover brings down the lash. Seven, eight, nine, ten— In the middle of the tenth step her left leg gave under her and she tumbled to the grass. She rose on hands and knees, tried to stand again, and cried out. Wandor sprang up with a cry of his own and started toward her. He'd covered only three steps when spiked clubs seemed to smash into his knee and thigh joints. He fell on his side, and saw dimly through a haze of pain Gwynna still trying to stand.

By the time the pain left him she'd given up and lay on her stomach on the grass, showing just enough life to prove she wasn't dead. Finally she rose and crawled back to him. This time they emptied the water bottle.

"I wouldn't care to do that again," she said when she could speak again. "I won't have to, fortunately. What Beon-Kagri's done is bind our bodies with a spell which won't let us go in any direction except north."

"That's—"

"True, to start with. I know. I wouldn't have believed it possible myself, but I don't think I've made a mistake. It's not a very subtle spell. Beon-Kagri learned how to put it on, but didn't learn how to make it unreadable. And the pain—that's a crude way of keeping us on course."

"I could use stronger words about it, myself."

"So could I, and so will Cheloth when he learns of it."

"You can't break it yourself?"

"No. I simply haven't the strength in my Powers or my body. Not now. Breaking this spell would be like battering down a city's wall. All I can do now is pick a lock. Cheloth can do both. Taking the spell off may hurt as much as fighting it, but it will only be once. Then we'll be free."

Wandor suspected she was overstating the certainty of Cheloth's aid and understating the dangers of taking off the spell, but it didn't really matter. With the weapons and clothing they had, obeying Beon-Kagri's sorcerous command to go north would be almost certain death. Even remaining where they were for more than a few days would put them in more danger than any work of Cheloth's Powers. Wild animals, snakes, insects, poisonous plants, and Chongan fevers would be all around them, and perhaps bands of Kerhabans still carrying on their city's fight.

Wandor refilled the water bottle from the stream, putting his shirt over the mouth before he shoved it under the surface. The cloth should keep out blood-eggs, young bristle worms, and other things which gave an unwanted seasoning to many of Chonga's rivers. While he did this, Gwynna pulled biscuit and dried fish out of the bag.

They were just starting to eat when Mitzon and Hawa found them.

Mitzon and Hawa were hardly surprised to find Wandor and Gwynna. After all, Telek the Fatherless had told them everything about his schemes, including where the two northerners would be left. At the time he spoke he'd had no reason to lie to them. In any case, the chance of Telek's having lied disturbed Mitzon much less than the certainty of his trying to take vengeance afterward, with or without the help of his fellow *mungans*. Telek's vengeance could mean death by torture or at least lifelong exile from Chonga for Mitzon and Hawa.

Then the canoe slid around a bend in the stream, and the dark man and the fair-skinned woman with the flaming hair leaped up from where they sat on the bank. Wandor snapped one spear up into throwing position and tossed the other to Gwynna. His arm was going back when Hawa stood up, dropped her cloak, and held out both hands.

"Peace, I beg you. Wait and listen to us."

The spear point was steady. Mitzon drew the horn lantern from beneath his seat and held it up. It showed his face and Hawa's black *mungan*'s garb. Both spear points dipped toward the grass.

"Did Telek send you?"

"In a way."

"Can you wait until we've finished our meal and reached Cheloth?"

"You must not use your Powers," said Hawa.

"Why?" Gwynna's voice shook with sudden anger. "We can't deal with Beon-Kagri's spells without—"

"You know Beon-Kagri's a sorcerer?" Both *mungans* spoke together.

"Yes."

"How?"

"We've been spellbound to go north, in *this*." She jerked her spearpoint at Wandor's clothing and her own.

Mitzon and Hawa looked at each other. "Damn Telek," said the woman. "I should have known he'd leave—"

"I'll be happy to join you in damning Telek," said Wandor evenly. "I'll be still happier if I know why. Come ashore, keep your hands away from your weapons, sit down, and tell us your tale."

Mitzon heard in Wandor's voice the anger of a man so beset by enemies whom he can't strike down that rage may drive him to strike at friends who don't prove their friendship quickly enough.

"As you wish," he said, and picked up his paddle.

Bad news is best exchanged the way rotten teeth are pulled and festering limbs amputated—quickly. The four sat in a circle around the oil lamp, and Hawa emptied a vial of powder into the flame. Foul-smelling smoke poured out, driving away the insects, as Mitzon and Hawa learned of the northerner's experiences. They learned some details unknown to Telek or at least untold by him, and how the meeting with the three Kerhaban judges looked through the eyes of the people whose life or death was being decided. They also learned of Beon-Kagri's spell, a complete surprise to them. If Telek had known anything about the Kerhaban's Powers, he certainly hadn't told them. And if he had known, why did he dare to lie about a matter of sorcery in the presence of a sorcerer? (Had Telek become so accustomed to lying that he did it by sheer force of habit, regardless of circumstance?)

It did not make much difference, now that Telek was their enemy. He'd urged Beon-Kagri to spare them, but had been careful to have *mungans* of his own choosing to take them out of the city. His orders were simple: give Wandor and Gwynna just enough to keep them alive until the Kerhabans find and kill them.

"Perhaps that spell of Beon-Kagri's saved your life," said Hawa. "Only an hour or two south of here, the land on both banks swarms with Kerhabans. Many escaped through the tunnel under the river—"

"Tunnel?" said Wandor.

"Built in secret over the last two years," said Mitzon. "Beon-Kagri used his Earth spells to bind the walls so that the weight of the river and the mud wouldn't collapse them. Without the soldiers from the city, there might be a chance for you to get through. The countryfolk would be poorly led, and most wouldn't know you by sight. As it is, if you fall among them you're doomed. If you call them north by calling Cheloth, you're at least in danger."

If they reached Cheloth, Kaldmor the Dark and his master would almost certainly learn of it. That meant Telek's learning it, and anything Telek knew which would harm Wandor's cause would be passed on at once to whomever could do the most damage with it.

If they didn't reach Cheloth, Beon-Kagri's spell would drive them north like a storm driving a crippled ship. If they did reach Cheloth, they'd be hunted through the forest by the Kerhabans. Even if they could reach Cheloth without drawing the Kerhabans on to them, they might still draw Kaldmor into another duel of sorcery, especially if he'd restored his *limar* by that time.

"Whatever comes of that duel, its happening at all will be a blow to you. Unless you would care to see Cheloth use all his Powers and try to destroy Kaldmor entirely?"

"No," said both Wandor and Gwynna together.

"Good," said Hawa. "If you'd said yes, we'd find it hard not to kill you ourselves. A duel like that would send half of Chonga mad with fear, and we don't have enough friendship for you to see that happen." Then she described the duel at the temple of Murorin. Watching Wandor and Gwynna, Mitzon saw that her words reached deep into them.

I'm glad of that. One reason I'm breaking with Telek and his passion for Cragor is that the Black Duke wouldn't care if half Chonga did go mad. Easier to rule the other half, he'd say. Wandor and Gwynna aren't of that mind, and neither are those they'll leave behind if the worst happens.

As Hawa finished, Wandor started laughing. The others looked at him, Gwynna with fear in her eyes. Wandor saw this and forced out words. "All I can do is laugh or weep. Weeping will do my enemies no harm and me no good. So I laugh." This time they all laughed, and Gwynna laid her head against his shoulder for a moment.

"So we go north," Wandor said. "If you can bring us food, better weapons, and something to put on our feet—"

"We can do better," said Mitzon. "We'll give you the whole canoe and everything in it. We weren't sure if we'd be returning to the city, so we brought—"

"You can't!" said Gwynna. "I know what you're facing for us. I say you've done enough already."

"I say we haven't," replied Hawa. "We have to give back to you as much as we can of the hope Beon-Kagri and Telek took away. It's a matter of honor, ours and the *mungans'*."

Mitzon nodded, but added, in case Hawa's words might pluck the wrong string, "It doesn't mean any danger for us.

Remember, we're Chongans, and we know the forest better than you do."

Wandor shrugged. Gwynna nodded and said, "Let's try to move south once more, in your canoe. If our bodies are being carried without doing any work themselves . . ."

"You think the spell might not act?"

"I don't know enough about it to be sure."

"It's certainly an idea."

It was not a good idea.

This time when Wandor's senses returned he was lying on the bank with fading pains in every limb as well as a pain in his head. Mitzon stood over him, while Hawa held Gwynna's shoulders as she vomited into the stream. The canoe was drawn up on the bank. Wandor closed his eyes and let the pains fade.

Mercifully the pains of Beon-Kagri's spells involved no tearing of flesh, twisting or straining of muscles, or breaking of bones. When the spell-bound body stopped fighting the spell, the pain faded.

The pain in Wandor's head wasn't fading. He reached up and felt a tender lump. "I'm sorry," said Mitzon. "Even after we turned in to the bank, you went on thrashing about. The three of us together couldn't hold you. So I had to use the hilt of my knife." Wandor sighed and sat up. He believed the man, although right now he couldn't have fought three kittens, let alone three other people.

In time, both Wandor and Gwynna gained enough strength to pull on boots, belt on swords, sling bows and quivers, and prepare for their march through the forest to the riverbank. While they were marching, Mitzon and Hawa would take the canoe and its load down the stream to the river, then paddle north to meet their friends. It was a slower and more dangerous way of beginning the journey than any of them cared for, but the only one Beon-Kagri's wretched spell allowed.

As sometimes happened, the mood Wandor tried to show to others became truly his. He felt ready to walk, let alone paddle, all the way to the mountains of Kalgamm.

"We may be back in Kerhab before you are," he said. "I'd be surprised if we don't meet a friendly ship within a day or two. Then we'll be safe from the worst the Kerhabans can do. If not, we'll make camp five or six days upriver and reach Cheloth from there."

Gwynna slipped her arm through his and stood close. "I

suppose it doesn't matter why Telek's turned against us. But—
do either of you know? He always seemed to love keeping the
pot boiling just to hear it bubble. Has he changed?"

Hawa frowned. "I'd say he hasn't and that's why he turned
to Cragor. Right now, if Pirnaush learned you were alive,
Cragor would be finished. With you dead, Pirnaush may still
need the duke."

"Cragor's no more likely to prove a friend to the *mungans*
than we are," said Wandor. "Less, I should say."

"Perhaps," said Hawa. "But the way Telek sees it, the true
friend of the *mungans* is the man capable of leaving the most
chaos in his wake. Telek thinks that man is Cragor. He is only
one man, and he has few certain friends at home. Allied with
you or your captains, Pirnaush could set about putting Chonga
in order until there was no place left for Telek."

"I hadn't thought of doing that," said Wandor grimly. "But
now I think I might. With luck, I may even be able to explain
this to Telek before I kill him. Until morning, then."

Mitzon and Hawa were climbing into their canoe as he and
Gwynna walked toward the trees.

TWENTY

━━━◆◆◆━━━

Dawn, the day after Wandor and Gwynna awoke in the forest.

Mitzon and Hawa found them only a little farther north than they'd expected. Gwynna was asleep, Wandor staring out over a Hiyako as bare of ships as if men had never been created.

"It's said Kobo's taking all his ships around to Shimarga," said Mitzon. "If that's so, few ships'll be sailing north of Kerhab until he returns."

Wandor shrugged and swallowed a mouthful of pork and seed cake. "It hardly matters. We'll find a safe camp within a few days, and after that everyone will know we're alive. Cragor, Kaldmor, and Telek together won't find anything easy after that."

Mitzon wished he could share that faith in Gwynna's Powers. If he did, perhaps he'd be better armed for what he was facing. "We can take a message to Count Arlor, so that if you don't reach Cheloth—"

Wandor and Gwynna both shook their heads. She spoke first. "No. You might make Arlor believe you, but there's nothing you could do which would let him convince Pirnaush. If we reach Cheloth, we can do anything needed to make Pirnaush know we're alive and ready to help him. We can even make a Showing for all Dyroka."

"Sorcery!" exclaimed Mitzon in spite of himself.

"Yes, sorcery," said Gwynna. "Sorcery which can harm no one."

"Except Cragor," said Hawa.

Wandor stepped forward and gripped Hawa's hands, then

Mitzon's. "Besides, you've already put yourselves in enough danger for us. So go back to Kerhab, watch your own backs, and wait until word comes from us."

"And if word doesn't come?" said Mitzon.

"If we don't return, you've earned a place among our people," said Wandor. "Go to Arlor, tell him your story, and also tell him—" what sounded like four or five words in a language Mitzon couldn't even recognize.

"That will be enough?"

"For Arlor, yes, and no one will go against him." Wandor repeated the words. "They're in the King's Tongue of the Sthi, so don't worry about understanding them. Just speak them until Arlor understands, then be welcome."

Mitzon repeated the words over and over again as they prepared the canoe, until he had them by heart. "We thank you," he said. "I'll remember the words. But if such a time does come, I'd rather earn my guest rights with Telek's head."

All four embraced, then the northerners climbed into the canoe and pushed off in silence. The silence lasted until the canoe was only a speck on the river to the north. Then it was broken by a rare sound—Hawa weeping. Mitzon held her until he heard muffled words, "If they don't gain the victory, I deny the gods. Those two are worth five of Cragor."

Mitzon shared her grief and her thoughts too completely to worry at her blasphemy. "Yes, but do the gods know this?" was all he would say. Then he remembered "the King's Tongue of the Sthi" and other tales told about Wandor. Perhaps the gods did know, but were no better than men in using their knowledge wisely.

Another dawn, five days after Wandor and Gwynna left Mitzon and Hawa on the bank of the Hiyako.

Wandor and Gwynna came up the river, traveling by night after the first day. They saw half a dozen bands of armed Kerhabans, one more than three hundred strong. Twice they saw galleys tied up to the bank, disguised with branches and grass, and once a small *kulgha* slipping across the river in the dawn light. They didn't see a single friendly ship or soldier.

"Now we know why there weren't more Kerhaban soldiers in the city when it fell," said Wandor. "They must have escaped through the tunnel or been clear of the city before the siege began. They're not giving up the fight, even though the city itself is in Pirnaush's hands."

"Pirnaush can't spare the time or men to harry every village and farm," said Gwynna. "And perhaps if the Kerhabans go on fighting, other cities will turn against Pirnaush."

Once they began traveling by night, the danger from the Kerhabans largely vanished. Even men who knew the river and the forest, fleeing from a captured city and hiding from their enemies, preferred the daylight. The wild creatures and sand bars had neither friends nor foes among men. So they paddled north along the river sometimes like black glass, sometimes dancing under the rain or rippled by the wind. Each night they covered at least three times the distance they could have made on foot. Each dawn saw them hiding the canoe and making camp on the most deserted stretch of bank they could find. After the third day they were north of the lands settled from Kerhab, and in peaceful times anyone fleeing the city could have found a safe refuge.

After the fourth day, they saw no Kerhabans on land or on the water. On the fifth day, they entered a stretch of river where the hills hemmed it close on either side. Steep banks left few good landing places for anything larger than their canoe. There were few fishermen and fewer villages, and any Kerhabans in this land would be hiding well inland. There was no really safe place in an enemy's land, but this stretch of the Hiyako was less dangerous than any other within reach.

Now it was a gray morning, and they stood by a spring which flowed from a patch of wild hare's ear and down a little bluff into the Hiyako. They'd bathed, drunk, and eaten lightly, then both stripped off their clothes. When the time came to break Beon-Kagri's spell, Wandor would be thoroughly drawn into the net of Gwynna's and Cheloth's Powers. He was not as frightened at the prospect as he'd expected to be.

My bond with Gwynna reaches farther and farther. This time it does so because a Chongan sorcerer who shouldn't have existed in the first place tried to kill us.

They joined hands as well as minds. Wandor felt Gwynna's Powers lifting up all their thoughts, hurling them across both physical space and the otherwhere which held Powers, gods, and nameless things. Then everything except the call to Cheloth left Wandor, and he felt himself soaring like an eagle on mountain winds. He became only a mind with a single thought and that thought a single image—Cheloth of the Woods, all in green except the pointed silver helmet with the eye and mouth slits.

Then the image was replying to the call of the two minds

holding it. ("You're alive. Where are you?") In anyone else but the sorcerer, the total lack of pleasure or even surprise might have been disturbing. In Cheloth, it would have been far more disturbing if he'd babbled with joy.

Cheloth listened to Gwynna describe their adventure with only three interruptions to ask polite questions on matters where Gwynna had spoken too briefly. He listened in silence to her theories about Beon-Kagri's Powers and spells, and that was rare. Perhaps Cheloth was capable after all of being affected by their return from the dead. Also, Beon-Kagri might be something new even to Cheloth—and if so, the sorcerer was certainly wise enough to listen in order to learn.

At last Cheloth interrupted a fourth time. ("You have much to say on this which is worth hearing, but I would rather hear it another time. Whatever we can do now must be done quickly.")

("Kaldmor?") Both of them asked.

("Perhaps. At least I cannot be sure that he has not restored the *limar*. So we must guard against the worst. Also, there are the talents of the Chongans themselves in Mind Speech. Other ears may serve Kaldmor to our disadvantage.")

("Can you take off the spell?") asked Gwynna.

("I will read it first. What you said could not be enough to let me judge. Let your minds go free of all thought, but hold your bodies rigid.") That was not an easy combination, and it took Wandor and Gwynna three or four attempts before Cheloth was satisfied.

Cheloth's reading of the spell involved nothing Wandor could detect, but it was different for Gwynna. Her eyes closed and her breathing quickened, and muscles along her right cheek and jawline started jumping like frightened mice. At last her eyes opened and Cheloth spoke.

("Certainly you described the spell correctly. It is hardly subtle, but it is enormously powerful. Beon-Kagri's Powers may be greater than Kaldmor's, and his knowledge is not less. I have no certain knowledge, because Beon-Kagri has ordered his Powers so that when he does his work underground, no one above ground can recognize that he is at work or what he is doing. It has always been known among great sorcerers that Earth Powers could take this direction. Beon-Kagri seems to be the first to put the knowledge to use. More than this, I can only say after I find a way to reach underground or Beon-Kagri comes into the daylight.") Cheloth's thoughts held no more feeling than before, but Wandor had the distinct idea that what Beon-Kagri was facing would be anything but a pleasant experience.

("Can you try to break the spell without having the keys to it?") asked Gwynna.

No reply.

("*Can* you?") in a sharp, commanding tone Wandor knew well.

("If you wish it.")

("We do.") With Gwynna in this mood, Wandor would hardly have dared to disagree. ("Unless there's a danger of Kaldmor hearing or breaking in?")

("Not at once, I believe. I suggest haste, though.")

Wordless agreement from both.

Again Wandor forced himself to lock his joints and muscles while leaving his mind a void. He wished there'd been time to ask Cheloth to explain what was going to happen. Now he could only prepare himself for more of the racking pains they'd faced trying to fight the spell.

Then Wandor felt a sharp throbbing in his belly, and a sudden warmth in the soles of his feet as if he was standing on sun-heated stone. Neither was natural, neither was comfortable, but neither was really pain. They lasted while he took six deep breaths, faded away, then returned.

He went through the cycle three more times; the last time he looked at Gwynna. Except for a frown she might have worn trying to read an ancient parchment, she seemed completely at ease.

He knew Cheloth's work was over when he heard Gwynna's thoughts. ("Thank you for your skill, Cheloth. You didn't have the keys, but you still worked with great care and subtlety.")

So that was why they'd felt no real pain. ("Did you break it?")

("No.")

("Can you use more strength?")

("Yes. But if I do there will be great pain, and perhaps danger to Wandor. Without Powers of his own, he cannot resist—")

Wandor knew what would come next even before he heard it. ("If we are not linked, can you break the spell on me, then let me work with you to take it from Bertan?")

Gwynna flinched at the force of Wandor's wordless cry of refusal, but it was Cheloth who put matters in order. ("It might

195

still kill you or leave you mindless. You could easily be helpless for some days.")

("Are you telling the truth?")

("I would not have expected you to doubt me.") The old Cheloth seemed to be returning.

("I believe him,") said Wandor. ("This is no place for either of us to need nursing. What's more, there's Kaldmor. If human enemies attack, I can defend you, but if Kaldmor attacks—")

She released what would have been a resigned sigh if she'd done it aloud. ("Very well. Should we stay here while you seek out Beon-Kagri, or continue north?")

("There is no more danger to you from Beon-Kagri if you stay where you are. Kaldmor is another matter. Safety from him lies farther to the north. So do the mountains of Kalgamm.")

And the Dragon Steed of Morkol. Gwynna's eyes widened as the thought reached her. Then the link with Cheloth broke, as sharply as iron splitting under a blacksmith's hammer and chisel. Wandor's legs folded under him, and Gwynna sagged into his lap.

The first thing Wandor did with his returning strength was gather up their clothes. Now that his awareness was no longer turned wholly inward, the dawn breeze from the river blew uncomfortably cool on his bare skin. Gwynna lay still, but he recognized the light form of the Seer Trance she sometimes used to quickly restore herself after unexpectedly demanding work with her Powers. In a few moments she also clothed herself, then spoke. "Are we going north?"

Wandor nodded slowly. "It's our best course. We don't need to go far. Four or five more days and we'll be far beyond the reach of any Kerhabans. The forest tribes won't have a blood debt to pay, and they're spread thin in any case."

"The tribes and the Kerhabans weren't all you thought about, Bertan."

"No." He leaned back against a tree, fighting an overpowering urge to sleep. A bout of sorcery and Mind Speech wasn't his choice to follow a night of paddling.

"The two of us should seek the Dragon Steed?"

He pressed the heels of his hands against his eyes, as if they'd fall out of his head otherwise. "We'll have to seek the Dragon Steed sooner or later. The Guardian of the Mountain hasn't yet sent me down a false path."

"Just the two of us?"

"No. We go north as far as we can go by water. Then we wait, until Cheloth breaks Beon-Kagri's spell and Pirnaush sends men north to us."

"Will he?"

"If he'd turned against us, Cheloth would have told us. Now that Cheloth can tell him we're alive, he may very well decide for us. Certainly he'll put the decision aside until we return. Even if he doesn't send his own men, he won't keep Berek and Sir Gilas from coming upriver with theirs."

"And when they join us, we seek the Dragon Steed?"

"Yes, with two or three hundred men at our backs. If Pirnaush has decided for us, we can safely do as we please. If he hasn't, he'll probably put off the decision again while we seek the Dragon Steed. Morkol's name is too honored for him to do anything else." He smiled. "In fact, we can have the men sent north at once and start searching for the Dragon Steed while Cheloth looks for Beon-Kagri."

Gwynna frowned. "Morkol created his dragon by Beast Magic, which makes it a creature of Earth Power. We have a powerful Earth spell on us, thanks to Beon-Kagri. I don't think it would be wise or even safe to approach the dragon until the spell is broken."

"Or at least until Cheloth knows more about it." Wandor would have agreed with her on a score of small matters now that he'd won his main victory. They would not go north merely because a sorcerer with more strength than skill had worked a spell into their bones. They would go north as human creatures to seek something which was part of his quest, not as the puppets of anyone's Powers.

They would be leaving behind them much work which had to be done, of course. They were also leaving behind men who could do all that work. And they'd leave behind Chonga's steaming lowland heat, its plots, its listening ears and ready daggers, its sullen friends and smiling enemies, its endless demands that Wandor be King or Duelist or both together at the whims of chance.

Wandor closed his eyes, and found that he could see the battered walls of Kerhab. A small figure stood on them, waving an impotent sword. It was King Wandor, cursing to no purpose as the Duelist paddled north, alone except for the one person he could trust in all things and in all the moments of his life.

* * *

Fifteen days after the fall of Kerhab.

Dehass loved his garden at dawn, and particularly the view of austere symmetry from the bridge over the fish pond—white gravel path, squat green trees in black stone tubs flanking the path, terraces of flowers rising to the vine-grown brick wall on three sides. This morning the view had less than its usual appeal. Kaldmor the Dark was late, and an idiot of a gardener was pruning a bush when everyone knew the garden was the master's alone at this hour!

Then the gardener shuffled up to the end of the bridge, pruning knife in one hand. He raised his head—then his face flowed and changed shape like oil on water. Suddenly he was Kaldmor the Dark. Dehass took two steps backward and made a gesture of aversion. Kaldmor smiled. "Yes, those deaf-mute litter bearers have their uses. But the deaf-mute still have eyes to see and minds to hold memories. My coming to you seemed better not remembered by anyone except the two of us."

"You think your—spells—were adequate for the purpose?" Dehass hoped to provoke a few moments of light talk, to give his unease time to pass.

"I think so. At least I can shape my whole head now, not just my face. I must bend my own back, and I can't produce a knife which looks real." He pulled up the left leg of his trousers and thrust the knife into an ankle sheath. "But I do not imagine you asked me here to talk of northern magic."

So much for the hope of gaining a little time. "You do that unasked. I would like to know if the *limar* is healed from its work at the temple of Murorin."

"Very nearly. In a few days I expect it will be as fit as it ever was. Will that be soon enough for whatever plot you wish to aid?"

"Baron Galkor would not have spoken so plainly, Lord Kaldmor."

"Baron Galkor would not have needed to speak that way, *Zigbai* Dehass. You would know he saw through your misty words to the reality beyond. You do not know that of me, therefore I must tell you in plain speech when I see a reality you try to hide."

"One does not expect to hear a sorcerer speaking of reality."

"Any sorcerer knows that he begins from reality and returns to it, wherever he goes between."

"But we Chongans are too ignorant to realize this?"

"Few men of any land realize this, and not all who do are

198

sorcerers. Bertan Wandor knows it, I think. So does the Black Duke."

Trying to pay back Kaldmor for his shape-changing was clearly going to use much time to little purpose. "How does your master?"

"Well enough. The camp is healthy, and after two weeks there the men give little trouble."

"They may not be there much longer."

"That will make the duke happy."

"I would not swear to that." Dehass knew that from this moment on he would find it hard to prove his innocence, and the moment was upon him sooner than he'd expected, thanks to Kaldmor's sharp tongue and sharper wits. "At the end of the next week, Chiero will proclaim his honor service for Wandor and Gwynna."

Kaldmor couldn't hide all his surprise and unease. "What sort of honor service?"

"No one except Chiero and his father knows. The treasury has been asked to provide three hundred *duquals* of gold for the purpose."

"It will not be a small service."

"No." Three hundred *duquals* in gold was enough to equip a fair-sized army.

"Will it also have the Lord *Bassan*'s approval?"

"The time for Pirnaush to disapprove has passed. He could not turn against his son's wishes now without causing talk among his doubtful friends as well as his known enemies. I think Chiero's plan has his blessing, and he will proclaim some honor for his son at the ceremony. He may even make a further proclamation, one which will please neither you nor your master."

"And you?"

"I serve the Lord *Bassan* Pirnaush. I have served him for many years. He is wise, but he can make mistakes."

"He will certainly make one if he lets Chiero declare a great honor service for Wandor and Gwynna. As for what else he may do—my master and I must guard ourselves against it."

"Your master has more enemies in Chonga than Wandor's men, and fewer friends. If those friends were to gather in secret, however, and strike first—"

"You call yourself such a friend."

"In this matter, I might be. You may judge that in time.

For now, I say only this. Alive, Chiero S'Rain is a barrier to what we both seek. Dead, he may be a path."

"If what you know is the truth, this may be so."

"Do you know otherwise?"

As Dehass expected, Kaldmor let the question pass. The sorcerer was hardly going to reveal to any Chongan how he might have used his Powers to penetrate their secrets. The *Zigbai* would not let this concern him. His own net of spies might seem a child's toy to Kaldmor, but he was sure it would give him good service without spreading fear among his sorcery-hating countrymen.

Kaldmor broke the silence. "We can work together, then?"

"We *can*, if each is willing to trust the other and bring to the work what he has. I bring knowledge of Chonga and its people. You bring your Powers and knowledge of their uses."

"At the moment, I trust you more than I do Pirnaush. The duke will say the same."

"You will—?"

"Speak of this to him? Discreetly, yes. I will not hold back until I hear his reply, of course. We do not have that much time. But I will certainly not put my Powers at your service without Cragor's word."

"I will be surprised if you do not have it."

"So will I. But I *will* have it." This might be loyalty or mere common sense, but Kaldmor seemed immovable. Fortunately Dehass knew he could persuade the duke to give Kaldmor a free rein.

Kaldmor was willing to give Dehass two days to reach a final decision. He himself would need that much time to be sure of finding ways to hide their work from the *mungans*. Dehass hoped that he'd succeed. Many *mungans* seemed to be with the army, including Telek the Fatherless himself, but even one *mungan* in the wrong place at the wrong time could bring them down. Although if guarding against the *mungans* meant strong magic...

"What about Cheloth?"

Kaldmor frowned. "I know that Cheloth is not dead, because his death would have made such a disturbance in the Spirit World that I could not have overlooked it. Nor did I give him any injury in the duel. He has withdrawn, deeply and for reasons which I refuse even to try guessing. We can only go forward and hope he will not come forth against us."

Fear made Dehass want to say, "Hope? Ridiculous!" but

common sense kept him silent. Kaldmor would hardly be admitting this much ignorance of his opponent if he wasn't telling what he saw as the truth. Besides, there was no way to completely avoid the danger from Cheloth except by sitting quietly while Pirnaush declared for Wandor's cause, which Dehass refused to consider. Even without Wandor and Gwynna, the Viceroyalty's chiefs would be fatally strong as Pirnaush's allies. Behind them stood lands and peoples who might give Wandor's memory the same good service they'd given the living man, and would certainly be slow to listen to his enemies. Cragor had only Kaldmor and Baron Galkor to trust in all things. Behind him stood a usurped land, with many who served him reluctantly and no small number who hated him.

The aid of either side might give Pirnaush the victory, but then how to keep the ally from becoming the master? Cragor's rear was vulnerable; any man with sufficient cunning and gold could make enough trouble in Benzos to bring the Black Duke to heel. Wandor's men had no such weakness. What they asked of the man they'd made king over Chonga, they would probably get. They would certainly get it, if Pirnaush died and was succeeded by the son who was about to do Wandor and Gwynna an honor service!

An alliance with the Viceroyalty meant that, in the end, there'd be only two powers in Chonga, the united northerners and the king. There'd be no place for Dehass to seek his own allies, and perhaps no place for him at all. How much did the men of the Viceroyalty know? If they came to ask Pirnaush for the *Zigbai*'s life, could they tell the king why they asked? If they could, Pirnaush would be one millstone, Arlor the other, and *Zigbai* Dehass Ebrun the rice ground between them.

The *Zigbai* did not remember how the talk with Kaldmor ended. He only knew that suddenly the sorcerer was a stooped old gardener again, and then he was completely alone on the bridge facing the sunrise.

High noon on the Mesti, twenty-six days after Wandor and Gwynna vanished from Kerhab.

Sir Gilas took off a broad-brimmed leather hat the color of moldy porridge and fanned himself with it. It kept the sun out of his eyes, to be sure, but nothing would really fight the Chongan sun except staying out of its reach altogether. The hat was also the only thing he'd allowed himself to bring away from Kerhab.

He was happy to be clear of the battered city, its sullen people and bored conquerors, its bare shops and ghost-haunted streets, with the stench of death hanging over everything. He'd have been happier if he hadn't felt he was turning his back on battles yet to come, if not against whatever Kerhabans might still have courage and weapons, then against Zerun or perhaps Shimarga of the Mines. He'd have been happiest of all if he and Berek were bringing back to Count Arlor some proof of what happened to Wandor and Gwynna.

He no longer doubted that they were dead (although he still couldn't ignore a small voice saying: *Don't kill them until you've seen their bodies*) and wondered why Count Arlor seemed unwilling to let the idea be written down. Nonetheless, the count was certainly letting Chiero S'Rain prepare the great honor service for the two absent ones, and perhaps that meant he knew the truth but couldn't bring himself to admit it. No great matter—the count was keeping his wits about him, and if they all did this, they might still bring home a victory which would mean a great deal to everyone except the two who should have been there to see it.

A village appeared on the west bank, with the usual huts and drawn-up boats, but with a stone quay and a wooden watchtower at its end. The quay seemed crowded, with more people coming down the bank onto it all the time. A second glance told the Knight that many of them were pointing at the passing ships. Reluctantly he stepped out of the shade of the sail for a better look. Four men hurried down to the beach and started pushing a boat into the water. This led to an argument in which several people were shoved off the quay. By the time they'd floundered back to shore, the boat was moving.

Something was wrong, though not wrong enough to need a call to arms. Sir Gilas sent an order to the men at the tiller, to hold a steady course; to the deck watch, to have their weapons ready; to Berek, to come on deck.

By the time Berek woke up and came forward, the boat was approaching fast. Berek moved slowly, still blinking sleep from his eyes, naked except for a loincloth and a leather speaking trumpet slung around his neck. He reached the foredeck, raised the trumpet, and hailed the boat.

"*Hoaaaa!* What news for us?"

"Chiero S'Rain is dead, lords!"

"Dead? How?"

"He was murdered this morning."

"Murdered?" roared Berek. The man in the boat echoed him, then the boat was dropping astern.

Sir Gilas stared at Berek. For once the big man's ability to let unwelcome news break over him like waves on a rock had failed him. He could not meet his Brother's eyes, and he looked as bewildered as if a snake had crawled out of the speaking trumpet and bitten him in the face.

The Knight felt much the same way. Chiero's death was stark unreason, with no place in the world Sir Gilas even wanted to try imagining.

TWENTY-ONE

───────◆◇◆───────

Armed men of Pirnaush's household guarded every door and stairway. At the door to the *Bassan*'s private chambers, Kaldmor recognized deaf-mutes, more alert than the others because they could only rely on their eyes for warning of trouble.

The guards led Kaldmor and Dehass into the chamber. As the door closed, Pirnaush stared as though he'd never seen them before. He looked like a man half out of his wits with grief and doubt. His feet and head were bare, his green robe was stained, and his hair hung down in a filthy tangle all around a face which seemed to have fallen in on itself overnight. His eyes were unnaturally large, and on his cheek tear trails and smears of ash combined to look like revolting skin eruptions. Kaldmor felt like cheering. This man might need only a small push to send him along the path he and the *Zigbai* wanted.

Pirnaush stood to greet his visitors. "Dehass, Lord Kaldmor. I don't really find anyone welcome today, but if you've brought what you promised—"

"We have, lord," said Dehass. Pirnaush thrust out a hand with black rings under all five nails. The *Zigbai* pulled a scroll from his belt pouch and handed it to Pirnaush. It was a short scroll. Dehass and Kaldmor had just time to exchange looks before the *Bassan* finished reading.

"Damn them," he said. "*Damn* them. Why? Chiero wouldn't have approached Gwynna, certainly not in any dishonorable way. The boy didn't have it in him to do that. Yet they killed him for what he didn't do! Lord Kaldmor!" His voice was the snarl of a wolf with his leg in a trap. "You're from the north.

205

What sent Arlor mad, to have Chiero murdered this way? You know the men of Benzos. What could have done it?"

"Well, Lord *Bassan*," said Kaldmor. "You ask me a question all my Powers couldn't answer for certain. I've never dealt with a man like Arlor. My master the duke is a man of honor, but I think he'd find it in him to ignore or forgive anything poor Chiero could have done."

"Arlor's a fool not to have done the same," said Dehass grimly. Pirnaush nodded.

"Perhaps Arlor wasn't such a fool after all," said Kaldmor, frowning as if the idea had just occurred to him and was only partly formed in his mind. "You know Sir Gilas Lanor offered twice for Gwynna, before she married Wandor?"

"I did not."

"Suppose he'd still been in love with her. Then—"

"Yes," said Dehass. "There were rumors of something like that, among the Viceroyalty men. Nothing I'd have thought worth taking seriously, but now—"

Pirnaush sighed. "Perhaps you did wrong, but the harm is done. It wasn't your hand that thrust the knife into my son. Go on, Kaldmor."

"If Sir Gilas started thinking he ought to avenge Gwynna's honor, he'd talk. Count Arlor would have to take him seriously. Sir Gilas is the sort of fool to do something like this, and Arlor would be afraid of his going ahead and doing it anyway. So he'd set to work and try to have Chiero murdered in a way which couldn't be discovered."

"Not wise of him," said Pirnaush, shaking his head. "If Sir Gilas lost his wits—oh, I'd have had his blood, but now . . ."

"Forgive me for reminding you of what we all know," said Dehass. "But—the way the Viceroyalty men stand by each other, Count Arlor would think he had to act. Otherwise he'd have to send Sir Gilas out of Chonga, or let him strike and die. Even if he was the only one punished—"

"Yes, yes, you don't need to use brushstrokes a hand's breadth high for me," said Pirnaush. Kaldmor didn't like the sudden briskness and alertness in his voice. "It's still the last thing I'd do in his case, striking down a man's son. Even if Sir Gilas went ahead and—"

"Forgive me, now," said Kaldmor. "But—I cannot find words for it you will care to hear—"

"Then use the words you can find, Kaldmor. I'm not a child."

206

"Your son—for many years you grieved that Chiero was unfit to be your heir, and that Kobo wasn't the eldest. All those years, it was well known you gave Chiero little thought. Arlor and the others of the north—they might have thought striking at Chiero wouldn't be striking at you. Not in any way to anger you, at least."

Before Kaldmor finished speaking, Pirnaush was giving a remarkably good imitation of a man about to have a fit. Both hands clutched at his hair and at his cheeks, improving the appearance of neither, and his eyes stared at everything without seeing anything. Then he buried his face in his hands again, and for a time there was no sound in the chamber but Pirnaush S'Rain trying not to weep.

"Arlor's wrong," he said finally. *"Wrong.* Now, when I'd found Chiero again, after he'd been lost all those years you talk about—to do this thing." He shook his head. "Wrong, I say." Kaldmor didn't dare exchange any more looks with his ally, but he could very nearly read the man's thoughts because they were so close to his own. *Pirnaush is angry now, as well as grief-stricken. Though neither anger nor grief have stopped all his thoughts, he still may choose himself to follow the path we wish.*

"At least I don't have to think Arlor's gone mad," said Pirnaush. "I'd find that hard to believe. Is the murderer still alive?"

"Yes, Lord *Bassan,*" said Dehass. "The executioners were careful."

"Good. I want that—river-pig's dung to die even harder than Chiero. There's no justice in his dying otherwise." Chiero S'Rain had taken a whole day to die, with his belly ripped open and torn far beyond the power of any Healer to repair. Kaldmor and Dehass could never have risked forcing their man to strike such a blow, but he had, making the effect of Chiero's death all the greater. Kaldmor remembered Pirnaush's face as he knelt beside the bed where Chiero tossed and twisted, trying to only moan instead of scream.

"Keep him alive and quiet, until I can see him," said Pirnaush. "Did he act alone?"

"Perhaps," said Dehass. "If one man is enough for a secret task, why tell more? But we think there may have been at least two others."

"You think?"

"He described two men in such a way that they might have

been helping him. But that was near the end, when he was not speaking clearly, and he mentioned no names. We are searching for them, however." If they needed to make the search successful, they could produce four men and one woman whose magically-planted false memories would support the accusation against the Viceroyalty men. That was as many as Kaldmor could influence without danger of Cheloth learning too much, or Dehass's men could bring to the sorcerer without the *mungans* becoming suspicious. To be sure, Cheloth and the *mungans* were still silent, but it was always best to be cautious against opponents whose return to the battle might only be discovered after they'd done fatal damage.

"Go on searching," said Pirnaush. "Dehass, it's in your hands now." He looked at Kaldmor. "I won't say anything against what you've done so far, but there won't be any more. Otherwise there'd be talk of your using northern sorcery, and—"

"Surely the people will forgive its use against Chiero's murderers?" said Kaldmor.

"—people won't stand for that, not after what happened in Kerhab."

"I fear not," said Dehass. Kaldmor wanted to glare at the *Zigbai*.

"I haven't heard that they suspect the Viceroyalty men, out in the streets," said Pirnaush. "What have you heard?"

"The same," the two men said almost in chorus. They'd both known that such rumors would certainly alert Arlor and perhaps bring him straight to Pirnaush, to ask awkward questions or have Cheloth ask them for him.

"Good," said Pirnaush. "We can leave matters that way. We'll see who talks and what they say for two, three days. Then I'll have Arlor and Besz come here, listen to what we've learned, and tell me what they've done."

"Here?" Kaldmor didn't need the quick glance from Dehass to know he shouldn't have spoken.

"Of course. Arlor and Besz'll be good hostages for getting the murderers delivered up and the rest on their way home."

"They may not submit tamely, Lord *Bassan*," said Kaldmor.

"I know. Dehass, I'll make you responsible for seeing they don't have any choice. Tell—" he named three *Hu-Bassans* "—to have their men ready to move on an hour's warning, night or day, and obey you as they would me."

The three captains named had five thousand men at most,

half of them *Haugon Dyrokee* who'd spent the Kerhaban war manning Dyroka's walls. They weren't enough for safety against the Viceroyalty's strength. Kaldmor decided he had to argue for waiting until Cragor's men came south.

"The duke would be happy to bring his men to Dyroka to help with—"

"I'm sure he would," said Pirnaush. "But I think we'd best move with what we have here in Dyroka. The duke's men are nearly a week from the city."

"True," said Dehass. "Also, I would be afraid of the disorder we might have, bringing into the fight men who don't know Dyroka."

Neither Kaldmor nor the Black Duke feared that disorder. They hoped to use it to conceal Kaldmor's spells from Cheloth and the duke's daggermen from Pirnaush and the *mungans*. Between spells and steel they had hopes of making sure that not one of the Viceroyalty's captains left Chonga alive. All these hopes had no meaning now. Kaldmor found himself sweating and forced his mouth to stay shut, his face to stay a mask. Pirnaush's grief hadn't made him ready to be led by the nose, and as for Dehass—it seemed he was the sort of man to be sure his allies had no power to act without him.

Kaldmor did not remember how the rest of the time in Pirnaush's chamber passed. He did remember his words to Dehass as they passed down the last flight of stairs to the entry hall. "Pray to your gods you don't need my master's men in the end."

Dehass's look was enough to tell Kaldmor not only that Baron Galkor wouldn't have said this, but that it was something best not said at all. However, saying it eased Kaldmor's anger and set his thoughts in motion. Instead of holding the Viceroyalty men in Dyroka until Cragor could strike, it was now a question of driving them out of the city and preferably out of Chonga, if that was the only way of blocking the *Bassan*'s plans. His plotting with Dehass could never survive the meeting of Pirnaush and Arlor. That meeting must not take place.

Fortunately, Kaldmor had resources for bringing this about, even without using his Powers. Half the duke's picked daggermen were already in Dyroka. Cragor had sent them, along with the names of those Dyrokan captains he'd bought, and gold, jewels, and pearls to buy more. Before dawn tomorrow it should be possible to make the meeting impossible. After that he might be able to win time for the duke to come south, or provoke a pitched battle which would do the work without the duke's help.

Best not dream of a great victory and let the small one go, however. Dehass obviously wanted the Viceroyalty men left not just alive, but ready to join Pirnaush if the *Bassan* found that an alliance with Cragor chafed him like ill-made armor. Even if he couldn't stop Kaldmor outright, he might easily find ways to strike back afterward.

He certainly wouldn't stop Kaldmor's work to prevent the meeting, however. The ax might not be as close to the back of the *Zigbai*'s neck as it was to Kaldmor's, but if Pirnaush learned of his old friend's plotting, it would be close enough.

TWENTY-TWO

———————◆•◆•◆———————

Gwynna awoke and began unknotting the sleep from her muscles as Bertan scrambled up the bank. He shook himself, doglike, and the water made a puddle around him as he wrung out his beard with both hands. His beard had grown longer than she'd ever seen it before, except during their captivity among the HaroiLina. *Does the climate of Chonga make everything grow faster?*

His eyes were admiring her as she finished her exercises. He untied the leaves holding the baked fish left over from last night and handed her a piece. She let it rest on her knee and looked at him.

"Yes?"

"It's been a long time since we heard from Cheloth."

"Too long, I think."

She nodded. "There might be good reasons for his silence. He's certainly managed to avoid a major duel with Kaldmor. But if he and Arlor had set matters in order, I think we'd have heard."

"I'm afraid you're right. At least we can't wait any longer to find out. Can you reach him?"

Gwynna frowned. Bertan's new ease with sorcery and her Powers was too fragile to endure a lie, even if there hadn't been so many other reasons for telling the truth.

"Not unless he's willing. If Cheloth has shielded himself against Kaldmor, I couldn't crack that shield—unless—"

"You worked so long and so hard that Kaldmor heard you and struck back. Then you might not have the strength to do your share, and even if Cheloth won, you might not escape harm."

"Yes. And if Kaldmor learned we were alive before Arlor did, it might be Cragor's men who came up the river after us."

"So where does this leave us?" he said. He threw down his fish and started jerking on his clothes, careless of half-rotted seams and worn spots. "We can't go south and we don't dare go north unless—" He stopped, one leg in his trousers. "Are you thinking of trying to take off Beon-Kagri's spell yourself?"

She nodded. "Beon-Kagri's working with the purest sort of Earth Power. So pure his spells have to be worked below the ground, and can't be detected above it. Suppose this means his spells can only be *taken off* by working against them underground?"

There was a long silence. She'd brought Bertan face-to-face with the unknown, and the unknown in sorcery still unsettled him more than the unknown in more common matters. Then he said slowly, "I'll suppose that. But if it could be true, wouldn't Cheloth have spoken of it?"

"Oh, he'd have spoken of it, if he'd known it and wasn't keeping his own counsel."

"Cheloth keeps his own counsel too much." A shrug. "I don't know whether it bothers me more, that he knows but won't tell or that he doesn't know." Another, shorter silence. "Now, our getting underground. There was a cave on the riverbank, about half an hour downstream. Will that be enough?"

"If getting there doesn't awaken the spell, yes. I don't think I want to try fighting the effects of the spell and finding a way to take it off at the same time."

"I wouldn't let you."

"You can't—"

"I can. And I will, when I see you being foolish about dangerous sorcery." He went on dressing in silence. After a moment Gwynna turned away and began to do the same, holding back sharp words. Bertan could be right, he certainly wouldn't change, and saying anything would keep alive a conversation best left to die.

Breaking Beon-Kagri's spells would almost certainly involve her using the Powers she'd encountered on Yand Island. She was no longer a passive channel for them, but even now she had to admit she couldn't entirely control them.

It was going to be a fiercely hot day even for Dyroka in the summer, and Count Arlor returned to his chambers wooly-mouthed, slimy with sweat, and hungry. Instead of breakfast, he found Cheloth of the Woods pacing back and forth beside the table, as though he was feeling impatient or uneasy. When Arlor learned why Cheloth was here, he could almost believe the sorcerer really was feeling some human emotion. He also wished he could believe Cheloth was lying about Kaldmor's plotting with Dehass.

Fortunately much had been done to gather the Viceroyalty men since Sir Gilas and Berek returned from Kerhab. What remained to be done needed only a few orders and then a few hours. After that the Viceroyalty's men would be ready to defend themselves against any number of enemies they could expect to face in the next day or two. Pirnaush had less than ten thousand men in Dyroka, of which half would be needed to keep the peace in the city. Not all of the rest would willingly march against the northerners.

"I'm sending a message to Pirnaush, asking for an audience tomorrow," Arlor concluded.

"Why not today?"

"I want to offer an honor service for Chiero," said Arlor. "I need a day to decide what it should be."

"Why do you need a whole day?"

"Would you rule here, Cheloth, or will you let me act as I see fit?" The sorcerer's head jerked back as if he'd been struck in the face and his gloved fingers hooked over his belt, but he was silent. Arlor explained the rest of his plans for bringing matters into the open and forcing Pirnaush to a decision.

"And if the decision is against you?"

"If we have more than a few hours' warning—"

"And if you do not?"

Facing a man, Arlor would have been close to drawing his sword. Facing Cheloth, he could only glare. If Pirnaush or Cragor fell on them without warning, their danger would indeed be great. Otherwise, they had a good chance to retreat down the Mesti to safety. Kobo S'Rain's fleet was still up the Hiyako, and Cragor's ships were farther up the Mesti along with his men. On the Mesti there were now only a few armed Dyrokan ships. So Captain Thargor would start downriver today in the fastest of the Viceroyalty's *kulghas*. He'd take command of the greatships in Jubon Bay and sail at once to the secret meeting

213

place in the Tok'li Islands. Here in Dyroka, they'd be ready to sail at an hour's notice.

With no more luck than an honest man could ask from the gods, they'd be able to retreat to safety and take counsel. They might look as if they'd run off with their tails between their legs, but Cragor would soon learn differently, even if he had Chonga's gold pouring into his hands. The war would go on.

Cheloth left without saying anything more to show either approval or disapproval of Arlor's plans. The count stared after him a moment, then thrust his head out the door and shouted for his breakfast, his scribe, and messengers.

The sun was approaching its peak when Wandor and Gwynna found the cave mouth. They had to cover only a few steps to the west to reach it, and any pain from the spell was lost in the itching of scores of insect bites. The mouth was so narrow that it was going to be a tight fit for Wandor. Inside, the rock wall dropped straight away for twice the height of a man. The visible part of the cave's floor seemed to be clean and firm.

Wandor reluctantly tore himself away from the cool air exhaled from the cave and started looking around the hillside for a solid place to anchor a rope. Below the cave there was a stout sapling, the grass was longer, and if—

Gwynna cried out, in surprise more than in pain, and went to her knees. Then Cheloth was in Wandor's mind as well, answering unasked and even unimagined questions. Chiero S'Rain dead. Pirnaush grief-stricken and suspicious. Dehass and Kaldmor playing on those suspicions with great skill and a twisted story of jealousy and avenged honor. Dyroka apparently calm on the surface, but underneath seething like boiling porridge and certain to see blood flowing before another dawn. Arlor and their other comrades preparing to argue their case, fight, or flee as might seem best.

Then Cheloth was gone, and Gwynna was standing close to Wandor, gripping his shoulders so hard he felt her nails in his skin as she shook all over. He started to take her in his arms, then looked into her eyes and knew she was shaking with rage.

"Cheloth didn't tell Arlor we were alive."

"We don't—"

"He certainly wouldn't admit it, would he? But how could all this—" she used a Yhang obscenity "—happen if he'd spo-

214

ken up? He—he—" Rage closed her throat and twisted her hands into claws.

The hands moved from Wandor's shoulder to the sling of her pack. "Bertan, I'm going down into the cave, test it for *luors* of old magic. If it's clean I'll—"

"You aren't going down there now."

"I'll go—"

"You won't, and by all the gods show some sense! You're going to be working with the Powers you faced on Yand Island, and that's bad enough. I won't let you work at all until you're fit to—"

Her hand came up, nails reaching for his face. He sensed that blocking her might trigger a real attack with all the skills he'd taught her and stood motionless. Before the nails scored his flesh, Gwynna's hand stopped, then fell to her side. She pressed her face hard into his shoulder, then stepped back. She sighed. "Bertan—I'm sorry. But—poor Chiero." Her voice was steady, in spite of the tears creeping down her cheeks.

"Don't be. Cheloth betrayed our faith in him, and Chiero's death is on his conscience, not ours. We'll have to do the best we can ourselves." He dropped his own sack and pulled out the long curved jungle knife. "I'll lower you down and you can test the cave while I try to anchor the rope."

The *kulgha* carrying Captain Thargor downriver finally vanished from sight. Sir Gilas Lanor turned back toward the ships at the quay, his eyes watering from the glare of the sun on the river, and saw Berek coming down the gangplank of the second ship. The Sea Folker was half-carrying two men barely able to walk. Making the ships ready meant working straight through the heat of the day, and not all the Viceroyalty men could endure it.

The Knight walked along the quay until he could hail Berek without shouting. It was too hot for raising voices, even when there was an urgent message. Berek turned from pouring a bucket of water over one of the heat-stricken men and nodded. Then he dismissed the two men, poured a bucket over himself, and came across to Sir Gilas. The Knight led Berek out of everyone's hearing and spoke quickly.

"Tonight a hundred of our men are going to the house of Naram Tekor and bring everyone there aboard our ships."

"What will Pirnaush say to that?"

"Not much, unless he's planning to forgive all Dehass's

plots. Naram learned most of what we knew about *Zigbai*'s work up to the time of Chiero's death."

"Yes. Cheloth could have given more, but he did not. I should like to know why."

"So would we all. Count Arlor isn't sure the *Zigbai* and Kaldmor know of Tekor's work, but even if they don't, we've promised not to leave him behind."

Berek nodded. "You are leading the men to Tekor's house?"

"Yes. Will you be with me, Brother?"

Berek frowned. "Yes, if you tell me why you are leading the men."

"It is my place, Berek."

"That is not all the answer, Gil. Not when there are a dozen other captains as fit for the work. Are you doing this because of what the people are saying, about you and Gwynna and Chiero's death?"

From some men those words would have meant a challenge. From most they would have been ignored. From Berek they were hardly even a surprise. To many, Berek seemed short-sighted and even slow-witted, but Sir Gilas knew that in fact he missed very little, though he said even less.

"Yes. I've heard the talk. At first I couldn't believe anyone would think something so stupid. Then I heard some of my own words about Gwynna on other men's lips." He shrugged. "I can't unsay those words and the men who talk won't unhear them, but I can stop their mouths."

"By dying here in Dyroka?"

There was no answer to that Sir Gilas could give with a clear conscience, at least to Berek. He shrugged again. Berek smiled. "Then if you are going into battle looking only to your honor, I must come to look to your back." The smile faded. "But I cannot look to all the other men. Do you owe them nothing?" His voice turned sharp. "Brother, if your wits do not clear, I must go to Arlor and tell him you're not fit to lead the men tonight."

"Arlor already knows why. I had to tell him."

"And not me, Brother?"

Sir Gilas winced. "Arlor also lives with love for a woman who cannot be his."

"Anya yet lives."

"Yes, as Cragor's toy. So perhaps he suffers more, knowing this. Gwynna was happy with Wandor, and now she is beyond joy or pain."

He reached up and gripped Berek's shoulders, as if he would shake the big man. "Brother, believe me that I'm telling the truth now. I won't throw my life away tonight. I won't be careless of the men under us. But not even by our oath of the Brothers to Serve can you ask me to live one more day with the whispers of 'daggerman' following me!"

"I won't, Gil. I won't." Berek laid one hand on the Knight's shoulder. At such times Sir Gilas felt something like a father's compassion flowing out of the Sea Folker—a strange thing, since Berek was only a year older.

Wandor slipped down the rope to the floor of the cave and turned to Gwynna. She sat in the fading patch of sunlight from the cave mouth overhead. The light had a ruddy sunset tinge. Their packs lay beside her.

"If there's anyone watching us, they're too well-hidden for me," he said.

"Then we may as well begin. This cave is clear, as far as I can tell." She read his face. "No, I didn't use any of the new Powers. Any *luor* which could put us in danger, I could read with my old skills." She raised one leg and started unlacing a boot.

Wandor picked up flint and steel and lit the torch tied to an arrow driven into a crack in the rock. The torch burned a pale orange, and its light drove the shadows back only a little way. Wandor felt uneasy about being naked in the presence of so many shadows crowding so close.

However, Gwynna already had her clothes piled on the ground and was sitting cross-legged on them. Her face was calm and her breathing steady as she prepared her body for the demands the coming work would make on it. Wandor started undressing, cursing under his breath as his hands shook in spite of himself. He ripped seams and cursed again, remembering how few fresh clothes they had now and the weather they'd be facing if they had to travel farther north. Finally he sat down on his pack and started slowing his own breathing. Gwynna rested one hand on his knee, and he felt a subtle Power already in her, ebbing and flowing like a slow tide.

"Are you frightened, Bertan?"

"Yes."

She smiled. "Try to control it. It makes the work harder for me."

He tried, and she helped him by gripping his hands and

forming a Mind Speech link. He read fear in her, too, but also a strangely pleasurable excitement.

("Gwynna, how can you—?")

Formless, wordless thoughts, questioning, then coming clear. ("When you were a Duelist, did you ever face an opponent you knew you might not defeat, but who would certainly teach you things you hadn't known before?")

He understood, but didn't quite agree. ("Yes. But I wasn't going to die in the teaching. Are we going to be safe if you fail?") Instead of answering she moved so that she sat facing him, still gripping both hands.

("Don't move unless I tell you.")

The shadows around them seemed to crawl closer. Gwynna's hair glowed softly, then flared so brightly that the torchlight vanished. Where Wandor's bare skin touched the bare rock, he felt a prickling like a thousand tiny thorns. He had time for one thought—*This time we go into the House of Shadows together, if we go*—then his mind was no longer enough his own to hold his thoughts.

TWENTY-THREE

Mitzon peered over the edge of the roof, which was raised enough to hide him as long as he stayed on hands and knees. He was high enough to see the street in front of Naram Tekor's house for a good long way in both directions, but low enough to reach the street swiftly.

Hawa crawled up beside him and made a hand signal. The other three watchers were in position too. Five *mungans* wasn't much for what might be tonight's work; Telek would certainly have been able to bring fifty.

A hot, still night was following a hot, still day. Mitzon felt the sweat band around his forehead growing damp and for a moment wished he'd darkened his face with grease rather than with a mask. But a mask could be snatched off in a moment, and that might be useful tonight.

Both the streets and Tekor's house were unnaturally quiet. The fear and unease hanging over Dyroka kept the streets clear of all except those whose business needed the cover of darkness. He was about to suggest to Hawa that they climb down and explore the house, when shadows moved far down the Street of the Four Taverns. Hooded lanterns revealed them as they reached the corner and turned uphill toward the house. In the lead was a giant, his coat of mail rippling with a watery sheen as he moved and an ax slung across his back. A smaller armored figure marched beside him.

Mitzon let out breath he hadn't known he was holding and gripped Hawa's shoulder. Berek and Sir Gilas Lanor were bringing up the Viceroyalty men in strength. That might keep anything else from happening, which would satisfy Mitzon entirely. He was ready to do everything which could be done against Telek and for Wandor, but how much could that be?

The stillness of Naram Tekor's house seemed to shout into Sir Gilas's ear. Berek heard it too, and his signals sent men to guard all the street approaches.

The silent house told them nothing. Most of the windows were dark and all were barred. Stones tossed up on the roof got no answer, and neither did Berek's and Sir Gilas's calling softly through the door in every language they knew. Finally Berek motioned the Knight to stand clear.

"If I thought nothing was wrong, we might take the time to go through the garden. As it is..." and he swung Thunderstone off his back. The great ax sighed through the heavy air and crashed into the lock. Half a dozen blows loosened it. Berek drew the small ax Greenfoam from his belt and used its spike to pry the lock free of the wood. Then he reached through the hole, felt around in the darkness, and heaved. A heavy bar clattered on the stone floor, and the door swung open.

Sir Gilas jumped back from the sight inside. Five bodies lay on the floor of the front hall, and the polished stones were caked with blood and vomit. The men behind the two leaders pushed forward, then also jumped back with curses and obscenities. A few looked sick.

Sir Gilas stepped forward, skirting the worst of the filth, then stopped as he saw that three of the five bodies had their throats cut. All three had knives or daggers in their hands. From the way they were holding the steel, it looked as if they'd cut their own throats.

The man behind Sir Gilas unhooded his lantern, and its light showed something else unnatural. All five faces were a pale blue—*like sun-bleached violets*, thought the Knight. Their eyes were so bloodshot they seemed to glow red, and their lips were as pale as the moss from a lightless cave. Some of the curses died, others took a new note. Battles against men do not always prepare one to face sorcery. Then Berek knelt down, lifted one of the staring blue faces toward him, sniffed at the mouth, then cursed in the tongue of the HaroiLina.

"Not sorcery—not sorcery alone," he said. "*Luk* smoke."

"I thought that was outlawed?"

"Daggermen still use it, when they need to kill several people at once. That is not often, so most have forgotten it."

"Dehass would have men who knew it, though."

"Yes, and Kaldmor's skills could make it stronger, until . . ." Berek shook his head and absentmindedly combed blood-caked hair back from a woman's forehead with his fingers. "They must have stabbed themselves in the throats to end the pain."

The uncertain murmurings behind Sir Gilas told him it was time to put the men to work. He turned. "These people died from *luk*weed smoke, strengthened by Kaldmor's sorcery. There's no danger to us, but I'm afraid our friends here are beyond help.

"Tzuran, take fifteen men and search the house in bands of five. If you see anything suspicious, send us word before you get too close! If you can, bring the bodies down. Elshor, take twenty men and search the streets for a wagon. We'll need it to take the bodies back to the ships. The rest—"

Elshor spoke up. "What's with takin' the bodies, Sir Gil? Can't help them much, can it?"

"No. But these people were our friends, and were murdered for that friendship. We owe them a better burial than they'll get here in Chonga. Also, if we can prove how Kaldmor took a hand in this night's work—"

"Ah, I see. Right you are, Sir Gil."

Mitzon saw the bodies brought out and laid in a neat row along the front of the house. Some men held up torches, while others cleaned the bodies as well as they could and arranged them decently. That was wise, Mitzon thought. The work could no longer be a secret, and darkness would only make it hard to tell friends from enemies. More torches flared, then lanterns in the windows. The darkness retreated until Mitzon hoped he wouldn't have to do the same. That might leave him and his people too far away to do more than watch if anything did happen.

Then there was a bobbing glow as though distant fireflies were coming up the hill. Hawa's breath hissed in his ear. If this was the trap, they'd have to wait for it to be fully sprung before moving. Otherwise they might end as only five more swords lost in the confusion.

The newcomers carried their lanterns unhooded. As Mitzon recognized faces and badges he began to doubt that this was the trap. It was the Ninety of Deijur Mimbran, a painfully honest middle-aged veteran, slow-witted, quick-tempered, but utterly reliable for almost anything except the sort of plots Dehass and Kaldmor were hatching.

Sir Gilas heard the rumble of wheels on the stones and the tramp of approaching feet at the same moment, then Berek's shouts. Tzuran's men came down the stairs as if the house were on fire, and the Knight followed them into the street as the Dyrokan Ninety came up.

Sir Gilas stepped up to the Dyrokan *Ki-Bassan*. The man was large for a Chongan, gray-haired, and though he wore green-enameled armor he did not wear a *paizar-han*'s sash.

"Why do you come here?" said Sir Gilas.

Being asked why he was about his duties in his own city left the *Ki-Bassan* speechless for a moment. "We come—what do you here, with these dead men?"

"They are our countrymen, murdered by Chongans."

"Mur—"

"No man breathes *luk* smoke for pleasure, I think."

"*Luk*—"

Berek stepped forward, holding Thunderstone. The glint from its dark metal drew eyes on both sides. "We came to the house of Naram Tekor to offer him a journey to the Viceroyalty. We heard he has enemies here, and it seemed best that no more blood be shed without good reason."

The *Ki-Bassan* tried to catch up. "With a hundred men, you came?"

"You know how the times are," said Sir Gilas. "We didn't want to be mistaken for criminals." No one laughed.

"Criminals or not, you must come with me," said the *Ki-Bassan*. "It is my duty."

"No," said Berek. Sir Gilas was tempted to draw his sword, but saw too many crossbows among the Dyrokans. They were not held ready, though, and many weren't even cocked. Suddenly he saw a way to avoid the worst of the danger, and repair his reputation as well.

"No," he said. "We will not trust ourselves to the Lord *Bassan* Pirnaush of Dyroka."

The *Ki-Bassan*'s mouth snapped shut. "This you do not say, in his own city."

"I do say it, and loudly." The Knight raised his voice. "Hear me. Pirnaush is lord of Dyroka, but he has not stopped the tongues which call me the murderer of his son. He has not stopped the hands which ended the lives of all the people in this house, or the sorcery which aided the killers."

That brought gasps from the Dyrokans, and a nod from

Berek. "Yes," said the Sea Folker. "It was *luk* smoke, but aided by sorcery. Some of you must know how the smoke kills. Look at these bodies, and see for yourselves." The Dyrokans began crowding forward, but a bellow from the *Ki-Bassan* stopped them.

"Enough! You will come with us, to a safe place under the Lord *Bassan*'s hand."

"That is not a safe place for us."

The Dyrokan took a deep breath. "I would not wish to have this come to blood."

"I also," said the Knight. He smiled, went down on one knee, spread his arms as wide as he could without getting his hands too far from his weapons, and turned his eyes upward.

"Hear me, Khoshi Swift in Battle, Staz the Warrior, Haro Sea Father, and all the other gods who watch over men who do battle. I ask you to judge between us." He clasped both hands over one knee and looked at the *Ki-Bassan*. "Let us do all the fighting ourselves, the two of us. If I win, I and all my people go safe to our ships with the bodies of our friends. If you win, we go with you under the Lord *Bassan*'s hand."

Again he aimed his words at the men behind the *Ki-Bassan*. "What say you? We have fought beside one another, and it would be godless to shed one another's blood. Yet a judgment is needed here. So your *Ki-Bassan* and I will put ourselves in the hands of the gods, and let the judgment be theirs."

Even if he'd wished to, the *Ki-Bassan* could not have stopped the shouts of his men. He had to shout himself, to make himself heard. "How will we know, who wins?"

"The loser is dead, wounded past fighting, or calls for quarter," said the Knight.

"No quarter for me," said the Dyrokan. His men cheered him.

"So be it," said Sir Gilas. He hoped he could wound the man past fighting without killing him; he could hardly be a part of whatever plans Dehass and Kaldmor might have laid for tonight. This would make the fight rather more dangerous, but Sir Gilas felt he had a perfect right to sacrifice his own blood to cleanse his reputation.

Berek called for the torchbearers on both sides to come forward and light up a fighting circle. Someone else suggested the two men toss a coin to see who'd start facing uphill and who down. Sir Gilas drew his sword and tested edges he'd sharpened this afternoon. He heard men on both sides exchanging tales of the siege of Kerhab and even a few wagers on the outcome of the fight. Then he stepped forward and the torchlight flamed on his blade.

Mitzon watched the unexpected duel with growing pleasure. The two men were a good match, but the northern Knight had a significant edge in speed. Of course there was always bad luck, but the worst had already been avoided. By the Knight's challenge, the northerners had made it clear their business tonight was honorable, fit to be blessed by the gods. That would weigh heavily with the Dyrokans and men elsewhere in Chonga. They'd also preserved the bodies of the dead as evidence of the sorcery involved in the deaths, which would weigh even more heavily.

Finally, Berek's bringing the torches forward left the rear ranks of both parties in shadow. From above Mitzon could see men slipping away from the rear of the northerners. If they reached Count Arlor, secret murder of these men in prison would be much harder for Dehass and Kaldmor to contrive.

Mitzon's gaze followed the men out of sight, then he cursed under his breath. Coming toward him from the north was the glow of massed torches and the gleam of armor. Another hundred paces, and Hawa was also cursing, not under her breath. The approaching men were not only marching with torches lit but with their Ninety's banner unfurled and aloft. It was the Ninety of Sekud Afaaro, and he was Cragor's bought man: at least he was if Telek had told the truth a month ago.

It was time to be ready on the ground. He spoke briefly to Hawa, then to his chosen partner for the work. Three or four men would be better than two, but a messenger was already gone and one man would have to stay up here with Hawa. With the darkness and *mungan*'s skills two should certainly be able to get in, and getting out again was always in Khoshi's hands. Mitzon embraced Hawa, then slipped back down the slope of the roof toward the rear of the house.

The duel ended by the common consent of both fighters as the new Ninety marched up, before either man had done much more than work up a good sweat. Deijur had a small cut over one eye, and Sir Gilas had two new dents in his armor. The Viceroyalty men drew into a circle around the wagon holding the bodies. The archers were inside the circle, where they could cock and load without being seen and then shoot over the heads of their comrades. Berek ordered that no more men were to slip off; there were enough messengers on the way already. Then he handed Sir Gilas a cloth to wipe his face and stood beside him while the two *Ki-Bassans* argued.

"—so I answered the Knight's call to let the gods judge. For my honor and the honor of Dyroka, what else could I do?"

"You've insulted our *Bassan*, Deijur," said the newcomer. "He's the judge of what the city's honor needs. As for your honor..." He shrugged. "That's between you and the gods. But now I give the orders here."

"Not to my Ninety, you bastard. I had it two years before you had a Thirty."

"You've had dealings with the Viceroyalty men. In the face of that, your years don't matter."

"I've had no dealings I wouldn't lay before the *Bassan*, and—"

"You'll be doing just that, when these people are safe in the Ekatabani Fortress."

Deijur's hand dropped to the hilt of his sword. "I've sworn they'd not be dishonored or treated as criminals, even if the Knight lost."

"You can't swear an oath to—"

"I can and I did. And I'll keep it, which is more than you've ever done with any oath you ever swore, Sekud Afaaro."

Sekud's breath went out in a snake's hiss. "Unsay that, you toad weaned on pig's dung."

"Not when it's the truth. I know what—"

"Traitor!" came a shrill scream from the ranks of Sekud's Ninety. "You've sold yourself to the northerners!" Deijur's men growled like hungry bears, but before any of them could act or their *Ki-Bassan* could draw his sword, a crossbow went *snik*. The bolt might have been aimed at Deijur, but it took the man standing beside him in the throat. Blood sprayed over his clutching fingers, he staggered, and as he went down a voice rose from the rear of the Ninety.

"Murderers! Cragor's bought you!" A second crossbow let fly. Its bolt drilled Sekud Afaaro squarely in the forehead. His mouth opened and his eyes closed, but before he could fall Deijur leaped forward, drawn sword in one hand, holding up his dying opponent with the other.

Perhaps he'd hoped to prevent a fight. Instead he made one inevitable. His men took his gesture as the signal to charge the other Ninety. War cries rose, along with death screams, the rattle of bolts on armor, and the screech and clang of clashing swords. Surprised and leaderless, Sekud's Ninety was driven back into the Street of the Four Taverns. Suddenly the Viceroyalty men had a clear street ahead of them and an open path downhill to the waterfront. Sir Gilas leaped up on top of the wagon.

"Downhill! Hurry!"

A dozen men tossed their weapons to comrades and gripped the wagon. It creaked into motion. Berek called the archers out to form a rearguard. Some of the Dyrokans in both Nineties saw that the northerners were getting away, but they were too busy fighting each other to do more than send a few bolts past Sir Gilas. The men at the rear of Deijur's Ninety shrank aside as the wagonload of dead rumbled past. Then the Viceroyalty men were past the corner and Berek gave a single order.

"Run!"

They ran down the hill until it was so steep that the men on the wagon were holding it back rather than pushing it. They ran until the torches began going out from the wind of their passage, and through narrow places where sparks flew as the wagon's hubs scraped stone and brick. They ran along wider stretches, where doors and windows flew open and half-naked Chongans stared at the wild procession.

Two-thirds of the way down the hill they met a Thirty of the *Haugon Dyrokee*. Berek saw them hastily trying to form a line across the street, and ran forward to try a parley. They'd managed to avoid shedding any Chongan blood tonight, and if they could keep it so—

Sir Gilas shouted his war cry. "Lanor and victory!"

The men handling the wagon gave a mighty push, and it seemed to fly down the street at the Dyrokans. They scattered before it, and it rumbled past them. Sir Gilas was shouting and waving his sword as if he were leading a mounted charge. Berek shouted, "Business of the *Bassan*! Make way! Make way!" and the other men took it up. The northerners pounded past, and those Dyrokans who wanted to pursue saw the rearguard of archers and thought better of it.

At last the hill ended, and they turned toward the quay where their *kulgha* waited. When they reached it, Sir Gilas leaped down, and the men on the wagon started unloading the bodies. Archers took posts to watch all the streets and rooftops, then the Brothers to Serve turned to look back the way they'd come.

An ugly orange glow was mounting into the sky, swelling higher as they watched. Tekor's house or something close by it was on fire. In the sudden silence after the rush downhill, Berek could hear the gongs of the watch and the *Haugon* posts sounding the fire alarm.

By the time Hawa and the last *mungan* slipped down from their roof, the fire in Tekor's house had broken through the roof. Fire-weakened beams collapsed, spilling tiles into the flames, while cinders and sparks flew high and drifted off into the night.

Sekud Afaaro's men must have used warfire on the house. Nothing else could have made it blaze up so fast or promised a sufficiently thorough destruction of the evidence of murder and sorcery. It still wouldn't do much good if the Viceroyalty men got clear with the bodies, and less good if the fire spread. There'd been ten hot, rainless days in Dyroka, and those sparks and cinders would find many dry resting places.

Hawa and her companion moved through the alleys and back streets at a brisk trot. Once they saw a Thirty of the *Haugon* hurry past, most of the men unarmored. Twice they saw *Ki-Bassans* of the Fire Guards urging along ragged bands of men with buckets and hooks. The fire gongs now seemed to sound from everywhere.

They passed a street where a Thirty was questioning some poor wretch who'd been caught too far from a hiding place. His shrieks drowned out the sound of their passing. Then they were coming up to the agreed meeting place, under the rear porch of Old Lilyu's house.

Hawa crawled under the porch, then crammed her fist into her mouth to stifle a scream. Mitzon was sitting facing her, propped against the wall. The left side of his face was all blood from eyebrow down to chin, one arm dangled uselessly, and his breathing was shallow and quick. A soldier's lantern flickered between his feet, and his sword lay across his knees. He was alone.

"Where—?" began the other *mungan*.

Hawa shook her head. "Don't know. Can't wait to learn either." She wished she could speak more calmly.

The other *mungan* started opening the pouch at his belt. "I have bandages and salves."

"Thank you." Her hand was almost steady as she took them. His staying at her back this way deserved more than thanks.

227

For now she could think only of Mitzon, and snatching him away from Kaldmor and Cragor, Dehass and Telek, bad luck, or even death itself.

Master Besz came up the gangplank from the quay, approached Count Arlor, and spoke briefly. There were no less than six Nineties watching the quarter, but for the moment there was no danger. Each of the Nineties seemed to have a different version of what had happened at Tekor's house. None seemed ready to trust any of the others on their flanks or in their rear. No *Hu-Bassan* had come, nor any orders from Pirnaush. However, this might change at any moment, and before it did—

"Yes. You've said this already. Is there any word of Cheloth?"

"No."

All the Viceroyalty men were aboard their ships now, except for the handful Besz had watching the Dyrokans—and searching for Cheloth of the Woods. The sorcerer had vanished as completely as if the Earth on whose Powers he drew had swallowed him. If there was little danger of an immediate attack from the Dyrokans, there seemed even less chance of enlisting the sorcerer's aid in learning exactly what might be happening in Dyroka or in predicting what dangers might come with the passing hours. After the *luk* smoke, Arlor was quite prepared to turn Cheloth and all his Powers loose, and Chongan fears be damned!

Should they go or stay? Retreat downriver to the open Ocean and whatever safety might be found there, or remain in Dyroka and fight for whatever advantage might be snatched from the confusion spreading since Chiero's death?

Certainly those counseling retreat—such as Master Besz—had much wisdom on their side. The Viceroyalty fleet was still the strongest fighting force afloat on the Mesti. Pirnaush had considerable strength in Dyroka, but tonight's events had shown that the *Bassan*'s men could be of divided minds about fighting against the Viceroyalty. Sir Gilas's challenge, the apparent treachery of Sekud's Ninety, and the evidence of sorcery would divide them still further.

Once they'd reached the Ocean, they could make for the Tok'lis, meet the greatships, fill their water barrels, and be ready to fight, flee, or invite Pirnaush to sit down with them and hear sense. Whether they won or lost the battle for Chonga, the war could go on. If all else failed and Pirnaush turned to Cragor, they would be in a position to negotiate with Pirnaush's enemies, and sow in Chonga a war which could at least keep Cragor from making much use of his victory.

On the other hand, there was much to be said for the Vice-royalty fleet staying where it was. If they retreated, the Chongans might call them cowards. Some would call the retreat a confession of guilt. If they stayed, they would look like men with clean consciences, and the Chongans had a sharp eye for such. Sir Gilas had proved that. If they stayed, they might find more friends even in Dyroka, and perhaps they could reach Pirnaush.

That was Arlor's highest hope. If he and Cheloth and Sir Gilas could sit down with the *Bassan* and show him by words and spells all they knew about the plots of the last few days—well, it would be the end for Dehass, and even Duke Cragor might need some luck to get out of Chonga alive. Pirnaush would certainly offer an alliance to the Viceroyalty. He *might* even permit Cheloth to go to work on Kaldmor—if Cheloth had not in fact vanished.

Arlor decided not to burden his mind with too many problems at once. He'd have to decide soon, Cheloth or no Cheloth. Even a short delay might see Cragor's friends winning in Dyroka, or Dehass and Kaldmor striking openly at Pirnaush. A longer delay might bring Kobo S'Rain and his fleet to the mouth of the Mesti.

Out on the river a Dyrokan galley crept across the silver-gilt moonpath on the water. On the far bank a new fire silhouetted a temple tower. Then a shout from the quay drew Arlor's attention. A strange party was coming along it at a brisk walk, toward Arlor's ship. Berek led it, Sir Gilas brought up the rear, and four men between them carried a litter. Beside the litter walked a woman, and on it lay Cheloth of the Woods.

Arlor met Berek at the head of the gangplank and drew him aside as the litter-bearers came aboard. The woman walking beside the litter Arlor now saw was one of the Tree Sisters who'd come with the Khindi.

"Where was he?"

"In his chamber. It seemed to me that he must be working dangerous spells. He would most likely do this in his chamber."

Arlor was about to reply, then saw Thunderstone slung across Berek's back. The huge ax smelled of hot metal, and its head was sooty black with the edge blunted and distorted. Arlor swallowed.

"You broke down Cheloth's door with your ax."

"Yes."

"You could have—"

"I swore the Oath of the Drunk Blood. Also, Thunderstone is sky-stone metal. Cheloth works his magic from the Earth. I thought the ax might protect me." He reached back and stroked the head as though he were caressing a beloved woman. "It did, but I do not know if it will be fit for battle again."

Arlor could neither move nor speak. He would never have dared order Berek or any other man to do this thing—to spit on the very doorstep of the House of Shadows. Berek shrugged. "One must accept the duties of service. I broke down the door and entered the chamber. Cheloth lay on the floor, as he lies now."

"Is he dead?"

"He breathes, and the Tree Sister says he also does other things he did when alive. She will not say what they are."

There seemed no bounds to the sorcerers' habit of treating Powerless humans as children. Arlor sighed. "Will he wake soon? And will he be fit when he does?"

"She says she does not know."

There it was. Cheloth might rise from his litter in the next moment, probably cursing those who'd seen him in his weakness. He also might be a living corpse for weeks. The world beyond the world held things which could strike back cruelly even at Cheloth of the Woods. Kaldmor the Dark might be able to call on some of them.

For a moment the hot night was cold. If Kaldmor could defeat Cheloth, then they were all dead men. Best that they act like living ones, though. If this wasn't Kaldmor's work, he might not yet know what had happened. He had to be kept from learning. But if Cheloth remained this close to Dyroka...

They were going downriver and out to sea. Staying here on the chance of Cheloth's quick awakening would be foolishly dangerous. Arlor smashed his fist hard into the railing. The pain and rage at Cheloth's state silenced him for a moment.

"We must leave, Berek."

"That is so, my Lord Count."

"I—you'll be rewarded for all you did tonight." Arlor nearly said, "I shall reward you," but he had the feeling that the moment he openly took Wandor's and Gwynna's place in giving rewards and punishments, they would die. He gripped Berek's arms. "Go to your ship." The big man turned toward the gangplank, and Arlor hailed the afterdeck of his *kulgha*.

"*Hoy*! Hang out all the battle lanterns and pass the word for all ships to prepare to cast off. We'll be on our way downriver as soon as Master Besz has his men aboard!"

TWENTY-FOUR

Wandor and Gwynna came down to the riverbank at dawn. It seemed to Wandor that life since they'd left Kerhab had been nothing but one dawn on a riverbank after another. This one was different. A breeze cooled the air, the night insects were asleep and the day ones not yet risen, and they'd come three miles straight south from the cave where Gwynna had broken the secrets of Beon-Kagri's Power and stripped his spell away from their flesh and bones.

Wandor didn't remember most of the details, doubted he wanted to remember them, and was sure they were now the least important thing in the world. In breaking Beon-Kagri's spell, Gwynna seemed to have nearly broken herself. She was pale and walked as though a cruel puppetmaster in her head was jerking her limbs along. Twice Wandor offered to carry her, and twice she refused. Wandor was half-glad of her refusal, for he was barely able to keep himself upright, let alone anyone else.

When he could make out colors on the flowers around them, Wandor realized they should get out of sight in case the river held enemies. He drew Gwynna behind two close-growing trees, and the last strength left both of them at the same moment. Wandor held her, and presently felt rather than heard or saw that she was weeping. He suspected that she was weeping from more than exhaustion, but knew he shouldn't press her for an explanation. Gradually she calmed, then spoke, and before long Wandor understood.

"What I did in the cave wasn't easy work," she said, wiping

her eyes on her sleeve. "Beon-Kagri is every bit as strong as we suspected. But everything I used against the spell in the end was something I already knew."

"Everything?"

"Everything. Most of it I've known for years, even before Yand. But I didn't *know* that I knew it, if you understand me."

Wandor wasn't sure he did. Gwynna continued in a brittle voice. "My Powers came to me when I was very young. I could do much with them, and I was proud of it. Zakonta warned me about that pride. Her grandmother even wanted to send me back across the Silver Mountains until I'd grown older."

Wandor now found something in Gwynna's words he could grasp. "It's—you were like a young Duelist who's either much faster or much stronger than the average. They usually have problems, thinking they can do it all with what nature gave them. A wise Master will hold them back, until they've learned that they need system and practice as well. If they aren't held back, they often die young."

He realized he'd said too much when Gwynna turned dead eyes to him and spoke softly. "Yes. Much like that. And I didn't die, but I think all the Power I used when I was too young has made me barren."

"It's too soon to—"

"After so many years? Is it? I wonder if the old woman was right, and Zakonta was wrong. If I'd been sent back—"

"If you'd been sent back, you'd have used your Powers with the same pride and even less guidance. None of us are very wise at fourteen, no matter what we're called on to do. As for your pride—you've much to be proud of."

"Not making myself barren. Not Chiero's death, or the other—"

"I *said* it's too soon to tell." Wandor wasn't tired enough to sit like moss on a rock and let Gwynna torture herself. "As for what's happened in Chonga, remember the Chongans' witless fear of northern sorcery. Remember all we could have lost if either you or Cheloth gave Cragor cause to call us oath-breakers. Remember how frightened I've been of your working with your—"

Green eyes turned hard as emeralds. "Bertan, I'm not a child to be led into a good temper with a handful of sweets. You know you've beaten down your fear of my Powers. By the time we left Kerhab, Kaldmor had already broken his oath. I could have done anything needed without frightening the

234

Chongans any more than they were already. I killed Chiero S'Rain as surely as if I stabbed him myself."

Wandor gave up. "We'll do him an honor service no one will forget, when we return."

Her head wobbled on her shoulders. "The best honor sh—service—it's to make sure this doesn't happen—again." When he was certain she was asleep, Wandor gently stretched her out on the grass, then covered her with his cloak and lay down beside her.

The Viceroyalty fleet went down the Mesti swiftly and unmolested. The heat grew damp, on the banks they heard priests chanting for rain, and there was a ring around the moon. But the rain did not come, the moon shone, and the fleet found safe ways around the sand banks and floating logs.

The lack of Chongan opposition was no surprise. Kobo's fleet and its master were still keeping watch on Shimarga, Zerun, and Kerhab. Only direct orders from Pirnaush could have welded the Dyrokans remaining on the Mesti into a force able to hold the northerners. There were bold captains in Pirnaush's service who under other circumstances would do what was obviously necessary without orders, but it was not obviously necessary to get oneself killed stopping the Viceroyalty men from leaving Chonga.

In fact, more than one of the Chongan captains who hailed Arlor's ship to learn the fleet's identity and destination was plain-spoken enough to say that he welcomed their departure.

"No one will say a word against your courage and war skill," one of them declared. "At least not where I can hear them. But your coming has the *Bassan* netted like a fish in six different plots, and we'll all be happier seeing an end to that. He needs the wisdom he's been too busy to show since you northerners came."

Arlor's main fear was of incidents provoked by Cragor's men or by Dyrokans in his pay. The Viceroyalty men were ready to avenge Wandor, Gwynna, and their dead comrades on any Chongan who gave them the slightest excuse, and to continue their vengeance until they could no longer swing their swords. Cragor's own men were still safely in the north, however, and his Dyrokan allies were too busy in the city. The Viceroyalty men kept their bows strung and their swords loose in their scabbards, but sailed down a river free of enemies.

In the darkness just after the watch change, when the second

235

day on the river became the third, Arlor stood amidships, too tired to sleep. He thought of wine, and remembered that there was none left except a few barrels reserved for the sick. He heard a voice calling softly, and turned to see one of the Tree Sisters who attended Cheloth of the Woods approaching.

"My Lord Count, Cheloth is awake and wishes to speak to you."

Since Nond's death Arlor had lost most of the power to be surprised. "How is he?"

"Well enough, I think," said the Khind woman. She hesitated. "I also think he has been awake for some time, but did not choose to make this known until now."

"Using his Powers?"

The woman shrugged. "Cheloth can easily shield his magic from us, and says little."

"He will speak to me," said Arlor. He followed the woman down the ladder to the hold, where Cheloth's stout-walled chamber filled one corner.

The sorcerer's door was ajar when Arlor reached it, with a trickle of reddish light creeping out. Arlor dismissed the Tree Sister and knocked.

"Count Arlor may enter."

Cheloth's voice was hoarse, like a man with a bad cold, and Arlor caught a heavy scent of spices. Inside the chamber, the air was not only scented but hazy with spice smoke, and the reddish light twisted colors. The sorcerer sat in his hanging chair, his head bowed, his hands clasped in his lap, and his legs locked rigidly enough to hold the chair completely still.

"You wished to speak to me," said Arlor. Cheloth silently raised one hand and pointed at the door, which promptly closed. "You wished to speak to me," the count repeated.

"Yes. I have news I must give to you first."

A cold hand closed on Arlor's loins. *Wandor and Gwynna are dead.* Now Cheloth's hoarseness made him think of a man who has wept until his throat is raw.

"Wandor and Gwynna are alive."

The cold hand unclasped so suddenly that Arlor had to clutch the door handle to keep from falling. "Alive?"

"Alive, far to the north. They—"

Arlor raised a hand, and the gesture silenced Cheloth. He was so surprised at the sorcerer's letting himself be interrupted by anyone except Gwynna that he forgot the words he'd been choosing. He didn't forget the thought: *There's more to come*

236

and it must be bad. He couldn't see any other reason for breaking the news here and now, except that—

"How long have you known this?"

Cheloth's silver-cased head rose. "Since a week after we took Kerhab."

Arlor's dagger came into his hands almost as if it had flown there. He took a step forward. All that kept him from the second step to within striking distance was Cheloth's passive silence. The sorcerer either had no need to ready himself for battle or no wish to, and the second notion shook Arlor more than the first. What lay behind whatever Cheloth had done or left undone, that he seemed ready to be sacrificed like a sow to Mother Yeza as punishment for it?

Arlor sheathed the dagger. Steel offered no answer. "Cheloth, whatever—" He fumbled for suitably harsh words, then gave up. "Cheloth, why in the name of all the gods did you do this?"

Something like a sigh came from the sorcerer. "The answer begins two thousand years ago, as you humans reckon time. It was—"

"Your duel with Nem of Toshak, after he defeated the Guardian of the Mountain and ended the line of the Five-Crowned Kings?"

"Yes. How—"

"Never mind how I knew. Just assume that I know more about sorcery than you have been willing to admit any human can know. Assume that *all* of us know more, and stop treating us like children. None of us will forget or forgive that again, not after this. We'd rather do without a sorcerer at all than deal with an arrogant, stubborn—"

"Yes."

The one word cut into Arlor's rage. The rage was quite satisfying, but it was teaching him nothing. "Your battle with Nem, you say?"

"Yes. May I show you?"

Arlor frowned. "You need to enter my mind?"

"Yes, but with nothing more than a form of the Mind Speech. Your mind will be your own at every moment." Arlor's frown deepened; Cheloth's tone sharpened. "Arlor, you do not care to forget or forgive what I have done. I cannot forget, and forgiving is something for humans. But both humans and I know the value of knowledge. Will you refuse to *know* what has happened, and why?"

237

"No." Arlor drew his dagger and held its point toward his throat. "But if I feel myself losing control of my own mind and body, I will stab myself. I do not think I could kill you even if I wished to, but I do not think you could save me either." He knew that he would be better off dead than to become Cheloth's puppet, or even to be rendered forgetful of what Cheloth might confess. Only if others—and above all, Wandor and Gwynna—knew what Cheloth had done, would there be any chance of keeping the sorcerer from doing it again.

"Very well," said Cheloth. He rose, motioned Arlor to sit down, then rested one hand on the count's shoulder. "Two thousand years ago there was a continent where the Tok'li Islands now lie. Its people . . ."

The cabin around Arlor faded into a gray mist. The mist lifted, and he looked down on a rolling, fertile green land. Rivers, streams, and canals curled around the bases of terraced hills, washed the foot of city walls built in blue brick, watered fields of crops Arlor had seen in Chonga—rice, Dead Man'. Thumb, ground nuts, sweetroot—and provided a path for scores of boats. The people at work in the fields, on the walls, in the streets and boats were a taller, darker version of the Chongans.

"They prospered," said Cheloth. "They even sent out colonists to settle the land to the north."

Arlor looked down on a log-walled town squatting on the bank of a river. By studying the hills behind the town, Arlor realized that it stood on part of what was now Old Dyroka. The hills were heavily forested, with only lonely huts and scattered fields where shops, houses, and temples now jostled each other. Further inland, there was only jungle instead of the Sea Jade Palace and the estates of the wealthy.

"They acknowledged the rule of the Five-Crowned Kings, and also had their own hereditary Defender. At this time, the Defender was Morkol Tecuri, who knew Beast Magic as well as war. After the overthrow of the last King, the leading men of the land wisely decreed absolute power for the Defender, for a term of three years. They knew war was coming."

A shaded patio appeared, with a green-tiled pool in the middle. Beside the pool a small brown man, hardly more than a youth and naked except for a tooled and jeweled leather loinguard, sat on silk cushions. Two slaves fanned him while he studied a scroll. More scrolls, bows, swords, and models of ships, siege engines, and castles littered the tiles around him.

"Nem of Toshak overthrew the Guardian of the Mountain. The Guardian still lived, but no longer in a form where he could aid men. I knew that Nem was not satisfied, that he would have Toshak become ruler of the world of men and then seek the rule of other worlds as well. He and I would meet, and sooner rather than later."

A fleeting image—Cheloth staring up at the slopes of a mountain. After a moment Arlor recognized the twin peaks of Mount Pendwyr, seen from an unusual angle. He recognized Cheloth's green clothing, but there was only a silvery mist in place of his helmet.

"I did not wear the helmet then, but it is not time for you to know my face."

"You read my thoughts."

"It was easy to read your thought: *Now I will see Cheloth's face.*"

"Show me what happened."

Another image. Arlor stiffened, suspecting his fear would be as easy to read as his curiosity had been. A deserted city, its buildings of granite blocks and slabs of purple marble still intact, but with even the fish in the ponds and the cats in the alleys stripped of life. Above a doorless gateway stood a man—the same man whose form and Powers walked again in Kaldmor's *limar*.

Nem of Toshak.

He wore purple robes, and jointed bracelets, collar, headband, and belt of polished silver. Each link was a geometrically perfect pentagram, and shimmered faintly from the Power lurking in it.

"Some of the Masters of Toshak who'd become part of Nem's bond still lived, though not in their bodies. Others were gone, their Powers sucked into Nem's like water into the sand of a desert. Everything else living in Toshak, human or animal, died to bring him victory over the Guardian."

"He was—what kind of victory—?"

"He was Nem of Toshak. He thought that when he had drawn all of the old Life into himself, with his Powers he could create a new Life according to his whims."

"He wanted—to be a—a *god*?"

"I would not quarrel with that way of describing Nem's desires."

Arlor was speechless, but once again his thoughts must have been easily read. Cheloth seemed sad. "Arlor, I ask you to believe that I cannot show you the battle between myself and Nem. It is not meant for human senses."

"I can—"

"Arlor, it is not a question of what you wish to know, or even have the right to know. It is a question of what you cannot learn without the learning killing you, or at least leaving you a mindless, senseless husk of flesh fit only to be tended like a baby until death is merciful enough to take you. You would lose much by this. Do not ask me again, Arlor."

An image—and Arlor sprang up with an oath. A curtained bed, and a woman whose blond hair spread soft and wide across a perfumed pillow. The woman turned toward him, raising one bare arm. "Arlor, my life..."

Anya, Anya. "Anya!" He cursed horribly. "Cheloth, you— twisting my mind with—" He had no words for the filthy thing the sorcerer had done; he could only hiss like a goose.

"I did not twist your mind. I have shown you the past. Sometimes I can also show a man the future, if it is one where his own thoughts can help my seeking through time." The idea of Cheloth's showing him a vision of a future with Anya dropped Arlor back into the chair as if he'd been clubbed. His anger faded, but he could not have found words to describe what took its place.

"I cannot show you how we fought, but I can tell you. We fought by drawing on all the Powers either of us could command, hurling them at each other without the least thought for what might happen elsewhere."

"Both of you?"

A sigh. "Both of us, myself as much as Nem."

"Ah."

"Yes."

Arlor saw a green fog and strange trees waving in that fog, then realized he was looking at the bottom of the sea. Silver and red fish darted past, then the whole scene shivered violently. A great boulder of coral rolled down the slopes, ripping the seaweed "trees" loose. A crack opened in the sea bottom, water found its way through to strike molten rock, and the scene burst apart in steam, bubbles, and mud.

"Earth holds its balance against Water only with difficulty at the best of times. If great Powers are drawing on the Earth, that balance will give way. This time it gave way in the south, and what the Chongans call the Old Land or the Sunken Lands vanished beneath the sea in two days and the night between them."

Images, coming so fast that Arlor forgot most of them. When he thought of the ones he remembered, he was glad.

—A hill, green and shining, with white flowers around its base—lovely, until he saw that the hill was a wave and the white flowers the foam as it marched across rice fields. It struck a village; suddenly the face of the wave was dotted with bits of thatch and broken timber.

—A smaller wave was marching up a canal, just as deadly in the confined space. A crowded torchlit boat rose on the wave and pitched end over end. The torches went out, but the darkness did not swallow the screams.

—A steep slope, with a road winding back and forth across it toward the top. From the base halfway to the top, the road was packed with carts, pack animals, and bundle-laden families on foot. Suddenly part of the road slipped down the hill, carrying its burden with it a little way before burying people and animals. Then a wave rose to lick the lower part of the slope clean. The survivors above panicked and the weak were pushed off, while below, the bodies and the wreckage floated away as the water receded for the moment.

—A boy, no more than twelve, struggled desperately to hold the head of an older woman, perhaps his mother, above water. The father paddled frantically toward them in a canoe, as the boy's hands slipped and the woman vanished. The father was almost up to his son when a black fin cut the water and foam and blood spread where the boy had been.

"Nine people out of ten in the Old Land were lost, and nearly all of its wealth. Most of those who survived, both there and in the Twelve Towns, owed their lives to Morkol Tecuri. He could not truly defend them against the rising of the waters, for there was no way to prevent it, and some would not believe him. Those who did believe went to work."

Now Arlor saw men in the Chongan forests building rafts for their household goods, driving their livestock to high ground, tying their boats with long ropes to trees high above the river. They did not look like doomed men, or at least not like men who would wait for doom to come to them.

"Morkol did his work well. The sea rose along the coast, and the rivers rose inland. But what would become Chonga survived, and even sent help to the south."

Three scenes, coming rapidly one after another:

—A long line of fishing boats, light galleys, and vessels Arlor recognized as ancestors of the *kulgha*, stretching across a twilight sea. Torches burned at the bow and stern of each boat.

—Dawn, and a family as naked as animals clinging to the roof of a floating house. They had barely the strength to shout as a fishing boat glided toward them out of a pearly mist.

—A camp on a riverbank, with strips of bark cloth on reed frames hung between trees to shelter the fugitives huddled below. Most of them were still nearly naked, but Arlor saw a Healer passing among them, followed by two men carrying steaming pots on shoulder yokes.

"Everything men could do to heal the damage done by the sinking of the Old Land was done, under Morkol's leadership. The work ended his life before he was forty, but he did not die before it was finished."

Another scene of the site of Dyroka—the log walls replaced by stone, wooden quays spreading along the bank, the familiar tangle of streets beginning to shape itself inside the walls. Inland, one hill after another lay bare, stripped to provide timber for the city or room for its growth. Then the gray mist flowed around Arlor, and when it cleared he saw Cheloth and the cabin.

"Morkol died, and his ashes were cast into the rivers. The Dragon Steed flew north into the Mountains of Kalgamm and out of human sight. I crossed the Ocean and aided Jagnar the Forest King to overthrow the Empire of the Blue Forest. After that I lay down in the Temple of the Dwarf God and slept until Bertan Wandor came seeking my aid."

Arlor felt as limp as if he'd been fighting all day in full armor. Cheloth drew something from a cask into a silver cup and handed it to the count. Arlor drank without tasting or even caring what he might be drinking. The drink was spicy and tasted of Chongan fruits; it restored him enough to listen attentively.

"Since the day the Old Land sank, I have never felt easy about what I did then, or about returning to Chonga. Yet I had to come, because my purposes and yours both demanded it.

"I came, but I could not forget. I felt shame, Arlor. Shame, and a sickness over what I had done, which grew every time I learned more of the Chongans' fear of sorcery. That fear is more real than even you can believe, Arlor."

The count nodded and found that he could speak. "So—

whenever it was a question of using your Powers against Kaldmor, you saw the Old Land sinking again?"

"Yes. Or at least this was so after the duel at the temple of Murorin, which I destroyed in my rage. The will a sorcerer brings to the use of his Powers is as important as the Powers themselves, and the will was not there."

He told the story of what had happened between the fall of Kerhab and the night of leaving Dyroka, without giving many details. Arlor did not press him for any. He believed the sorcerer, because he did not believe Cheloth would otherwise have revealed so much of his life, his shame, and the errors into which the shame led him. Even worse for the sorcerer, his errors meant that he had to admit them to Arlor, not to Wandor and Gwynna.

"The time came when I knew we might have to leave Dyroka and put ourselves beyond Pirnaush's reach, also beyond my reaching out to aid Wandor and Gwynna. I could still do nothing against Kaldmor, but I knew that I might do something useful against Beon-Kagri of Kerhab. Him I could study without much use of my Powers or any danger of Kaldmor's learning anything."

So Cheloth had gone underground, put himself into a trance, and reached out toward Beon-Kagri. The battle was longer and harder than he'd expected, but it had ended in victory. Beon-Kagri's tunnels collapsed as their binding spells faded, and he himself was left too weak to restore the spell on Wandor and Gwynna when it later was removed.

"In winning that victory, I weakened myself so that I knew I might not survive against Kaldmor if he used all his Power and knew where to strike me. So I returned to my chambers and once again entered a trance. It would be easy to find my body, but not the rest of me, which remained in the Power sphere."

"Couldn't Kaldmor guess where the rest of you was, if he learned about your body from spies?"

"Only Nem and I among sorcerers can find the Power of another sorcerer merely from knowing where his physical body lies." Cheloth seemed amused. "Also, if Kaldmor struck at me, he would have to leave off watching Dehass and probably offend Pirnaush as well. He would put in danger not only himself but his hopes of replacing Galkor at Cragor's right hand."

"True." *Thank the gods for Kaldmor's pride and Galkor's*

being in Benzos these past few months. Baron Galkor was born knowing more about intrigue than Kaldmor would learn if he lived a hundred years.

"When I came out of the trance, it was time to help Gwynna break Beon-Kagri's spell. I reached out to her only a few hours ago." The hoarseness was back in Cheloth's voice. "She broke the spell herself. With her own Powers and her knowledge of their use, Gwynna did all the work. I gave no help. She needed none. None."

The silence lasted long enough for Arlor to seek words which might ease the sorcerer's pain and shame, realize he wasn't going to find them, and decide that he wouldn't have said them anyway. Not while Wandor and Gwynna were still in the north, seeking what might not be there to be found.

They would have to stay there, too, whether or not the Dragon Steed flew out of legend to aid them. Pirnaush would let the Viceroyalty fleet return only if he knew Wandor and Gwynna lived, and what he knew, Kaldmor and Cragor would know as well. If Wandor and Gwynna remained hidden behind a fog of mystery, they would find it much easier to survive until their comrades in the south found allies and reinforcements.

However, there was no need for the fleet to go south in the belief they were leaving behind a Viceroy and his lady to be avenged. "Cheloth, in the morning I'll pass the word of this to—"

"No. Even if you swear everyone to silence, there are enough Chongans with traces of the Mind Speech to put the secret in danger. Not until we reach the Tok'lis."

"I won't let—" He nearly said, "I won't let our people weep to spare your pride or turn aside awkward questions." He shook his head. "Perhaps. But the captains must be told. They—"

"Even they could be read, Arlor. They have powerful minds, true, but the Mind Speech is subtle and not entirely understood. Unless I could enter their minds, one by one, and shield them against the Mind Speech? This is possible, and if they let me—"

Arlor groaned and rubbed eyes which seemed to be filled with red-hot sand. "You know the answer to that, Cheloth. They would only permit it if I told them beforehand why I was asking it—"

"—and they must be shielded before you tell them. Can't you—?"

"No, I can't order them."

"You mean you won't."

In another moment there would be no peace between them. Arlor started to rise, and found Cheloth's hands pressing him back into the chair. He began to struggle, then the sorcerer spoke.

"Arlor, forgive me. I have done much wrong. I will do no more, if I can help it. Perhaps I can even do some good, at least for you."

His grip on Arlor tightened, and gray mist swirled around the count again. He found himself in bed, with a quilt over him, perfume in his nostrils, and Anya's face on the pillow beside him. Her blond hair was tangled and damp, the wide mouth relaxed, almost slack. He remembered fierce loving not long past, knew there'd be more not far in the future. In the meantime there was the warmth of her body beside his—a warmth different from the warmth he'd felt in other shared beds. It seemed to be rising around him like a friendly tide, or else he was sinking down into it.

When Arlor's eyes closed and his mouth curved into a smile, Cheloth called men to take the count away to his own cabin.

The fleet passed Bezarakki in a rainstorm which had the priests out ringing gongs again, this time in praise to all the Eight Gods for the rain. Occasionally Dyrokan ships would slip out of the gray veils and challenge the fleet, but always let them pass after learning their business and course. Once again, no one was prepared to fight to keep the northerners in Chonga when they seemed to be peacefully removing themselves—not without orders from Pirnaush or Kobo. Two days out of Bezarakki the wind died, but the rain held and rowing even the overladen ships was not the ordeal it might have been.

A week later they'd dropped anchor in the bay at the northern end of Sow's Belly Island in the Tok'lis, and Arlor was being rowed across to Captain Thargor's greatship.

TWENTY-FIVE

The excitement in the fleet when Cheloth told his news was great, but did not last long.

Few believed that Cheloth was lying outright; fewer still trusted him completely. Also, the idea that Wandor and Gwynna were safe in the forests of northern Chonga did not come easily even to those who most trusted their ability to survive any and all perils. Finally, there was simply too much work to be done.

Cheloth retired into seclusion on the island, after publicly swearing to follow Wandor's and Gwynna's wishes in the matter of telling the rest of his story. The men of the river fleet moved aboard the more capacious greatships and started catching fish, or landed to start building huts, store-houses, and catch basins for rainwater. Sentries were posted on all the ships, on boats rowing around the anchorage, and all around the island. The nearest Chongan fort was a half-rotted relic with fewer than three hundred fit men, but it was only three days' easy sailing away in a small boat. Everyone knew that one spy escaping might be death for Wandor and Gwynna, and nobody grudged the effort involved in this vigilance.

"Indeed," said Master Besz, "the problem will be to keep the men from tearing comrades apart on the mere suspicion of spying."

In Chonga:

Cragor brought his men south to Dyroka, thanked Kaldmor in public and Dehass in private, and set to work. He found that without orders from Pirnaush, the Dyrokans were no more willing to risk a fight with his men than with Arlor's. Since he couldn't know how long this would last, he found it best to have his men walk as softly as their sense of being victors would let them.

The duke did openly place under his protection the survivors of the men who'd help drive Arlor out of Dyroka. Scores of Dyrokans thus escaped the consequences of things they'd done not only to the Viceroyalty men but to their fellow Dyrokans. Kaldmor did not care for this, but could not see that his master had much choice. The Chongans had an exceptionally acute eye for the balance of risk and profit; if the duke did not exert himself to tilt the balance in favor of profit, few Chongans would risk much for him. Dehass also publicly agreed that the duke had no choice, but privately rejoiced at seeing the duke make enemies in Dyroka while trying to protect his friends.

Pirnaush gave no orders against any northerners because he had no wish to fight them until he'd settled matters with his fellow Chongans. This was proving to be more difficult than anyone had expected. Kerhab itself was held down by a garrison strong enough to squash any signs of resistance like a cockroach. The forests to the north and west still swarmed with Kerhabans, and it was said that if you went far enough to the north you might even find Shimargans secretly aiding the Kerhabans.

None of Pirnaush's men got far enough to find out for certain. Scouts entering the forests either didn't come back at all or came back minus half their strength. Once *Hu-Bassan* Meergon himself led the scouting party, and while this one returned, it also brought Meergon back with a poisoned arrow in one knee. Sheer toughness and a good Healer saved his leg, but did not restore him to his master's service quickly.

Eventually Pirnaush decided that he could hold Kerhab and overawe Zerun with his army alone, as long as the men could retreat eastward to the valley of the Mesti if they had to. Shimarga had only a small fleet, so most of Kobo's ships and their men could sail down to the Ocean and be free for other service. The couriers started riding out with the necessary orders.

Hawa nursed Mitzon back to health in a village on the west bank of the Mesti, half a day's sailing below Dyroka. Soldiers kept coming and going, but Hawa feared only Telek, and their friends said he seemed to be spending most of his time in

Kerhab or in Dyroka itself. They could not be much safer unless they fled to the Tok'lis, which Mitzon refused to consider.

In Benzos:
Word that Wandor and Gwynna were dead spread rapidly among those who cared about the matter.

The Grand Master of the Duelists always spoke of "their disappearance" rather than "their death." "Until someone sees the bodies, I won't say they're dead," he told one trusted young Master.

"Will everyone in the Order have your faith?" said the Master.

Gray eyebrows rose. "They'd better, or else remain silent. Anyone who lifts a finger in the belief Wandor is dead will answer to me."

Queen Anya continued to perfect her archery and supervise the royal household. Now that Lady Helda was dead, she seemed to have no other interests. It was noted, however, that whenever she did make a remark on some larger matter, it was an intelligent and judicious one. Some who heard her praised the continued soundness of the blood of the House of Nobor, although they were always careful to emphasize that they were thinking of Anya's children by Cragor, rather than of the queen herself. Others, more cynical, simply assumed the queen had found her own spies.

Baron Galkor agreed with the cynics, but refused their requests to help hunt for Anya's spies. They might be anywhere or anybody, and he had other and more urgent matters to deal with. A small army of reinforcements for Cragor in Chonga had to be gathered, equipped, loaded aboard ships, and sent off, and Galkor's share of this work was big enough for six men.

For a while he was spending a third of each day meeting with nobles and captains, a third inspecting troops, ships, animals, and equipment, and a third in the saddle. When he staggered up one castle's stairs at dawn, red-eyed and unshaven, a steward stopped him.

"My Lord Baron, when did you last sleep?"

The reply was a thin-voiced "Sleep?"

The force grew and grew, until Galkor had more than six thousand men and ships to carry them. He decided that it would be best if he went south himself. So many of the men who'd held aloof until now were going to Chonga that there would hardly be enough prospective enemies left for a drinking party, let alone a conspiracy. Galkor would have been flattered at the prospect of leading so many grandsons of dukes and counts, and him the grandson of a slave, but he knew the sudden rush of men had little to do with his merits. It had much more to do with the news of Wandor's and Gwynna's death. It was now possible to believe that the Black Duke was on the edge of victory in Chonga, and many wanted to be remembered as having helped him deliver the last few blows.

In the north along the Ponan border, Count Ferjor launched raid after raid with the united bands, both before and after the news came. Most of the men under him and Hod ranFedil had long since burned all their bridges; Cragor could not kill them twice. Only a few knew that Count Ferjor sometimes walked alone in the forest, weeping or cursing or both.

One of the raids killed the captain over Cragor's soldiers in the mid-border country. He'd been brave and skilled enough, but foul-tempered and fond of torturing prisoners. He was not greatly mourned, but until another man was sent in his place it was not clear who commanded along this stretch of the Nifan.

Of the five surviving captains, Tagor was the youngest but knew the country the best. He might have become the chief captain, but he refused even to try for the post.

"Why?" asked Jaira one night, when she'd learned of his lack of ambition.

"Safer, Jaira. Much safer. Best thing for me is to be big enough to protect myself and you, not so big somebody's going to notice me or get jealous."

"But if you are captain over the whole land, can't you stay in the duke's service after the war?"

Tagor laughed and pulled Jaira down beside him. "Gods, woman! Are you that fond of living around soldiers?"

The news reached the Viceroyalty some time after the new fleet of reinforcements sailed for Chonga. Streets and houses were filled with the sounds of weeping, temples with the sounds of prayer.

Jos-Pran and Zakonta were only a few days from their wedding, but thought seriously of putting it off. "This news is a bad omen for starting anything new," said Jos-Pran. "We could be putting a curse on our children." Zakonta would have disagreed with him if she could; the thought of her hopes falling apart now made her want to scream, even in her grief and fear for Wandor and Gwynna. Her knowledge told her that Jos-Pran might be right.

Baron Delvor saved them. If he wept over the news, he did so alone. But one night after dinner, muddleheaded from grief or wine, he became so dizzy that he had to be put to bed. He slept late, and when he woke he called the two Yhangi to his bedside.

"You people think this is cause to stop your wedding. You're wrong. I don't know your Red Seer witchcraft, Zakonta, but I do know my daughter. Maybe I know her even better than you. Just because she's gone doesn't mean she's dead. No one will put her in the House of Shadows until she's ready to go. Bertan's the same, or she wouldn't have taken him.

"Even if they're dead, it's not so bad an omen. Not if they died well, and they wouldn't do anything else. Whatever Yhang custom says, I say you go and marry."

Jos-Pran smiled in spite of himself. "Is that your command, as Viceroy?"

"If you want to call it that, yes it is."

So Jos-Pran and Zakonta gripped the lance and drank the wedding ale after all, in spite of the long faces at the short feast.

Wandor and Gwynna sought the Dragon Steed of Morkol.

They took their canoe up a tributary of the Hiyako until it became a creek, then up the creek until it became only a stream flowing over patches of mud and gravel. There they picked a well-hidden spot for a permanent camp; without the dragon they'd be spending the winter here in the north. They hid the canoe and everything else they couldn't hope to carry on their backs, made themselves rough snowshoes, and started on the long walk north.

At first it was almost an idyll. The days were warm and the nights cool, and there was plenty of game. As they dressed out each day's kill and retrieved the arrowheads, they considered what it was they sought in the north. Not much had survived about the Dragon Steed, most of what had survived was legend, and Wandor privately doubted much of what was called truth. However, when one examined the story from all sides, it went something like this:

Morkol Tecuri the Defender was a master of Beast Magic, as skilled as any of the Beast Wizards of Yand Island or the Blue Forest and much more honest. He used his Powers to improve the livestock and pond fish of the Old Land, and made only one creature for his own use. Always traveling between the Twelve Towns and the Old Land, he wanted a faster way of making the journey than a ship.

So he created the Dragon Steed, which carried him from Dyroka to the shore of the Old Land in half a day. The scales on its body were ruddy brown on the belly and pale brown on the back, and blue green feathers gleaming like jewels covered its wings. The eyes were golden, it did not breathe fire, and it could eat an entire cow at a meal. It was even said that Morkol held Mind Speech with the dragon, as though it had the wisdom of a man or at least more than that of a beast.

All the tales about the dragon's size had in Wandor's ears the sound of men either frightened out of their wits or trying to make a good story even better. Its body was as long as a small ship, and its wings larger than the ship's sails, while its head was as large as a man's body.

"I don't doubt that it was larger than anything else that ever flew," said Wandor. "But that big?"

"It carried Morkol on its back."

"Morkol was supposed to be a small man. What was needed to carry him?"

"I don't know," said Gwynna. "I do know that I saw the Beasts of Yand from as close as you did. I also know more about the sort of magic which created both the Beasts and the Dragon Steed. I won't doubt anything about the dragon until I've seen it."

Wandor did not add to himself *if we see it*, and wondered why. Was it that the Guardian of the Mountain had never yet sent him questing for that which did not exist? Or was it that he simply didn't want to believe that he and Gwynna were off on a wild dragon-chase? Certainly he found the rest of the Dragon Steed's legend no easier to believe than the first part.

The Dragon Steed was a great help to Morkol in all the work he did when the Old Land sank and Chonga became a new homeland. When Morkol died, the dragon watched by his funeral pyre until the last ashes grew cold. Then it leaped into the sky, circled three times, and flew north as fast as it had ever traveled. Some hunters in the north saw it circling again, above a tall three-peaked mountain. Then it flew onward again, apparently still bound north, and no human eye had seen it since. Later chroniclers identified the three-peaked mountain as Mount Reakka, the southernmost of the great summits of the Mountains of Kalgamm, but added nothing else to the tale.

"At least we know how to reach Mount Reakka," said Wandor. "Perhaps we can even do it." Their map suggested that they could cover most of the distance to the mountain without climbing out of the forest with its water and game. The mountain might not be the end of their search, but it would certainly be the best place to begin it.

They came in sight of the three peaks of Mount Reakka after thirteen days of walking and thirteen steadily colder nights of huddling by small fires. The trees grew thinner, and there seemed to be something lacking in the very air they breathed. The game was still abundant enough to feed two people who could catch and eat almost anything. Some of the animals and birds acted as if they'd never seen a human being, let alone a hunter, in their lives.

Perhaps they hadn't. This land was seldom visited, probably not visited at all since Pirnaush's great wars began twenty years ago. There were passes across the Mountains of Kalgamm into the Heshar Desert, but these were seldom used and all of them were far to the south and east of Mount Reakka. North of its three peaks, the mountains of Kalgamm marched off in an unexplored wilderness of rock, snow, and ice, stretching no one knew how far and rising no one dared to guess how high. Of course, this made the mountains a nearly ideal hiding place for a large creature which shunned men. If the Dragon Steed really had more than a beast's wits, it might very well have known this, and so—

No! Wandor shook his head. *I have enough trouble believing the legend as it is. I won't try adding my own fancies to it.*

On the sixteenth day of their march, they came to the foot of Mount Reakka. Unlike the hunters of the dragon's legend, they camped outside its shadow, to catch what little sun the day offered, but close enough to the mountain so that it broke the rising wind. Mount Reakka was a magnificent sight, the three peaks all crowned with snow and the valley between them half-filled with a glacier. It was even somewhat terrifying, when the wind blew hard enough so that one heard the moan from the distant crags. Wandor understood perfectly why men doubted that everything about Reakka and the other mountains to the north was entirely natural. For all this, nothing he saw, heard, or felt gave him the slightest hint of what to do next.

Gwynna usually had an idea if he didn't, so he turned to her. "End of the quest?" He spoke aloud. There might be no Chongans to listen to their Mind Speech, but there might be something even less friendly bound into the rocks around them.

"Do you want it to be the end?"

Both her face and her voice had grown sharper the past few days. Wandor didn't blame her, hoped the long march after great sorcery hadn't drained her strength, and knew he couldn't ask her outright.

"I don't want it to be the end unless it *is* the end. Is it?"

Gwynna sighed and lay face down on the leather blanket spread across the rocks. Wandor reached to massage her legs, then realized she was trying to read any magic which might be lurking in the earth. Hoping she wouldn't have to strip herself bare to the rising wind, he rose and stood back. It seemed a long time before she sighed again and sat up, frowning.

"I'm no more sure than you are. The legends are right, though. Reakka is a place of magic. Very old magic, I think, and either very weak or some kind I can't read." She stared at the sky as she often did, trying to catch some elusive memory. "It is said that there used to be such things as natural—oh, call them *wells*—of Earth Power. Sorcerers and creations of Beast Magic could sometimes draw on them. But they were always rare. Most of them were destroyed when Cheloth and Nem fought, and the rest died with the passage of time. I'd always heard of them as a legend, so I never learned how to deal with them."

"That isn't something—"

"I should torture myself about?" She smiled. "I feel foolish, all the same. Here I am, with what might be one of the great discoveries in magic in our day, and I can't even tell whether we're near the center or on the edge of the well!"

Wandor started stretching the cloaks which did double duty as improvised tents between two boulders. "It seems to me that we can try finding the center on foot. We'll cast around in the mountains, keeping Reakka in sight. You can read the ground as often as you need, and judge the strength of the magic. By the time we've gone completely around Reakka, you should have a better picture of the well."

"I might. And if the Dragon Steed is still alive—an Earth Well is the best place to start looking. Even if it isn't laired up within the circle of the well, it might be close by. A creature of Beast Magic should be able to draw on the well for strength no matter how old it is."

"If it hasn't come to feed like a natural animal."

"I don't think it does. A beast the size of the dragon would have eaten half the game in this land and made the rest as wary as mice in a kitchen."

"Yes. If—" He broke off, shook his head, and laughed.

"If what, Bertan?"

"I was just thinking something very foolish. How are *we* going to feed the dragon if it comes to us?"

"Don't call that a foolish thought. Not yet."

TWENTY-SIX

As usual they started off at dawn on their fourth day in the mountains. Gwynna read the ground and said they were still within the limits of the well, and Wandor sent a Mind Speech message into the cold sky without getting an answer. They'd done the same several times during each of the last three days.

When they started off, they could easily see the three peaks of Reakka to the southwest. By midmorning the peaks were gone and so was half the sky, behind gray clouds marching in from the north. By what might have been noon they could see neither peaks nor sky, and the first few flakes of snow whirled down on the wind. They stopped, ate dried meat and rice biscuits, read the ground and called the sky, and moved on again.

By midafternoon they could see barely two hundred paces in the swirling snow and a sullen twilight. Gwynna stopped, brushed the snow from her hood, and shook her head. "I think we'd better look for a cave or a cleft while we can still find one. This storm can't do us much harm unless we're foolish enough to tramp around in it until we're exhausted."

"You think it's going to last?"

"Two days, at least."

He was willing to follow her lead. She knew the Silver Mountains in the Viceroyalty, and like the mountains of Kalgamm they were high enough to make their own weather. They had food for two days' sitting and waiting, with enough left over for the march out to open ground, and there would always be ice for water.

Before the light failed they found a cleft driven so deeply into the face of a rocky slope that toward the rear it was almost a cave. With their leather cloaks they could cover a portion large enough to hold both of them. By the time they'd made camp, both minds and bodies were screaming for rest, and they promptly fell asleep.

On the third day of the storm, Wandor began to feel he'd seen something like its steady, implacable work before. On the fourth day he remembered where. He'd been a young Duelist then, just advanced from apprentice. The Trorim House was invited to attend an exhibition of weaponscraft featuring several visiting Masters.

One of them was a very ordinary man, in size, appearance, and even in the pattern of scars on his face and arms. He was neither particularly strong nor particularly fast, but he was precise, unhurried, and indefatigable. An opponent could meet a hundred of his attacks, then the hundred and first would break through a defense which was no longer able to meet it. Meanwhile, the Master neither spoke nor smiled, and hardly seemed to sweat.

The snowstorm was like that Master. It had no howling winds or bitter cold, it merely went on piling up snow, to the depth of Wandor's waist and then deeper. Nothing its victims could do seemed likely to make much difference to their ultimate fate; it would only make a difference in the manner of their dying.

Certainly there was nothing they could do about traveling while the snow still fell. Even the snowshoes hadn't helped much when Wandor tried them on the second day. After two hundred paces he nearly fell into a hidden crevice wide enough to swallow a horse. After four hundred paces he was so completely lost that only Gwynna's Mind Speech helped him fight down panic and struggle back to the shelter, to be stripped of his sodden clothes and warmed by her body under the furs.

The fifth day came, and Wandor knew they were going to have to break out of the mountains soon, even through the storm. If they didn't, they could be too weak to reach the forest even if they struggled through the drifts. At the same time, he was desperately reluctant to simply turn his back on the well and plunge into the storm. They'd also be turning their backs on the Dragon Steed—

"—at least until spring, and the gods only know what could happen between now and then."

Gwynna sat up. "Bertan, I've been reading the ground here more thoroughly than I did while we were on the march. If we are going to try calling the Dragon Steed, we should do it from here."

"I've been using the Mind Speech every time I felt I could send a clear message. Nothing's happened."

"I think we'll need more than the Mind Speech. Or at least the Mind Speech will need some help."

"From the well?"

"And from us."

She explained. They were close to the center of the well. The Earth Power would almost certainly grow weaker if they moved on, and they would need it to call the Dragon Steed. From everything Gwynna knew or could reasonably assume about the well, the Dragon Steed, and magic in general, the dragon did draw heavily on the well. It was a creature of magic, and if a sorcerer wasn't on hand to work on the spells built into its substance, it needed to take magic from a natural source. The Mount Reakka well was probably the only one in this part of the world; if it was, the dragon must either lair up within the limits of the well or visit it at intervals.

"How long between visits?"

"Perhaps years, perhaps centuries." Wandor swallowed, both at the sheer size of the world beyond the world and at Gwynna's ease with it.

"I don't think the Dragon's in the well itself. It would have heard your Mind Speech. So the Dragon Steed should be somewhere in the mountains, not within the well but continuously *aware* of the well, its magic, and any changes in that magic. Wandor's Mind Speech, hurled out into the mountains by the magic from the well, would be such a change, one which should bring the dragon if it lived at all."

Unfortunately, the Mind Speech was not true magic, drawing on Powers. Wandor could not link his Mind Speech directly to the well except through Gwynna. But Gwynna could link herself to the well on one hand and to Wandor on the other. The magic of the well could reach Wandor through her, and her own Powers could help shape its work and perhaps even increase its strength. With this double linking, Wandor's Mind Speech could fly out to the dragon with ten, twenty, fifty times its normal strength.

"Even if the dragon doesn't understand a message, it will understand that something is disturbing the source of the magic it needs. It will come to learn if there's any danger."

Wandor thought he understood. With the double linking, his Mind Speech would be like a catapult mounted on a siege tower, or an archer perched in a tree. Raised higher, it could reach farther.

"Yes. That's the logic of it." Gwynna started unhooking her jacket. Knowing that he'd understood the logic of what he was facing eased Wandor less than usual. This time he would not be the willing *object* of magic brought into existence by Gwynna's Powers, controlled by her knowledge, and hopefully responding to her hard-won skills. Both his Mind Speech and her Powers would work with and be worked on by a source of magic entirely outside themselves and almost outside Gwynna's knowledge and experience. He did not need Mind Speech to know that she was frightened herself, and grimly aware of the amount of guesswork and improvisation she would need in a matter where both were dangerous. Gwynna was shivering from more than the chill in the cave by the time she lay huddled under the furs, waiting for Wandor to finish undressing. He stroked her hair.

"How—"

"Dangerous?" She shrugged. "I can't be sure. I do think I can control the link or if necessary break it before there's any danger to you."

"To *either* of us." Their eyes met in mutual understanding, if not in complete agreement, and Wandor sighed. If Gwynna really thought she could save him by sacrificing herself, she would do it, and use all her skill to hide what she was doing until it was too late. He couldn't really resent this, since he knew he would do exactly the same thing if the situation was ever reversed.

Wandor helped Gwynna sit up. "I know we can do this once," she said. "I think we can do it a second time, if we're willing to gamble on reaching the dragon. Otherwise we should make this effort our only one, and save our strength for the walk out." Wandor was silent. Gwynna might know it anyway, but he didn't want to admit that he'd rather die in the storm than in the grip of magic gone wrong. In this, King Wandor and Duelist Wandor were united.

Gwynna sat with her knees up, legs apart, hands on her knees, and gooseflesh all over her dirt-darkened skin. "Lean back against me, until the top of your head is touching my throat."

Wandor found he could just hold the position without throwing his full weight back on Gwynna. "Like this?"

"Yes. It's the best position I know of, for closely linking two people working with high Earth Powers."

Wandor felt Gwynna's flesh cold against his, then felt the rise and fall of her breasts steadying as she brought her breathing under control. Her hands slipped into place, thumbs just above his ears and fingers curling forward to cover his eyes. He closed them.

"No." A sleepy voice. "Leave them open."

Silence, except for Gwynna's slow breathing. Wandor found his own matching hers without his willing it. He began to form the Mind Speech pattern he'd used in the past, a simple picture of the dragon flying with him and Gwynna on its back. He hoped his image of the dragon was accurate. He'd taken it from a painting made at least five centuries after Morkol's death.

"Not yet," in a still sleepier voice. "When you do—again—*call*."

A familiar light filled the shelter as Gwynna's hair began to glow. Then the glow and everything else drifted away into a cool darkness. Deep inside that darkness Wandor sensed veins filled with warmth; still deeper inside it was Gwynna's voice saying:

("Now.")

Come to him who seeks you, thought Wandor.

("Stronger, as though you were talking to me.")

("Come, dragon. I seek you. I need you. I shall work with you as Morkol did.")

("Yes. Like that.")

("Come. Come. Come, dragon. I call you to me. Come. Come. Come.")

With part of his mind Wandor called, over and over again. With another part he reached down into the cool darkness toward the veins of living warmth. He felt the darkness against his skin, and realized that it was rock.

He touched the veins—except that his hands seemed to be Gwynna's; he recognized the scar on one thumb and the twisted nail on a little finger—and the veins writhed sluggishly, like basking snakes disturbed. He drew some of the warmth out of the veins and into his own body, and willed it to flow upward into his head. As it did, the ("Come, dragon. Come!") became so loud that he expected echoes, as if he was shouting madly into a vast cave.

("Come, dragon. Morkol's work must be finished. I have come to finish it, but I need your help.)

("Come.)

("Come.)

("Come?")

It wasn't exactly the word. It was more like the *idea* of something moving from farther away to closer at hand. It was also so faint that for a moment Wandor thought it was only the echo he'd expected.

("Come!")

(The faint idea again.)

("Dragon!") Wandor felt like screaming with his body as well as his mind.

("Why?") Again it was more of an idea than a word.

("Come.") Gwynna's hands which were also his clutched at the warmth flowing from the veins in the rock and squeezed it until it pulsed and sprayed sparks like resin-rich wood in a fireplace.

A new image now: Mount Reakka, seen as if from a mountain still higher. Clouds trailed gray capes over it, and the wind whipped feathers of snow into the sky. Wandor felt a cold which seemed to banish the very idea of warmth plucking at him like tiny pincers and slashing at him like tiny knives. He felt Gwynna begin to shake in both body and mind, heard her cry out with both.

("Come!") he howled.

Silence. Then the silence of the world beyond the world gave way to the sounds of the shelter—the sigh and hiss of the storm outside, two pairs of lungs fighting for air, Gwynna sobbing. Wandor tried to sit up and fell backward helplessly, carrying Gwynna with him. His head found its usual place between her breasts, and he beat off the wave of comfort this sent through him.

He managed to drag himself into most of his clothes, and Gwynna into some of hers. Then he pulled her against him, pulled the furs over both of them, and stopped fighting the desire to sleep.

Wandor awoke feeling oddly warm, as though he'd slept next to a brazier of hot coals. He crawled out of the furs and peered through the gap under the tent. The snow had stopped, and it was nearly dark. They must have slept most of the day. Then he saw that the darkness had a subtle but unmistakable edge. Beyond that edge, the snow was pale gray. Wandor took a deep breath, considered waking Gwynna, then on hands and knees crawled into the open.

Beyond the shadow was the grayness before dawn, not the grayness of evening. The shadow itself was cast by a wing the size of a *kulgha*'s sail stretched across the cleft. Wandor rose to his feet, stepped out of the shadow, and watched as the Dragon Steed of Morkol turned its head to look at him.

The head was indeed larger than a man's body, with a horn on top and a shorter horn over each eye. The eyes—yes, you could say that they were golden and leave it at that. You could also go on describing them and all the colors in them which seemed to have been left by what they'd seen, until you had no breath left.

The dragon lowered its—no, *his*; a creature with those eyes was not an "it"—head toward him. It was within easy reach before Wandor gathered his courage to pat the scaled muzzle. The touch flooded Wandor's mind with emotions and images— more warmth (and now he understood why he'd felt warm on awakening), a strength which was magnificent and terrible at the same time, quiet courage mixed with doubts over facing a world grown two thousand years older, and finally a clear picture: the dragon in flight, with two men riding on either side, just above the forelegs.

Wandor thought a question at the dragon. The dragon wanted to fly as soon as possible, but how were Wandor and Gwynna supposed to hold on? Even through his gloves and boots, Wandor felt the cold at work.

The dragon opened his mouth, sending out a wave of amusement and warm spicy breath, and confronting Wandor with an impressive array of stained teeth and a coal-black tongue. The teeth had broad edges, like carpenter's chisels, rather than needle points, but those edges looked as sharp as swords. Again the image of the dragon in flight reached Wandor, with a note of irritation in it.

As Wandor stood blank-faced, the dragon apparently realized his message wasn't getting through. He folded his wings and shifted position, gripping rock with his shorter forelegs while he moved his longer hindlegs. For a creature who really was the size of a small ship, the movement was careful, almost delicate. It still dislodged several tons of snow, which plummeted into the cleft and completely buried the tent with Gwynna inside.

Wandor let out a howl of pure anguish, like a wolf seeing his mate taken by the hounds. The dragon quivered all over, then shifted position again until he could cling to the edge of the cleft with one hindleg and both forelegs, his tail drooping down into the cleft. Then the scaly hide quivered like the head of a drum as the muscles of back and hindquarters tightened. A moment later, Wandor found himself completely swallowed in a cloud of the snow the dragon was hurling out of the cleft with furious strokes of his tail. In another moment, he half-expected to see her come flying through the air like a bird, along with the snow.

Gwynna staggered out of the cleft, except for her hair, nearly as white as a children's snowman. She opened her mouth to spit out snow and curses, then closed it abruptly as she saw the reason for her rude awakening. Slowly she brushed the snow away, but the face underneath stayed white.

Again the dragon showed himself in flight, and at the same time pointed to his back with a five-clawed foreleg. At last Wandor saw what he'd been meant to see. Along the dragon's spine ran low vertical plates, set in threes. Holes were drilled clean through two sets of plates. When the image of the dragon in flight came again, Wandor could see hints of some sort of carrying harness, held in place by ropes through the holes in the spinal plates. The men rode forward of the wings, their weight balanced by the hindquarters and tail.

It took a good deal of guesswork, and after that much slashing with knives held in stiffening hands, before Wandor and Gwynna had enough leather strips for their purposes. One set of strips went through the rear holes, to make loops for their feet. Two more sets met in the middle, to support waistbands padded with fur.

Wandor sat in the snow by the piled harness, tying knots on top of knots until he found himself staring into a pair of golden eyes the size of drinking bowls. The dragon rumbled low in his throat, and Wandor sensed a mixture of emotions in which irritation and eagerness to be gone stood out most clearly.

Gwynna finished digging their weapons out of the snow and joined Wandor in tying the harness in place on the dragon. All around them was frozen stillness, shapes blurred by the snowdrifts, with a dreary sky overhead. Wandor couldn't see Mount

Reakka, or anything else to tell him that they were still in the world where they'd gone to sleep, rather than transported by the dragon's own magic into some other world where he had lived these past two thousand years.

This might be what had happened, but Wandor doubted it. *You came to our call*, he thought, as he settled into place on the dragon's flank. *You saved Gwynna. You told us what we needed to know to ride you. We trust you.* He didn't know if his words could be understood, but what lay behind them seemed to reach the dragon. He got back understanding, almost affection—and once again, impatience to be gone.

Very carefully, Wandor projected the image of the dragon in flight, with himself and Gwynna in their places. Just as carefully, the dragon sought a patch of firm snow, spread his wings, and crouched down. Wandor felt a hurricane's wind around him, an earthquake's shock under him, and through the swirling cloud of snow he saw the ground suddenly falling away.

The dragon's wings thrashed hard, then found a steadier rhythm, and he rose into the cold sky.

TWENTY-SEVEN

As the dragon climbed above the cliff top, Mount Reakka appeared in the distance. A moment later Wandor's stomach rebelled against the new sights and sensations of flight. With the wind roaring in his ears he couldn't hear if Gwynna was also suffering, but knew that the dragon felt more amusement than anything else at his riders' sickness.

The dragon climbed steadily as he flew toward the mountain, and at first Wandor found it best not to look down. Then the dragon made a complete circle around the mountain, just below the summits. Forcing himself to look, Wandor recognized that the picture he'd seen while they were trying to call the dragon was simply Mouth Reakka from the sky. The dragon had been trying to ask where the people calling him might be.

Wandor realized that this must be the way the dragon spoke to others. He sent pictures and feelings—amusement, anger, impatience, no doubt many others—into their minds and received the same from them. He suspected that before much longer he'd need Gwynna's help in talking to the dragon. This way of talking held as much of true magic as it did of Mind Speech.

Then fear was in him again as the dragon soared into the clouds over the mountain. A clinging wet grayness was all around him, nothing had any shape or form, and for a moment he lost all sense of direction and even of up or down. His stomach knotted, and when he licked his lips he felt ice on them. Then the dragon climbed out of the clouds, and fear vanished as Wandor saw the sky world for the first time.

267

The clouds rolled away toward the rim of the world in ranges of gray and white hills, the crests silvered by the rising sun and the valleys still deep in purple-tinted shadow. Far away on the rim, a great pool of gold and orange and crimson was spreading across the cloud crests, and above, a flawless sky held all the colors men had named and many more only the gods had seen. Then the sun leaped above the cloud crests, gold and orange flame dazzled Wandor, and he looked away.

He would have looked away even if he hadn't been dazzled. This sky world—it was part of the same world as the ground, now farther below him than Wandor cared to think. It was also a world of its own, where men the gods allowed to enter at all should come with the sense of how great it was and how small they were.

("It's like the world the gods saw on the First Morning,") came Gwynna's thoughts. ("They've separated the World from Chaos, but no more.")

Wandor would have replied, but the lack of vitality in this high air was making him gasp for breath and was slowing his thoughts. He had to give the dragon a direction and a destination. Somewhere in the south . . . Slowly he decided on Kerhab. Even more slowly and with much trouble, he sent the dragon images of the city—the clearest map he could remember and a view of the city's walls from the river.

The dragon wheeled in a vast circle, one wing high, until Wandor found himself swinging out over empty space and cloud crests. Then the dragon straightened out, and from the position of the sun, Wandor knew they were now headed south.

A long formless time followed, with nothing Wandor remembered afterward except diving back into the clouds. When the world took shape around him again, they were flying over what seemed to be the treeless foothills of the mountains of Kalgamm. He managed to twist his neck, and saw the three peaks of Mount Reakka far behind them.

Wandor and Gwynna still had to use the Mind Speech; the wind-roar of the dragon's flight made anything else impossible. Wandor only hoped the dragon wouldn't listen.

("Kerhab?") It was Gwynna's question. ("Why not straight to the Tok'lis?")

("I want the word spread that the Dragon Steed flies again. It will spread from Kerhab as fast as from anywhere else. Also, we owe the Kerhabans a debt.")

She was satisfied. Wandor looked down, and noticed that

the grass on some of the hilltops was pale with frost. It would soon be late in the year for any sort of campaign, although it would be later still before the Viceroyalty men could move in force. They would still move, however. He had to pay as much of his debt to the Kerhabans as he could, and there were debts owing to other Chongans as well.

They were back over the valley of the Hiyako by mid-morning, flying south under a watery sun. Mist still clung to the low places, and Wandor gave up thinking of seeking their canoe and heavy equipment. He could now tell land from water, forest from open ground, and hills from valleys, but he could hardly tell one patch of forest from another.

As the mist burned off the river, they passed over an oddly-shaped clearing, which Wandor suddenly realized must be some city's northern outpost. Rectangles must be huts, a smoke-belching square might be a smithy or cookhouse, irregular lines could be a log wall with perhaps a ditch at its foot. He was tempted to have the dragon descend and circle, but decided not to take the time. Friend or foe, the soldiers would at least have the unexpected and unsought honor of being the first to know that Morkol's dragon flew again.

He had the dragon circle high over Kerhab when they reached it around noon. Wandor didn't know how high one of the big Dyrokan siege bows would shoot if it was aimed vertically, and didn't want to find out at the dragon's expense. The dragon's reply to that decision was unmistakable—relief, and praise for his caution.

Pirnaush's siege camp was virtually abandoned. A new fortified camp commanded the road to the east, and earthworks stretched along the riverbank to the north of the city. Gangs of workers were building similar earthworks to the south. The breaches in the walls were blocked off with rubble and timber. From the number of soldiers Wandor saw scurrying about in the streets, a good part of Pirnaush's army here was now inside Kerhab itself.

There were few ships at the quays. To the north of the city, a line of boats moored abreast stretched clear across the river, with a plank bridge laid across them. An earth-walled fort rose at the Kerhab end of the floating bridge, another was rising on the far bank, and in the water upstream Wandor saw the long shadow of a floating boom of logs chained together just below the surface.

Pirnaush was preparing his defenses, at least around Kerhab. Who was going to attack? The Shimargans? Perhaps, although not soon, or their ships and men should have been visible from the sky. The Kerhabans? More likely, although would they be striking after Beon-Kagri's defeat? Except that Pirnaush might not know of the sorcerer's defeat or even his work, unless Kaldmor—

Wandor sighed. These were only the first few of a hundred questions whose answers lay no nearer than the Tok'lis, if there. He sent the dragon an image of the southward course of the Mesti. The dragon broke out of his circling and began to climb.

When the wagonmaster for whom Telek was chief guard took most of his beasts and wagons back to Dyroka, he left the *mungan* in full charge of the rest. This made Telek's life much easier. He could go where he pleased, and if he needed to be alone he could arrange it with a few orders.

By the time the dragon flew out of sight, Telek found himself alone on the bank of the Hiyako without having given any orders. Half his men seemed to have vanished entirely, while the rest were either praying or standing in little clusters, talking in low voices. So when Telek saw the *mungan* Isir Hodro sitting on the tongue of a wagon and waiting for him, he knew there would not be even a moment's delaying what Hodro must have come to say.

Isir stood up as Telek approached, and crossed his arms on his chest. "Telek, Wandor is Dragon Lord in Morkol's footsteps. Gwynna is—"

"Do you know that they have anything to do with this coming of the dragon?"

"Do you know that they do not?"

Telek's face and voice could not support some lies. "No."

"Then will you end your war against Wandor the Dragon Lord?"

"The dragon gives him nothing he has not had before."

"Do you believe that?"

"Yes."

"I am not so sure. Others will believe it does. Count your men, Telek."

"They are not *mungans*."

"The *mungans* are not all there is in Chonga."

270

"You could not have come here, knowing the dragon would appear. Who sent you?"

"I sent myself, Telek."

"I did not ask for you."

"I have worked with you, Telek. That does not mean I come or go only as you wish. I am not one of the slaves Wandor freed in Bezarakki."

Telek shrugged. Whatever had been in Isir's mind no longer mattered. "You have come here. What do you have to say now?"

"That the hunt for Mitzon and Hawa will cease."

"Is that all?"

"It is enough for now. I also say that I never saw great wisdom in the hunt. Mitzon and Hawa offended you, but they did not betray the *mungans* with blood as you seem about to do."

Telek realized his hand was on his sword hilt without his knowing how it got there, and saw Isir ready to draw. Isir was shorter, but had a longer sword and he was famous for his quick draw. Now there could be no quick killing which might pass unquestioned, and possibly not even victory.

Telek made a noise low in his throat. "Mitzon and Hawa will go free." Perhaps there were ways of letting them live but keeping them powerless or even making them suffer. "I swear it by Khoshi and by this sword." He cautiously touched the hilt.

Isir nodded. "That is enough for now." He walked away from Telek, but did not turn his back until he was nearly out of sight.

Wandor did not want to fly over Dyroka or even within sight of it. ("Seeing the dragon might tempt Kaldmor to strike.")

("Yes. Or it might tempt whatever friends we have left in Dyroka into doing something even more foolish.")

Wandor thought he detected the dragon expressing approval of this exchange, but he wasn't sure. He was sure that in the next moment the dragon's thoughts almost glowed with hunger and eagerness, as he swooped down toward the forest. Wandor thought a furious protest, but the dragon seemed to be suddenly as mindless as a hunting shark.

As the dragon spread his wings to land, Wandor's full weight came on the harness and he heard leather creak ominously. Frantic squealings told him what had brought the dragon down—a herd of pigs. Around here, they probably belonged to some village allied to Kerhab, driven into the jungle to save them from Pirnaush's hungry soldiers.

Hanging at an angle, Wandor saw that the dragon had a dozen or so of the pigs penned up in the curve of his long tail. A quick grab with both forefeet, and Wandor was nearly shaken out of the harness as the dragon rose on his haunches. He held a squealing pig in his claws, and started munching on it like a man chewing on a length of sausage. If there'd been anything left in Wandor's stomach, the sounds and smells of the dragon's feeding would have brought it up.

Eventually the dragon finished his meal and hinted he was ready to go again. Wandor and Gwynna dropped to the ground, massaged and twisted feeling back into wrenched and numb limbs, and made sure their harnesses were still sound. A pond lay beyond the matted, bloody grass where the dragon had fed, but a brief look ended Wandor's hopes of a bath. The pond was stagnant and scum-covered, reeking of unwholesome things in the water and in the mud on the bottom. It also looked like the outflowing of a slaughterhouse with the remains of the dragon's meal.

The dragon flew southeastward toward the Mesti as he gained altitude. They crossed over a village Wandor recognized from the forest-shrouded octagonal ruins on the hillside above it. When the *paizar-hans* had been an independent power in Chonga, those ruins had been the largest temple of Khoshi Swift in Battle ever built. Then the merchants and priest of each of the Twelve Cities took their own warriors firmly in hand, and the *paizar-hans* could no longer maintain their own fortresses or temples outside the walls of the cities. The village which once flourished as the home of the temple's servants now lived modestly from its fields, the winding canal which linked it to the Mesti, and the occasional pilgrim to the ruins.

The village fell behind, and ahead the gray-green Mesti took shape out of the haze. Wandor gave the dragon a picture of flying south along the river, and he swung onto the desired course, climbing slowly.

Distance and the forest silenced the cries from the village at the foot of the hill. Hawa had a good view of it from between the tumbled blocks of the old temple, but didn't take her eyes off the dragon until it vanished toward the southeast. Even then she gave the confusion in the village only a brief glance before turning back to Mitzon.

He'd finished his prayers to Khoshi and was standing up, brushing dirt off his chest and trousers. He still favored the arm hurt the night of the battle in Dyroka, and he'd carry the scars on his face for the rest of his life. Otherwise he looked fit and ready for whatever might follow from the return of the Dragon Steed of Morkol.

Mitzon sat cross-legged and looked up at her. "Do we want to find a new place?"

Hawa swatted at an insect and frowned. The ruined temple was a maze of stone and trees which hid them well, but it was also far from anything except Dyroka itself. At last she shook her head. "Not unless you think we're likely to be needed some place other than Dyroka."

"No. I asked Khoshi for a sign whether we might be. He didn't send one."

A day ago Hawa would have pointed out that she didn't need a god's help to see the wisdom of staying close to Dyroka. Today she had seen the dragon come again. She'd never doubted that the coming of the northerners might sow strange crops in Chonga; now she wondered if some of those crops might be sown by the gods.

Mitzon suddenly smiled as much as his scars would let him, and continued in an entirely different voice. "Also, this place has enough room to hide all our comrades, if we need to bring them together. And it will hide our fighting exercises."

"You're ready to start them again?"

"Yes."

"Telek?"

Mitzon ran two fingers along the scars. "This blood debt's been paid, and anyway it was never Telek's. But there is another debt, for what he's done to the honor of the *mungans*. I won't seek him out over that, but if our paths do cross I want to be the one who walks away."

Between midafternoon and early twilight, the dragon flew the length of the Mesti south to Bezarakki, then east to Jubon Bay. This flight across land and water he knew well told Wandor more than he'd realized before of the dragon's speed. He shrank days of traveling into hours, while his high climbing shrank men and all their works to ants scurrying about an anthill. How did a man ride the dragon and still remember he was of the same flesh as these ants?

The tales of Morkol Tecuri told Wandor little. Morkol rode the dragon for nearly half his life, and that life ended while he still seemed at the height of his powers. Did his dragon-riding and his early death go together, and if so, how? Had he simply burned himself out from too much work with the necessary Powers, as Gwynna thought she'd made herself barren? Had he possibly let himself be corrupted, paid the price, and lived on as a spotless hero only because the Chongans in later years scoured him clean with lies? Or did death and the dragon go together, like the hilt and blade of a sword? Wandor felt a chill which did not come from the wind, and an upswelling of the doom-sense.

They flew to Jubon Bay to be sure the greatships were gone, and circled over it while Wandor and the dragon had a voice-less, wordless argument over what to do next. The dragon wanted to find a landing place along the shore of the bay and spend the night there. He was tired, it would be dark before they could reach the Tok'lis, and there were any number of places where they could land which would be safer than risking a night flight over water.

Wandor held to his own opinion as stubbornly as the dragon held to his. The dragon might be tired and night was definitely coming on, but surely it would be better to leave the mainland behind? By now everyone around Jubon Bay would have seen the dragon circling against the westering sun. There were sev-eral of Pirnaush's garrisons within a few hours of any place they might choose for a landing. Flying back inland far enough to be safe could mean as much more time in the air as flying south. Did they have any real choice, if they wanted to sleep in peace?

It took several increasingly irritated exchanges before Wan-dor realized what the dragon was asking. It didn't take him long after that to find himself safe among the Viceroyalty's people the next time he touched ground. At the same time, he couldn't deny that the dragon really seemed tired, or that it was only his hopes which had the fleet waiting for them in the south.

In time they hammered out a compromise. Of the two hundred named islands in the Tok'lis, less than half had any people. If the dragon could fly as far as one of the uninhabited islands, they could land unseen in the darkness, sleep safely through the night, and be on the wing again by dawn, before anyone could even notice them, let alone attack. What did the dragon say to this?

What the dragon said was very clearly approval—approval not just of Wandor's idea but of something more Wandor couldn't grasp. He wasn't sure if the dragon couldn't find a way to say it or if the day's events had muddled his own wits until he couldn't understand. He did know that it seemed a good idea to bind thongs firmly around one arm, so that if they fell asleep they'd be jerked awake before slipping from the harness.

Wandor was knotting a thong as the dragon flew over Cape Sagomara and headed out to sea. He was too busy to see the long lines of ships stretching across the water to the east. Perhaps he'd have missed them anyway, for the gathering shadows to the east and the rainclouds overhead made them dim in all eyes except the dragon's, and he had no way of knowing that the ships might interest his riders.

To the men on the decks of Kobo S'Rain's fleet, however, the dragon was clearly silhouetted against the blazing sunset. It seemed a long time before that silhouette merged with the Ocean horizon to the south.

Kobo S'Rain's own *kulgha* was almost the farthest to the east in the fleet, and he was walking its deck with his thoughts turned inward when the dragon flew by. So he did not see the dragon himself. Even when he learned what the shouting from the ships to the west was all about, his thoughts were still more on the orders he'd received from his father.

"Sail to Tok'lis. Make our men there safe. Then cause the Viceroyalty men and ships to leave Chongan waters, but without giving them any provocation."

The ambiguity was perhaps justified, since there were hardly any secrets left in Chonga these days. By now the orders would be known to Duke Cragor, among Wandor's friends, and probably in Kerhab! His father did not want to write his plans across the sky for all to read.

But "cause the Viceroyalty men and ships to leave"! Did his father use such soft words because he still believed that there was hope of an alliance with the Viceroyalty? If there was, it certainly wasn't great enough to be worth risking the fleet, and that was what he'd be doing if he did anything but surprise Sow's Belly Island with all his strength. The Viceroyalty men could defend themselves well enough, and they might have been reinforced until they would have the edge in numbers.

No. He would obey the first part of the orders, because it was foolish to leave the half-armed, half-naked garrisons in their rotting forts exposed to Arlor's vengeful strokes. After that he would do nothing at all, until he could devise a way of provoking Arlor into some action which would justify destroying the northerners. Arlor was only a little less capable than Wandor himself of coming to rule Chonga in all but name, something which could not be allowed. There was no such danger from Cragor, in spite of his pet sorcerer.

Kobo went below, and was considering various means to this end, when there was a knock on his cabin door.

"*Ki-Bassan* Komarn, lord."

"Enter."

Komarn was a nephew of *Hu-Bassan* Meergon, one of the man's horde of legitimate, illegitimate, and adopted relatives. Some weren't above using their family ties to win an easy life, but Komarn had earned his rank fairly, by cool-headed courage in half a dozen battles on land and sea.

Komarn entered and bowed. "Lord, you know that the Dragon Steed of Morkol flies again."

Kobo smiled. "I did not see it with my own eyes, but men whose eyes I trust saw it. I know."

Komarn bowed again and licked his lips. Kobo sensed an unease in him and a reluctance to speak. "Say what is to be said, Komarn. I doubt if it is fish sauce, likely to improve with age."

"No, lord, it is not." He took a deep breath. "What are your orders, when we reach the Tok'li Islands?"

"They are secret, Komarn. Surely you know that?"

"We—I—"

"We?" Komarn seemed ready to bite his tongue over the slip. Kobo nodded. "Have you come to speak for others besides yourself?" Komarn nodded. "That is mutiny." Kobo's hand dropped to his sword.

The *Ki-Bassan* shrugged. "You may call it what you please. You will not prevent it by killing me."

"What is asked?"

"You need not even reveal all your orders. Only tell us— do you have orders to move against the Viceroyalty men?"

Kobo laughed. "No. I have no such orders. I swear this by Khoshi and by my brother's memory."

"Good. I do not think you could trust the fleet to obey you otherwise."

"Because of the dragon? What does that prove about the Viceroyalty men?"

"It proves that we are under the eyes of the gods in a way we were not before, lord. Until we know what they mean by this, it would be wise to move cautiously."

"This is true, but I will not be pleased if you insist on telling me this over and over again. You have done your duty and shown honorable courage. Now go."

Komarn bowed himself out. Kobo drew his sword and placed it on the table in front of him, point toward the door. He frowned. He was not going to reverse course merely at Komarn's words, but he suspected that his own inquiries would quickly tell him the same thing. Komarn was not the kind of man to come as he had to tell less than the truth.

He would not reverse course at once. Now it was all the more important to strengthen the scattered garrisons of the Tok'lis, then keep the fleet united. Neither dragons, dukes, nor Duelists could bring disaster to the fleet of Dyroka if it stayed united under his rule.

The dragon flew down the path of the moon on the Ocean. Both his riders were asleep, and he would not presume to read their dreams now that he knew enough about their waking thoughts. He banked to avoid a patch of moon-silvered clouds and began to climb slowly. He was tired, but not so tired that he could not carry his riders all night and most of the next day without harm. His argument with Wandor as he circled over the—Jubon Bay, men now called it?—had been of the nature of a test for his new lord.

It was one of the commands Morkol had left with him, to set such a test to anyone who would ride him. There were many other commands, and the dragon did not pretend to understand all of them. Many of them would surely need deep thought, in this world grown two thousand years older. Fortunately the lord Wandor would be able to help him, and he thought the woman Gwynna might be able to help him more, although he could not have said why he thought this.

He needed no help to know why he should test those who would ride him. To use the dragon as a mere tool, like a sword or an adze, was to put the dragon, the world, and the man himself in danger. This danger could be prevented, merely by testing each rider to make sure that he could think of the dragon as a being like himself.

Wandor could do this. He did not hide his desire to return to his own people, but he would not ask the dragon to submit blindly to that desire. With wisdom in him, he was as safe a lord to serve as Morkol Tecuri, although in many other ways he was so different from Morkol that the dragon suspected he would never learn them all.

Meanwhile, there was the first service Wandor had earned—a swift return to his own people. The dragon cautiously read his riders' bodies, and sensed that he'd carried them as high as they could endure for long. Higher still, he could have flown faster, but this was high enough. He willed strength into his wings, and they took up the great sky-eating beat he had not found occasion to use since he flew north after his vigil by Morkol Tecuri's pyre.

TWENTY-EIGHT

———◆◆◆———

From the clearing on the hillside, Arlor watched the east turn gray and the night lanterns aboard the ships in the anchorage below wink out one by one. The air was close and heavy, and Thargor was probably right in predicting a storm.

Best not send out the fishing boats yet. They'd only risk being caught at sea, and we don't have enough salt to save a really big catch anyway.

He looked seaward again, shifting his gaze along the horizon. Something flickered on—no, just *above*—the northern horizon, then flickered again. Too high for a ship, too small for a cloud, and in any case it was moving faster than any cloud—

Arlor saw the long body and the great wings, and though a good many early risers heard his shout, none was ever able to really describe it. They could only say there was no fear in it.

The dragon came out of the dawn and swung in circles just above the mastheads of the fleet. All the lanterns which had just gone out lit up again, and more besides. Then the dragon broke out of its circling and swept inland, passing so low over Arlor's head that he saw Wandor waving feebly on the dragon's shoulder. It turned, and Arlor's hat took wings in the storm of the dragon's landing.

It landed on its hind legs, flowed gracefully down onto all fours, and raised its head to look at the count. He met the stare of immense golden eyes more easily than he would have imag-

279

ined possible. It helped a great deal that he was too curious about the dragon's expression to really have time to be afraid.

If I had to put words to it, I'd say the dragon was smiling.

Then the dragon lay down, and there was no mistaking its weariness. Arlor stepped around the great head and started tugging at the knots of the leather harness holding Wandor's limp figure in place.

"Cut the damned thing apart!" Wandor said hoarsely.

"Lord?"

"We're not sick—hurt. Just—stiff. He flew us all the way from near Kerhab—"

"He?"

"It's true what the legends say, Arlor. The dragon's no animal. He was tired, but he flew us all the way here because he knew we wanted to come home."

"Home?"

"Arlor," came a familiar voice from the other side of the dragon. "Arlor, you haven't lost your wits, have you?" Gwynna giggled, making Arlor realize that he did indeed sound more like a simpleton than he'd care to have anyone overhear. He started cutting Wandor free of his harness, but it was slow work under the gaze of the golden eyes and in the shadow of the shining, blue green feathered wing.

Wandor was able to sit up before Arlor had finished cutting Gwynna free. He struggled to stand, but he was still holding on to one of the dragon's horns when Berek ran up the path at the head of a mob of armed men. The dragon reared back on his hind legs, and Berek started to raise Thunderstone.

Wandor shouted, "No, hold!" and pressed both hands against the dragon's shoulder, then stood that way for a moment. The dragon took three steps backward, then squatted on his hind legs, forelegs still displaying five-foot-long claws but wings folded.

"I talk to him with—call it Mind Speech," said Wandor. "He hasn't lived with people for two thousand years, so—"

"Two thou—" Arlor forced his mouth shut. Berek unpinned his cloak and tossed it to Master Besz, then bent down to pick up Gwynna. Besz ordered six of his men forward to take the cloak and make a litter of it for Wandor. Arlor found his voice to order everyone to stand clear of the dragon, then joined the rear of the procession as it wound its way down the hill.

* * *

Wandor and Gwynna slept through the day in the captain's cabin of Thargor's greatship. There was nothing wrong with them not to be cured by a hot bath, sleep in a bed, and another hot bath, with several large meals in between. By evening they were ready to face Cheloth of the Woods.

Gwynna spoke for both of them, after Wandor decided that he really had nothing to say which Count Arlor had not already said better. If Cheloth had shown that he really didn't understand how his failure looked to a human who had the task of ruling, Wandor might have found something to say. As it was, he knew Arlor had spoken in a way which would have penetrated the awareness of an ox, let alone a sorcerer.

Gwynna herself did not find it particularly easy to speak. If she hadn't been led almost as far astray from her duty as the sorcerer, she might have felt righteous indignation. As it was, she knew Chiero's blood was as much on her hands as on Cheloth's. In the end all she could say was, "Don't *ever* do this again," over and over.

Silence fell at last in the cabin, and an oil lamp guttered out to leave a smoke-stench behind. Gwynna shook her head. "Cheloth, you say Beon-Kagri's Powers are chained?"

"For use against us, yes. I did not try to take them from him for all time."

"The brotherhood of sorcerers strikes again?" said Wandor.

"It would have meant a great battle, enough to put the Chongans in fear and draw in Kaldmor. Such a battle is foolish, when it is not needed."

"Are you sure it wasn't needed?"

After a moment's silence, Cheloth shrugged. "It did not seem so. But Wandor is right. I saw in Beon-Kagri a man who'd devoted himself to his Powers in a land where such devotion would find little reward. I could not bring myself to take away all the fruits of his life's work."

Gwynna said nothing. Beon-Kagri's pride in his Powers and all he'd learned to do with them might be equal to hers, and she knew too well what her pride was. Only Bertan's death could hurt more than losing the fruits of so many years' work. And who could say that in time they might not get help or at least useful knowledge from the Kerhaban sorcerer?

"Cheloth, I want your help in bringing some system and order to my work with my Powers. I want you to help me learn what I know, if you understand what I mean?"

"I do." The eye slit turned toward Wandor. "Do you accept her learning this?"

"I do."

"You do not enjoy it, though?"

"Cheloth, you ask rude questions."

"Only when I need answers."

A thin smile. "I am uneasy each moment Gwynna spends exploring the world beyond the world. I shiver at the thought of what she may bring back from there. But I know she doesn't go there for the pleasure of it, and that what she brings back may make the difference between our winning and losing. Is that enough?"

Cheloth nodded. "It is."

"Good," Gwynna said briskly. "Now the first thing I want to learn is the various Powers connected with the dragon. It must—"

"No, love," said Wandor. "The first thing is for us to show ourselves to our people, so they'll stop worrying about us."

The celebration the next day was both sober and short. There was no wine left and not much ale, and there was still a great deal of work staring everyone in the face. The soldiers and sailors shouted themselves hoarse and carried Wandor and Gwynna up and down the beach on their shoulders for the better part of an hour, but that was all.

In the afternoon, Wandor, Gwynna, and Cheloth walked up the hill to speak to the dragon about learning his magic. Gwynna already had learned most of the secret of speaking to the dragon and found it easy to learn the rest. It was even easier for her to learn that the dragon would have nothing whatever to do with Cheloth of the Woods.

Facing Cheloth, the dragon radiated fear, hostility, and stubbornness so powerfully that Gwynna ended the day with an agonizing headache, Cheloth nearly lost his temper, and the Tree Sisters and even Count Arlor sensed some of the dragon's thoughts. The next day Wandor and Gwynna were able to argue the dragon into showing something besides images of the sinking Old Land and monstrously distorted figures of Cheloth. Then they grasped the reasons behind his attitude.

He did not trust Cheloth enough to come within reach of even the least of his spells or Powers. Perhaps Cheloth was not willfully evil like Nem, but had that made any difference for the Old Land and its people? He was a sorcerer who gave no proper thought to what his Powers might do to the innocent. That would always make him dangerous, and the dragon would not trust him. Wandor and Gwynna, on the other hand, he trusted entirely.

But Wandor had no Powers.

Then Gwynna should work with the dragon.

Perhaps. With Cheloth's help, her Powers might be—

Not even with *help* from Cheloth. Alone. The destroyer of the Old Land must stand utterly apart from all work with Powers in which the dragon was expected to join.

This last thought was so emphatic that it gave Gwynna another headache, and everyone thought it better to end work for the day. That night, Gwynna lay in her husband's arms and they talked.

"First we had a reluctant sorcerer," he said. "Now we have a reluctant dragon. Perhaps we'd better do the work with our men's swords. *They* haven't been reluctant."

"I don't think we'll have to go that far."

"You can master all the dragon's magic?"

"Don't I have to, now that the dragon has decided to be stubborn about Cheloth?"

Bertan ran his hand down her back. "Love, I wouldn't care to have this carved on my tombstone or shouted from the rooftops. I'll say it to you, though. The dragon is right. Cheloth is a great sorcerer, but he's also selfish enough so that I won't fault anyone for wanting to keep well away from him."

She wriggled, but less from his touch than from happiness. The dragon's distrust of Cheloth had given her a chance she would not have dared to ask for outright. Now she could work with only her own knowledge and Powers in a matter of great sorcery. Perhaps it was only pride, but—

No. No "perhaps." She had to know that she could explore a new use for her Powers and master it. The work against Beon-Kagri's spell hadn't been enough. She needed more if she was to feel that in learning all her magic, she'd truly done something worth the sacrifice of becoming barren.

She also wanted to know if she could ride the dragon by herself, or if he was so much a part of Bertan's quest that he would obey no one else. The dragon was not an ax or a spear or a helmet, nor was he a Sea Folker who'd sworn the Oath of the Drunk Blood. He was himself, as Morkol and two thousand years in the mountains had made him, and what this was she badly wanted to know.

She also wanted the freedom of the high skies, and wanted it more than anything else she'd ever wanted in her life. Flying could not be as important as her desire made it seem, but this made no difference—except that such a desire was also something she would not care to have carved on her tombstone or shouted from the rooftops.

Bertan's hand moved in a familiar pattern, but she stopped it long enough to say, "The first thing I'll try to do is learn how he feeds."

"Not on half a herd of swine a day, I hope."

"He may eat less when he's not flying. The legend hints that Morkol's Beast Magic somehow let the dragon feed mostly on grain and vegetables. I'll try to find that magic again."

Then his hands started moving again, and this time she did not stop them.

At first the dragon went through three or four barrels of fish a day, but this did no harm. The fishermen of the HaroiLina were into the rich grounds off Sabo Island, where they could have netted enough to feed twenty thousand men and thirty dragons. As long as the Viceroyalty men were content with a monotonous diet, they would never starve.

There was also three months' salt rations stowed in the holds of the ships, but Arlor had very early decided to save this for times of greater need. Even if they had to retreat all the way to the Viceroyalty, he wanted everyone to get there alive. Wandor found no reason to quarrel with the count's logic.

Indeed, he found very little reason to quarrel with anything Arlor had done since the fall of Kerhab. He was not surprised to hear Berek say, "Master, there is hardly a man here who would not swear to Arlor all he has sworn to you and Firehair if the count asked it."

"He would not ask."

"No. That is one reason why we would swear it."

Arlor had the Viceroyalty camp and anchorage on Sow's Belly Island in such good order that for days at a time, Wandor had little more to do than massage the aches and tension out of Gwynna at the end of each day's work with the dragon. She was closemouthed about her progress, but seemed happy enough about what she was learning so that Wandor did not press her.

Then the seal ships bringing the catch from the fishing grounds returned to anchorage escorting a large Dyrokan *kulgha*. Her mostly Bezarakkan crew had mutinied, seized the ship, and slipped away from Kobo's fleet in the darkness. Wandor sent Besz and Berek aboard her to get the mutineers' stories, then called a council of war.

Besz told what he'd learned with his usual frugality of words. "Some don't want to fight against the dragon lord. They say doing so is cursed by the gods. Others think the dragon's coming will give too much courage to Dyroka's enemies. They don't want to fight in a lost cause." It was the common Chongan mixture of superstition and brutal common sense.

They decided to let the mutineers stay without asking them to fight on either side, since most of them still had families within Pirnaush's reach. Captain Thargor spoke up for the Dyrokan officers.

"The crew only locked them up, instead of just pitching them overboard," he said. "When a Bezarakkan crew does that with Dyrokans, the Dyrokans have to be good-headed men. When they speak, people are going to listen."

Gwynna nodded. "Yes. Even if they don't do anything else, they might help keep Pirnaush from punishing the mutineers' families. I'm with Thargor."

Two days later the surprised Dyrokan officers found themselves being loaded into a fishing boat and given water, food, and courses for both the fleet's anchorage and the fastest trip home to the mainland.

"Just in case you'd rather be out of Kobo S'Rain's reach when you tell what happened," said Wandor as he dismissed them. They seemed too stunned to say more than, "Thank you, Lord Wandor," but he hoped they'd be a little more talkative when they reached home.

Four days after the fishing boat's sails dropped below the horizon, another fishing boat came with news from the mainland. There was war again around Kerhab.

TWENTY-NINE

———————◆◆◆———————

The Shimargans began the new war. They knew they had to be among the first to strike if they wanted peace with Kerhab after Pirnaush fell. They also knew they had to strike hard at the Dyrokan army in the valley of the Hiyako, or pay a high price for victory.

The Dyrokans had built a fort at the mouth of a stream flowing into the Trinopo, a day's march north of where it joined the Hiyako at Zerun. The fort commanded the only practical ford of the stream near the river. Farther inland, the forest was so rank that no *Hu-Bassan* in his senses could have expected to get an army through it.

No *Hu-Bassan* did. One night four thousand of Shimarga's best soldiers marched south, carrying with them the pieces of a portable bridge. No word of the Shimargan plans reached Dyrokan ears from the *mungans*, who had been strangely silent since the coming of the Dragon. That meant no word at all, as Pirnaush's spymasters had come to take for granted the service of the eyes and ears of the *mungans*.

The Shimargans laid their bridge across the stream, and three thousand men crossed it to storm the fort under cover of a morning fog. The other thousand formed small bands and slipped north, to join the Kerhabans already in the forest.

Word of the trouble quickly reached the *Hu-Bassan* commanding the Dyrokans around Kerhab. Without waiting for orders, he crossed the Hiyako and marched north toward the captured fort. Two days later he fought the Shimargans. They had only three thousand men, but half the Dyrokans were *Hau-*

gon Dyrokee and a thousand were untrained Bezarakkan levies. The Shimargans were picked men, fighting from carefully dug positions, well-supplied with arrows and warfire.

At nightfall the surviving Shimargans retreated across their bridge, then carried it off. Half the Dyrokans were gone, and the one surviving *Hu-Bassan* led them south. Then the Shirmargans and Kerhabans swarmed out of the forest, and no more than five hundred men of the Dyrokan force returned to Kerhab.

The Shirmargans also planned attacks to the north and south of Kerhab. The attack to the south depended on the men of Zerun, and many held that its fate proved the wisdom of the old saying: "Trust a snake before a northerner, and a northerner before a Zerunite." Five thousand men from Zerun tramped north along the river, to meet a force of two thousand Dyrokans under *Hu-Bassan* Meergon's eldest son, newly raised to the same rank as his father. The *Hu-Bassan* promptly launched a furious attack on the Zerunites, broke not only their ranks but their courage, and drove half of those who didn't die by the sword into the Hiyako to drown. Meergon's son paid for the victory with his life, but his men rounded up nearly two thousand Zerunite prisoners and nearly all the equipment the city had ready for war in the open field. Zerun was still safe enough behind its walls, but was now impotent outside them.

The northern attack was never intended to be more than a diversion, but might have done a good deal of useful work if it had been delivered on time. However, the Kerhabans making it reached the river three days late, the galleys to carry them were two days later still, and by then the Dyrokans were ready for them. Most of the Kerhabans never recrossed the Hiyako, and the only noteworthy damage done was the burning of the wagon park to the north of the main camp. Many of the teamsters died there, either killed outright or thrown alive onto their burning wagons. No one could ever say whether one of the charred corpses found in the ashes was Telek the Fatherless or not. It was certain that his orders to the *mungans*, rare enough since the coming of the dragon, now ceased entirely.

Word of the battles along the Hiyako reached Dyroka swiftly. The news was the first thing Baron Galkor heard when he rode into the city from the east.

Baron Galkor had left the six thousand fresh men from Benzos waiting in their ships at Tsur-Kymana, at the mouth of the Kymana. He'd heard the news of the return of Wandor and Gwynna on the dragon's back from fishermen on the day he sighted the Chongan coast. At once he had decided he should not take his men straight up the Mesti to Dyroka, where the route home could so easily be cut behind him. Instead he had taken them to the mouth of the Kymana, the easternmost of the four great rivers of Chonga, rising in the hills east of Dyroka. Then he took his fastest galley upriver to the head of navigation, hired horses, and rode across the hills to his master. When he reached Dyroka he'd been in the saddle for a whole day, without sleep for two days, and without food for three.

"You've done well, Galkor," said the duke. "Once we have enough river craft on the Kymana, we'll rule it as if it was part of Benzos. Then you can bring the men up to Dyroka and we'll have more than ten thousand ready to hand."

"That will be a stronger force than the *Bassan* himself has around the city, I think."

"Yes, but what of it?"

"Will the *Bassan* let us gather it?"

The *Bassan* would not, at least not unless Cragor took his own men out of the city and to the south of a line running from the Sea Jade Palace to the southernmost fortress of Dyroka itself. Otherwise the *Bassan* would have to send men from the Sea Jade Palace to hold the pass through the hills to the valley of the Kymana.

"—and the baron knows, Lord Cragor, that a thousand men can hold the pass against many times their number."

"For how long?" The duke tugged at his beard, which Galkor saw now held nearly as much gray as black.

"For long enough, if the stronger force is in haste."

The duke and the baron looked at each other. Pirnaush looked at both of them and smiled. Galkor would have preferred a stream of obscenities to that smile. "Come, lords. If you're thinking of putting your men into Dyroka, or between Dyroka and the army on the Hiyako, stop thinking. I won't have it, and you wouldn't gain from it. Maybe you think you'd be a dam in the river. I'd call you the grain between the millstones."

"Your men—" began the duke.

"Are mine." Galkor wished his back was turned to a solid wall as Pirnaush smiled again. "My lords, friendship is best between equals. Let's remain that way. Now—do you agree to put your men where I've asked?"

They did. After they were alone, the duke slumped into a

chair. Galkor poured him wine. "My Lord Duke, it could be worse. Our men will be together, and we'll be almost two to one against Wandor." The duke emptied his cup and held it out. Galkor poured again. "Also, we'll still outnumber Pirnaush's men around Dyroka. And we will have a clear road to the pass and down the Kymana."

The duke seemed to brighten. "Yes. We'll have the Kymana for the taking, if we must go that way. We can leave it a wasteland, so that Wandor will get no use out of it. No Chongan will ever forget us either."

Galkor hoped the duke had finished with the wine. Chonga seemed as full of ears as ever.

Getting Cragor's men out of Dyroka and Galkor's men up the Kymana was easier than either man had expected. Several of the *Hu-Bassans* of the *Haugon Dyrokee* were generous with information on good camp sites, guides to lead Cragor's scouts to them, and wagons and porters to carry his men's baggage.

Kaldmor was fairly certain that these *Hu-Bassans* were supporters of Dehass. If they were, Dehass was probably trying to win the duke's alliance for himself. This did not mean that he was planning to betray his master outright, the sorcerer explained, merely that he wanted the duke on his side if there ever was a rupture between him and Pirnaush.

"The idea of being in Dehass's debt turns my stomach," said the duke. "But if you think it would be useful to hint that we are grateful—"

"Useful, I'm sure. But safe—that is another matter. Pirnaush is not a child, my lord, and—"

"Neither am I, Kaldmor."

"Forgive me, my lord."

"Continue."

"Pirnaush is not likely to ignore the *Zigbai*'s trying to become our friend, but I cannot say what he will do about it."

"Why not?"

"I do not know if Wandor hopes to leave Pirnaush in power, or whether his Chongan allies will let him do so if he wishes it. That is why Dehass is seeking to gain strength of his own. He wishes to be able to offer himself ruler of Dyroka if Pirnaush falls."

"Wandor is too honorable to accept that, and he also has too much sense to trust Dehass."

"I agree. But when all is said and done, Dehass still disdains northerners as barbarians, and Pirnaush does not understand them as well as he should. Neither has the measure of Bertan Wandor."

Cragor refrained from adding that the same might be said of Kaldmor, and began pacing back and forth. "Dehass is throwing out a bait to us, hoping for our gratitude. He'll have it; meanwhile, we'll fortify the camp. Kaldmor, can you read the ground to find the best site, without being detected at work?"

"My Powers are more of Air than Earth, but—"

"Can you or can't you?"

"I can."

"Good."

"Is the *limar* fit for work?"

"Entirely, my lord."

"Even better. Test it while you're testing the ground. We may find ourselves needing it before long."

"Ah."

The duke began pulling on his hooded rain cloak. "Have the ground completely tested by the time Galkor's men come. While you're doing that, also consider what might make a suitable gift for Dehass. I think you know him better than I do."

Realizing he'd been dismissed, the sorcerer turned away. The Black Duke belted on his sword and watched him go. Reading the ground would keep Kaldmor too busy to indulge his growing appetite for intrigue. Kaldmor was still not much beyond the point of being able to extricate himself skillfully from situations he should never have been in at all.

The fortified camp would also be a warning to the Chongans that the men of Benzos would not be easy prey. With a proper site and plenty of men, the labor would be no more than good exercise for Galkor's reinforcements after their weeks of shipboard confinement. When the camp was finished, there would be much less risk of "incidents" and little risk of surprise attack.

Building the fortified camp took sixteen days. During that time an army of Shimargans and Kerhaban exiles openly made camp opposite Kerhab, and Kobo S'Rain brought the fleet back from the Tok'lis to anchor in the harbor of Aikhon, at the mouth of the Pilmau. There was no report of Wandor's activities, natural or magical.

When the camp was finished, Cragor gave a banquet for

Galkor, Kaldmor, and the chief captains. Less publicly, he sent a gift and a message to Dehass.

Galkor sat up late that night, drinking with his fellow captains. When he finally slept, it was nearly dawn. He fell at once into the sound sleep of a man who has worked hard to some purpose.

Kaldmor left the banquet early and also slept, but not soundly. Three times he dreamed that the *limar* of Nem of Toshak had disobeyed one of his commands, but he could never remember what the command was.

Cragor was still on his feet at dawn, the last man to leave the banqueting table. When he lay down he found he still couldn't sleep, and thought of calling for a woman. Then he remembered they were not in Dyroka with its ready supply of easy women. At last he decided not to sleep at all, rose, bathed, and set about the day's work.

Dehass Ebrun greeted the knight who brought Cragor's message and the duke's gift of a jeweled battleax. He read the message, tested the ax's balance, and dismissed the knight with a gift of his own. Then he sent messengers to his most trusted men, for once wishing he had a sorcerer's help in speeding those messages. If he could reach a decision tonight, Pirnaush might not have time for any useful reply.

Pirnaush S'Rain walked in the garden of the City Palace all night. He'd ended the immediate danger from Cragor by pushing the Black Duke's men out of the city. They'd gone peacefully, but probably only because the duke's alliance with Dehass wasn't yet firm enough to allow for open defiance. Now they'd be more determined than ever to seal that alliance.

The simplest course would be to eliminate Dehass; for now it was also the least practical. A trial would be out of the question, daggermen might fail, and even if they succeeded there were enough of Dehass's friends to take vengeance which would bring chaos to Dyroka.

What else could be done? Pirnaush knew his greatest weakness: more than half of Chonga wanted his blood and a clipping of Dyroka's wings. Would they choose one or the other, if they couldn't have both? Pirnaush knew he'd lose some friends in Dyroka if he admitted that his dream of kingship over Chonga was dead, but he'd gain many elsewhere.

Dead the dream certainly was. The best he could hope for now was to be head of an uneasy alliance of cities, perhaps aided by Cragor, fighting a continuous war with a more solid alliance of other cities, certainly aided by Wandor. *Khoshi forgive me, but why should I spend the rest of my life fighting for so little?*

No. Better to make peace now, and use that peace to assure Kobo's undisputed succession as *Bassan* of Dyroka when Sundao called his father onward. With peace, few except perhaps the Kerhabans would be calling for Pirnaush's blood. That would break the strongest weapon Cragor and Dehass now had, in the struggle for the favor of the Chongans. Wandor already had the Dragon Steed of Morkol, and all that meant. Cragor and Dehass would have nothing to match that, if the Chongans ceased to place much value on the head of Pirnaush S'Rain.

He would still have to move cautiously, even though his life depended on speed, and leave more to luck and the good will of others than he liked. But after forty years of gambling he'd look foolish if he refused to gamble once more to save his city and his life.

There was no safe way of sending a message to Wandor now, and this was unfortunate. Until Wandor chose to speak, few Chongans would be likely to listen to any appeals from Pirnaush the Bloody. Many would regard them as a further sign of weakness.

However, he could start gathering a new army around Dyroka. Twenty thousand men, if he could find that many, under a trusted *Hu-Bassan*. The man he wanted was Meergon, if he was fit to command in the field again. He'd get the soldiers by stripping the young and fit from the fortress troops all along the Mesti, and adding more from the *Haugon Dyrokee*, the garrison of Bezarakki, the fleet—no, not the fleet. Kobo shouldn't expect reinforcements, but neither should he be asked to fight half of Chonga with undermanned ships. Besides, the strength of the fleet was the only thing which made it safe to bring men north from Bezarakki.

Then—put the twenty thousand somewhere to the north of Dyroka, where they could move south to defend the city against *anyone*, or west to fight around Kerhab. There'd be less danger than if they were corked up in the city itself, and less danger of disease, if they made their camp in the hills.

Pirnaush began to walk rapidly up and down the gravel paths as forty years' experience in war fed his thoughts and plans. He sobered slightly when he realized he'd be stripping the city of defenders and almost stripping himself. But with another thousand men he could make himself impregnable in the palace quarter; with the gates closed, two hundred old women with brooms and kettles of hot water could hold it! If Dehass opened the gates of the city, of course, Cragor's men would be inside in a moment—but they would still have to reckon with Meergon's army ready to come down on their rear. Meanwhile the men of Benzos could certainly be trusted to fight Wandor, if it came to that.

By dawn, Pirnaush's captains and messengers were already riding into the hills and sailing down the river.

THIRTY

◆━◆◆◆━◆

After Gwynna began working regularly with the dragon, what everyone called the Dragon's Nest was moved to a clearing farther inland. There the dragon was invisible from the sea, sentries at a discreet distance could guard all the approaches, and Gwynna could sink herself into the next world as completely as she wished without any danger from this one.

It was still an unpleasant surprise for Wandor to walk into the clearing one evening and find it empty.

In the fading light he at first saw nothing except that both Gwynna and the dragon were gone. Then he saw a pile of Gwynna's clothing tucked half out of sight under an arching tree root. He ran over to the pile and started fumbling through it, looking for bloodstains until he realized surprise was making him foolish. He'd believe many things about the dragon, but not that he would turn killer. He noted that Gwynna had taken cloak and boots, her silk bag of magical apparatus, and the tooled Yhang leather belt and loinguard which let her do most work with her Powers. Everything else was there, including her sword and knives.

Of course the fact that the dragon hadn't eaten her didn't mean she was safe. Wandor sat down on the root and concentrated his thoughts for Mind Speech. Then he called out, using both words and pictures so that he might reach either Gwynna or the dragon.

No one answered.

He called again, with the same result. After he'd called a third time, he began to wish he'd remembered some of the new things Gwynna had learned about Mind Speech while they were calling the dragon. He suspected he'd allowed himself to forget them, but picking that particular scab would get him nowhere. Gwynna wasn't answering his call, but she might have linked herself with the dragon in some new way. Wandor remembered how she'd been shut out from Mind Speech with him while he was linked to the King Horse during his testing before the Yhangi. It could be something like that, and it could be something else quite unimaginable, but it could not be that Gwynna was dead. Wandor knew he would feel the moment of Gwynna's death, dragon or no dragon.

He started walking back and forth across the clearing, telling himself that he was looking for signs of what might have happened. He'd crossed the clearing twice when he heard running feet on the path. He turned, saw half a dozen men burst into the clearing, and drew his sword before he recognized Berek and the sentries.

A long-legged Hond youth Wandor didn't recognize ran up to him and knelt at his feet. "Lord Wandor, Lord Wandor. Great good news! The fleet from the Viceroyalty is in sight. Five thou—"

Berek and the sentries ran up. Berek reached for the youth, who jumped up and ran around behind Wandor for protection. Berek looked at the empty clearing, then at his master's face, and reached for Greenfoam.

"Lord Wandor, I beg you!" the youth squealed. "I only wanted to bring the good news—"

"It won't be good news for you," growled Berek, raising the ax.

"Berek, let him be!" There was no cure this side of the House of Shadows for Berek's determination to protect his Master, and nothing to be said to him here without humiliating him. Mercifully the sentries were already on their way back to their posts.

"Now," said Wandor to the youth. "The fleet from the Viceroyalty is in sight, you say?"

"Yes. Forty ships, five thousand men, and they'll be here in the morning." No captain in his right mind would take such a large fleet into an unknown anchorage in darkness. Wandor opened his purse. "You've earned some reward for good running, but none for good sense. The sentries have strict orders, and if you'd come running up in the dark I might have killed you myself. Think twice next time, or you may not live to spend this."

The youth was just taking the coins when Berek cried out. Wandor looked up, to see the Dragon Steed plunge out of the clouds with Gwynna on his back. Her hair was glowing like a red-hot coal, and she was lying facedown on the dragon's back between the wings. Her cloak was folded under her for padding, and she seemed to be guiding the dragon with hand movements as well as thoughts.

There was no time for Mind Speech and barely time to get out of the dragon's way before he dove straight at the clearing. Berek picked up the youth by his collar and carried him off like a dog carrying a dead rabbit, with Wandor at his heels. At the last possible moment the dragon's great wings snapped out, cupping the air and bringing both mount and rider gently to the ground. Wandor stepped back out into the clearing, then stopped abruptly as he saw Gwynna.

She was sitting up on the dragon's back, and now the dragon twisted his head around to look at her. Wandor would have given much to know what passed between them in the moment when the dragon's face and Gwynna's were no more than an arm's length apart. Then the dragon lay down, stretching out his neck. Slowly and jerkily, Gwynna rose, picked up her cloak, then walked down the dragon's neck until she could step easily to the ground. She walked toward Wandor as though she was treading on an invisible carpet a finger's breadth above the ground; he doubted that she saw the grass at her feet and was quite sure she didn't see him. He heard the messenger muttering words of aversion and Berek invoking Haro Sea Father.

Slowly the glow from Gwynna's hair died and life came back to her face. With fumbling fingers she shook out the cloak and draped it over her shoulders. Then Wandor reached her, putting his arms around her to reassure himself that this was really Gwynna. Through the cloak he felt chilled flesh, and he pulled her tighter against him to warm her.

"The h-h-high skies are cold," she said, shivering. "But Itr'ell suggested I should go up ready to use my Powers. He—"

"Itr'ell?"

"The dragon's name is Itr'ell."

"I didn't know he had a name. The story—"

"I don't think he had the name from Morkol. I think he chose it himself."

"And told you?" Wandor caught himself before adding, "And not me?" No good would come of sounding jealous, even if he had cause. "So—Itr'ell said you might need your magic?"

"Yes. I didn't, after the first moments. But then we—I didn't want to land again, and the high skies are cold." She shivered harder.

Half the questions Wandor wanted to ask sounded petty and the rest could wait. "Boy!" he shouted at the good-news bringer. "Run to the sentries and tell them to build up the fire and heat some soup." The youth ran off, clearly eager to get out of reach of both Berek's ax and Gwynna's magic.

With forty new ships the anchorage was jammed, and with five thousand more men there was barely room in the camp to turn around. To balance the crowding was the fact that Wandor now had ten thousand fighting men ready to hand, with ships to carry all of them anywhere in Chonga, and stores and war gear enough to keep them in the field for half a year. Baron Delvor had worked with a lavish hand; one ship carried nothing but pikes and arrows, while another carried enough tools and timber to set up a fair-sized shipyard.

Nearly half the new men were Yhangi, carrying shortened pikes instead of their lances, as well as the usual swords and bows. The pikemen were not Royal Army infantry, but they would give the archers a fair amount of protection, while the Yhang bow had as much range as the lighter Chongan crossbows and four times the speed in shooting.

Even if the Yhangi hadn't been so well-equipped, their presence would have been encouraging. To get a Yhang off his horse was hard enough; to get him to go into battle in a strange land on foot was a near-miracle. The coming of the Yhangi was a high tribute to their courage and sense of honor, and probably also to what Jos-Pran threatened for those who held back.

Wandor now had the strength to take a hand in the Chongan wars at once, without waiting on any Chongans. But whether this would be wise was a many-edged question. It could be dangerous to act without knowing what possible Chongan friends might want, other than the overthrow of Pirnaush. On the other hand, waiting on the Chongan might give Cragor time he could put to good use. It would certainly not be taken in good part by the Viceroyalty's men, most of whom had little patience left for Chongan intrigues even when they didn't have blood debts to pay.

Weighing the risks, the War Council decided to wait a month. If the Chongans hadn't offered an opportunity by then, the men of the Viceroyalty would make one.

As it happened, the wait was only a few days. The new men had barely time to learn their way to the cookhouse and privy pits when three *kulghas* arrived from Shikaramani. They bore envoys from Timru, with a complicated tale of what was happening in western Chonga and a request for Wandor's aid.

Jifo, at the head of navigation on the main river of western Chonga, the Bokito, was trying to stay neutral. It hadn't renounced its oath to Pirnaush, but it hadn't stopped trading with Timru either.

Giraska, on the Bokito's major tributary, the Vigan, was following Timru. It usually did, in much the same way as Bezarakki usually followed the lead of Dyroka.

Timru, traditionally ranking second only to Dyroka, had openly thrown down a challenge to Pirnaush. The *Bassan* of Timru had taken a fleet and an army down the Bokito to Magasla at the river's mouth and summoned it to surrender.

Magasla refused. A Dyrokan garrison held its citadel and port, and there was also genuine sympathy for Pirnaush in the city. The rulers of Magasla were a tightly-knit band representing the various seafaring trades and crafts, from captain and pilot down to carpenter and sailmaker. Twenty years before, Pirnaush had led Dyrokan troops to beat down a rising of the wealthy merchants, supported by Shikaramani. Since then the sailors had ruled well enough so that there was little discontent with the Dyrokan alliance in Magasla—certainly not enough to make the city yield before the strength Timru alone could bring against it.

So the men of Timru marched overland to Shikaramani, moving fast and carrying wagonloads of spare weapons. The weak garrison of Shikaramani was all Magaslan; when the Timruans came in sight, the city's people opened the gates. The garrison barricaded itself in the citadel, while the Timruan envoys set sail for the Tok'lis.

"So now some of our men stand before the citadel of Shikaramani, and the rest before Magasla. If you will come with all the strength you have here, both will fall, and all the Bokito valley will be united against Pirnaush the Bloody."

"Also under the rule of Timru?" said Wandor. After a moment the man nodded.

"I have sworn the Duelist's Oath," Wandor said, and repeated it for the benefit of the Chongans. "So I will promise nothing until I have seen at least Shikaramani, Magasla, and Timru with my own eyes."

"Lord Wandor!" exclaimed the oldest envoy. "Is there time for you to travel among us? Pirnaush will be—oh..." His voice trailed off and Wandor nodded.

"Yes. I ride the Dragon Steed of Morkol. However much or little this may mean in the eyes of gods or men, here it means that I can visit all three cities in a single day if I choose. My lady and I do so choose. Can you noble gentlemen write letters which will assure us a proper reception on the mainland?"

When the envoys recovered their wits, they could not agree too eagerly. Arlor was a good deal less eager to see Wandor and Gwynna flying off to the mainland, into the gods alone knew what danger of traps and treachery, and said so in plain Hond. Wandor heard the count out, then was equally blunt.

"Arlor, do you truly think it's only pride or the Duelist's Oath which takes me to Timru?"

"No, but—oh, curse it, if we only had the time..."

"Do you think we do?" Arlor shook his head. "Then the dragon is our best hope, and for now only Gwynna and I can ride him. Furthermore, we're not completely helpless if the Timruans do prove treacherous."

"We hold the envoys as hostages?"

"Yes, though politely and without using the word. Also, Gwynna and I will speak to Cheloth before we go. If we're held or harmed on the mainland, we'll reach him if it's the last thing we do. You'll have the bad news as soon as he does." Wandor did not expect he'd have to tell Arlor what came next, and wasn't disappointed.

The count smiled one of those smiles enemies wouldn't care to see. "If Timru proves treacherous we sail to Shikaramani and release the garrison, then to Magasla—"

"And destroy Timru's fleet. Without the ships, the army will be cut off, and we can present them on a platter to Pirnaush."

"Along with a request that since we've dealt with his enemies, would he be so kind as to deal with ours?" asked Gwynna, with a grin similar to the count's.

"Yes. I'm willing to help Pirnaush stay in power if he's

300

willing to accept our help. Of course we can't approach him about it now, or the other allies we may need will slip away at once. But I'd rather make a friend of Pirnaush than fight for Timru's dreams of becoming the first city in Dyroka."

"Shimarga and Kerhab will certainly oppose that," said Arlor. "Perhaps not while they're facing Pirnaush's army, but certainly as soon afterward as they dare."

"Yes, and we'd be caught in the middle of a whole new war without allies we can trust, and without having put Cragor out of the game." Wandor threw up his hands in mock disgust. "Rather than face that, I'd become king over Chonga myself!"

They all laughed.

THIRTY-ONE

Hu-Bassan Meergon was more than willing to command Pirnaush's new army, but he was the strongest part of it. Many of the unblooded *Haugon Dyrokee* and fortress Nineties were already too weak from desertion to provide many men for service under Meergon. The *Hu-Bassan* commanding in Bezarakki also begged to be spared from sending any men north. The city was restless, he said, and reducing Dyrokan strength there might dangerously encourage the foolish or the hotheaded. Pirnaush was willing to believe the man; he'd also received letters from Kobo that the Bezarakkan ships of the fleet were losing sailors and even officers. Day after day, they slipped away to wait out the war or even to join Wandor in the Tok'lis.

If Bezarakki revolted, Pirnaush reflected, the Mesti would be open all the way to Dyroka unless Kobo brought the fleet over from Aikhon. But that would leave the Pilmau open for enemies to sail up to Kerhab, join with the Shimargans to free it, and march overland to the Mesti. Either way, the final battle would then be fought before Dyroka itself.

The other cities will be as happy as pigs in a sweetroot patch, and even Wandor might be willing to see it happen to finish off Cragor. There's nobody who cares what happens to Dyroka except me.

Before long, Pirnaush knew that if he kept back the strength he'd need to hold the palace quarter, he'd be giving Meergon barely ten thousand men, few of them well-trained. He considered bringing them into the city, then decided against it.

Meergon still had to be where he could move to Kerhab easily. North of the city Meergon could also more easily train his men, prevent desertion, and keep out Dehass's spies.

However, Pirnaush did not lack weapons even if he might lack men. He had enough spears, bows, and swords left in secret hiding places all over Dyroka to arm fifteen thousand men. Only a few trusted captains knew where all of them were. If all else failed, Pirnaush could now arm the people of Dyroka against his enemies. Against either the northerners or the rest of Chonga, Pirnaush knew he could trust the people in Dyroka's streets as long as they had enough weapons to give them a chance for their lives. He wasn't sure if he could trust them to fight Wandor, but with luck there would be no such fighting.

Cragor and Dehass no longer kept their alliance a secret, and were as honest with each other as could reasonably be expected. The one matter Cragor refused to discuss with the *Zigbai* was Kaldmor's plans for sorcery in the coming battle. He wanted to hide his own fears and also the fact that he didn't really know what Kaldmor's plans were. When he considered that the sorcery in the coming battle might involve a full duel between Kaldmor and Cheloth, even the duke found it hard to be calm. He knew that any Chongan, even the *Zigbai*, would be frightened half out of his wits and quite possibly out of his enthusiasm for their alliance.

"But can we be sure that such Powers will not affect this world, as they did before?" Dehass complained one night.

"I doubt that even a sorcerer can be sure of anything, when such great Powers are involved," said Cragor with a shrug. "I would not think better of Master Kaldmor for claiming knowledge he does not possess."

"I would think better of him if he at least swore to be careful," said Dehass.

"Do you wish victory or not?" said the duke, imitating Kaldmor's voice. "That is all he would say to such a question."

"He would be keeping a rare guard on his tongue if he did."

The duke shrugged. "Kaldmor does talk too much. But it is purposeless to ask him to be careful. A sorcerer who works with such Powers as he does is either careful or dead."

Mitzon and Hawa went down the Mesti to Bezarakki with a dozen sword followers, leaving as many more behind in Dyroka. The *mungans* were even more confused than the rest of Chonga, between the coming of the Dragon Steed and the disappearance of Telek the Fatherless. Mitzon and Hawa did not fear open enemies, but they knew they'd have few real friends until they'd won a major victory.

Bezarakki seemed the best place to start looking for that victory. It was already restless, a few incidents could lead to open war, and Wandor and Gwynna would quickly hear of anything which happened there.

Wandor and Gwynna spent many exhausting days on the mainland of Chonga. With proper harness and clothing, riding the dragon was no longer the ordeal it had been; the exhaustion came from their experiences on the ground.

They flew first to Shikaramani, where they met the leaders of the city and the *Hu-Bassan* of the Timruan army besieging the Magaslan garrison in the citadel. Their next visit was to the Timruans before Magasla. The *Bassan* of Timru was a merchant's son who knew his limits in war and relied heavily on the advice of four experienced mercenary captains and the *Hu-Bassan* of the Timruan fleet. It also helped that the "siege" of Magasla was a calm, polite, and nearly bloodless affair, with everyone trying to avoid driving a permanent wedge between Timru and Magasla.

At last they flew on to Timru itself. The Timruans spent two days on their beloved ceremonies, determined to honor properly the riders of the sacred Dragon Steed, before settling down to serious talk.

The Timruans were ready to aid Wandor, to the limits of their resources, in overthrowing Pirnaush, in destroying Cragor in Chonga if possible, and otherwise, in carrying the war to Benzos. In return, they expected him to recognize them as the first city of Chonga and to help them keep that position. This meant first of all sacking Dyroka so that it would not recover for a century, and they had other plans almost as bloodthirsty. Wandor soon realized that the rest of Chonga would shortly hate Timru more than it had Dyroka if Timru won the kind of victory it wanted, and probably hate him as well.

Unfortunately, the Timruans were not only offering a generous price for his alliance, they were making veiled threats about turning to Cragor if they couldn't buy him. Wandor couldn't ignore these threats; Cragor would certainly have no qualms about leaving Chonga a shambles if it would deny the land to his enemies. So he fought down the temptation to tell the Timruans exactly what to do with their alliance for several more days. Then one night two secret envoys from the miners of Shimarga came to him and Gwynna. Suddenly the Chongan puzzle began to appear something a merely human mind could hope to understand.

The twelve thousand copper, tin, and iron miners of Shimarga wanted to arm themselves and join the army before Kerhab. That would give the Shimargan army a decisive advantage in numbers, but the city's leaders didn't want them to join in the war.

"I'm not sure they aren't right," said Wandor at first. "You're among the strongest and bravest men in Chonga, but you aren't trained soldiers. You might be throwing your lives away."

"Perhaps not. We are, as you say, strong. Some of us are strong in ways not common in this land."

Gwynna's eyebrows rose. "Earth Power? It is said that some of the miners of Shimarga can work with it."

"Much is said. Some of it may even be true."

"Such as Beon-Kagri of Kerhab having once been a miner of Shimarga?"

The two envoys looked at each other in a way which made words superfluous. "You knew Beon-Kagri?"

"And will know him again, I think," said Gwynna. "He is not dead, unless Cheloth of the Woods has lied to us."

For over a century the miners of Shimarga had wanted to become one of the Lawful Bodies of the city, along with the merchants, moneylenders, craftsmen, and priests. If they marched out to fight for the city, they could win this honor. "We will stand by our city regardless," said the envoys. "But much might happen to everyone's benefit, if the riders of the Dragon Steed came to Shimarga."

"Indeed," said Wandor. That was all he said to the envoys before he dismissed them, but before dawn he and Gwynna were on their way to Shimarga. It was a gamble, flying north with so little preparation or warning, but if they came down among the miners they should at least be safe, and they might win a notable victory. Also, delay might prove a gift to the Timruans, who seemed to want the dragon, Wandor, and Gwynna only as new tools to re-build their old power.

In Shimarga, many of the miners were reluctant to march unless they could be sure of good captains, protection from Kaldmor's sorcery, and aid for their wives and children. Many

306

Shimargans feared the cost of these measures, even though they knew that every day's delay was a gift to Pirnaush. When they learned that delay would also be a gift to Timru, all parties agreed to submit the matter to the judgment of the dragon's riders.

"The miners have a just claim, but Shimarga should not have to bear all the cost of it," Wandor said. "I will see about finding other ways of paying the miners, if all Shimargans will promise me one thing."

"And that is . . . ?" asked a miner.

"Shimarga must stand beside me in protecting the Sailors Council in Magasla against Timru."

"Why not?" said a *Hu-Bassan*. "If that means they'll stand by us. . . . But if you're thinking of going to Magasla—"

"We are," said Gwynna.

"—then you should go up to Jifo first. The woodworking trades there have a position like the one the sailors have in Magasla and the miners want here. Pirnaush has promised to support their claim if anyone tries to beat them down by force. If you'll just make the same promise—"

"Will they join us if we do?" said Gwynna.

The soldier shrugged. "They may not join us against Pirnaush. But we'll certainly have them with us against Timru, now and afterward."

So Wandor and Gwynna reached Magasla by way of Jifo, where they stayed two days, letting the dragon rest and feed while they talked with the city's leaders. Virtually everyone in Jifo either worked in wood or was a blood kin of someone who did, so swearing that they would keep Pirnaush's promises and letting it be known they were not friends of Timru did everything which needed doing. After that they flew south to Magasla, passing over Timru without landing.

The Magaslans were a harder nut to crack than Shimarga or Jifo. They feared Timru, they had a Timruan army before their walls, and several thousand of their soldiers were trapped in the citadel of Shikaramani. If Wandor and Gwynna hadn't carried letters from Shimarga and Jifo to prove what they'd done, the Magaslans might even have held them prisoner while they negotiated.

As it was, the Magaslans admitted that if Pirnaush was no longer able to control Kaldmor, he was not as good a friend as he had once been. If Wandor and Gwynna wished only to remove Pirnaush without giving his power to Timru, they had

307

much wisdom. Above all, they had the Dragon Steed of Morkol. Like the miners of Shimarga, the sailors of Magasla were more at ease with magic than most Chongas, in their case, with the Powers of Air—since they knew that the Powers of Water were not for men's knowledge. They feared sorcery because they knew it could do more harm than good, not because they knew nothing about it at all. If Wandor and Gwynna had the same Powers as Morkol Tecuri, this was not all bad, when Kaldmor the Dark was threatening to loose the magic of To-shak.

In the end, Wandor and Gwynna flew back to Timru with letters from Magasla, as well as from Shimarga and Jifo.

Various delays still cost time. They had to get the Shimargan envoys out of prison by threatening to fly back to the Tok'lis. Rumors of their threat led to riots in the city, which took several days to subside. Rumors of the rioting nearly produced a mutiny in the fleet and army before Magasla, which was prevented only by the cool head and quick work of the *Bassan* and his captains. Wandor was glad of that; the masters of Timru needed a lesson, but wrecking the fleet and army which had to be one of the main pillars of the alliance against Dyroka seemed an expensive way of teaching them. Finally he and Gwynna had to fly on the dragon to Jifo, Giraska, Shikaramani, and Magasla, and bring back from each city an envoy with the courage to ride the dragon and full powers to negotiate.

The terms of what came to be called the Alliance of the Dragon were simple enough. The Viceroyalty, Timru, Shimarga, Kerhab, Giraska, and Shikaramani bound themselves to make war on Dyroka until Pirnaush submitted without conditions, and use all their strength in that war. Magasla and Jifo would not join in the war, but they would give Pirnaush no aid, let their citizens serve in the war without punishment, and give Wandor money for the families of the Shimargan miners. Wandor would be *Bassan* of the alliance, with Arlor taking his place if necessary. Under Wandor, the *Bassan* of Timru would lead the fighting men. Gwynna would have no voice in matters of war, but she would have the title *Eremen-Bassanar* or War Lady of the Dragon, and the chief voice in all matters of sorcery.

The allied fleet would have to unite and stay together, because Kobo S'Rain not only outnumbered either Wandor or the Chongans separately but had a central position at Aikhon. So Wandor's ships would leave the Tok'lis and sail an offshore

308

course to Magasla. After uniting there, the allies would sail east.

What happened after that would depend on Kobo S'Rain. If he brought the fleet of Dyroka out to sea and was defeated, the allies would then sail up the Pilmau to Kerhab and destroy the Dyrokan army there. If Kobo refused to meet them at sea, they would sail to Bezarakki, capture it, and open the Mesti. That should draw Kobo into a battle where the allies would have the advantage, and once he was defeated the allies could go where they wanted.

Wandor knew this plan meant thrusting all his men and ships among a mass of Chongans whose tempers might suddenly turn. It also meant a bloody naval battle against an able and ruthless leader. On the other hand, it offered a good chance of ending the war without overthrowing Pirnaush or fighting a battle before Dyroka. No Chongans seemed to realize this, and Wandor did not see that it was his duty as *Bassan* to tell them.

Wandor and Gwynna flew back to the Tok'lis, and the Viceroyalty men started boarding their ships. The fleet was about ready to sail when a *kulgha* full of women and children arrived from Bezarakki. The city was in open revolt against Pirnaush. A series of incidents had led the people to storm a prison, and the Dyrokan garrison had replied with a massacre. The arsenal had burned, most of the ships there had been taken or sunk, and the Dyrokans were preparing to leave the city. Bezarakki itself was a slaughterhouse where it wasn't a pile of rubble, and famine and plague would soon be joining steel and fire to strike down its people.

Suddenly the Mesti lay open for anyone who moved fast enough.

"All the way to Dyroka?" said Gwynna.

Wandor shook his head. "Going upstream alone would strain the alliance and risk Kobo's blocking the Mesti behind us." He saw the further question in her eyes. "We couldn't do more than save Pirnaush's life, either. After what's happened in Bezarakki, not even Shimarga or Magasla will trust him against Timru."

"But they'll still need an ally, and where—oh, I think I see."

"Yes. They'll turn to us. I'm afraid we're not getting out

309

of Chonga as easily as I'd hoped we might." He stood up. "You and Arlor take the fleet straight to Bezarakki, but don't go upriver until we join you. I'll take the dragon to Magasla, and stay there until it's safe to land at Bezarakki."

THIRTY-TWO

Dawn over the Mesti:

The fleet of the Alliance of the Dragon lay downstream from Dyroka, just out of sight of the city and waiting for the order to advance. The clouds were scattered but low. Gwynna didn't see the dragon until he swooped down to land in a spray of sand on the riverbank to port. Hawa came up to stand beside her at the railing. They saw Wandor scramble down from the dragon's back and hurry toward the waiting boat.

"We should have brought a *viba*," said Gwynna. "With the masts cut down, Itr'ell could land on it."

"*Vibas* are hard to take upstream during the winter," said Hawa. "The dragon will be safe enough where it is. Cragor's men will stay on the Dyrokan side of the Mesti as long as the fleet's here, and no Chongan will attack the Dragon Steed."

Gwynna doubted there was anything Chongans wouldn't do, but trusted Hawa's judgment more than most. During the voyage upriver from Bezarakki the two women had become good friends, their friendship beginning when Hawa had confessed she was glad Mitzon wasn't with them. During the fighting in Bezarakki, he'd fallen through a rotten floor into a pigpen and been trampled by its inhabitants. Now he was bruised and sore from head to foot, quite unfit to do more than sit in a chair and give orders to the surviving *mungans*.

"He's already avenged the honor of the *mungans* three times over," said Gwynna irritably. "What drives him now?"

"He doesn't call the work done," said Hawa with a sigh.

"Besides, he wants to sacrifice a few Dyrokans to Khoshi in memory of the people we lost in Bezarakki."

"He sounds very much like Bertan."

Wandor's boat bumped against the side of the *kulgha*. He scrambled up onto the deck and into Gwynna's embrace.

"Are we ready?"

"We will be when Cheloth says he is," he replied. "The Bezarakkans are a little slow in going ashore, but their ships will still have time to catch us before dark."

"Good. How many people are there left in Heidrispon?"

"I didn't land to ask, but the city looks completely deserted. I think most of the people must have come north to Dyroka along with the garrison."

"Even better." Without Mind Speech, they still shared a single thought. The fewer Dyrokans or Dyrokan allies within reach of the vengeance-mad Bezarakkans, the better for everyone. That was why they'd decided to land the four thousand Bezarakkans in Heidrispon the moment they'd heard the city's garrison had gone north to Dyroka. Now the Bezarakkans were safely out of the fighting, unless Pirnaush tried retaking Heidrispon. In that case they'd have all the fighting they wanted.

Not that either Wandor or Gwynna thought badly of the Bezarakkans for wanting vengeance. Gwynna would have cheerfully gelded the Dyrokan *Hu-Bassan* there with her own hands. She remembered a little canal, so choked with floating bodies that a mangy dog walked out on them and started gnawing at trailing guts. Putting an arrow through that dog had been one of the few pleasures of her days in Bezarakki, along with meeting Mitzon and Hawa again and seeing the faces of newly freed slaves.

A sharp *crack* made her turn. Green smoke was rising from the forecastle of the big galley to starboard, and as the light breeze blew the smoke away they saw a familiar green-clad figure with a silver head standing on the deck. Today Cheloth was going to do his work in the open, on the galley's foredeck. Gwynna suspected that for once he needed to see with the eyes of his unhuman body as well as the eyes of his magic. He'd be safe enough as long as the galley stayed out of bowshot; Dyroka's heavy siege engines were still at Kerhab.

A black ball soared up one of the halyards of Wandor's ship, and his new dragon banner slowly spread itself on the breeze. Oars splashed into the water, capstan chants rose as anchors came in, and the fleet began to move.

From the tower of the New Palace, Pirnaush could see farther than any other man in Dyroka. So he saw the dragon flying up the river and was not surprised soon after to hear that the allies' fleet was on the move. He sat down on his campaign chair and called a girl to sponge his forehead with cooled rice water.

It would have been easier if today's battle was going to be like any of the others he'd fought. To be sure, he hadn't expected to fight before the walls of Dyroka, and knew now that he should have pulled men away from Bezarakki. If he'd done that, the *Hu-Bassan* there wouldn't have grown overconfident and provoked the rebellion which in the end had opened the Mesti to Dyroka's enemies. The man had done well enough afterward, getting his men overland to join Kobo at Aikhon, but if the Dragon allies wanted his head they could have it!

Even for a fight before Dyroka, he was ready. His men were in order and each was where he would do the most good or, in Cragor's case, the least harm. Meergon and twelve thousand men who'd come in from Kerhab were north of the city. The *Haugon Dyrokee* and the fortress troops held the northern part of the city itself. Cragor's men held the southern part of Dyroka and guarded the cliffs along the Mesti toward Heidrispon.

Taken all together, Pirnaush had as many men as the allies. Under the circumstances, they would have had little choice but to land either north or south of the city and besiege it, knowing that Dyroka hadn't fallen to a siege in five centuries. Pirnaush could have sat in his tower all day, watching the fleet parade past up the Mesti.

All this could have been, except for Kaldmor the Dark. Pirnaush cursed the sorcerer, cursed Cragor for using him, and cursed his own lack of courage in not having the sorcerer killed. It might have meant his own death, but it would have spared Dyroka the ordeal it now faced, trapped like the Old Land in a duel between mighty sorcerers.

Now it's too late, and if there's a disaster they'll say it's my fault, because I thought until it was too late that I could save both my city and my own power. He laughed. *It's also too late to worry.*

He called for a bowl of nuts, and told one of the girls to take down the brass screens on the river side of the tower. They wouldn't keep out arrows and bolts, and they spoiled his view.

* * *

As the allied fleet started passing Dyroka, Baron Galkor rode back to his post at the tavern in the Street of the Bone Carvers.

He'd been up before dawn, the work of getting the duke's men into the city having been finished well before sunset the day before. Bread, pickled pork, and wine made his breakfast; then he talked briefly with the *Hu-Bassan* of the *Haugon Dyrokee* on the other side of the Street of the Bone Carvers. The street was the dividing line between Cragor's men and the Dyrokans, and it was always better to study the man on your flank before the fighting started. Then Galkor rode south to meet the duke in a tower on the south wall.

The duke was uneasier than he usually was before a battle, but not so much so that Galkor thought anyone but himself had noticed. Nor did he blame the duke. They faced a choice which was at best disquieting: fight an uncertain battle against half of Chonga, or be spared the need to fight that battle through Kaldmor's victory in a still more uncertain and murderous battle of sorcery. It would have eased Galkor a trifle to have some idea what the sorcerer was planning to do with his *khru* medallion, *limar*, and Toshakan Powers, but that was hardly something he expected Kaldmor to reveal. Indeed, neither he nor the duke had seen or spoken to Kaldmor for three days.

Since there was nothing to say about Kaldmor the Dark, the two men talked of other subjects. At last there seemed nothing more to say, and giving an ear to his master's simple need to talk wasn't enough to keep Galkor from his post with his men. When he rode back, the streets of Dyroka were still almost deserted at a time when they would normally be swarming with men and animals.

Like every other Chongan city, Dyroka had a plan which gave each citizen inside its walls a place and a purpose if the city came under attack. Being Pirnaush's city, Dyroka had a better plan than most. However, like all the other plans its first order was for everyone not already carrying a weapon to stay home until they received their next order. So far the Dyrokans seemed willing to obey. Would they do as well when the Viceroyalty men were scaling the walls or Kaldmor's spells were thundering overhead?

The baron rode up to the tavern and one of his guards hailed him. "Lord Galkor! We've a prisoner, a Dyrokan we caught sneaking out back."

"Who's his master?"

"Hasn't said yet. There's more, too."

Galkor dismounted and followed the man around to the rear of the tavern. Where a shed had stood against the brick wall, a hole deeper than a tall man's height now gaped, filled almost to the edge with swords, crossbows, sacks of bolts, spears, and empty firepots. Everything was carefully wrapped, oiled, and laid in place, as though whoever put it there wanted it to keep for a while.

"He was looking at that shed all the time," said the guard. "That's why we stopped him—thought maybe somebody was inside it listening to us. He went crazy when we started ripping up the floor. We had to hurt him some before he'd stop. He's down in the cellar now."

"Take me to him."

The prisoner was a short man with calloused hands, light skinned for a Chongan, but well fed and well groomed. His lip was cut and his nose broken, but he managed to glare at the baron when he came down the stairs.

"Strip him," said Galkor. "Now, my men here are fairly good with stubborn prisoners. They'll work on you first. If they don't get the answers we need—"

Another guard scurried down the stairs, his face pale and working. "Lord Galkor, Lord Galkor! The *limar*'s on the walls and Kaldmor's working through it!"

Galkor swallowed. "What is he doing?"

"He—he—it's like a whirlwind, out over the river—"

"And the enemy fleet?"

"He hasn't hurt it yet, but—"

"Any sign of Cheloth?" The man gaped. "Any green light or green clouds?"

"N–n–no."

Galkor turned back to the prisoner in time to see a look of resignation settle on his face. "My lord Galkor," said the man. "Those weapons are from Dehass. He put them there, so he could—if he wanted to—"

"Arm the Dyrokans against us?"

The man buried his face in his hands. "Yes. To—to take you—turn you over to Wandor, so—"

Galkor's inarticulate growl and the guard's sword cut off any further words. The man toppled from the bench, his head split down to the bridge of his nose. Galkor turned to the guard.

"Next time we have a prisoner who's talking don't kill him until he's finished!"

"Yes, my lord."

"Put our friend in the pit under the weapons." He thought of calling for pen and paper, then hesitated. Anything written down could fall into the wrong hands, which now meant any Dyrokan. And were the man's words even something to be taken seriously?

Yes.

Chonga was Chonga. More important, Dehass was the king of intriguers, and putting himself in a position to buy his safety by turning Cragor over to his enemies—yes, that was far too like the man. Even if the plot was still shapeless, the duke needed to be warned, and those weapons suggested it had a fairly solid shape.

Galkor called down the captain of his guards. "Ride to the duke. Tell him that Dehass may be planning to betray us to Wandor. I suggest we should avoid giving him any chance to hurt us, but also try to let him start any fighting." Dehass wasn't so popular in Dyroka that even the best-armed mob would follow him blindly into a fight he'd provoked against an alert opponent.

Galkor went upstairs to watch the captain ride off. As the clatter of hooves on cobblestones died away, the baron became aware of a deep-toned roar. At times it broke into a whistle, and it came from the west—from the Mesti.

Kaldmor's magic.

The baron found the knowledge didn't make him quite as uneasy as it once would have. Perhaps Kaldmor had changed; certainly he had.

"What does it look like now?" came Gwynna's voice up through the hatch.

"Like—oh, imagine a snowball, but made of air and as big as a greatship. It seems to be spinning slowly."

"I think it is a *hairom* vortex. When the wind inside is blowing hard enough to tear a ship apart, he will move it against us."

In the time it took Gwynna to say this, the spin of the vortex increased noticeably. She was speaking slowly, because she was talking to Wandor while linked with five Red Seers, ready to complete the link to Cheloth if he called on them for aid. She could concentrate better if she was below.

The ships crept up the Mesti. Every man aboard Wandor's *kulgha* seemed to be staring aft so intently that the ship could have sailed off the rim of the World and fallen halfway to Chaos before anyone noticed. They were now approaching the northern wall of Dyroka, but the fleet's advance was slowing. The wind had died so suddenly that Wandor suspected Kaldmor's magic might have had something to do with it, and the rowers were slacking off as the *luor* of great sorcery spread north and south along the river. No one said aloud that Kaldmor might now be Cheloth's equal, but no one was able to watch the vortex without feeling a chill within him.

Suddenly the vortex rose high into the air and darted out over the river, bobbing and weaving like a butterfly. It stopped close to the opposite bank of the river. The roar and whistle of the vortex reached Wandor clearly now, but the water underneath barely rippled. Kaldmor must be containing the winds tightly as he called them up and brought them to their full strength.

Then Wandor saw another sort of rippling in the air above the city wall, not far from where he'd seen the vortex appear. The rippling became a sphere, then began to spin slowly.

"There's a second vortex forming," he called down.

"Ah," said Gwynna. "He must hope to let the *limar* rule one while he rules the other and guides both. If he does that, he can sweep the whole river clean."

A Tree Sister standing by the railing trembled as the *luor* became more intense. Thargor came forward, picking a path around the men kneeling in prayer on deck. The sound of the oars died away completely, and Wandor desperately wanted to be holding Gwynna's hand.

He called down again, but only silence answered him. He desperately hoped her need to learn more magic hadn't led her to try reading the spells Kaldmor was building. Cheloth could certainly protect himself in the coming duel, but he might not be able to protect her unless she was linked to him.

For Kaldmor the Dark, nothing existed except the elements, the magic he was using to shape the Powers drawn from them, the *limar*, and the two *khru* medallions. He not only sensed nothing else, he could not even spare the effort to remind himself that anything else ever *had* existed.

The most delicate moment of this spell-building was at hand. He would transfer the first vortex and all the Power needed to

317

keep it active to the *limar*, build the second vortex to full strength, break the link between himself and the *limar*, and send both vortexes down upon the fleet, to smash ships and drown men. He'd tested the *limar* as well as he could without Cheloth's detecting him; it could do its part of the work. With two vortexes feeding on two bodies of Powers, Cheloth would have to strike down both to save the fleet from ruin or at least crippling damage. Even for him, that would not be easy.

Kaldmor started gathering the totality he would be transferring to the *limar*, sending it through the *khru* medallion so that the transfer would take place in the space of a few heartbeats. He chanted without hearing, danced without feeling the floor under his feet, raised his staff without knowing his muscles worked, breathed deeply without smelling the herbal smoke filling the cellar.

He drove the totality out of himself, through his own *khru* medallion, into the *limar*'s medallion—then cried out without sound as he sensed something blocking the last step of the transfer. He poured more of his own awareness into the other medallion, and found an impurity in its metal he hadn't detected before. He started gathering new Earth Power to purify the metal; at the same time he began transferring the totality to the *limar* through other, slower channels. This was dangerous; it meant he was trying to do a great deal at once and while he was doing it the totality would not be dangerous to others and perhaps would be dangerous to him. Yet he didn't want to give up having two vortexes at work on the fleet. That would double the damage, and no one would ever say again of Kaldmor the Dark that—

Green, green, greenness—nothing else at any level of existence or awareness.

Kaldmor cried out. This time his body's voice reached his spirit's ears. Cheloth had been watching for his enemy's weakest moment, and using all his Powers to hide that vigilance. Now he was striking back.

Kaldmor felt the totality losing stability and the *limar* struggling to join in his efforts to fight back. But the *limar* was weak without absorbing the totality; Kaldmor could almost hear laughter from Cheloth as he struck at the *limar* and drove it and the totality apart with dreadful ease.

The totality began to disintegrate. Kaldmor tried to shield the *limar* from the disintegration, and understood too late that instead he should have tried to break the link between himself

318

and both the *limar* and the totality. The totality's disintegration was not only destroying the *limar*, it was sending a dangerous backwash of Power along the link.

Kaldmor abandoned the *limar*, heard it cry out as the *khru* medallion melted a path into its body, and threw himself wholly into breaking the link. If the *limar* would just die a little faster, the link might break without any more effort on his part. He reached out to twist the life from the *limar*—

—and through the link Cheloth struck again, driving his own Power into it, driving the Power of the disintegrating totality before him like a wave hurling a ship onto the rocks. Kaldmor's defenses were overwhelmed before he was fully aware that they were under attack, and he felt control of the second vortex being pulled out of him like a limb out of its socket. He felt unbearable pain at every level of sense and existence.

Kaldmor howled like a wolf, and knew briefly that the physical world was returning as his cry echoed from the stone walls of the cellar. Then his body seemed to turn liquid, bowels and bladder voided themselves, and all the worlds of either men or magic left him.

THIRTY-THREE

All over the deck of Wandor's *kulgha*, men were rising to their feet as if invisible ropes were pulling them, too fascinated by what they saw to go on praying. Even if this was death coming at them, they wanted to see it.

Both vortexes were now glowing and pulsing with raw green light. The spinning had stopped, and they looked like immense bladders. Wandor knew that the greenness meant Cheloth's Powers at work, but there was still something foul in the color.

Then the vortex over the river vanished so suddenly that Wandor drew blood biting down on his tongue. The greenness flashed blindingly, and before Wandor could see again a thousand thunderclaps rolled over him. Half-dazzled, he saw the surface of the river heave and toss like a shaken blanket. Small steep waves rose and gusts of wind tore them into spray which drove horizontally across the deck of the *kulgha*. He kept his eyes narrowed and watched the ships roll and pitch until men were thrown off their feet or against the railings. He saw a mast go overboard and heard the screams of the men carried down with it. Then the tiny, savage storm was gone, as the second vortex fell out of the sky onto the walls of Dyroka.

It seemed that the wall was sucked up into the sky, struck by a hammer blow from the river, and shaken apart from underneath all at the same time. The roar and grinding of falling stones didn't drown out a scream from Gwynna, and a wall of dust towered where the wall of stone had been. It looked as if a large part of the city had caught fire, and Wandor didn't dare to think what might be happening behind the dust. Was all this Cheloth's work?

Whatever acted upon the walls of Dyroka, the forces were balanced so that few large stones flew out into the river and none struck ships. The waves rose again, more oars were swept away, more masts carried men down into the Mesti, but nothing more than gravel pattered down on decks like hail.

By the time the dust settled, the river wall of Dyroka had crumbled into rubble for three hundred paces. What lay beyond the rubble Wandor still couldn't be sure, but for now Dyroka certainly appeared entirely open to a swift stroke.

Pirnaush stood at the railing watching the ball of green light and fierce wind over the river vanish and the surface of the water turn white. Then the green ball over the city's wall tore apart, and all the girls screamed. The tower was moving under their feet, swaying and lurching from side to side like a drunken man on a rain-slicked street. Thunder and wind tore at Pirnaush's ears until only the fact that he didn't dare let go of the railing kept him from clapping his hands over them. He saw a long stretch of wall and all the buildings for a hundred paces behind it shiver, crumble, and vanish in the dust spewed up from their fall. He saw water rushing in where the walls had been, laying the dust. Then he felt the tower move again, tilting over to an angle from which he knew it could never recover.

The girls were now too frightened to scream. Pirnaush slapped two of them smartly across the rumps. "On your way, little ones! Hurry! This damned tower won't last long enough for another party." The lightness he forced into his voice did its work; the girls broke apart and ran for the stairs. Pirnaush waited until the last was gone before leaving the railing. He'd always made sure he was the last man out the few times his armies had to retreat, and the five girls were just another army now.

Probably the last I'll ever lead.

As he turned his back on the city, the tower tilted still further, so that he knew it could not stay upright much longer. Perhaps the girls would be able to scurry down the winding stairs at least as far as one of the lower windows, but he himself was too late. If he went down now he'd be crushed under the falling stones.

Pirnaush clung to the railing until the tower swung slowly and inevitably past its final point of balance. Then he climbed

322

onto the railing, closed his ears to the screams of the girls, and threw himself out into space.

If I land in the garden, something might break my fall. If not, it's still a cleaner death.

By the time Wandor's *kulgha* approached the breach in the walls of Dyroka, a dozen ships had already put men ashore. All of them were the Viceroyalty's, but some had grounded on new reefs of tumbled stone or the remains of quays and were landing their men in small boats or over planks laid on the decks of luckier ships.

Wandor paced the deck uneasily. Too many ships crowding the breach might delay getting men into the city long enough for the Dyrokans to recover their courage and fight, or lose it entirely and confront the invaders with several hundred thousand people all trying to flee at once. However, the Chongans in the fleet seemed to be holding back, as if uncertain whether they should approach a place of such great magic.

Gwynna finished arming herself and came on deck just as the *kulgha* ran aground. Wandor's impatience drove him to scramble over the side and wade ashore in water up to his chest. Gwynna, still pale from the backwash of Toshakan Powers, waited for a boat.

Wandor picked his way across the stones, water trickling out of his armor, until he met Berek. The big Sea Folker had a score of the strongest men he could find at work making paths over the rubble. Berek seemed to be learning how to command: he only picked up rocks himself when they were too large for anyone else to move.

From the roof of a half-wrecked house the Dragon banner drooped in the still air. In the shadow of the house Wandor found Sir Gilas Lanor, who was pushing his scouts ahead as fast as he dared. "Many of the houses along the wall seem to have been emptied last night," Sir Gilas said. "In the rest, everyone who could walk or crawl must have been moving before the dust settled."

So there might not be as many bodies to dig out of the rubble as Wandor had feared. He heard Gwynna calling him, and saw not only her and Hawa but the *Bassan* of Timru and his guards approaching. Gwynna sat down, breathing deeply, head between her knees while Hawa massaged her neck and shoulders, leaving Wandor and Sir Gilas to speak to the *Bassan*.

"Lord Wandor," he said. "The—the magic seems to have

driven the Dyrokans from most of the wall. I've ordered a score of ships to send their men up on ladders south of here."

"Well done," said Wandor. "I think we'd best call this breach the dividing point between our men. Mine will take all to the north, yours to the south."

"Very good," said the *Bassan*. "I must say—some of us are not easy about coming so close to where great sorcery may have left—what can still do harm."

Wandor looked at Gwynna and saw that she also was suppressing a smile. If the *Bassan* wasn't willing to trust Cheloth to control any aftereffects of his own magic and Kaldmor's, and instead preferred to leave Wandor the half of Dyroka which included the palace quarter and Pirnaush himself—well, they would certainly not try to cure his ignorance of sorcery now.

Wandor advised the *Bassan* to leave a few thousand men aboard ship, to scale the cliffs to the south of the city, "—or at least to pin down Cragor's men by the threat," he whispered to Gwynna. He had no objection to fighting Cragor's men at the right time, but the more he dealt with in Dyroka first, the better.

As the *Bassan* left, the dragon Itr'ell passed low overhead, thinking urgent questions about Wandor and Gwynna but with no fear of magic in him. Wandor thought reassurance and hope at the dragon, heard him reply, then saw him turn. This time Itr'ell passed so low overhead Wandor felt the golden eyes on him. As the dragon passed out of sight, Wandor realized that Itr'ell's presence here was the best sign imaginable that the duel of sorcery was over and no traces of magic left behind. The dragon's fear of Cheloth was the Viceroyalty's secret, though; the Chongans could learn nothing from seeing him. They would go on being content to fight in the south, leaving Wandor free to arrange matters in the north.

Galkor had learned before he was a man grown that you do two things when a battle is going on and you receive no orders. You keep your men together, and you send scouts out to find either the enemy or your leader.

So he kept his men south of the Street of the Bone Carvers and sent scouts north toward the breach in the walls. They soon learned that Wandor's men were pouring into Dyroka in such strength that moving against them would be bloody, and, unless Pirnaush and Meergon moved from the north at the same time, nearly useless.

Galkor had just learned this when word came of the Chongans moving against the river wall. He was mounting to ride down there himself when Dehass Ebrun appeared, carried in a litter and escorted by some thirty hard-looking fighting men including four *paizar-hans*. Neither master nor men looked particularly friendly, and after a moment Galkor dismounted. If he'd had a trained war steed of Benzos under him, he would have stayed in the saddle, but being mounted on a skittish Chongan horse would only make him a larger target.

"I've ordered your men to move to the riverside wall," said Dehass sharply. "They—"

"Refused to obey you?" said Galkor. "Of course. They have their orders from Cragor himself."

"Are those the orders a friend would give?"

"A wise war captain, yes."

"Are you saying you are no longer friends to Dyroka?"

Galkor stepped close to Dehass. "Are you a friend we can trust in our rear, when you've placed arms ready so your city can turn against us?"

Elsewhere than in Chonga, Galkor would have been ready to believe that the confusion on the *Zigbai*'s face was real. "Arms? I don't know what you're talking about." He took a step backward; Galkor saw that several of the guards were moving so that in a few more steps they could get between the baron and his men. He raised his hand to the rim of his helmet.

"Lord *Zigbai*, your plan is known to us. You want to push our men up to the river wall, let them be caught up in fighting against the Chongans, then call out the people and trap us. Perhaps Wandor would call the duke's head a fair price for letting you rule in Dyroka."

The *Zigbai*'s jaw dropped and he staggered rather than stepped backward. A *paizar-han* shouted, "Hands off the *Zigbai*, you northern pig!" and touched his sword hilt. Galkor frowned. "Dehass, we have no cause for a quarrel if—"

Galkor had spent the first three years of his service for the duke in the streets with Cragor's daggermen, and learned among other skills to keep his eyes moving without appearing to do so. Now he saw off to his left what looked remarkably like a man raising a crossbow. At the same moment Dehass sat down in his litter, giving both the crossbowman and the *paizar-han* a clear path to Galkor.

Galkor jerked his hand down and threw himself backward, clear of a dozen crossbow bolts which suddenly whistled down

325

from above. The *paizar-han* and the bowman died without a sound. Dehass took three bolts in the stomach, opened his mouth to gurgle indignantly at Galkor, took a fourth bolt in the chest, and died with a look of utter confusion on his face. Galkor drew his greatsword from the sling across his back and shouted:

"For Benzos and the Black Duke—lay on!"

The late *Zigbai*'s men had the advantage of numbers, but Galkor's men had the advantage of surprise and grim determination. Although the battle was not one-sided, none of the Chongans was breathing when Galkor wiped his greatsword on the nearest corpse and slung it again. He'd seldom ended a battle more thoroughly splattered with other men's blood, or more completely satisfied at having fought it.

The bodies were still being gathered up when the Black Duke arrived. He reined in, started to dismount, saw what lay at his feet, and stopped with one foot still in the stirrup and one hand on the saddle.

"Galkor—what—?"

The baron told him. The duke's face turned nearly the color of Kaldmor's robes, and his hand lifted from the saddle to clench into a fist. Galkor took a deep breath.

"My lord. We had little chance of victory before. Now I think we have none. It would be best if we left the city before Pirnaush and Meergon hear of this. As long as we hold the Brass Gate, we should have a clear road to the pass."

"Yes. But if we're caught divided—what then? We might do better to barricade ourselves in the city and bargain. We can lay Dyroka in ruins if we wish. The Timruans and Bezarakkans at least will give us some reward for that."

The duke's words were sensible, if you didn't hear his voice or see his eyes. Galkor knew his master wanted to lash out at the Chongans, regardless of what might come of it. He remembered his own battle-lust, understood Cragor's, but still would not let the duke condemn them all to death.

"My lord—that would unite Wandor, Pirnaush, and all Timru's enemies against us. We won't even take a good price for our deaths, and we'll give Wandor his final victory. I love the Chongans as little as any man, but they're not our *first* enemies!" Galkor realized he was nearly shouting, but wondered if there was any other way to break through the madness he saw on the duke's face. Still, he went on more quietly.

"It will take hours for Pirnaush and Meergon to learn what

happened, reach Wandor, stop the fighting, and move their men against us. If we start out of the city now, we'll have several hours' lead before dark. If we march all night, they'll never catch us."

For a long moment the duke looked as if he wanted to vomit in sheer disgust at the whole world. Then he sighed. "No doubt. No doubt about your wisdom. But— No. We'll go."

Once he'd made his decision, the duke had messengers riding off like bolts from crossbows. Hold the Brass Gate at all costs, without letting the Chongans know why. Burn all papers, divide all treasure, abandon everything too heavy to be easily carried. Sick and wounded who couldn't travel would be left in the fortified camp; volunteers would be needed to hold it until Wandor's men could take their surrender—

"Wandor?"

"Wandor swore to give our men honorable treatment, and Duelists keep their oaths. I'm not going to leave a camp dog for the Chongans!"

Messengers ahead to the ships on the Kymana. A horse litter and a healer for Kaldmor, even if they had to steal the first and capture the second—

"I thought Kaldmor was dead."

"No. Stunned, perhaps mindless, but still alive."

"Then why not leave him in the camp?"

"Kaldmor may not be Cheloth's equal. But if we lose him we don't even have protection against Tree Sisters and hedge-sorcerers!"

Unfortunately the duke was right. Even more unfortunately, getting clear of Dyroka and even to the Kymana would not ensure complete safety. They still had to get down the river to Tsur-Kymana and out to sea.

However, a battle is fought one blow at a time. Galkor unslung his greatsword and called for a mace, his horse, and his guards.

Wandor's men fought their way north against the Dyrokans with all their skill and determination, although most of them would rather have been fighting their way south against Cragor's men. Some Dyrokans fought to the last, but many were willing to yield if promised their lives and protection both from their fellow Chongans and Cheloth's sorcery. Both promises were easily made; Wandor hoped both could be as easily kept.

When word came that Dehass was dead and Cragor's men

were leaving the city, many Dyrokans became even more willing to surrender, but not all. Dehass's men seemed to lose all hope of doing anything except selling their lives as dearly as possible, and it took hard, ugly fighting before they were dead. "More like rat-killing in a midden than honest war," Sir Gilas Lanor called it.

Word also came that Cragor's rearguard had completely stopped the Timruan advance into southern Dyroka. Wandor sent Count Arlor with a message to the *Bassan* of Giraska, commanding him to land his men still aboard ships at once in order to scale the cliffs, and then to act as he saw fit. This would cost few men and might at least shame the Timruans into fighting harder.

Wandor decided not to take any of his own men south against Cragor. As long as the Dyrokans hadn't yielded, he couldn't divide his army. Otherwise he'd lose the ability to stand between the Dyrokans and his own allies, without doing much harm to Cragor. At the same time, Wandor also decided that he would not put himself out to please the Timruans and anyone who followed them.

Both the afternoon and the fighting went on. The last survivors of Dehass's men were rooted out. Now the piles of rubble from collapsed buildings and the clouds of smoke from fires were greater obstacles than the Dyrokans still in arms. Fortunately the city was wet enough from the last week's rains to slow the fires, and with Dyrokan prisoners hauling buckets from the wells and canals they were soon out.

Dealing with the rubble was less easy, but Cheloth came ashore and from behind a stout guard of Khind archers he put binding spells on most of the weakened buildings along the main streets. That at least would keep the problem from becoming worse, and might provide shelter for homeless Dyrokans if they could overcome their fear of sorcery. Even if they couldn't, the binding spells would bear witness to Cheloth's not being the legendary monster of destructive sorcery.

Late in the afternoon, they learned of a rumor among the Dyrokans, that Pirnaush was dead or dying. Soon afterward the Dyrokans began surrendering so fast that by twilight Wandor's scouts were approaching both the northern wall of the city and the inner wall around the palace quarter. Wandor and Gwynna went forward along with Cheloth, to summon the palace to yield.

Only silence greeted the first summons. Then a torch flared

atop one of the gate towers. The armored man standing there looked familiar; as more torches glowed, Wandor recognized *Hu-Bassan* Meergon.

"Lord Wandor!"

"I am here, Meergon."

"If it is lawful for you to accept Dyroka—"

"Is it lawful for you to give it?"

A strained silence, then: "Yes, it is. Pirnaush fell with the palace tower. He is dying. By his wish, I lead the fighting men of Dyroka. The city fights or yields by my word."

"Good." Wandor turned to Gwynna and saw her nod. "As *Bassan* of the Alliance of the Dragon I accept Dyroka and all in it. All lives and wealth are safe. You may also keep five thousand men under arms, to move only at my orders. By Staz, Alfod, Sundao, and Khoshi I swear this."

"I thank you. And now—will you enter the palace, and—speak to the—to Pirnaush?" Meergon's voice was now somewhat less steady. "He wishes it."

Wandor would have gone even if Gwynna hadn't nodded again. Besz and Sir Gilas led fifty men forward, as the gate squealed and creaked open. Surrounded by the guards, Wandor and Gwynna entered the palace.

They found Pirnaush in a tent pitched in the middle of the garden, clear of any walls or trees which might still fall. A light spell told Gwynna that Pirnaush was indeed dying. His spine and both legs were broken, and so many organs had been abused that it was no longer a question of healing the sick but of bringing life back to the dead, and that was beyond the bounds of any magic. He could still move his eyes and lips, however, and both were as eloquent as his strength allowed.

"You came. Thank you. Dyroka and all that was mine—it is yours now." He got his breath back, then asked, "The magic—how did it smash the walls—shake the ground?"

While he was recovering his breath again, Gwynna explained as well as she could without having talked with Cheloth, trying to use only words Pirnaush could understand. She felt that this was another test of her skill in magic, but it still took so long that by the time she'd finished it was hard to tell if Pirnaush was still alive.

Then his eyes opened and he licked his lips. "But—if To-shak's magic is—air." A deep breath. "If it's of the Air—why—so much trouble from the Earth when Kaldmor's spell—broke?"

Gwynna gripped Wandor's hand to steady herself. "I wish I knew for certain. I do know that when a spell that powerful breaks up, it's always hard to keep Fire, Air, and Earth apart." She was almost certain that Cheloth had ruthlessly thrust a great deal of his own Earth Power into the final attack on Kaldmor, but the less said of this to any Chongan the better.

"Curse Kaldmor," said Pirnaush. "A dying man's curse on him. And Cheloth—he thinks of how not—not to hurt..." His voice trailed into silence, and again they thought he was dead. Then, rallying his strength as he'd rallied his men in a dozen battles, he went on. "I need a *kunduru*, Lord Wandor. Can't use the knife myself. I want you for *kunduru*."

A *paizar-han* would not let himself be captured; a dedicated one would not let himself die a natural death. If he could not kill himself, he would ask for a *kunduru* or "last friend" to cut his throat. The *kunduru* was usually someone bound to him by blood or oath. To ask an enemy to be *kunduru* was a form of deathbed reconciliation which no one could thereafter set aside without risking Khoshi's curse and the contempt of men.

Wandor had two boot knives and a belt dagger, but they all wore a light coat of rust from their bath when he waded ashore. Gwynna had kept her weapons dry, and now handed him one of her boot knives.

"If a woman's blade is lawful—" began Wandor, but Pirnaush interrupted him with a cough which made blood trickle from his mouth. Gwynna wiped it away with a corner of the blanket, and the *Bassan* smiled.

"Steel is steel, Wandor. And a warrior is a warrior." He started coughing again but stopped himself. "Don't let Dyroka suffer for my death, Wandor."

Gwynna held Pirnaush's hand while Wandor drove in the dagger. There was surprisingly little blood, and only a faint death rattle and a slow closing of the eyes to mark the end.

THIRTY-FOUR

The Black Duke got away from Dyroka with most of his able-bodied men. The all-night march left the road to the pass littered with abandoned gear and exhausted stragglers, but took the army of Benzos out of easy reach of its enemies. The duke and Galkor led them over the pass and down to the ships on the Kymana with nothing more than a few mounted scouts watching them from a safe distance.

Wandor was frustrated rather than truly angry over Cragor's escape. He didn't like the prospect of further warfare, but he was far from certain he could have made things come out any other way short of turning Cheloth and Gwynna loose with their Powers. There were rumors of Kaldmor's death, but they were only rumors. If he was still alive, he was Gwynna's match, and even without the *limar* and the *khru* medallions could probably defend himself well enough against Cheloth to provoke an open duel of high sorcery before the eyes of all Chonga. What might come of that no one could say; certainly it would do much to keep the Chongan fear of sorcery alive and dangerous.

This did not seem worth it, when Cragor might still be caught by a blockade of Tsùr-Kymana. By leaving his sick and wounded in the camp for Wandor, Cragor had shown himself willing to observe the oaths he'd taken before Kerhab. Even if he changed his mind later, not only would the devout call him an oath-breaker, but his soldiers would protest his putting them in danger from Wandor's vengeance. The duke now seemed to be an opponent who could be fought as a man rather

331

than as an animal. Would he perhaps yield peacefully if he found the Ocean road home held against him at Tsur-Kymana?

Wandor wished he knew where this thought came from. Did it come from his Duelist's coolness toward senseless fights to the death? Or had fighting beside Cragor with the North Riders and on the walls of Kerhab shown him a face of the Black Duke which he hadn't seen before, perhaps because it wasn't there to be seen?

Within days Wandor and Gwynna moved themselves and the Dragon Steed to the Sea Jade Palace, and most of their men and prisoners to Cragor's fortified camp. Meergon moved his five thousand men into Dyroka, and all the Dragon allies moved out, except for Timruans holding the palace quarter and Vice-royalty men holding three important gates.

From the Sea Jade Palace, Wandor and Gwynna faced a still-confused situation in Chonga. Pirnaush was dead and Dyroka had fallen, but Kobo S'Rain was still alive and ruling nearly half the city's fighting strength. A hundred ships and fifteen thousand Dyrokans lay at Aikhon, apart from the city's own fighting men. Twenty-five thousand men held down Kerhab, and fifty ships guarded the Hiyako.

Kobo himself refused to even promise safety to envoys from the Alliance of the Dragon. A third of his men in Aikhon were the Dyrokan garrison of Bezarakki, who knew that their *Hu-Bassan* had a price on his head and doubted that they themselves could expect any mercy. The army before Kerhab remembered that it had not only taken the city but won two of its three battles in the new war, and considered that Dyroka had fallen to sorcery and not in lawful battle. It would be many months before the Dyrokan armies melted away of their own accord, and no one cared to wait that long. The Chongan cities could hardly afford to keep their fleets and armies at war strength for the better part of another year. Wandor would not lack gold now, but feared that Cragor would find in Kobo a valuable ally or at least a priceless opportunity for making mischief.

At the same time, the allies seemed unable to agree on the best way to finish the war. No one enjoyed the idea of fighting at least forty thousand men apparently determined to sell their lives as dearly as possible. The Chongans also had doubts about fighting Dyrokans in the field while leaving the city itself almost intact in their rear.

"Of course, Meergon has only five thousand men *now*," they said. "But certainly he can put his hands on arms for three times as many, and raise them in two days." The Timruans were heard to add, "And if he does this, can we trust the *Bassan* Wandor to resist him?" There were times when Wandor suspected that he'd made a mistake in being so determined not to lay Dyroka in ruins. It was too soon to know if this had prevented a long, bloody war, and it was certain he'd weakened the Alliance of the Dragon.

Wandor ordered a blockade of both Aikhon and Tsur-Kymana—the best ships to go to Aikhon, since Cragor's fleet was not really fit to fight at sea. He and Gwynna flew to visit the Shimargans and Kerhabans on the Hiyako, and were feasted by the armed miners and cheered politely by the Kerhabans. He dealt with a thousand and one petty details rising from being ruler of Dyroka in all but name. Finally, he held three secret meetings with an eye to carrying on the war in ways which might not meet with the approval of all the Dragon allies.

The first was with Mitzon and Hawa. Mitzon was nearly fit now, and desperate to throw himself back into the fight to make up for lost time and what Wandor suspected he saw as lost honor.

"It seems to me that Kobo S'Rain is the heart of your enemies now," said Mitzon. "What if the knife was thrust into that heart?"

No need to ask who would do the thrusting. No need either to ask what the look passing between Hawa and Gwynna said. "The gods save women from men too brave and virtuous to think."

Wandor shook his head. "That would be a death sentence for you, and Kobo's enemies may throw up another daggerman in time. There is other work for you and Hawa. Does anyone know if Telek the Fatherless is truly dead?"

"His body may still live, as long as no one knows where it is," said Mitzon. "But he is surely dead as leader of the *mungans*."

"I thought so. Would you and Hawa care to take his place?"

The two *mungans* exchanged looks, then nodded slowly. "At least we'll lead as much as anyone can now," said Hawa. "Telek's failure has shaken many *mungans* so badly they may take to peaceful lives or leave Chonga altogether. If there are more than two or three hundred left who can be trusted, I'd be surprised."

"We'll certainly make matters easy for those who do wish to settle down," said Wandor. "As for those who may want to leave Chonga, if they're willing to swear some proper oath they can enter our service."

"They will be leaving the ranks of the *mungans* if they leave Chonga, I think."

"We'll need interpreters and arms instructors too," said Gwynna. "I'd like to find someone to teach me the use of the Chongan sword. There's much to be said for it, when one is not tall."

"You have a teacher," said Hawa. After that the talk and the wine went back and forth mostly for pleasure.

The talk with Meergon was more sober. Gwynna was not present, and to put the *Hu-Bassan* at ease, Wandor spoke of many other things than the one on his mind—the campaign of the North Riders, the etiquette of Dueling in Benzos, the fate of *Zigbai* Dehass.

"It's a pity we'll never be able to honor either Galkor for putting an end to Dehass, or the man who lied to the baron and made him suspicious," said Meergon.

"The man who lied?"

"Yes. He was one of Pirnaush's arms masters, who was seeing to the hidden weapons. He must have thought he could at least sow distrust among the *Bassan*'s enemies if he couldn't save his own life."

"So Dehass Ebrun the master of lies meets his own death through one."

"Do you mourn?"

"About as much as I do for Telek the Fatherless."

Meergon sighed. "Pirnaush deserved more such good servants."

This was as good an opening as Wandor could expect. "He had many, nonetheless, and I'd like to make one of them his successor in Dyroka. You, if you're willing."

"Lord Wandor, I . . ."

"If you're willing, tell me what I should do in order to have everything according to Dyrokan law. I want no questions asked about your right to call yourself *Bassan* of Dyroka." It was hard to keep his voice cool when he wanted to beg.

At last Meergon was able to speak. "Lord Wandor, for Dyroka—for Pirnaush's memory—I'll do it. Thank you, thank—"

"Don't thank me. Thank Khoshi, your master, and your own honor and good sense if you're passing out gratitude." Wandor poured two cups of wine, saw that Meergon's hand shook as he picked up his, and went on as if he hadn't noticed. "As soon as you're the lawful *Bassan*, you can arm another five thousand men and move into the palace quarter."

Meergon drained his cup and set it down. "You understand that making me *Bassan* gives me rank above Kobo?"

Those heavy-browed eyes would not miss a lie. "I do."

"Would you perhaps like me to order him to yield?"

If Meergon was going to refuse this, it was best discovered now. "Yes."

Meergon smiled. "I thought so. Indeed, I've already written privately to Kobo, asking him if he thinks continuing the war is wise. If you want me to *order* him, though, I'll ask you for a close guard."

"Striking at you doesn't avenge his father."

"No, but it could frighten any Dyrokans thinking of serving the Dragon allies. That could keep you from ruling Dyroka, without making you let the Timruans and Bezarakkans ruin it. A Dyroka which his enemies can neither rule nor ruin will be a great help to Kobo."

"He has lost!" Wandor felt like cursing.

"He does not see it that way," said Meergon. "I do not say he is right, but I must tell you what he thinks."

Wandor sighed. "Very well. I'll have Mitzon and Hawa pick a dozen of their most trusted comrades to guard you."

"That will do well enough for now," said Meergon, and held out his cup for more wine.

Wandor and Gwynna spoke to Beon-Kagri of Kerhab together. Wandor thought the little sorcerer walked up to the northerners like an old Duelist facing an unwanted death match with a younger opponent whose character he despises but whose skills he knows will end his life.

"Last summer you alternately saved our lives and nearly took them," said Wandor. "In the end we saved ourselves, with the aid of friends and my lady's Powers. Whether we treat you as a friend or an enemy is your choice. We have preserved your Powers, and would like to see them at work for us."

"I know your story," said Beon-Kagri. "Cheloth hammered it into me so often that it has become boring."

I have yet to meet a sorcerer whose manners wouldn't get a common man stamped into the floor of any tavern, thought Wandor. "Very good. Then you should know why we would like your aid."

"What will you do if I refuse it?"

Gwynna smiled. "Why should we tell you? If we're going to do it, that will give you warning, and we respect your Powers too much to want to do that. If we aren't going to do it—well, I don't think you're a man to be moved by idle threats."

"You are wiser than Cheloth, I see," said Beon-Kagri. "He spent some time threatening me with painful ways of losing my Powers."

"I shall speak to him about that," said Gwynna.

"Yes, but will he listen?" Beon-Kagri smiled for the first time, as if he'd heard that what had been announced as a death match would now be fought on points. "What sort of aid do you want?"

They wanted him to teach both Cheloth and Gwynna all the secrets of his underground Earth spells. They wanted him to use those spells on a tunnel under the Hiyako north of Kerhab, so that the army of Shimarga could cross under the river. The miners could easily dig such a tunnel if he would strengthen its walls. They also wanted him to use his Earth magic in rebuilding the cities of Chonga—starting with Kerhab, of course.

"And if I'm still alive after all this?"

Gwynna looked at Beon-Kagri in a way Wandor had seldom seen her look at anyone but himself. "Then I want you to help me with an honor service for Chiero S'Rain. I know it's rather late, but he deserves one nonetheless." She took a deep breath. "I want to see a school, where all the best teachers in Chonga gather to pass on their knowlege to the best pupils from each city. I want you to teach sorcery there."

Wandor was as surprised as Beon-Kagri, but he was not shaken as Beon-Kagri was, to the point of weeping. Gwynna rose and laid a hand on the sorcerer's shoulder. "It takes more than you've done to us, to make me want someone to end his life in dishonor."

Beon-Kagri said nothing, and at last they had to call a pair of Tree Sisters for him. It would take more than words to restore him, after he'd seen the chance to teach his knowledge to his own people in the light of day. When the sorcerer was gone, Wandor looked at Gwynna.

"Did you think of that just here and now?"

"Yes. It came to me—somehow, I don't know. Is something wrong with it?"

"No. Not at all. Chiero deserves an honor service, and he

336

loved learning, even if he never learned everything he should have known."

The Shirmargan army never marched through Beon-Kagri's tunnel under the Hiyako to free Kerhab. Kobo S'Rain struck first.

The day after Meergon was installed in the City Palace as *Bassan* of Dyroka, word came that Kobo and seventy ships of his fleet were out of Aikhon. They'd given the blockaders the slip in a heavy fog, and were now lost in the maze of the Tok'lis. Wandor had the feeling that they hadn't seen the last of Kobo, and promptly set the allied fleet into motion. Some ships landed men to take the submission of Aikhon, others sailed to Tsur-Kymana to strengthen the blockade, and the rest started up the Pilmau to join the Shimargans and Kerhabans.

All these movements came to nothing. With picked ships and crews of desperate men, Kobo easily outdistanced his opponents. He came out of the dawn onto the blockaders off Tsur-Kymana like the wrath of Khoshi. Forty Timruan ships were sunk or taken. Kobo fought at the head of his men, killing more than thirty opponents, uttering inhuman war cries, and giving no quarter. Swimmers from the sunken ships were picked off by archers or left for the sharks. Then Kobo sent a message to Duke Cragor, and Cragor's men went aboard their ships. The two fleets met off a terror-stricken Tsur-Kymana, then sailed north for Benzos.

After hearing reports of the butchery, Wandor wasn't easily consoled, even by the submission of all the Dyrokans at Kerhab.

"If I'd thrown all our men after Cragor, we'd have won more than we have now!"

"Even with Dyroka in ruins? Even if we lost half our men?"

"Yes, as long as we killed Cragor. Kobo would never have done this without hoping for Cragor's alliance."

"Perhaps. But did the Chongans care that much about Cragor?"

"They will now, at least those who want Kobo's blood."

"Exactly. Now they'll be more willing to follow you wherever you lead them against Cragor. Or they will, if you don't go around telling everyone what a fool you are."

She wasn't joking. Wandor unclenched his fists a muscle at a time, then sighed. "Very well. But *you* know I was a fool, and so do I."

"I don't admit that, Bertan," she said, reaching across the

table to stroke his cheek. "But even if I did, consider this. Do the Chongans really deserve to be told the truth all the time?"

After that he could not keep from laughing, although it was some weeks before he again could laugh easily.

THIRTY-FIVE

The northbound fleets had a rough passage, and fevers, bad water, and storms took their toll. Nine men out of ten still lived to reach what was home if they were of Benzos, exile if they followed Kobo S'Rain. Kaldmor the Dark not only survived but recovered most of his strength on the voyage. His ordeal at Cheloth's hands seemed to have made him immune to seasickness.

The sorcerer offered no explanation of what had happened, but instead retired at once to his castle and began to work on a new *limar*, new *khru* medallions, and several other skills and devices to make sure this defeat would be the last. Cragor was far from hopeful about Kaldmor's success, but even making the effort spoke well of the man. Certainly his time was better spent trying to win the next battle than explaining why he'd lost the last one in a way the duke might not even fully understand.

There was also enough in the affairs of Benzos to keep the Black Duke fully occupied. There was the Council of Governance to be ended and its papers examined. There was the report that the outlaw Count Ferjor now ruled his land along the Nifan like a great noble, treating the duke's tax gatherers like poachers and welcoming fugitives even from the Order of Duelists.

Then there was Anya. She was as coolly polite as before, but the months of work with the bow in all weathers had done marvels for her. She was tanned, fined down, and handsomer than she'd been since the birth of their first child. Several times the duke found himself almost on fire with wanting her, and without any dreams of degrading or tormenting her. Setting aside the horrible notion that he might be developing a passion for his own wife, what was happening?

The duke decided the question would have to remain unanswered. Kaldmor, no doubt, could break through the barriers against sorcery in Anya's mind. But it was even truer than before that the sorcerer had more important work at hand, and that there would be a dangerous uproar if by some chance he destroyed Anya's mind.

No, the secret could wait, particularly when the duke still had ample resources to gain the victory. Perhaps it would not be the victory he'd begun by seeking—the destruction of all his enemies—but certainly it still could be the victory of forcing his enemies to admit that they could not destroy him. He had most of what he'd had before he went to Chonga, and now he also had Kobo's eight thousand Chongan exiles. They had no home but Benzos, no enemies who were not also his, and nothing to live for but vengeance. Above all, he still had the trust of the soldiers, for he'd brought most of them out of Chonga and not spared himself in doing so. Galkor's spies reported this from all the soldiers' taverns; the duke only hoped that certain other men's spies were also listening to the soldiers' talk.

Wandor kept his mouth shut about his sense of having made a mistake in letting Cragor escape. Indeed, Gwynna threatened to have Cheloth cast a spell of muteness on him if he didn't. He wasn't sure that she was joking, and in the end she was right in predicting good results from his silence. The Chongans said very little against him for either Kobo's escape or Cragor's, and the Dyrokans praised him loudly for his honorable dealings with them.

Indeed, it soon became clear that the escape was not entirely a curse. The battle of Tsur-Kymana and the alliance of Kobo and Cragor brought the Timruans quickly to heel. With more than four thousand dead to avenge and that vengeance possible only through victory over Cragor, they quickly assented to measures they might otherwise have fought with words and perhaps with swords for months or years. They accepted Wandor as *Bassan* over all Chonga, they accepted a share in the cost of rebuilding Kerhab and Bezarakki, they contributed more than one-third of a *Bassan*'s war treasury which ended all of

Wandor's problems in paying any of his men, and they promised a hundred ships and ten thousand men for the war in Benzos.

It struck Wandor that being *Bassan* of Chonga on such terms was almost the same as being king over the land. Had he won his fourth crown? He remembered his declaration that, rather than see chaos in the land, he'd become king over Chonga himself. Did anyone besides himself and Gwynna remember those words?

Men might forget. The gods were another matter.

There are also victories not won on the battlefield or even in the council chamber.

Winter was about to turn into spring when Wandor returned one evening from watching the masons at work on Pirnaush's tomb in the gardens of the Sea Jade Palace. Four Tree Sisters met him as he turned into the hall leading to the private chambers. One of them called out to him.

"Lord Wandor, are you going to your lady?"

"Why? Is she ill?"

"Are you going to her?"

Many Tree Sisters had the manners, if not the Powers, of sorcerers. "Yes."

"Good. She wishes to see you. She—" Wandor outran the rest of the woman's words.

He found Gwynna sitting up in the bed, propped against a hillside of cushions, her eyes blanker than Wandor had ever seen them except when she was working with her Powers. Her mouth quivered.

"How is the tomb, Bertan?"

"It goes well enough. The sculptors aren't really equal to their work, but—"

"We—when the school is founded, perhaps we can hold a contest for sculptors and stone carvers. The one who does the best work for the tomb becomes the teacher at the school. We—"

"Gwynna! *How are you?*"

Her mouth became completely shapeless, and she blindly reached out to him with both hands.

"Bertan, I'm going to have a baby."

Wandor felt as if someone had clubbed him across the base of the skull and at the same time poured half a cup of fruit spirits down his throat. The world jumped away to a great

341

distance. "At—last," he said softly. "After so long—our child."
To his own ears he sounded rather like the dying Pirnaush.

Then the world leaped back at him. He saw Gwynna's face
twisted and tear-streaked, knew that these were tears of joy,
and also knew that she was trying to smile with a mouth completely out of control. He sat down on the bed beside her and
held her gently until she muttered, "I'm not turning into glass,
Bertan." Then he held her tighter, until she stopped crying and
he was reasonably sure he wasn't going to start.

She was a little more than a month gone, the Tree Sisters
had said. It wasn't certain that her long barrenness would make
it difficult to carry the child, but she should be careful, more
so than most women. A first child sometimes cured many
female troubles, however, and further pregnancies might be
both easy and safe. They would read her body at intervals
during the pregnancy, and very thoroughly after the child came,
then advise her.

"I suppose that means I can expect to spend most of this
year locked up like the war treasury," she said sourly.

"Only if you want to."

She gripped his tunic. "Bertan, I don't want to. But I *need*
this child." She seemed about to cry again, but laughed instead.
"I could almost wish he—she—it hadn't started for another six
months. There was so much I was all ready to learn. Beon-
Kagri's spells. More dragon magic. Chongan sword fighting."
She grinned. "Would you believe I was even thinking of having
Hawa teach me some of her dances?"

"The ones she does for—carefully chosen audiences?"

"Of course. Don't you think I chose you carefully?"

When he'd stopped laughing and hugging her, a thought
struck him. "Did the Tree Sisters say anything about our—
joining?"

"Yes." An imp's face.

"What?"

"We should do it at least once a week until I start getting
big. They have ways of making it a mild spell to help the
child." Then for a moment she forgot he was still looking at
her. The imp vanished, and what came onto her face—he
couldn't say anything except what was in his heart.

"Gwynna, to keep that look on your face I'd be celibate for
a year after the baby comes."

She gripped his hair and pulled his face down to hers. "Don't
be foolish, love. How would we get the other children?"

Chronology

AUTUMN

Chonga:	*Benzos:*	*The Viceroyalty:*	*Tok'li Islands:*
Pirnaush's council meeting in Dyroka *Mungan's* meeting			

WINTER

| | Jaira and Tagor; Count Ferjor and Hod ranFedil; Kaldmor the Dark; Grand Master of the Duelists in Tafardos; Lady Helda Odomorna's fall | | |
| | Baron Galkor | | |

Chonga:	Benzos:	The Viceroyalty:	Tok'li Islands:
	meets the *kulgha* from Chonga		
	Cragor, Galkor, and Kaldmor meet	Zakonta with Jos-Pran; Wandor and Gwynna share their fears for the future	
		Meeting of War Council of the Viceroyalty	
Galkor sails up the Mesti and meets Kobo S'Rain			
Wandor meets Kobo S'Rain off the Chongan coast			
Wandor buys and frees the slaves in Bezarakki			
Meeting with Pirnaush at the Sea Jade Palace			

Chonga:	Benzos:	The Viceroyalty:	Tok'li Islands:
	Anya's archery practice		
Hawa's dance at the White Plum Tree			
Wandor and Gwynna bathe together and receive Pirnaush's invitation			
Kaldmor receives the challenge of the priests of Sundao	Galkor sends off reinforcements for Cragor		
Cragor reads Anya's letter			
Wandor and Gwynna watch archery practice			

SPRING

Arrival of Galkor's

Chonga:	Benzos:	The Viceroyalty:	Tok'li Islands:
reinforce-ments; second meeting with Pirnaush; Hawa's dance for Cragor; Wandor's sleepless night			
North Riders leave Dyroka			
North Riders cross Mesti			
Battle by the ships on the Hiyako; Wandor saves Cragor			
Pirnaush arrives before Kerhab; North Riders' assault on the river walls fails			
Cragor takes oaths to give Gwynna honorable			

Chonga:	*Benzos:*	*The Viceroyalty:*	*Tok'li Islands:*
treatment if she is captured			
Arrival of Count Arlor; the oath-taking of the royal troops of Benzos			
Siege of Kerhab			
Cheloth's withdrawal from the world over fear of provoking another disastrous duel of sorcery			
Storming of Kerhab; Cragor talks with the *limar*; Wandor and Gwynna vanish from the Temple of Murorin; Cragor's treachery leads to a duel of sorcery and the destruction of the temple			

Chonga:	*Benzos:*	*The Viceroyalty:*	*Tok'li Islands:*
Wandor and Gwynna face Beon-Kagri and are sentenced to seek the Dragon Steed of Morkol in the north			
Arlor speaks with Chiero S'Rain			
Wandor and Gwynna awake in the forest, discover Beon-Kagri's spell on them, and are aided by Mitzon and Hawa			
Mitzon and Hawa see Wandor and Gwynna paddle north up the Hiyako			
Cheloth reads Beon-Kagri's spell on Wandor and Gwynna,			

Chonga:	*Benzos:*	*The Viceroyalty:*	*Tok'li Islands:*
and finds that he cannot remove it			
Kaldmor and Dehass meet to plot			
Sir Gilas Lanor and Berek learn of Chiero S'Rain's assassination			
Kaldmor and Dehass meet with Pirnaush			
Wandor and Gwynna discuss removing Beon-Kagri's spell			
Cheloth warns Count Arlor of Chongan treachery; Wandor and Gwynna learn from Cheloth of the crisis in Dyroka; Sir Gilas and Berek talk on the quay; Wandor and			

Chonga:	Benzos:	The Viceroyalty:	Tok'li Islands:
Gwynna prepare to fight Beon-Kagri's spell			
Battle around Naram Tekor's house; wounding of Mitzon			
Escape of Viceroyalty men down the Mesti			
Gwynna explains her Powers to Wandor			
Arlor confronts Cheloth and hears his confession			
			The fleet of the Viceroyalty reaches the Tok'lis and the army makes camp
Cragor, Kaldmor, and Dehass plot while Pirnaush's men fight	Word of Wandor's and Gwynna's death spreads	The bad news reaches the Viceroyalty, but Jos-Pran	

Chonga:	*Benzos:*	*The Viceroyalty:*	*Tok'li Islands:*
the Kerhabans in the forests; Mitzon's wounds heal	throughout Benzos as Anya practices archery, Galkor raises troops, and the fighting in the north continues	and Zakonta reluctantly go ahead with their wedding	
Wandor and Gwynna reach Mount Reakka			
Wandor and Gwynna call up the Dragon Steed of Morkol and fly south; they are seen far and wide in Chonga			Wandor and Gwynna reach the Tok'lis and take counsel with their comrades

AUTUMN

| The Shimargans open the | | | |

Chronology (continued)

Chonga:	Benzos:	The Viceroyalty:	Tok'li Islands:
new war; defeat of Zerun			Gwynna learns the dragon's name and how to ride him; reinforcements arrive from the Viceroyalty
Return of Baron Galkor			
Cragor's new camp outside Dyroka; Pirnaush tries to regain his freedom of action			Envoys arrive from Timru to seek Wandor's support; he decides to fly to the mainland to negotiate an alliance
Meergon's army assembles; Pirnaush prepares to arm the Dyrokans			
Wandor and Gwynna reach the mainland and begin to form their alliance of Chongan cities			
Revolt of Bezarakki			
Wandor's fleet reaches Bezarakki			

352

Chonga:	Benzos:	The Viceroyalty:	Tok'li Islands:

Chonga:

and sets it free

The fleet of the Alliance of the Dragon under Wandor reaches Dyroka; battle of sorcery; defeat of Kaldmor, destruction of the *limar*, and collapse of city's walls

Fall of Dyroka to Wandor, with the death of Pirnaush and Dehass and the escape of Cragor and Galkor

Wandor and Gwynna meet with Mitzon and Hawa; then separately with Meergon and Beon-

Chonga:	*Benzos:*	*The Viceroyalty:*	*Tok'li Islands:*
Kagri of Kerhab			
Kobo's fleet breaks the blockade off Tsur-Kymana and releases Cragor; the two fleets sail north for Benzos			

WINTER

	Cragor reaches home along with Kobo's Chongan exiles		
Wandor proclaimed *Bassan* over all of Chonga			
Gwynna learns that she's pregnant			

Chonga:
A Short Glossary

ash-water Water in which the ashes of certain poisonous plants have been dissolved. When thrown down on men climbing walls, it can produce blisters, often blindness.

Bassan Literally, "great war chief." The supreme commander of the fighting men of a city, or (more rarely) the commander of a large part of a city's strength operating independently.

Dead Man's Thumb A commonly cultivated plant in Chonga, named for the shape and color of its seed pod. The seeds are edible, the dried seed pod is a powerful seasoning, the leaves are good animal fodder, and the stalks can be used for thatching huts.

druno The homemade rafts of the nomadic river families of Chonga, made of whatever logs come readily to hand, bound together with various waterproof reeds.

Fifteen of Kerhab The elected ruling council of the city of Kerhab.

Five Masters of Dyroka The ruling council of the city of Dyroka, formerly elected but under Pirnaush S'Rain appointed by the *Bassan*.

Haugon Dyrokee "The Shield of Dyroka." The citizens' army of Dyroka raised by Pirnaush by quota from each quarter of the city. Intended to free the better-trained permanent troops for the field army.

Healer General term for anyone permitted to practice the healing arts. When capitalized, refers to one allowed to use sorcery in his work.

Hu-Bassan   "Lesser war chief." The rank of an officer normally commanding a detachment of an army, a section of a city's walls, or one wing of an army in battle.

Ki-Bassan   "Least war chief." The rank of an officer normally commanding a small detachment, a single fort, or a small unit of an army (such as the fighting men aboard one ship).

Khoshi Swift in Battle   The Chongan god of war.

kulgha   The most common type of Chongan ship, with two masts, a broad beam, and a draft shallow enough for the rivers but deep enough to let her go to sea. Can carry either passengers or cargo, and be used in war.

kunduru   The "last friend," who cuts the throat of a *paizar-han* who will not be taken alive but who is too weak to commit suicide.

Lawful Bodies of Shimarga   A guild, craft, or other group of Shimargan citizens with the right to elect representatives to the city's ruling council, maintain its own temples to the Three High Gods, and send its own contingents to the army and the fleet in war.

luk **smoke**   A *mungan*'s weapon: the poisonous smoke of the *luk* weed. Produces agonizing pain in the throat and chest and kills by making it impossibly painful to breathe.

mungan   A "death bringer," a member of the order of assassins and spies that seceded from the *paizar-hans* when the warriors submitted to the rulers of the Twelve Cities.

Murorin   Chongan god of wealth and patron of merchants.

Old Lands/Sunken Lands   Common names for the continent from which the ancestors of the present Chongans came, and which sank into the Ocean as a result of the great duel of sorcery between Cheloth of the Woods and Nem of Toshak.

paizar-han   A Chongan fighting man who has been instructed by another *paizar-han*, sworn the Four Oaths to Khoshi, and is allowed to wear both sword and long dagger. The *paizar-hans* were once an independent order, but were reduced to subordination by the rising merchants of the Twelve Cities about one thousand years after the sinking of the Old Lands.

qual/duqual   A *qual* was originally set as the value of the land needed to feed a family of five for one year. A *duqual* is ten *quals*. Inflation has affected the value of both.

river-pig   A species of wild swine, semiamphibious and eaten by the poor of Chonga.

Sundao River Father   The principal god of the Chongans, lawgiver and ruler of the rivers.

sweetroot   A fist-shaped tuber, which when boiled yields a sticky juice used in Chonga both for sweetening and as a glue.

torchball   A ball of rope impregnated with any one of several light-giving chemical compounds; when ignited and thrown from the walls of besieged cities, it illuminates attackers.

Thirty/Ninety   Units of the *Haugon Dyrokee*, both commanded by *Ki-Bassans*. In the field, six to ten Nineties are grouped under the command of a junior *Hu-Bassan*.

Turtles of Kerhab   An elite corps of Kerhaban fighting men, heavily armored and primarily armed for repelling attacks on the city's walls.

viba   A common type of Chongan rivercraft, broad-beamed, flat-bottomed, propelled largely by slave-manned sweeps, and used for carrying heavy or bulky cargoes.

warfire   A chemical compound, the exact formula one of Chonga's most closely guarded secrets, yielding an adhesive compound whose flames can only be extinguished by sand or urine.

Wasra Mother of Life   The Chongan goddess of love and fertility.

Zigbai   Literally, "wisest friend." A common title for the principal minister or adviser of a Chongan ruler or council.

THE FALL OF WORLDS TRILOGY
BY FRANCINE MEZO

The FALL OF WORLDS trilogy follows the daring galactic adventures of Captain Areia Darenga, a beautiful starship commander bred for limitless courage as a clone, but destined to discover love as a human.

THE FALL OF WORLDS   75564 $2.50

Captain Areia Darenga is brave, beautiful, intelligent and without passion. She is no ordinary human but part of a special race bred for a higher purpose—to protect the universe from those who would destroy it. For without the blinding shackles of human emotions, Areia can guard her world without earthly temptations. But when she leads a battle against a foe, Areia finds her invisible control shattered—her shocking transformation can only lead to one thing—love.

UNLESS SHE BURN   76968 $2.25

A tragic battle in space has transformed Captain Areia Darenga into a human and leads her to a death she would have never known. Exiled to the hostile planet of M'dia she lives in the desolate reaches of a desert, struggling for a bleak survival. But then she is rescued by M'landan, a handsome alien priest who awakens in her a disturbing passion and mystical visions of a new and tempting world.

NO EARTHLY SHORE   77347 $2.50

Captain Areia Darenga has found life-giving passions in the arms of M'landan, high priest for the M'dia people. Forced from their planet, M'landan and his people are threatened by an alien race who seek their total destruction. As they are mercilessly tracked across the universe by their enemies, Captain Areia, M'landan and his people search for a world where the race may be reborn.

AVON Paperback

If you like Heinlein, will you love Van Vogt?

A READER'S GUIDE TO SCIENCE FICTION

by Baird Searles, Martin Last,
Beth Meacham, and Michael Franklin

Here is a comprehensive and fascinating source book for every reader of science fiction — from the novice to the discerning devotee. Its invaluable guidance includes:

*A comprehensive listing of over 200 past and present authors, with a profile of the author's style, his works, and other suggested writers the reader might enjoy

*An index to Hugo and Nebula Award winners, in the categories of novel, novelette, and short story

*An outstanding basic reading list highlighting the history and various kinds of science fiction

*A concise and entertaining look at the roots of Science Fiction and the literature into which it has evolved today.

"A clear, well-organized introduction."
Washington Post Book World

"A valuable reference work."
Starship

AVON Paperback

46128/$2.95

G8clFI 6-81 (2-9)

THE EPIC OF WANDOR
by Roland Green

"Roland Green . . . has mastered the art of writing continuously fresh and picturesque series of character novels . . . entertainment it is."
Chicago Sun-Times

The mighty hero Wandor is given a perilous task by the last of the Five Crowned Kings. He and the beautiful sorceress Gwynna must find five legendary weapons—the Helm of Janar, the Ax of Yevoda, the Spear of Valkath, the Sword of Artos and the Dragon-Steed of Morkol. Their travels take them through magical and monumental battles of flashing swords and fantasy. Their dangerous task must be completed—or peace will never reign in their land again.

WANDOR'S RIDE	45658	$1.95
WANDOR'S JOURNEY	45641	$1.95
WANDOR'S VOYAGE	44271	$1.95
WANDOR'S FLIGHT	77834	$2.75
WANDOR'S BATTLE		Coming soon